John Atkinson Hobson

John Ruskin

Social Reformer

John Atkinson Hobson

John Ruskin
Social Reformer

ISBN/EAN: 9783337296315

Printed in Europe, USA, Canada, Australia, Japan

Cover: Foto ©Raphael Reischuk / pixelio.de

More available books at **www.hansebooks.com**

SOCIAL REFORMER

BY
J. A. HOBSON.

BOSTON
DANA ESTES & COMPANY
PUBLISHERS

CONTENTS.

✦

PREFACE.

A BOOK which professes to be primarily an exposition of Mr. Ruskin's social teaching may seem at first sight to be needless and unprofitable. No master of impassioned prose has endowed his writings with more perspicuity of meaning and more force of utterance, or used a fuller liberty of reiteration in placing his chief thoughts before the reading public. And yet these very qualities of brilliance and amplitude have helped to hide from many the supreme value of Mr. Ruskin's criticism of life, especially in reference to social reform, by giving too great emphasis and attractiveness to unrelated individual thoughts, set in single jewelled sentences, or in purple patches, and by thus concealing the consistency of thought and feeling which underlay and gave intellectual unity and order to his work. Though Mr. Ruskin, like Matthew Arnold, would probably disclaim the title of a system-maker, as implying too mechanical a conception of his intellectual life, and though his mode of composition seldom leans towards severity of arrangement, yet no great modern thinker exhibits in his writings a more definite and conscious adjustment of ideas, both in the order of their growth and in the maintenance of their relations towards one another.

Mr. Ruskin will rank as the greatest social teacher

of his age, not merely because he has told the largest
number of important truths upon the largest variety of
vital matters, in language of penetrative force, but
because he has made the most powerful and the most
felicitous attempt to grasp and to express, as a com-
prehensive whole, the needs of a human society and
the processes of social reform. To assert that he has
attained or even approached complete success, either in
his delineation of the social ideal, or in his estimate of
particular measures and movements of progress, would
be to prefer a foolish claim. But it may be justly said
that he has done more than any other Englishman to
compel people to realise the nature of the social problem
in its wider related issues affecting every department
of work and life, and to enforce the supreme moral
obligation of confronting it.

In seeking to mark this unity and consistency of
conscious design in Mr. Ruskin's work, and, at the same
time, to furnish a critical estimate of the whole and of
the parts, I shall run the risk of offending some by
tedium, and others by the presumption which attaches
to the most cautious censorship of the great. In drawing together and imposing argumentative order upon
thoughts which flit self-poised and with bright irresponsibility among the pages of Mr. Ruskin's brilliantly
discursive books, I shall seem to some to be guilty of
literary desecration. My defence must be that I am
claiming for Mr. Ruskin, as the chief among his virtues,
one which has not yet been admitted save by a small
section of his numerous readers, the distinction of being
a philosophic thinker upon the nature and modes of
social progress, particularly on its economic side.

The very qualities which have pleased the body of his readers most, the brilliant word-painting (which he has vainly repudiated), the superb freedom of passionate utterance in praise and blame, the immense variety of swift and telling illustration, the gifts of rhetorical exaggeration which he employs, have done him this injury with sober-minded thinkers of a more practical or scientific turn, that they have concealed the close and accurate texture of his deeper thought. Thus the selfish interests and the false passions which he so constantly and bitterly assailed have, in part at any rate, succeeded in persuading large sections of the thinking world that, while Mr. Ruskin is a valuable art-critic and a brilliant litterateur, he has no claim to serious consideration as an economist and a thinker upon social reform. Particular phrases and judgments have been distorted and abused, the grossest misrepresentations of a general character have been employed, in order either to pretend that Mr. Ruskin did not really mean what he has plainly said, or that his fundamental notions and valuations are too unsubstantial to deserve the attention of thoughtful practical reformers. This is the common price paid by literary genius to the dull-witted multitude, who have always been easily persuaded that a man who writes well cannot think clearly or deeply.

Some even among his lovers and admirers may hold their master to blame for a certain perverse ingenuity of waywardness in the intentional disorder of his reasoning. That he has in fact carried this disorder so far as to hide from many the full appreciation of his logic is my chief excuse for this work.

To crib, cabin, and confine in a dull array of formal

propositions the rich exuberance of Mr. Ruskin's thought would be a needless injury. This I have endeavoured to avoid. But, however one may handle so delicate a writer for purposes of exposition, some considerable loss of the finer flavour of his work is unavoidable. As we draw together from diverse quarters the compact order of his thought, the spell of his eloquence is broken, the all-pervasive charm of his rich free utterance is dissipated. To some it may seem that the establishment of a sound logical reputation is no adequate compensation for such a loss. My answer is that every reader who would appraise his work aright, in all its breadth and fullness, must in some fashion do for himself this work of formal analysis and synthesis, must seek a wholeness and a harmony in Mr. Ruskin's art of life. This central fire of inspiration which gives vitality to all his works, this art of life, issuing as it does from his supreme sense of spiritual brotherhood, is identical with the passion of social reform, which is the aspect of his work that here engages us. Some account of the outward circumstances of his life, and of the more distinctively artistic and literary interests which absorbed much of his time and attention, is here given. But neither biography nor art philosophy is treated for its own intrinsic interest, but only in so far as it helps to explain, historically or logically, the order and nature of his social teaching. My design is to render some assistance to those who are disposed to admit the validity of the claim which Mr. Ruskin has made to be first and above all else a Political Economist, and who are willing to give careful consideration alike to the strictures he has passed upon current economic theory and prac-

tice, and to the schemes of social and industrial reconstruction which he has advocated with zeal and
persistency for over thirty years.

The main part of this book is devoted to a statement ⌐
and a vindication of Mr. Ruskin's claim to have placed
Political Economy upon a sounder scientific and ethical
foundation than it had hitherto possessed, and to have
built upon that foundation an ideal of a prosperous human
society. The particular qualities and defects of Mr.
Ruskin's criticism and constructive policy are examined
in some detail, his repudiation of democratic ideas and
institutions receiving special attention. The important
contribution which he made to educational theories and
experiments, and its bearing upon the wider social
polity, are separately discussed, and chapters are accorded to certain themes, such as his attitude towards
machinery and his view of the position of woman, which
seem to demand separate treatment. Finally, some
account is given of the constitution of the Society and
Guild of St. George, and of the industrial and educational experiments either directly associated with the
Guild or animated by the spirit of Mr. Ruskin's social
teaching.

For many of the biographical facts I wish to express
my indebtedness to the admirable work of Mr. Collingwood, " Life and Work of John Ruskin."

I have also to acknowledge the kindness and courtesy
of Mr. Ruskin, and of Messrs. George Allen & Son, in
permitting me the use of copious excerpts from Mr.
Ruskin's published works.

J. A. HOBSON.

JOHN RUSKIN.

CHAPTER I.

FORMATIVE INFLUENCES OF EARLY LIFE.

§ 1. "An entirely honest merchant" and his wife. § 2. First
impressions from literature and art. § 3. Education of nature
and of books. § 4. A home-keeping youth — Dawn of the
literary faculty. § 5. Undergraduate days at Oxford.

§ 1. ONLY those who are familiar with John Ruskin's
estimate of the mercantile life and of the art of home-
keeping can understand the full significance of the
phrases in which he summed up the distinctive and
essential virtues of his parentage. The first great "formative influence" in his life was the fact that he was
the son of "an entirely honest merchant" and of "a
consummate housewife."

Scotch blood entered his veins from both parents,
with some infusion of the Galloway Celt. Those who
attach importance to the powers of "race" as deter-
minants of individual character and work may find an
interest in tracing the Celtic qualities in Mr. Ruskin's
art and literature, and will attribute to this source the
vivid imagination and the impulsiveness which give
such brilliant colour to his social criticism. A surer

influence was exercised by the Jacobite traditions which
prevailed for generations among his ancestors, and
which in Scotland often coalesced with a deep enduring
strain of evangelical religious sentiment. John James
Ruskin and his cousin-wife, when they came South, in
1809, brought with them in powerful measure the
qualities of grit and foresight, the commercial and
intellectual acquisitiveness which have brought so many
of the North Britons to the front in the struggle of life.
The two great departments of business and home-life
were ordered by them with equal diligence and success.
Mr. Ruskin contributed the brains and energy to a great
wine business with a famous reputation for high-class
" sherry."   " Entire honesty " he found to be an excellent policy, for he soon began to amass considerable
wealth, which enabled him to satisfy, with an ample
margin, all the demands of a luxurious home and a
dignified social position. The status of a successful
wine-merchant, even in an age when " trade " was less
irreproachable in its respectability than now, was always
good, being that of a responsible adviser to the aristocracy and gentry in one of the most important and
critical departments of gentlemanly conduct — the selection of their wine. This fact, more than any other,
enabled the wine-trade, in its upper grade, to escape
some of the demoralising effects of excessive competition,
which have broken down the responsibility of a merchant
to his " customers " in most trades.

Though closely devoted to his business, Mr. Ruskin,
however, was never absorbed in it. Having received
a sound and liberal education in Edinburgh, he enjoyed
ample leisure and means for cultivating literary and

artistic tastes, and the reading aloud of good books and the collection and study of pictures form a large part of the early recollections of his son. Mrs. Ruskin seems to have been the stronger character of the two, determining with somewhat autocratic power all the larger issues, and exercising a constant and minute supervision over the early life and conduct of her only child. Her nature, as revealed to us in many scattered passages of John Ruskin's books, is too acutely positive, too unyielding in its power, to be very prepossessing, seeking and winning more respect and admiration than affection. As we read the story of his childhood, we feel his mother's "principles" are too obtrusive to be wholly pleasing or wholly profitable. "My mother's general principles of first treatment were, to guard me with steady watchfulness from all possible pain or danger; and for the rest, to let me amuse myself as I liked, provided I was neither fretful nor troublesome." [1] The words, "as I liked," however, require serious qualification, for "toys" were forbidden; and a sorrowful story is told of a carnally-minded aunt who gave the baby a splendid Punch and Judy, which was promptly confiscated by his mother, who said, "'It was not right that I should have them,' and I never saw them again." Old-fashioned views about the place of punishment in education prevailed in the Ruskin household. "I was always summarily whipped if I cried, did not do as I was bid, or tumbled on the stairs." When it is added that her earliest conception of her special duty in education took the form of forcing John to acquire long chapters of the Bible with perfect verbal accuracy every morning, and

[1] Fors, Letter li. (iii. 38).

to read the book right through, once a year at least, from Genesis to the Apocalypse, every syllable, at a time when no skill of interpretation in the teacher and no precocity in the pupil could have imparted a right understanding of many portions, the opinion we form of her judgment and discretion is not too favourable.

But the imaginative reconstruction of a personality from episodes is seldom reliable, and, in the case of Mr. Ruskin's mother, evidently gives a most unjustly biassed view. The fuller and more general picture is that of a singularly peaceful and gentle home, parents closely attached to one another, and in ever kind and anxious sympathy with all that made for the interest and welfare of their child. The strong evangelical leanings of the mother admitted the relaxations of " a lighter self " capable of a free and honest enjoyment even of the stories of Fielding and Sterne, which Mr. Ruskin's father, a devoted student of literary masterpieces, read aloud in the evenings.

§ 2. This family life was self-centred to an unusual extent; and the extreme care which both parents took of their boy kept him from many of the childish interests which might have thrown him freely amongst other children and have widened the area of child-life. As we read his early story we are reminded of the title he has given to one of his own books, " Hortus Inclusus." To the physical care bestowed upon him by his mother, John, with his delicate constitution and mental precocity, owed very much. To the early training he received in literature and art he owed still more. Too much is often made " of books that have influenced me." But no careful student of Mr. Ruskin can fail to see the extraordinarily powerful impact upon his sensitive imagination and his retentive memory of the "great books" which taught him his earliest wider lessons of life and humanity. The Bible, Sir Walter Scott, Homer (in Pope's version) not only formed his early outlook upon life and history, but stored his childish mind with images and words which made an imperishable impression upon his literary work.

Art, too, crept early into his life, for his father was not merely a collector but an amateur painter of delicate taste, and pictures and engravings were objects of serious interest to him. The somewhat austere habits of this Scottish household seem to have admitted a good deal of material comfort which, under the pressure of a rapidly expanding income, included many expensive luxuries, though never degenerating into show or magnificence.

Born in London, John Ruskin was yet no city-bred boy. In 1824, when he was five years old, the family moved to a comfortable mansion in Herne Hill, then a charming rural spot, upon which the speculative builder had not begun to lay unholy hands. Here the Ruskins kept almost entirely to themselves, rarely entertaining, never "entering society," giving their son John the best of everything, as they understood it, in physical and mental culture. In such an atmosphere, fenced round by parental solicitude, there was indeed grave danger lest a sensitive, precocious child might develop into a portentous prig. That he escaped this fate must in part be imputed to his native modesty, and to the powerful early interests in books, art, and nature which took him outside of himself.

§ 3. Had the elder Mr. Ruskin been possessed by that

same genius of mis-education which was driving another
Scottish father [1] to attempt the ruin of another distinguished son, it would have gone hard with John Ruskin.
Fortunately, the strict physical regimen of young Ruskin
was mitigated by abundance of free leisure, that "broad
margin to life" which is so essential to healthy growth.
From books and the routine of a too carefully ordered
home, John found wholesome relief in the beauties
of Nature, which were the objects of his earliest and
most abiding passion. The woods and streams and
trees in the charming country round Dulwich became
his familiar friends, and their free beauty formed a
healthy counterpoise to the "luxury and formalism"
which in later years he recognised as chief dangers of
his early years. Moreover, each summer, the peaceful
monotony of residence at Herne Hill was broken by
long and delightful travels, in which the child became
familiar with all the varied scenery of his native land.
There is an irresistible quaintness in the picture of little
John packed away in the post-chaise with father and
mother, leisurely traversing England and Scotland as
they drove from one stately home to another, to take
orders for sherry. Mr. Ruskin was his own traveller,
and worked in pleasure and business most successfully.
It was indeed a splendid education for such a child, who
saw all the famous sights, the cities, cathedrals, rivers,
mountains, castles of his native land. His first love, he
tells us, was for castles and ruins, not for pictures; that
came afterwards. These travels, to be supplemented
later by Continental journeys, fastened the realities of
history upon his imagination, and early reflections and

[1] James Mill.

judgments began to stir his childish mind. From Homer and Scott he had already gained "strange ideas about kings," and in "Fors Clavigera" [1] he tells how "a painful wonder soon arose in my child-mind why the castles should now be always empty. Dark yearning took hold of me for a kind of Restoration" — a seedling of the later hero-worship and new feudalism which were to figure so strongly in his scheme of social reform.

Too much, however, must not be made of these dim foreshadowings. Ruskin's early love was the pure romantic passion for beautiful scenery and historic associations. This soon took further shape in the beginnings of scientific curiosity. Not content with a "superficial sentiment," derived from the "grandeur" of mountains, he wished to know about them, became a searcher into causes. Mountains thus led him to mineralogy and physical geography, and one by one other branches of the natural sciences began to interest him, and he sought to give more definite meaning to the rivers, the clouds, trees, and all the objects of the external world.

This early scientific spirit belongs to the "analytic" talent which Mr. Ruskin in manhood has always justly claimed as his most distinctive gift. His was never a mere delicately receptive mind; to accurate sensation he added this power of analysis and the attendant faculty of creative imagination. Those, however, who regard him distinctively as of a poetical imaginative nature have no justification for this view. Of the faculties just named, the creative imagination was always weaker than the faculties of observation and analysis.

[1] Fors, Letter x. (i. 193).

§ 4. Later in life Mr. Ruskin brought this rare analytic power to bear upon the moral education of his
early life. Its virtues and defects are clearly and justly
indicated by him. Peace, obedience, and faith were the
moral atmosphere he breathed; truth, honesty, and perfect exactitude of conduct were taught in the example
of his parents; the foundation of justice and consideration for others was laid in his home life. It was a safe
but hardly a stimulating moral atmosphere. It furnished, he tells us, " nothing to love," and " nothing to
endure:" the " judgment of right and wrong and powe
of independent action were left wholly undeveloped."
Nor was any corrective to this somewhat enervatin
calm furnished by school life. Except for a brief seaso:
in a small day-school, his " education " was conducte
by private tutors under the same close parental care
The best " individual attention " of skilled teachers wa
secured for him both in the ordinary branches of learn
ing and in art. It is impossible to assess the gain ar
loss arising from this policy of home education. On t
whole, however, it is probably a matter for congratu
tion that young Ruskin escaped the hardening ordeal
a great public school at a time before modern notio
of humanity had softened the asperities of mechanic
discipline. Brutal injustice is ill compensated by a roug
sense of comradeship; and to thrust into the educationa
cock-pit a sensitive nature such as Ruskin's in order
that he might " find his level," and " have the nonsense
knocked out of him," was a fatuous policy, which the
good sense and affection of his parents forbade them to
entertain. Thus he escaped the fate of being turned out

¹ Fors, Letter liv. (iii. 109).

of an educational factory at nineteen, a "man of the world" with fixed habits, ideas, and associations.

The result of excessive home-keeping was a lack of comradeship in work and play, and a premature excessive cultivation of the arts of self-expression in literature. There was none of the coercive over-pressure which went near to ruin J. S. Mill. But the solitary leisure of childhood awakened too early and too rapidly the thirst for literary expression. At six years old "graphomania" seized him; even before he had learned to write he taught himself to copy print, and the reading and making of books became his constant passion. Fiction with long descriptive passages and fraught with morals, in imitation of an early favourite, Miss Edgeworth, sometimes interspersed with dips into "hydraulics, pneumatics, acoustics, electricity, astronomy, mineralogy," were his earliest products. But from his eighth year the passion for metre and rhyme gained such a hold that he spent most of his leisure in composing poems, not wholly unambitious in their scope, as the title of one begun in his ninth year indicates, "Eudosia: a Poem of the Universe." As he advanced in boyhood, the diligent habit of putting into literary form, chiefly poetic, a close record of impressions and thoughts never quitted him. Even when much time was of necessity accorded to lessons, this activity did not much abate. The constant strain of mental energy does not seem to have been seriously discouraged by his parents, though it was undoubtedly the formation of a habit of restless intellectuality fraught with grave consequences in his later life.

Thus compassed in boyhood by all the luxuries of an

upper middle-class home, where wealth was visibly swelling, enjoying the best books, the choicest art, the most
interesting travels, picked teachers, and the constant
care of devoted parents, Ruskin grew up to manhood.
This tranquillity was but once subjected to serious disturbance, when an early attachment to a sweet young
visitor, daughter of his father's French partner, was
nipped in the bud by his discreet parents, who discovered
with no slight alarm that their young prodigy, whom
they destined for the Church, with secret hopes that he
would one day be a bishop, was intending to pledge his
affections to a Roman Catholic! This severance was
John Ruskin's first taste of deep sorrow, and his suffer-
ings of body and mind testified to the unusual intensity
of his emotional nature.

Among the many varied interests of boyhood — art,
literature, science, travels, history — we find no distinct
traces of any gathering of moral and intellectual forces
of criticism which took the direction of social reform.
Herne Hill was no rallying-place for those statesmen
and economists whose earnest projects stirred the enthusiasm and exercised the understanding of young
John Mill, who was to be Mr. Ruskin's protagonist in
the field of social politics. His father, content with the
political philosophy of Homer and Scott, stood rooted in
a Toryism so firm and simple that the gathering clouds
in the political horizon caused him neither interest nor
fear. His son pithily sums up this attitude, describing
him as " utterly hating Radicals and devoted to the
House of Lords." [1] Though England was passing through

---

[1] See this passage, " On the Old Road," vol. i., p. 11, for an interesting vignette of the elder Ruskin.

the most critical phase of her modern political history in the struggle of the reform period, there is scarce a mention of politics in the full and free reminiscences of the home at Herne Hill. Public events, unless of a specially literary or artistic character, scarcely found entrance to this peaceful household.

The few visitors who penetrated this " self-engrossed quiet " were, with the exception of two or three artists, all business acquaintances, whose conversation hardly contributed to broaden the social views of the boy. Yet from this source some early enlightenment regarding the nature of the business world seems to have come upon young Ruskin, for he tells us in " Præterita " how from these business dinners he formed " an extremely low estimate of the commercial mind as such." [1] Nor did the outer world supply what was needed for social education. A rich London suburb is perhaps the least favourable soil for the cultivation of genuine social sympathies. The Ruskins, moreover, appeared to have had but slight intercourse with neighbours, rich or poor. Neither theatregoing nor other public entertainments drew them out, and they seemed to have confined their public appearances to attendance at an unfashionable chapel on Sundays. They had few friends, still fewer intimates, " my father and mother in their hearts caring for nobody in the world but me." [2]

Even in the travels over England and the Continent the chief and absorbing topics of interest were scenery, churches, castles, works of art, — the life and manners of the people being of quite subordinate and incidental import. Though John Ruskin, in his journeys over Britain

[1] Præterita, i. 328.   [2] Ibid., i. 240.

in the post-chaise, must have passed over the land during the period of intensest misery and degradation we have ever known, when " the condition of the people" was beginning to force itself upon the governing classes by insurrectionary movements of impotent despair, there is nothing to indicate that the poverty and degradation of a people widely lapsing into hopeless pauperism, or congested in loathsome disease-swept areas of new manufacturing towns, claimed the attention or deeply stirred the feelings of our travellers. Engels, in his " English Working Classes in 1844," has given an appalling picture of the great " Cottonopolis." But young Ruskin's boyish record confines itself to telling us that " Manchester is a most disagreeable town." [1]

It was the England of romantic castles and cathedrals, of fair streams and majestic hills, that absorbed the boyish passion. Perhaps it was best that it should have been so, that the ugliness and misery of life should have been so carefully kept from spoiling the dreams of golden youth. Yet, as we read the eloquent denunciation and commiseration of Mr. Ruskin's later years, we sometimes feel that the note of close, detailed familiarity from personal experience, which gives such actuality to his treatment of inanimate nature and art, is lacking ; though deep inherent truths are presented, there is a suspicion

---

[1] Later improvements only induced Ruskin to expand this judgment, for in " Fors " (iv. 201) we find him declaring that, " taken as a whole, Manchester can produce no good art and no good literature ; it is falling off even in the quality of its cotton ; it has reversed and vilified in loud lies every essential principle of political economy." It is only fair to say that this Rhadamantine judgment was evoked by the proposal to annex the lake of Thirlmere for the supply of water to Manchester.

of unrealism which would not have been there if
John Ruskin had grown up from infancy in frank, close,
personal contact with the life of the masses, whose
claims upon a life worth living he champions so powerfully.

This tardy experience of the darker side of life Mr.
Ruskin himself clearly recognises. Summing the experiences of his first twenty years he says, " 1 had never
seen death, nor had any part in the grief or anxiety of
a sick chamber ; nor had I ever seen, far less conceived,
the misery of unaided poverty." [1]

This is significant of much, for it points to a late
revelation of the meaning and entire character of
life.

§ 6. Many a lad, his schooldays ended, is plunged into
the battle of life, to fight his way in business or profession
or in the university, and to stand or fall largely by his
own efforts. But his parents fenced round John
Ruskin with almost the same protecting care in his
Oxford career as in his home. His mother lived in
lodgings at Oxford during all the terms he kept, and
his father's figure became a familiar one in the High
Street. The choice of a college was a momentous question. The best that care or money could procure had
always been his. Christ Church must be his college ;
the life of a commoner, even in an essentially aristocratic college, is not good enough ; he must be gentle-
man-commoner, wear a gold tassel, and consort with the
scions of noble families. Though it is suggested that
some doubt about his ability to pass a preliminary examination contributed to this decision, Mr. Ruskin him-

[1] Præterita, i. 431.

self does not conceal the fact that the worthy wine-merchant with all his admirable qualities, was something of a snob, and gives a humorous sketch of his parent's secretly cherished ambitions.

"My father did not like the word 'commoner'—all the less, because our relations in general were not uncommon. Also, though himself satisfying his pride enough in being the head of the sherry trade, he felt and saw in his son powers which had not then full scope in the sherry trade. His ideal of my future — now entirely formed in conviction of my genius — was that I should enter at college into the best society, take all the prizes every year, and a double first to finish with; marry Lady Clara Vere de Vere; write poetry as good as Byron's, only pious; preach sermons as good as Bossuet's, only Protestant; be made, at forty, Bishop of Winchester, and at fifty, Primate of England." [1]

John fortunately seems to have inherited nothing of this propensity, for though in "Fors" and elsewhere he sometimes playfully admits his liking for a lord, the irony is sufficiently patent to deceive nobody. Aristocrat in the true sense of the word as Mr. Ruskin always boasted himself to be, no one great Englishman of this century had in his nature less of that quality which Thackeray pronounced to be the essence of snobbishness, "a mean admiration of mean objects."

It is frequently remarked, though generally without due regard to the size and accessibility of our universities, how small a number of those whose minds have made a powerful mark upon the intellectual history of the century have been educated at Oxford or Cam-

[1] Præterita, i. 141.

bridge. A fairer stricture upon university methods has reference to the defective capacity which our universities have shown for the detection, stimulation, and direction of any special talent or genius in those who have entered the academic gates. Mr. Ruskin was a true lover of Oxford, and he got and gave much profit and delight from the years he spent there; but his love for Oxford regarded it as a storehouse of great historical associations, a seat of learning, a "home of lost causes" rather than a curriculum of studies for modern young English gentlemen. Ruskin and Matthew Arnold in Oxford, like Tennyson and Darwin at the sister university, drew their best intellectual sustenance beyond the limits of the prescribed routine, and neither sought nor won great academic distinctions in the orthodox studies of the university. The detection of grammatical subtleties, which was then called "scholarship," and the dissection of historical and philosophic corpses, with no serious endeavour to rekindle the spirit of the past or to shed serviceable light upon the present, gave little satisfaction to the strenuous demands of such a mind as Mr. Ruskin's. Something he learned from the great ancient books, especially from Plato, whose quenchless glory has always shown through the crassest and most filmy methods in interpretation, and from the first great living historians, Herodotus and Thucydides; but all true guidance and assistance of a university in the organic development of an individual mind was entirely wanting. Looking back from later years he sums up this period as follows: "Oxford taught me as much Greek and Latin as she could. For the rest, the whole time I was there my mind was simply in the state of a squash before 'tis a peacod — and remained so there a year or two afterwards." [1]

Allowing for a certain strain of exaggeration in all Mr. Ruskin's more familiar writings, it is right to conclude that he took little from that training for which the university authorities made themselves responsible. But he seems to have been fairly industrious and acquisitive in other studies than the classics, though a breakdown in health precluded him from seeking " honours " in the schools. The only formal academic distinction which fell to him was the Newdigate prize for an English poem. But the indirect and extra-academic services of his residence in Oxford were many and invaluable. The social education of mixing with many men and many minds, the formation of some close personal attachments, the free intellectual atmosphere of the place, were particularly profitable to a home-keeping youth. The beginning of a life-long friendship with Mr. Henry Acland, who was one of the pioneers in the introduction of the modern branches of physical science into the university, brought him into touch with one of the powerful intellectual movements of the age, and helped to widen his outlook upon life. With the more absorbing religious interests, which at that time were gathering force, and which soon became so dominant a power as to arrogate to themselves the title " Oxford Movement," John Ruskin had no sympathy. Grounded in Scotch evangelicism, he does not yet appear to have experienced the earlier stirrings of that religious feeling which took distinct form a few years later in his curious and interesting tract, " Notes on the Construction of Sheepfolds,"

[1] *Præterita,* ii. 34.

and which was to manifest itself thoughout his life in a
series of concentric circles of ever widening religious
sentiment. Nor did the interests of his Oxford group
of friends draw him into the consideration of grave
political and social issues. Though among his Christ
Church comrades there were individual minds of distinguished calibre, there was no such brilliant gathering
of ardent spirits as Tennyson had found ten years before
at Cambridge, who —

> " held debate, a band
> Of youthful friends, on mind and art
> And labour and the changing mart,
> And all the framework of the land."

On many subjects young Ruskin seemed to have
reached a startling maturity of conviction; his earliest
writings show an unusually wide acquaintance not
merely with the technical treatises of the art subjects
with which he chiefly deals, but with ancient and modern
history and literature, and even with the great writers
upon morals and theology. But in all this early
thought and study, no signs appear of any specific application of his opening views of art and life in the direction of social reform. During his undergraduate time,
and for some years afterwards, no clear convictions
regarding economic wrongs, or the miseries arising
from them, appear to have forced themselves upon
his understanding, or to have stirred the passion of
revolt within him. For the most part he remained
absorbed in art, literature, and travel. At first sight
this may seem unnatural. It is not really so. The
larger superficial features of the economic and political

life of a nation acquire a constant and customary import
to us at such an early age, that, unless the course of our
education is particularly directed to them, or some
sensational illustrations break our emotional apathy,
all personal appreciation of their significance may
be deferred indefinitely.   There was nothing in John
Ruskin's early life and training to focus his curiosity
on social phenomena, or to stir his emotions to social
sympathy ; every circumstance of his upbringing, both
the negative condition of an almost total lack of social
experience, and the positive condition of an early and
deep absorption in interests far removed from social
reform, tended to screen from him the " mission " which
he was destined to fulfil, and for which he was making
sure but unconscious preparation.

CHAPTER II.

§ 1. If we use the term social reform, in its broad
sense, to describe those larger changes in the structure
or working of society which aim directly at some general
improvement of human life, as distinguished from such
work of reform as attacks narrower and more specific
defects, we shall find that social reformers come to this
work by widely different paths. Often it is the personal
experience of some concrete evil that first awakens a
sense of social wrong, and a desire for redress; reform

energy once generated is fed by a natural flow from various neighbouring channels of activity, the stream broad-
ening as it goes, until the man whose early activity was
stimulated by the desire to break down some little barrier
which dams the stream in his back garden, finds himself
breasting the tide of some oceanic movement. So it was
with such men as Cobden, Lord Shaftesbury, and Cob-
bett; a necessary organic association of related interests
and sympathies drew them from some specific " cause "
into the wider paths of philanthropic statesmanship.
Other instances there are of men who, entering public
life as a profession or a pastime, have come to discern
underneath the chicanery of party moves, and those
brief expediencies of legislation and administration
which have usurped the honourable title of politics,
the deeper needs of a continuous organic social policy,
and have set themselves earnestly to the larger task.
Men such as C. J. Fox and Gladstone may be placed in
this order.   Others again are social reformers *à priori*,
entering through some gateway of large philosophic principles into the practical service of society.   The Utilitarian School of Bentham and Mill, and modern Socialism
furnish not a few instances of men thus deductively impelled to social reform.   Literature, art, and theology
have each contributed leading impulses to social revolt,
accompanied by more or less definite suggestions of
social transformation.   Byron, Wordsworth and Shelley,
Hugo, Whitman, Tolstoy, Ibsen, illustrate the flow of
free literary forces in the same direction.   Pre-Raphaelitism, Wagnerism, and the subsidiary art currents of
naturalism and impressionism, have their wide social
implications, and have contributed many of the most

powerful prophets of revolution or reform. Wagner himself, Burne-Jones, and Morris in England, are leading
members of a great body of men in strenuous and radical
revolt against some of the most distinctive features of
recent civilisation.

For the influence of theology I now only allude to the
Christian Socialism of the broad church clergy of this
country in the middle of this century, and to the strong
and spreading spirit of reform which prevails in a large
section of the High Church in England, and in the
Catholic Church of Austria, Germany, France, and Bel-
gium at the present time, to say nothing of that most
intense passion of revolt which animates the Russian
sects who hazard their lives to embody in their social conduct the spirit of primitive Christianity as they interpret it.

§ 2. Now, politics, as we have seen, had no particular
interest for Mr. Ruskin. He always spoke of himself
as an "old Tory," and the making of democratic machinery was always repellant to his instincts of political
order. The radical philosophy of Bentham, Austin, and
the Utilitarians formed the object of his sternest denunciation from the earliest time when his attention was
called to it. Indeed, it must be said that his mind
had no natural affinity for political thought, and he
early developed a rough intuitive philosophy of his
own, grounded in natural piety, which disinclined him
from the endeavour to explain either individual or
national conduct by laws owing their discovery to
rationalist analysis. It might indeed have seemed
natural that the contemporary literature of his early
life should have sown seeds of social revolt in so sen-

sitive a nature. But no clear signs of such an influence
are discernible. Byron was indeed an early favourite,
but it was his penetration into the facts of nature, and
not the sentiments of " Byronism," which impressed him.
Byron's true gifts he held in high, perhaps unduly high,
esteem, writing of him thus : " Of all things within range
of human thought he felt the facts, and discerned the
natures with accurate justice." [1]   This love of fact, and
the felicity of song which gave it voice, he received from
Byron ; the effervescent cynicism, together with the
nobler sentiments of a great spirit in protest against
the conventions and inhumanity of society, he failed to
assimilate.

Shelley never got that mastery over him which he held
over so robust a genius as Browning ; he seems to have
always been to Mr. Ruskin what he was to Arnold, " a
beautiful but ineffectual angel beating in the void his
luminous wings, in vain." The full human worth of
Wordsworth was to bear fruit later in his life, though
from the first the nature-worship of this poet was a
constant fount of joy.

The brief sketch given in the last chapter of the outer
circumstances of Mr. Ruskin's early life, and of the order
of growth in his interests, will explain what has seemed
to some the strange absence of all visible signs of sympathy with social movements of any kind in his early life.

It was not a case of retarded emotional or intellectual
development. On the contrary, a perusal of the early
tracts on Architecture, or vol. i. of the " Modern Painters," shows a quite astonishing maturity of refined
emotional analysis. How comes it that one who had

[1] Præterita, i. 269.

seen so much, had thought and felt so deeply and so widely upon so many matters, should have no inkling of that work which in middle life he came to recognise as his supreme mission ? The answer to such questions is perfectly conclusive and satisfactory. Though incautious and sometimes extravagant in words, John Ruskin was a plodding and careful thinker; his thoughts had never L been directed, by necessary contact with his early interests, to the social and economic structure of societies, and therefore he had never formed any definite convictions relating to them.

Never being thrown into the eddying tide of any of the radical movements in politics or philosophy which marked that restless age, he was not impelled by contact with other fervent souls into hasty speculations or cheaply acquired convictions upon the fundamental problems of society. Yet it is none the less true that throughout his studies of nature, art, and history, he had been sowing the seeds which, deeply buried for many years, were destined by necessary process of thought and feeling to grow and ripen into the ideals of his social teaching.

§ 3. No great writer has shown a more contemptuous disregard for those literary arts of concealment commonly used to secure an appearance of consistency, no one has so freely and so loudly proclaimed his repudiation of past pronouncements upon important topics ; in no case has this serviceable frankness been treated with such lack of courtesy and understanding. Because Mr. Ruskin has always striven to confer upon the public that greatest service which a thinker can confer, by making everything he writes " part of a great confession;" because he has set down all his thoughts and feelings in their natural order, without exaggeration or extenuation of their form and intensity, many of his critics have chosen to represent him as a loose and reckless thinker, borne along by sudden gusts of sentiment, and void of any stable unity of thought or clear order of development. Now the utter groundlessness of such criticism is demonstrable by any one who takes the trouble to read his representative books in the order of their publication.

§ 4. Such a study will disclose, even in his earliest writings, certain prime and fundamental laws of thought and feeling which enable us to see all his later work in its true light as a multifarious and harmonious application of these same principles. This true, deep consistency is not impaired by change of view leading to new lights upon important subjects, or by the inherent difficulties of getting lucid arrangement in the expression of ideas. This latter difficulty Mr. Ruskin always felt to be responsible for much misunderstanding. " It is strange that I hardly ever get anything stated without some grave mistake, however true in my main discourse." [1]

The intelligent and minute love of Nature which showed itself so early in Mr. Ruskin's life must be taken as the starting-point in the just appreciation of his work. In time and in intensity it took precedence of his interest in art. " The beginning of all my own right art-work in life depended, not on my love of art, but of mountains and sea." [2] His childish pursuits, the collection of stones, — which began his geological and

---

[1] Letter quoted, Collingwood, ii. 138.   [2] Eagle's Nest, p. 45.

metallurgical studies, the minute devotion to wild flowers, the study of river-beds, cloud-forms, the shape of hills, were not merely his early passion, but his chief intellectual training. At the same time, in his literary education it was the same detailed attention to the forces and forms of words, the units in the natural history of literature, which was laying the foundation for the "absolute accuracy of diction and precision of accent in prose," [1] which he attributes to his mother's teaching, and which are the chief sources of his literary power. In later life, as we have seen, the intellectual capacity to which he laid especial claim was analysis, and this capacity was grounded in the "patience in looking and precision in feeling" which marked the youthful lover of Nature. It was no mere accident, but a just instinct which led young Ruskin to attach to his earliest publication of importance the *nom de plume* κατὰ φύσιν (according to Nature).

It was inevitable that a close student of Nature, gifted with power of analysis, who turned his attention to any of the orthodoxies of English art half a century ago, should take up an attitude of radical reform. By natural disposition an upholder of established order, and a man of peace, Mr. Ruskin was yet driven by the conditions of his age and country into as many " heresies" as he had interests. Though not till later did he discover the deeper nature of the malady which made this inevitable, he could not fail to find the evil symptoms in each separate art of human life.

The " violent instinct for architecture" [2] which first drove him, while still an Oxford undergraduate, into

---

[1] Præterita, i. 208.   [2] Ibid., i. 206.

the field of battle,[1] is significant alike for its title, and
the scathing criticism it contains of the thraldom of
architecture to narrowly conceived principles of utility.
This early treatment of " The Poetry of Architecture ;
or the Architecture of the Nations of Europe considered
in its Association with National Scenery and National
Character," is chiefly noteworthy as containing the first
germs of that splendid exposition of the true human
uses of architecture in " The Seven Lamps," and as
indicating his early sense of the principle that honest
adaptation of material to the true needs of life is the
basis of rightness and of beauty in buildings. The
first germ of his special thought, that " realism," or
study of the facts of life, and " idealism," or the use
of the imagination to impose forms of beauty which
shall appeal to taste, are not contradictory but complementary processes, is traceable in embryo, even in
this boyish work. The full relation, however, between
architecture and national character which " The Seven
Lamps " was to disclose and illustrate is yet hardly
traceable.

§ 5. To the first of Mr. Ruskin's two great masters,
J. W. Turner and Thomas Carlyle, allusion has already
been made. Making all due allowance for the enthusiasm of hero-worship, it may fairly be said that these
two men were chief instruments in determining Mr.
Ruskin's career. Turner made him an art prophet,
Carlyle, a social reformer. Mr. Collingwood, in his

---

[1] Earlier boyish essays, published in the " Magazine of Natural
History " (March, 1834), and elsewhere, as well as an unpublished
early draft of the leading ideas of " Modern Painters " contained
in a reply to a criticism on Turner in *Blackwood's Magazine,* show
the same early spirit of defiant scrutiny of established opinions.

admirable work, " The Life and Work of John Ruskin," traces the focusing of these rays of art-truth in a swift process of conviction, almost of conversion, in the year 1842, when his eyes were opened to the true mission of higher art as the interpreter of Nature in her deeper attributes and motives by the capacity of human sincerity. It was the perception of the distinctive qualities of Turner's landscapes which drove this conviction home, and Mr. Collingwood tells us how young Ruskin renounced henceforth his poetic aspirations, his capacities of art production, and his hopes to be a man of science, taking on him the mission " to tell the world that Art, no less than the other spheres of life, had its heroes; that the mainspring of their energy was Sincerity, and the burden of their utterance, Truth." [1]

This carries us to the first great art crusade. [2] John Ruskin was only twenty-three years old when he wrote the first volume of his " Modern Painters ; their Superiority in the Art of Landscape Painting to all the Ancient Masters proved by Examples of the True, the Beautiful, and the Intellectual, from the Works of Modern Artists, especially from those of J. M. W. Turner, Esq., R.A."

With the effect of this bombshell upon the world of painting we are not here concerned ; nor need we discuss the extraordinary brilliancy of literary style, and the display of art learning it contains. What does con-

[1] Life and Work, vol. i., p. 103.

[2] Though "Modern Painters " is rightly taken as the first full teaching of Mr. Ruskin's art-criticism, the character of that teaching amply justifies the claim which the author, in reviewing his life's work from the wider human standpoint, assigns it. "'Modern Painters' taught the claim of all lower nature on the hearts of man." (Fors, Let. lxxviii.)

cern us is the clear exposition of root principles in art-criticism, which were afterwards to inspire his social teaching. In this first volume of " Modern Painters," published in 1843, we find stated, in language of uncompromising vigour, the three main canons which Mr. Ruskin later carried from art in its narrower connotation to the art of life. All art must be based upon patient, thorough, detailed knowledge of the facts of its subject-matter in Nature. This is the groundwork of " realism," the lack of which forms one of the two chief heads of his indictment against most of the great " masters " of the post-Raphaelite schools in Italy and in England. In enforcing this canon against reputations so great as Claude and Poussin, Mr. Ruskin exposes the deadly sin of conventionalism. The object of art is not to imitate, nor to deceive the senses, but to tell the truth. But is art to tell all truths, to give a literal transcript of all individual phenomena of the outer world? No; such realism is not art. On the con-trary, art is concerned with the rendering of ideals. Nature is the servant of this idealism by furnishing ideas of truth and beauty. " Ideas of truth are the foundation, and ideas of imitation the destruction of all art." [1] These " ideas of truth " are the essential characters of any object where all that is accidental or merely individual is brushed off from the type. We need not pause to consider how far Locke or how far Plato was responsible for this doctrine of ideas, but it is important to discover that these ideas, which are strictly Utopian (for, like Plato's, " they have no exist-ence upon the earth, but are found, if anywhere, in

[1] Modern Painters, vol. i., p. 29.

heaven"), supply the true subject-matter of artistic workmanship. To bring out these "specific" forms in landscape is the first aim of art. The preface to the second edition of this volume contains the more mature statement of this essential doctrine, and presses home the second head of the indictment against the post-Raphaelite school on the one hand, and the Dutch school on the other. Whereas the former generalised so widely as to destroy all specific truth, producing trees that belong to no recognisable species, rocks which have no geological existence, the latter overload their pictures with the cumber of individual trivial detail. Now, Mr. Ruskin insists that "there is an ideal form of every herb, flower, and tree; it is that form to which every individual of the species has a tendency to arrive, freed from the influence of accident or disease."[1] Again, "Every herb and flower of the field has its specific, distinct, and perfect beauty; it has its peculiar habitation, expression, and function. The highest art is that which seizes this specific character, which develops and illustrates it, which assigns to it its proper position in the landscape, and which, by means of it, enhances and enforces the great impression which the picture is intended to convey."[2] The fuller teaching of this idealism of art is found in the second volume of "Modern Painters," published some years later, where the functions of the imagination in art receive maturer treatment; but its essential features are found in the earliest of Mr. Ruskin's great books.

§ 6. Still more important is the introduction from the very outset of the moral sense as the criterion of art, at

---

[1] Modern Painters, Preface, xxvi.   [2] Ibid., xxx.

once the standard of valuation for ideas and the fountain of pure taste. " The picture which has the nobler and more numerous ideas, however awkwardly expressed, is a greater and a better picture than that which has the less noble and less numerous ideas, however beautifully expressed," [1] was a bold sentence for a young art critic to write. Again, " Perfect taste is the faculty of receiving the greatest possible pleasure from those material sources which are attractive to our moral nature in its purity and perfection," [2] while " Ideas of beauty are the subjects of moral, but not of intellectual perception." [3]

The fuller exposition of the second volume, in which the essentially moral and religious basis of the " specific ideas " in nature on the one hand, and the capacities of the imagination of the artist on the other hand, is disclosed, is but the maturer growth of these same conceptions.

In a word, Mr. Ruskin as art prophet shows from the beginning an organic harmony of the powers of Realist, Idealist, and Moralist, the imagination working upon an intellectual and emotional basis of close knowledge of reality, under the supreme control of the spiritual faculty.

Having once reached the position that art is the representation of true and worthy ideas seen in nature by the penetrative and constructive power of the imagination, Mr. Ruskin never swerved from it. Steadily he proceeds, his feet upon the earth, his head amid the clouds of heaven, peering through for glimpses of a beatific vision.

---

[1] Modern Painters, vol. i., p. 12.   [2] Ibid., vol. i., p. 32.

[3] Ibid., vol. i., p. 34 ; *cf.*, vol. ii., p. 15.

Thus humanity is at once the standard and the end
of art. The later volumes of "Modern Painters" continually enforce this truth. Mere realism, the presentation of natural truths, however accurately, is not
worthy art. "All art which involves no reference to
man is inferior or nugatory. And all art which involves misconception of man, or base thought of him,
is in that degree false and base."[1] So art must justify
itself by human service. "The difference between
great and mean art lies wholly in the nobleness of the
end to which the effort of the painter is addressed. . . .
So that true criticism of art never can consist in the
mere application of rules ; it can be just only when it is
founded on quick sympathy with the innumerable instincts and changeful efforts of human nature, chastened
and guarded by unchanging love of all things that
God has created to be beautiful, and pronounced to be
good."[2]

This reference of art to the demands of human life
has an intimate bearing upon Mr. Ruskin's valuation of
the two great sources of art-work. Greece, with its
sincerity, its sense of the sufficiency of nature and of
human life, its love of harmony and order in the bearing of the individual, and in the establishment of civic
life, produced the most absolutely perfect forms of art-
work within the classic limits, the most faithful presentation of fact and of idea. But here was found no
adequate provision for the spiritual education of man.
"The Greek frankly took what the gods provided, and
enjoyed it. His heaven was here. The other world, if
there were any, was a thing to be staved off as long as

---

[1] Modern Painters, v. 203.   [2] Ibid., iii. 23.

possible. At best, death was a sad necessity, but there was no thought of any preparation for it which could interfere with his duty in the present. True, the shadow of Fate haunted him; but Fate was not an external law, but a part and parcel of his own life. For the most part his gods were glorified men, who, as men, were either indifferent or appeasable."[1]

This open-eyed but restricted outlook upon life did not satisfy Mr. Ruskin, who had no sympathy at any time with the "frankly pagan" attitude of modern "æsthetes." Gothic art, painting, and architecture, under the inspiration of Christian influences, supplied what Greece lacked, — the deeper seriousness, the sense of mystery and spiritual strife. Beauty as "the expression of the creating Spirit of the Universe" is inadequately, because too finitely, rendered in Greek art. The master-works of Gothic art, seldom if ever attaining the flawless execution of the greatest work of Greece, were rich in witnesses to divinity in man and in appeals to humanity through nature, containing a deeper, more stimulating view of life, and hallowing by spiritual associations the common material facts. "Gothic architecture was, at all times, the architecture both of the church and of the tavern: the house of God and the house of man showing thus their integral connection."

Thus the root of Mr. Ruskin's theory of art is its service to humanity through the presentation of noble ideas. Technique is taken for granted as the instrument of art, and not its essence.

---

[1] "A Disciple of Plato," by William Smart (p. 25), a most luminous study of the deeper teaching of Ruskin.

"In these books of mine their distinctive character as essays on art is their bringing everything to a root in human passion or human hope. Every principle of painting which I have stated is traced to some vital or spiritual fact; and in my works on architecture, the preference accorded finally to one school over another is founded on a comparison of their influence on the life of the workman, — a question by all other writers on the subject of architecture wholly forgotten or despised." [1]

In this stress upon the primary significance of work in its reaction on the life of the workmen, we trace in "Modern Painters" a chief driving force of the later social teaching.

§ 7. In speaking of Mr. Ruskin's moral standard of ideas, it is essential to recognise that his foundation is not ethics but theology; moral sentiments are not ultimate and self-existent things, but are effluences of divinity. The religious tone of his art-treatment in "Modern Painters" is not due to a general orthodox recognition of the divine supremacy in the order of the world, still less is it to be regarded as a literary expression of youthful piety. It is the first deliberate and philosophic statement of that doctrine of theocratic government of nature and of human life, which remained a fixed principle in all his work, and which we shall perceive as dominating his conception of a sound social order. There is, indeed, a stern enthusiasm in his early statement of this creed, which bears the marks of his Calvinist ancestry, and sometimes reminds us of that famous Scottish document, the "Shorter Catechism."

[1] Modern Painters, v. 201.

" Man's use and function (and let who will not grant me this follow me no further, for this I purpose always to assume) is to be the witness of the glory of God, and to advance that glory by his reasonable obedience and resultant happiness." [1]

A period of spiritual struggle marked his sojourn on the Continent in 1845, and he tells us in an interesting passage of " Præterita " how, during this summer, spent largely in the small Alpine village of Macugnaua, he " began the course of study which led me into fruitful thought, out of the till then passive sensations of merely artistic or naturalist's life." [2]

The theology of the second volume of " Modern Painters " (published 1846) is one among many indications of a ripening moral and religious fervour at this period of his life. The theology of Barrow and Hooker, the glowing piety of George Herbert, laid hold of his mind and spirit, as he wandered over Switzerland in 1844; and a period of intense devotion in 1845 to the Italian masters of painting and architecture in the twelfth and thirteenth centuries fastened upon him an abiding sense of the truth that moral character is the root of art. As art exists for man, and its greatness consists in what it can do for man, the power of all great works of art must come from some source of greatness in the artist. The voice of Mr. Ruskin is here the voice of Carlyle; art is an inspiration, " not a teachable or gainable thing, but the expression of the mind of a God-made great man : that, teach or preach, or labour as you will, everlasting difference is set between one man's capacity and another's, and that this

---

[1] Modern Painters, vol. ii.   [2] Præterita, ii. 245.

God-given supremacy is the priceless thing, always just as rare in the world at one time as another." [1]

§ 8. When we turn to Mr. Ruskin's conception of a true social system we shall perceive how this hero-worship of art is applied in the wider art of social life. The rarity of the great artist, and the infinite worth of his work (" For the difference between that 'all but finest' and 'finest' is an infinite one "),[2] is the necessary foundation of Mr. Ruskin's aristocracy in the order of social life. A letter written in 1845 shows how this spiritual ferment was swiftly bearing him along towards a wider mission than the vindication of Turner and the modern landscape school. " With your hopes for the elevation of English art by means of fresco I cannot sympathise. . . . It is not the material nor the space that can give us thoughts, passions, or power. I see on our Academy walls nothing but what is ignoble in small pictures, and would be disgusting in large ones. . . . It is not the love of fresco that we want; it is the love of God and His creatures; it is humility, and charity, and self-denial and fasting; it is a total change of character. You want neither walls, nor plaster, nor colours — *ça ne fait rien à l'affaire;* it is Giotto and Ghirlandajo and Angelico that you want, and that you will and must want until this disgusting nineteenth century has — I can't say breathed, but steamed its last." [3] Here we have an early glimpse of the wider social outlook.

Indeed, we may regard the definite moral and religious fusion of this period in some sense as a bridge

---

[1] Modern Painters, iii. 147–8.   [2] Queen of the Air, § 141.
[3] Collingwood, " Life and Work," i. 126.

from æsthetics into social criticism. To a young man
of broad sympathy and analytic temper much pondering
upon the deeper issues of religion inevitably proved a
solvent of early orthodoxy. Mr. Ruskin himself thought
it sufficiently important to record how in 1845 he first
" broke the Sabbath " by climbing a hill after church.
In fact, churches " built with hands " were beginning to
lose something of their old significance, and he was
working his way towards that broader conception of a
Church based upon a deeper harmony of spiritual convictions, the federation of all Protestants, which he
proposed in his pamphlet of 1851, entitled " Notes on
the Construction of Sheepfolds." Though his position
of broad Protestantism was but a half-way house which
he later on regarded with contempt,[1] it serves to
indicate a growing liberation of thought upon high
matters. Heretic in painting, architecture, geology,
Mr. Ruskin now came to be regarded by his parents
and his orthodox friends as a religious heretic.

§ 9. But in all these early writings upon the philosophy and practice of art and its vital relation to morality
and religion, widely discursive as they are, we find no
definite conception of the pressure of social problems.
The second volume of " Modern Painters," with its
astonishing width of scope, finds no place for society
considered as an object for the exercise of art and the
imaginative faculty. In that book we find indeed an
eloquent recognition of humanity. Its chapter " Of Vital

---

[1] See, for instance, his first " Letter on the Italian Question,"
written July, 1859 (and reprinted in " Arrows of the Chace," vol.
ii., p. 3), for an already clear recognition of the narrow arrogance
of Protestantism.

Beauty in Man" is perhaps the first clear evidence in
Mr. Ruskin of a deep-rooted dissatisfaction with man's
condition as a physical and moral being. The " right
ideal " of human nature is an object of passionate conviction, and can only be obtained for art " by the banish-
ment of the immediate signs of sin upon the countenance
and body." The power whereby the imagination of the
artist can compass his task is Love. " Nothing but
love can read the letters, nothing but sympathy catch
the sound." But Mr. Ruskin is thinking of the individual alone. When he tells us, " There is a perfect
ideal to be wrought out of every face around us," he
declines to apply his idealism to collective man. In
" Modern Painters," then, we have ideals of inorganic
nature, of vegetable and animal life in their several
species, of man the single human being, but not of
humanity.

An occasional glimpse, indeed, is to be found of
truths regarding the essential relation of work to man.
The pamphlet on " Pre-Raphaelitism," written in 1851,
opens with this striking sentence: " It may be proved
with much certainty that God intends no man to live
in this world without working, but it seems to me no less
evident that He intends every man to be happy in his
work." But though this sentence contains implicitly all
that is expressed in his later more vigorous pronounce-
ment, " Life without work is robbery: work without art
is brutality," he is yet far removed from the state of
social indignation which gives its sting to this forceful
epigram.

The wider implications of the " gospel of work " were
yet hidden from him: the art interest in the main still

absorbed his thought. And yet it was through his distinctively artistic studies that Mr. Ruskin came to know the supreme need of social reform.

§ 10. Entering his maturer study of the history of architecture and painting with the conviction that "the sensation of beauty is not sensual on the one hand, nor is it intellectual on the other, but is dependent on a pure, right, and open state of the heart both for its truth and for its intensity,"[1] Mr. Ruskin was driven to certain conclusions regarding the influence of political and industrial institutions and habits upon the character of art. Nowhere is the nature and vital capacity of a people expressed so permanently in such diverse forms, in such impressive fashion, so unconsciously, and therefore so truthfully, as in its architecture. In regarding the churches, palaces, and houses as great documents of national character, Mr. Ruskin could not fail to get new and powerful lights upon the meaning of history.

Applying his moral principles of art to the history of this specific art, he was led to deep reflections upon the moral causes which underlay the destiny of nations and were responsible for their rise and fall. The work embodying these reflections, "The Seven Lamps of Architecture," was written in 1848, and though Mr. Ruskin, newly married, with a quiet home of his own, suffered none of the rude shocks of this tempestuous year to break his outward tranquillity, the writings of Carlyle had already begun to stir the dark depths of his soul, and he writes with gloomy vaticination, "The aspect of the years that approach us is as solemn as it is full of mystery; and the weight of the evil against which we

[1] Modern Painters, vol. ii., p. 15.

have to contend is increasing like letting out of water. It is no time for the idleness of metaphysics or the entertainment of the arts. The blasphemies of the earth are waging louder, and its miseries heavier every day." [1]

§ 11. " Stones of Venice " — the work he undertook in 1849 — marks a perceptible advance in his social teaching. Here he definitely set himself to a concrete illustration of his theory of the dependence of national art upon national character.

" The ' Stones of Venice ' had, from beginning to end, no other aim than to show that this Gothic architecture of Venice had arisen out of, and indicated in all its features, a state of pure national faith and of domestic virtue ; and that its Renaissance architecture had arisen out of, and in all its features indicated, a state of concealed national infidelity and of domestic corruption." [2]

A fairly isolated instance of national development in art, commerce, and political power, Venice could hardly fail to throw a direct and powerful flood of light upon the " condition of England," a country which, actuated by the same evil pride of Mammon-worship that ruined the bride of the Adriatic, was visibly plunging into the same slough of enervating and degrading materialism. Mr. Ruskin clearly recognises the important educative influence of this study upon himself. In a passage of " Præterita " he describes how Tintoret led him to study the fate of the Venetian republic, " So forcing me into a study of the history of Venice herself ; and through that into what else I have traced or told of the laws of national strength and virtue." [3]

[1] Collingwood, " Life and Work," i. 137-8.
[2] Crown of Wild Olive, § 65.   [3] Præterita, ii. 250.

§ 12. There are passages in the earlier books and lectures where Mr. Ruskin seems to insist upon the moral character of the individual artist as an essential condition of true art-work. But his maturer thought leads him to lay more stress upon social than individual morality, as he came to realise the power of heredity, tradition, and the direct social support accorded to the individual by the spirit and institutions of his age. His true doctrine is thus summarised: "Let a nation be healthy, happy, pure in its enjoyments, brave in its acts, and broad in its affections, and its art will spring around and within it as freely as the foam from a fountain; but let the springs of its life be impure, and its course polluted, and you will not get the bright spray by treatises on the mathematical structure of bubbles." [1]

This clear and growing recognition of the organic relation between art and national character was the bridge from Mr. Ruskin's art mission to his social mission.

How can the springs of English national life to-day be purified so that a true national art may once more be possible? What are the taints of conduct and character, what are the vices and defects of social order which must be removed before a true national life blossoming in art is attainable? Such questions beset Mr. Ruskin now. Read the chapter upon "The Nature of Gothic" in the "Seven Lamps," and the whole process of his social teaching appears in embryo. Read "Stones of Venice," and his whole policy of social reform becomes inevitable.

§ 13. The earliest expressions of social revolt consisted in sharp outbursts against the vulgar utilitarianism,

[1] On the Old Road, vol. i., § 276; *cf.* Lectures on Art, p. 26.

the " corrupt, over-paupered civilisation," [1] the mechanical conception of progress which marked the age. The denunciations of Carlyle swept Mr. Ruskin's heart with a passionate storm of sympathy, and from their first close acquaintance, in 1850, he may be accounted a disciple. In 1851 he found himself unable to share in the chorus of self-congratulation which the English nation were raising over the apotheosis of manufacture at the great exhibition, and the editor of a keen-scented trade journal already detected signs that Mr. Ruskin was " inimical to sundry vested interests."

Some years elapsed before his social views took the form of definite criticism.

In 1855 we find the first mention of serious attention to political economy. Writing in that year he says, with cheerful self-confidence, " My studies in political economy have induced me to believe that nobody knows anything about that; and I am at present engaged in an investigation, on independent principles, of the nature of money, rent, and taxes in an abstract form which sometimes keeps me awake at night." [2]

These economic studies perhaps helped to interest him in the various philanthropic schemes of working-class education, in which he now began to take an active part. In 1854 we find him giving his first lectures to workmen in the decorative trade; and in the same year began his connection with the Working Man's College, where he enlisted, under the Rev. Frederick Denison Maurice, in a gallant and not unsuccessful attempt to get into close touch with working men. For some years

---

[1] Modern Painters, vol. ii., p. 3.
[2] Collingwood, " Life and Work," i. 194.

he was most assiduous in his attendance at the drawing-classes, and, even after he abandoned his regular tuition, he maintained a close interest in this work. Such experiments, attended by the publication of simple hand-books, the " Elements of Drawing" (1856), and the " Elements of Perspective" (1859), may be taken as evidence that he had not yet abandoned all belief in the possibility of an art revival among the people without any radical disturbance of the present social and industrial order.

§ 14. The results of his recent economic studies began to take more definite shape in 1857, when, invited to lecture at the Art Treasures Exhibition at Manchester, he chose for his subject "The Political Economy of Art." These lectures, afterwards incorporated in " A Joy for Ever," contain his first exposure of the essential defects of competitive commercialism in its bearing upon the production and distribution of that species of wealth classed as art. Here for the first time we find the fundamentally socialistic assumption that it is the business of the State to educate, organise, and in every way economise, the artistic ability of the nation in order to get and keep for the national good the largest number of the best works of art. Many of the schemes which find fuller development in after years are lightly sketched in these lectures, as, for example, the establishment of co-operative guilds of craftsmen responsible for the regulation of each skilled trade. But though the seeds of Mr. Ruskin's most " revolutionary" doctrines are all to be found in these discourses, there is no reason to suppose that their author was yet conscious of their full logical implications. The deep-rooted attachment to the existing order, and still deeper rooted distrust and

alarm at the gospel of liberty and equality which stimulated most of the agitations of the age, made him reluctant to follow out the logical sequel of his thought. A
lecture given about this time thus represents his view,
" He thought existing social arrangements good, and he
agreed with his friends the Carlyles, who had found that
it was only the incapable who could not get work " [1] —
a shallow judgment which he was soon destined to
abandon.

§ 15. A rough but serviceable classification divides
Mr. Ruskin's work and life before 1859–60 from the
period which follows, assigning to the earlier period his
art-work, to the latter his social work. The close of
his fortieth year seems to have brought a growing sense
of inward struggle. He seems to have " gone out into
the wilderness," and to have been engaged in terrible
conflict with those spectres of the mind which have
always arisen to tempt prophets from the way which
they should go. We have no such record of this spiritual conflict as Carlyle has given us of his valley-struggle,
but Mr. Ruskin's " Everlasting Yea " was, if less boister-
ously triumphant, more positive and definite in character
than his master's.

His social and economic criticism was now visibly
quickening in his mind. A series of lectures written in
the autumn of 1859, and suggested by strikes in the
London building trades, formed the embryo of the papers
which took final shape in " Unto this Last." In the
literary history of Mr. Ruskin these papers are of pivotal
importance. Thackeray, actuated partly by admiration
of Mr. Ruskin's works, partly by private friendship, con-

[1] Life and Work, i. 214.

sented to insert them in *Cornhill*, which he was editing. But after the first three had appeared, Thackeray wrote to say that he could only insert one more, assigning as his reason the unanimous condemnation of his reading public.

The interesting preface attached to "Unto this Last" shows the spirit in which Ruskin took up this public challenge. The "gentle reader" gladly accepted Mr. Ruskin as teacher of art; his eloquent interpretation of pictures and architecture was entirely welcome; but let the apostle of culture stick to his brush, and let him not attempt to instruct the hard-headed, practical Englishman upon the conduct of his business life.

What is Mr. Ruskin's reply?

"The four following essays were published eighteen months ago in the *Cornhill Magazine*, and were reprobated in a violent manner, as far as I could hear, by most of the readers they met with. Not a whit the less, I believe them to be the best, that is to say the truest, rightest worded, and most serviceable things I have ever written."

It might almost be said that he devoted the rest of his laborious life to substantiate this claim. The history of literature contains no more heroic example of a single man fighting, almost alone, against the indifference of the public and the unconcealed contempt of the mass of the educated classes: openly taunted as a fanatical ignoramus by arm-chair economists who dogmatised on the principles of political economy without possessing any practical acquaintance with the arts of production and consumption on which they theorised; bewailed by his artistic and literary friends as one who had aban-

doned himself to a wild and fruitless crusade; accounted
a Utopian dreamer by most of his readers, who condoned
his offensive opinions on account of the beautiful language in which they were expressed. Against such a
torrent of hostility, against such an impenetrable bul-
wark of indifference or misunderstanding, Mr. Ruskin
set himself in stout defiance for thirty years, essaying
with every weapon of his literary arsenal to find an
entrance to the heart and intellect of the people. As
we cast our eyes down the list of his published writings,
we still find that astonishing variety of subject-matter
which we trace during his earlier years. But whatever
the titles, whatever the immediate object — lectures
upon the history of painting, rock formations, the technique of drawing, poetry or prose fiction, education,
religion, or war; whatever the audience — Oxford undergraduates, Institute of Architects, business men, school-
girls, working men, military students — the spirit of
social criticism is always dominant, always inspiring,
often overwhelming, the formal topic of his treatment.

Though his theory of political economy underwent
some modifications in later years, its substance is contained in " Unto this Last," which still ranks as the
most powerful popular presentment of his critical as
distinct from his constructive theory. This criticism is
two-fanged; on the one hand it is engaged in exposing
the insufficiency and inconsistency of the current " Political Economy " considered as an explanation of existing
industry, and on the other hand it assails the character
of the industrial system — its waste, injustice, and inhumanity. This double process is characteristic of Mr.
Ruskin's criticism, though at certain places the two

streams flow together, namely, where political economy is arraigned for the support and approval it accords to the competitive basis of industrial activities.

The remedial suggestions in " Unto this Last," slight though they are, indicate that even amid the early ferment of his destructive criticism he was already thinking out the new social order to be expounded in his later books. [" Unto this Last," not merely in its thought but in its style, was too original to win early acceptance. Its conjunction of Mr. Ruskin's distinctive literary qualities, swift, close analysis of propositions, passionate appeal, biting humour, and quaint etymological research, was calculated to produce surprise but not conviction in the torpid mind of his " cultured " readers.

§ 16. But Mr. Ruskin knew no discouragement. He planned in 1861 a new series of papers, which were to set in closer reason and somewhat ampler form the same substantial truths. The body of this work he accomplished at Mornex in the Alps, and the editor of *Frazer's Magazine* plucked up sufficient courage to promise publication. But after three papers had appeared, the irate public and the publisher himself would have no more of "such rubbish." These lectures, the most brilliant and effective exposition of his social theory, were thus laid aside, and only in 1872 were republished under the title " Munera Pulveris." Mr. Ruskin's reply to such rebuffs may be read in the address he gave before the Institute of British Architects in 1865. This address is a formal abandonment of his earlier hopes for art and the art-mission to which he had set himself; and it assigns as a reason for this change the necessity of a radical reconstruction of industrial society, as a prior condition of true progress in art. In the history of Mr. Ruskin's thought this is a most important document. Speaking to architects, he couches his indictment of the present disorder in an appropriate illustration from the outward structure of the modern industrial town, and points his " moral " in the following words :

" But our cities, built in black air which, by its accumulated foulness, first renders all ornament invisible in distance, and thus chokes its interstices with soot; cities which are mere crowded masses of store, and warehouse, and counter, and are therefore to the rest of the world what the larder and cellar are to a private house; cities in which the object of men is not life but labour; and in which all chief magnitude of edifice is to enclose machinery ; cities in which the streets are not the avenues for the passing and procession of a happy people, but the drains for the discharge of a tormented mob, in which the only object in reaching any spot is to be transferred to another ; in which existence becomes mere transition, and every creature is only one atom in a drift of human dust and current of interchanging particles, circulating here by tunnels under ground, and there by tubes in the air ; for a city, or cities, such as this, no architecture is possible — nay, no desire of it is possible to their inhabitants." [1]

The personal conviction to which these passionate reflections lead their author is thus expressed : " For my own part I feel the force of mechanism and the fury of avaricious commerce to be at present so irresistible, that I have seceded from the study not only of architecture, but nearly of all art ; and have given myself, as I would

[1] On the Old Road, vol. i., § 277.

in a besieged city, to seek the best modes of getting bread and butter for its multitudes." [1]

The genuineness of this renunciation is attested by the fact that for many years, indeed until the completion of " Fors Clavigera," he refused to have his early art-works reprinted, hoping thereby to give increased prominence to his social writings. But while Mr. Ruskin henceforth took " the condition of England " for his theme and made reform of economic structure a first consideration, he always shunned fanaticism. Those who speak of him as a " fanatic " do not measure words. A man who feels and speaks strongly is not necessarily a fanatic. The unerring test of a fanatic is that he becomes the slave of a fixed idea, the owner of a panacea which is applied indiscriminately to cure all evils. Now Mr. Ruskin was never for one moment subject to this narrowing tendency, the result of a distorted and defective vision. That he gave dramatic emphasis to the seamy side of modern civilisation, and denounced the evil more strenuously and persistently than he approved the good, is no more than to say that he wore the cloak of a prophet and a practical reformer. But he never allowed his passionate abhorrence of some particular phase of evil to absorb his thoughts and his activity. When the conviction of the essential dishonesty of the competitive system of industry came home to him with its full force, it neither bred in him, as it has bred in many, a bitter class resentment, nor did it weaken his broad moral grasp of social problems, by impelling him to trust overmuch to structural reforms. Even when he came to hold that " all social evils and religious errors

[1] On the Old Road, vol. i., § 291.

arise out of the pillage of the labourer by the idlers," [1]
he never lost faith in the necessity of education as the
hopeful method of redress. In a word, his social mission
was distinctively an ethical rather than a political one;
and he never lost sight of the first requirement of all
valid ethical teaching, the need " to see life steadily and
see it whole." *see things as they really are*
While the need of social honesty, and the conviction
that the industrial order of the day rested upon dishonesty, became the central ganglion of his system of
teaching, he spent an ample share of his energy and intellect in tracing the course of the more distant nerves
of the social body, their relations among themselves and
to the centre, and the specific modes of health and
disease which belong to each of them. The confusion,
even chaos, of which some careless readers of Mr. Ruskin complain, yields to a clear unity of system as we
regard the meanderings of his versatile intelligence from
the standpoint of social justice, a plea for honesty of
transactions between man and man. This unity of system is not indeed a mechanical unity, an objective
system of thought, but rather a unity imposed by personal temperament and valuation. When we understand
it, we understand John Ruskin, his personality, his view
of life. Its worth consists in the variety, depth, and
accuracy of the " sensations " it records, and their ordering in accordance with prime principles of honesty and
humanity.

§ 17.   These general remarks may afford some explanation of the nature of the change which took place
in the period 1860–1865 in Mr. Ruskin's life.   He did

[1] Fors, iv., Letter lxxxiv.

not abandon any of the interests which had occupied him
in earlier years; he still figures as art critic, litterateur,
botanist, geologist, historian; but his intellectual and
emotional centre of gravity is shifted, with an alteration
in his sense of practical morality.

All his future work really consisted of applications of
this morality.

In this spirit his lectures upon " Kings' Treasuries "
and " Queens' Gardens," delivered in 1864 and published
in the book " Sesame and Lilies," must be interpreted.
" Munera Pulveris " had posited " certain conditions of
moral culture " in individuals as essential to the achievement of the reform of industrial society required by the
true Political Economy.   " Sesame and Lilies " is an
attempt to teach these conditions to members of the
pseudo-cultured classes.   " The Crown of Wild Olive,"
a collection of lectures published in 1866,[1] takes as its
special theme the question, What is Work ? tracing the
chief implications of one of the leading thoughts of
" Unto this Last," that the true end of work consists in
making " wealth " and not in earning profits.   Since Mr.
Ruskin's technical indictment of false industry consists
in his arraignment of competition as a false base, and
since the *raison d'être* of competition is individual profit,
the central interest attaching to " The Crown of Wild
Olive " lies in the full statement it contains of the fallacy
of profit as the motive of industry.   The stubborn and
eloquent defence of war and militarism which he
appends to this volume serves to show how, in shifting
his centre of gravity, he had kept fast hold of some of
the most debatable among his earlier judgments.

[1] Republished with another lecture and other new matter in 1873.

Mr. Ruskin's political economy, as we shall see, left the barrier between theory and practice peculiarly thin. The "Political Economy of Art" was full of "practical" suggestions, and the two broader treatises which followed possessed many fragments of constructive thought, while "The Crown of Wild Olive" contains an early draft of those practical reforms in education and in agriculture [1] which were the objects of Mr. Ruskin's own experiments a few years later. The full pressure of his desire to do "something practical," and especially to get into close communion with intelligent working men, is seen in the series of letters addressed to a working cork-cutter in Sunderland, first published in the early months of 1867 in the *Manchester Examiner* and the *Leeds Mercury*, and collected shortly afterwards in the volume entitled "Time and Tide by Weare and Tyne." Mr. Collingwood speaks [2] of this book as "the central work of the life of John Ruskin," containing, as it does, his ripest and most important thoughts in their most widely serviceable form. In simpler language, to be "understanded of the people," he sets forth the substantial criticism of "Munera Pulveris," but attaches to it, as a natural outgrowth, a full free account of a right social system, as he conceives it, and of the leading steps by which the necessary changes may be wrought. In particular, "Time and Tide" is notable as containing three of the proposals which Mr. Ruskin deemed essential to a sound society, — a renovated Guild System, Captains of Industry, and State Regulation of Marriage and of Population.

[1] See Lecture iv. on "The Future of England."
[2] Life and Work, ii. 74.

§ 18. "Fors Clavigera" was designed as complementary to "Time and Tide,"[1] relating to "the possible comforts and wholesome laws of familiar household life, and the share which a labouring nation may attain in the skill and the treasures of the higher arts." Such a sentence, however, gives a most inadequate suggestion of the real scope of "Fors," which is a miscellany of all his thoughts which relate directly or indirectly to social reform during the periods which they cover in their publication.

The title "Fors Clavigera," a noteworthy example of Mr. Ruskin's grave word-play, gives standing emphasis to the dominance of moral motives in all his social teaching. The triple meaning of "Fors," contained in the three English words Force, Fortitude, and Fortune, embodies the whole substance of this teaching, — the activity of manly exercise in work, capacity of endurance, and the Power outside ourselves which seems Fate or Providence, according as we regard its origin and nature.

Purposely loose and even familiar in style, "Fors Clavigera" is charged with passionate earnestness from cover to cover. The pressure to go out and preach the gospel of social righteousness had grown almost unbearable. The misery and injustice of the life he saw around him were goading him to action. In one of the earliest letters he writes thus: "I cannot paint, nor read, nor look at minerals, nor do anything else that I like, and the very light of the morning sun has become hateful to me, because of the misery that I know of, and see signs of, where I know it not, which no imagination

---

[1] See Preface to 1872 edition of "Time and Tide."

can interpret too bitterly. Therefore I will endure it no
longer quietly; but henceforward, with any few or many
who will help, do my poor best to abate this misery."[1]

So far as any closer design is preserved, it may be
stated in the following words from Letter xliii. :

"The current and continual purpose of 'Fors Clavigera' is to explain the powers of chance or fortune
(Fors) as she offers to men the conditions of prosperity;
and as these conditions are accepted or refused, nails
down and fastens their fate for ever, being thus 'Clavigera'—'nail bearing.' The image is one familiar in
my theology; my own conception of it was first got from
Horace, and developed by steady effort to read history
with impartiality and to observe the lives of men around
me with charity. 'How you may make your fortune or
mar it' is the expansion of the title."[2]

At the outset, however, it is made evident that social
reform in its practical aspects is to be the *pièce de resis-
tance*. There is, indeed, no close orderly adhesion to this
or to any other theme in "Fors." During the years of
its monthly appearance it supplied Mr. Ruskin with a
free instrument of expression upon all sorts of passing
events.[3] Topic after topic usurps the lead and holds it
for a while, suddenly disappearing and anon taking its
place again; large scraps of early autobiography are
embedded there, rich deposits of art-criticism, Bible
commentary, heraldry, poetic criticism, suggestive words
are tracked to their inmost lair, the elements of drawing

---

[1] Fors, i., Letter i.   [2] Ibid., iv., Letter lxxxv.
[3] "By the adoption of the title 'Fors,' I meant (among other
meanings) to indicate this desultory and accidental character of
the work" (Letter lxxxv.).

and of several sciences are followed for a while. We
have, in fact, a faithful reflection of the multitudinous
interests of this most fertile mind, given with an artless
fidelity that makes " Fors Clavigera" one of the most
valuable confessions in the whole of literature. But
though other purposes often overlay the directly social
teaching, this latter always reappears and occupies the
largest space throughout the volumes.

This teaching, however, no longer seeks merely to
inform the mind or to inflame the heart with an understanding of and a passion for social justice, it aims at
directly stimulating readers to join him in experiments
of practical reform. This is made clear in the opening letter (January, 1871) by the following declaration
of his purpose: " I must clear myself from all sense of
responsibility for the material distress around me, by
explaining to you, in the shortest English I can, what I
know of its causes; by pointing out to you some of the
methods by which it might be relieved; and by setting
aside regularly some small percentage of my income, to
assist, as one of yourselves, in what one and all we shall
have to do; each of us laying by something, according
to our means, for the common service; and having
amongst us at last, be it ever so small, a National Store
instead of a National Debt." [1] This craving to " do
something practical " is the animating spirit of " Fors."
To get a piece of land and to put upon it willing workers
who should till the soil and ply useful handicrafts, living
a wholesome family life in sound neighbourly co-operation and with obedience to rightly established authority,
with leisure and mind to cultivate and practise the true

[1] Fors, i., Letter i.

graces and joys of life — such an experiment in social
life Mr. Ruskin now strove to set on foot. The Society
of St. George, formed to carry out this work, or to help
with sympathy and money, plays a large part throughout
these letters, several of the early letters being devoted
to defining the objects, method, and structure of the
society. After a start in practical work was made next
year, " Fors " serves as a chronicle of progress and an
instrument for discussing the various educational and industrial projects which Mr. Ruskin hoped to further by
means of the Company. A statement of these schemes
is reserved for a later chapter. Here we need only
observe that they form a sort of backbone to " Fors
Clavigera," imposing a certain continuity of interest,
and serving to emphasise the growing pressure to pass
from theory into practice which beset Mr. Ruskin in
his later years. The Company, once formed, also made
a certain inner circle which he could address with the
authoritative familiarity of a loved and recognised
master, and whose education in the art of life was a
constant object of solicitude.

But this central position occupied by the work of
St. George's Company did little to restrict the topics or
the treatment of " Fors." The wider exoteric preaching
of his social gospel, the driving home of the great truths
of justice and humanity as he saw them in the multitudinous affairs of life, into as many minds as he could
reach, by every method of appeal which the astounding
versatility of his mind could command, is, after all, the
prevailing character of " Fors." The fragmentary and
irregular mode of its production, written as it was in
every variety of place and circumstance, makes it a

peculiarly vivid and truthful reflection of innumerable facets of his mind, while the familiarity of its style gives much which the dignity of literature commonly conceals, the passing moods of thought and temper, the quick impulsive judgments of events as they pass by, an impressionism which, rightly interpreted, is among the greatest services a man of sensitive and widely cultivated tastes is able to confer. That portions of the later volumes of " Fors " are darkened by the gloom and even embittered by the anguish which for seasons darkened and distracted the mind of the author, is visible enough to every reader. But even through such passages the ultimate and indomitable sanity of Mr. Ruskin's view of life shines with clear persistency; the confusion and obscurity is but occasional and superficial. On the whole, " Fors Clavigera " holds a unique position not only in Mr. Ruskin's writings but in modern literature. Crowded with brilliant and pertinent satire, with tenderest and most penetrative pathos, with cunning researches into words and things, with profound analysis of cause and effect in life, it is the fullest, freest, and, on the whole, the most effective " criticism of life " in England of the nineteenth century that we possess. Like all great books, it must be taken as a whole; for, in spite of large irregularities of form and wide gaps of time in its composition, it is a whole by virtue of the unity of that personality of which it is the most truthful expression.

In making this claim for " Fors " we must of course insist that its focus and its object shall be kept in mind, and that the criterion of unity and effectiveness applied to it shall be those rightly applicable to works of auto-

biographic form, and not those which are applied to
books whose composition proceeds by carefully ironing
out every crease of inconsistency so as to present a
smooth finality of well-ordered thought.

This position of importance I claim for " Fors "
because it contains the fullest and most mature presentment of the social teaching of the man who, by
the conjunction of the keenest sense of justice with
the widest culture and the finest gifts of literary
expression, has succeeded in telling our age more of
the truths it most requires to know than any other
man.

In Mr. Ruskin's own works it occupies an architec-
tonic place, marking his highest and fullest growth of
thought.

The following passage from the last volume of
" Fors " gives succinctly Mr. Ruskin's own view of the
development of his teaching through his five most representative works.

" 'Modern Painters' taught the claim of all lower
nature in the hearts of men; of the rock, and wave
and herb, as a part of their necessary spirit life; in all
that I now bid you to do, to dress the earth and keep
it, I am fulfilling what I then began. The ' Stones of
Venice' taught the laws of constructive art, and the
dependence of all human work or edifice, for its beauty,
on the happy life of the workman. ' Unto this Last'
taught the laws of that life itself, and its dependence on
the Sun of Justice; the ' Inaugural Oxford Lectures,' the
necessity that it should be led, and the gracious laws of
beauty and labour recognised, by the upper, no less than
the lower, classes of England; and, lastly, ' Fors Clavi-

gera' has declared the relation of these to each other,
and the only possible conditions of peace and honour,
for low and high, rich and poor, together in the holding
of that first Estate, under the only Despot, God, from
which, whoso falls, angel or man, is kept, not myth-
ically nor disputably, but here in visible horror of
chains under darkness to the judgment of the great
day: and in keeping which service is perfect freedom,
and inheritance of all that a loving Creator can give
to His creatures, and an immortal Father to His
children." [1]

Such is the general growth of Mr. Ruskin's thought
and labours, from Nature to Art, through Art to Human Life, in the Art of Life a growing sense of the
demands of Eternal Law in the making and governance
of Human Society founded on principles of justice and
humanity.

[1] Fors, Letter lxxviii., vol. iv.

CHAPTER III.

§ 1. THERE is a curious notion still widely prevalent, that Mr. Ruskin abandoned his proper work as an art teacher in order rashly to embark in Political Economy, for which he had neither natural aptitude nor the requisite training and knowledge. In order to show how ill founded such a notion is, it may be well to enumerate some of the special qualifications he possessed for this work of social and economic criticism. Political Economy, even in that narrow connotation of industrial science from which Mr. Ruskin sought to release it, takes for its subject-matter the work which men put into the

raw material supplied by Nature in order to furnish necessaries or conveniences for human consumption. Now
Mr. Ruskin's first qualification is that of being a skilled
specialist in the finer qualities of work on the one hand,
and of enjoyment or consumption on the other hand.
Both from personal practice and from long habits of
close observation of the work of skilful men in many
places, he obtained a wide and varied knowledge of the
handling of different tools and materials for the production of useful and beautiful goods. This experience was
by no means confined to painting, sculpture, and the so-
called " fine arts," but comprised the practical work of
architecture, wood and metal work, pottery, jewellery,
weaving, and other handicrafts.

His investigations into agriculture, both on the Continent of Europe and in Britain, were minute and pains-
taking; and though his experiments in reclaiming and
draining land were not always successful, they indicated
close knowledge of the concrete facts.

Moreover, Mr. Ruskin made a life-long study of animal and vegetable life, and of the structure and composition of the earth, thus gaining an intimate acquaintance with the nature of the raw materials of that wealth
which formed the chief subject-matter of commercial
economy. He had spent most of his laborious life in
patient detailed observation of nature and the works of
man. Both from contemporary observation and from
study of history, the actual processes by which large
classes of goods were produced and consumed were familiar to him. How many of the teachers of Political
Economy who have been so scornful of Mr. Ruskin's
claims possessed a tithe of this practical knowledge?

How many of them had studied the growth of the different arts and handicrafts in the history of nature as he had studied them? Most of those who sought to laugh him out of the field of controversy, or to ignore him, were either arm-chair economists, whose knowledge of present industrial facts was almost entirely drawn from books, and whose acquaintance with industrial history, even from books, was then extremely slight, or else business men engaged in some special branch of machine production or finance, whose personal knowledge, sound enough doubtless within its limits, covered but a very small section of the whole industrial field. Of certain large typical modern forms of industry Mr. Ruskin indeed possessed neither experience nor special knowledge ; but how many of our most authoritative writers on Political Economy have ever had their training in a cotton-mill, a mine, a merchant's office, or a retail shop? So far as first-hand knowledge of work and its results is concerned, Mr. Ruskin enjoyed an immense superiority over his opponents.

§ 2. Another advantage which Mr. Ruskin enjoyed in a supreme degree was his mastery of language. In no study have " masked words " (to adopt his own familiar phrase) played so much havoc as in Political Economy ; nowhere have " idols of the market-place " so often darkened counsel, pompous well-rounded phrases, which, usurping the dignity of scientific laws, browbeat the humble inquirer who seeks to get behind them to the facts they claim to represent.

This defect was inevitable in a science hastily improvised by gathering together the general results of a number of previously unrelated studies of agriculture, finance

and taxation, political philosophy, foreign trade, population, etc., into a science of "the wealth of nations,"
drawing its terminology partly from current politics,
partly from philosophic text-books, and largely from the
loose language of actual business intercourse.   That
much of the reasoning conducted by means of such ill-
arranged and shifty terms should be illicit was inevitable,
and it can be no matter for surprise that text-books of
Political Economy should be largely occupied in detect-
ing the loose arguments of predecessors based upon
verbal duplicity, and in constructing, by similar methods, new arguments, destined in their turn to similar
treatment by some not remote successor.   Now in such
a study Mr. Ruskin's finely trained instinct for language
served him well.   His passion of delving down to roots
sometimes, it may be admitted, led him into false paths,
and some of his work of literary " restoration " was too
fantastic to be really serviceable.   But, making all allowance for the deceitfulness of philology, his habit of
intelligent scrutiny applied to such terms as "value,"
" capital," " profit," " consumption," was really useful in
exposing the ambiguity and falsification of facts to which
these terms have lent themselves.

§ 3. Two other intellectual and moral qualities belonging to Mr. Ruskin's equipment deserve a word.   First,
his fearless honesty in dealing with all seen facts.   No
one who has faithfully followed the development of Political Economy can have failed to note how political or
business interests, or else some academic bias, have
warped and distorted the free natural growth of the
study, making it subservient to the conveniences of some
class or party cause.   Now, Mr. Ruskin's absolute sin-

cerity of sight and speech was quite unimpaired by such
obscuring or distorting influences. Neither was he ever
found servile to authority, though generally willing to
defer to the reasonable and well-grounded judgment of
others. The same originality by which he claimed to <
set aside the wrongful authority of Reynolds in art, he
applied to the authority of Ricardo and Mill in Political
Economy. This fearless exposure of insufficiently established authority, this insistence upon the right of independent inquiry into facts and principles, which is
undeniably the source of his most valuable achievements
as art critic, was equally serviceable in Political Economy, where the extreme paucity of intellects belonging
to the first order had foisted into the seat of authority
names quite undeserving of such high consideration.

§ 4. Finally, without endorsing the claim that Mr. 4
Ruskin is "the most analytic mind in Europe," all
who have closely read his books from "Modern
Painters" on to "Fors Clavigera" must admit his
wonderful faculty of minute analysis. How many
Englishmen of this century have evinced such intellectual vigour and subtlety as appears in the philosophic
handling of the origins of art in the second volume of
"Modern Painters," or such genius for classification as
appears in "The Seven Lamps of Architecture"? This
same faculty, heightened by wide experience, Mr. Ruskin
brought to bear upon social science. When we consider
his combats at close quarters with trained economists,
we shall see how well he was able to hold his own, and
though his constructive reasoning may not always prove
sound, his exposure of the fallacious reasoning of others
is generally forcible and convincing.

The foregoing considerations will serve to dispel the popular illusion which represents Mr. Ruskin as an ill-equipped knight-errant entering the lists of economic controversy in a spirit of sentimental bravado. Alike in possession of material facts, in command of language, and in trained capacity of argument, he was quite competent to discuss economic problems with Senior, Fawcett, and J. S. Mill. His leading defects he only shared in common with most economists of the last generation, viz., a lack of opportunity of early free contact with the labouring classes, whose work and life is of prime importance in economic study, and an insufficient grasp of evolution in the structure of industrial and political institutions.

§ 5. Even had Mr. Ruskin, accepting the limits of economic science laid down by earlier authorities, confined himself to criticism of the inconsistencies and errors to be found there, the powers we have enumerated would have enabled him to do yeoman's service. But in the far larger task to which he set himself these rare qualities of nature and experience were of unique value.

His arraignment of current Political Economy may be formally divided into two parts. Firstly, he accuses the science of commercial wealth of wrongfully assuming the title and function of Political Economy. Secondly, he impugns the accuracy of many of the fundamental doctrines of this commercial science, and imputes to them an injurious influence upon the happiness and morality of society.

Under this latter count may be included the attack which he makes upon the justice and the utility of industry conducted competitively for individual profit; for the gravamen of this indictment of Political Economy has reference chiefly to the support it has yielded to the existing industrial system.   The first head of the indictment alone will occupy this chapter.

§ 6. Failure to understand the nature of Mr. Ruskin's attack has led many to assert that he has wrongfully imported sentiment into matters where it has no proper place.   This charge, however, boldly begs the question, for his contention is, firstly, that sentiment does rightly enter, and ultimately dominates, a true science of Political Economy; and, secondly, that current Political Economy is largely sentimental both in its origin and influence, but that its sentiments are false.

First let us turn to the charge he brings against current Political Economy of wrongly arrogating to itself this title.   The subject-matter of this " science " consists of " wealth " defined as " utilities embodied in material objects," and possessing a money value.   Here are two assumptions, first that wealth is rightly confined to material embodiments, and secondly that it is to be estimated by reference to a monetary standard.

Researches into the right meaning of the terms " wealth " and " value " form the most vital criticism of " Unto this Last."   Mr. Ruskin's mode of etymological inquiry, with its frequent assertion of fanciful analogies and its undue emphasis on roots, should not mislead us into supposing that the distinctions he makes are " purely verbal."   In reality he always looks through words to things.   In his pertinent question, " What right have you to take the word ' wealth,' which originally meant ' well-being,' and degrade and narrow it by confining it to certain sorts of material objects measured by money?" he is not ultimately concerned with the perversion of a word, but with the perversion of an idea. His real arraignment is of the process of segmentation, which takes a particular sort of material objects as a subject of separate scientific investigation, and professes to found upon such science an art of national and individual conduct. For it must be distinctly understood that Political Economy has always claimed to be both a science and an art, — the art being, as is only natural, historically prior to the science.

Now Mr. Ruskin does not deny that a hypothetical science may be framed, upon the assumptions that every man is idle and covetous, and that the maximum quantity of wealth embodied in material forms and measured by money is the sole object of his endeavour, in order to investigate the laws of the production and distribution of such wealth. A science based on these assumptions as to the nature and aim of men may be consistent in its parts and correct in its reasoning. But when he is invited to accept this as a science relating to actually existent men and their conduct, Mr. Ruskin flatly refuses
> to do so. How, he asks, if man be not wholly idle and "a covetous machine," but is endowed with a liking for good work and a capacity of self-sacrifice, is not moved entirely by money but also by affections, seeks not only material marketable goods but other goods that are neither material nor marketable? What is the use of a science which begins by assuming that man is what he is not?

In "Unto this Last," Mr. Ruskin unduly presses the charge that political economists assert the existence of this economic man, and the utility of covetous action. The most rigid of the old economists, with their doctrine of the social utility of enlightened selfishness, would have admitted that the " economic man " was more or less a hypothetical creature. But Mr. Ruskin's over-pressure of this point does not really impair the validity of his criticism. The statement of the assumption of orthodox Political Economy contained in a quotation at the opening of " Unto this Last," is a substantially correct account of the prevailing mode of " working" the science :

" The social affections are accidental and disturbing elements in human nature ; but avarice and the desire of progress are constant elements. Let us eliminate the inconstants, and, considering the human being merely as a covetous machine, examine by what laws of labour, purchase, and sale the greatest accumulative result in wealth is obtainable. Those laws once determined, it will be for each individual afterwards to introduce as much of the disturbing affectionate element as he chooses, and to determine for himself the result in the new conditions supposed." [1]

The pages of such writers as James Mill, M'Culloch, and Ricardo furnish ample verification of this description of the method of argument in common use. First work out your problem by isolating the self-seeking forces, and afterwards make allowance for the " disturbing influence " of other motives. Indeed, only by such method of procedure could the old economic " laws " be made plausible.

§ 7. Mr. Ruskin laid his finger accurately upon the root-fallacy of this mode of reasoning. It is found to

[1] P. 2.

reside in the assumption that " the accidentals afterwards to be introduced were of the same nature as the
powers first examined," *i. e.* " allowance for friction "
will work correctly in a mechanical problem where all
the forces can be subjected to quantitative measurement,
and where the problem is essentially mathematical, but
it will work wrongly when the forces differ qualitatively,
and are combined not mechanically but organically. It
is not, however, difficult to understand how a purely
mechanical science of Political Economy seemed plausible to those who confined their attention to certain
large fields of industry in the earlier nineteenth century. In most departments of the new manufacturing
industries, in mining, railways, and many branches of
low skilled manual labour, generally in trade and in
finance, the desire to " buy in the cheapest and sell
in the dearest market," to " do as little as one could
and get as much," was, in fact, so general, so persistent,
and so dominant that, in considering the production and
distribution of these sorts of wealth, all other motives
seemed negligible quantities. Once assume, and in all
those cases the assumption seemed not unreasonable,
that work is in itself and for itself both undesired and
undesirable, and that the sole object of such industrial
energy is to get the highest wages and profits that are
obtainable, the " covetous machine " idea of Political
Economy seemed intelligible. If all industrial energy
both did and necessarily must conform to this type, a
science of Industry might reasonably be founded upon
the assumptions actually made, though even then the
claim of such a science to be Political Economy would
be open to challenge. The economic problem, as it

presented itself in practice to the average mill-manager half a century ago, was of a purely mathematical order, how to buy at cheapest price the raw materials, coal, machinery, and labour power, requisite for turning out his goods, and how to find a ready market for them at the price which would yield the largest margin of profit. The idea of allowing considerations of humanity ∠ to affect the price at which he bought the commodity of labour did not normally enter his mind, and the notion that owing to the peculiar nature of the human machine it might actually " pay " in the long run to give wages above the lowest competitive standard, was a daring novelty that had not reached the average sensual man. Since the buying, the handling in various mechanical processes, and the selling of quantities of goods was to the individual business man a matter of calculation upon the strict economic assumptions we have indicated, it seemed not unreasonable to Ricardo, Mill, and other believers in the universal application of the " inductive method " to generalise from this experience of the single business man to business as a system. Thus it was that the old economics, with its purely mathematical applications of a Law of Rent, a Wage Fund, a Law of Population, etc., came to hold the field.

§ 8. Now, Mr. Ruskin approached the problem from an entirely new point of view. Even the narrow connotation given to wealth and industry by the economists included many kinds of work and many commodities which were not found to conform accurately to the general laws of their system. Mr. Ruskin had early ∠ come to recognise that work is not an evil to be shunned, but a good to be desired, provided it is in

kind and quantity desirable; and he was himself familiar with many kinds of work engaged in producing the
finest kind of material wealth which did not at all
accord with the assumption of the political economist.
✗ Not only in the fine arts, where work may be a source
of supreme delight, but in the professions, and in many
handicrafts, he saw that the assumption of the natural
and normal idleness of man was false, and that profit or
money wage was in many cases not the only or the
strongest incentive to industry.   Convinced also that an
educated and well-ordered society could, both by the
direction of industry and by the reaction of refined
tastes upon the production of wealth, indefinitely increase the proportion of work which should conform
to this higher standard, he denied the normal and
eternal validity of the economic laws which were
derived from an exclusive observation of the lower
grades of industry during a period of transition.   This
was the first of a series of radical objections urged by
Mr. Ruskin against the current teaching, viz., that its
fundamental assumption of human motive visibly broke
down when applied to large departments of industrial
activity.

The attack of Mr. Ruskin and other critics upon the
unscientific method of abstracting certain purely " economic " forces, and making allowance later on for the
friction of other non-economic forces separately estimated, has operated in leading later teachers to endeavour to " humanise " their science by admitting into the
order of economic forces all sorts of motives which affect
man in getting and spending money, and which are
measurable in money.   Professor Marshall, for example,

is willing to include in his economic investigations the " affections " and other " disturbing influences," just in so far as they can be placed upon a common economic footing with the main driving forces of idleness and greed.

If early local attachments, for example, tend to keep a man at work in his native village, and this tendency can only be overcome by a certain remuneration, these feelings of attachment are economically represented by the increment of money wage which is sufficient to induce him to leave his village for work in the neighbouring town. So, in the spending of money, it is possible to compare and measure the desire for material " wealth " with a desire of a wholly different order : a person attending a missionary meeting with ten shillings in his pocket, who decides to give five shillings as a subscription, spending the other five upon his lunch, must be considered to have an exactly balanced effective desire for the spread of Christianity and the satisfaction of his appetite. A careful and rightly-specialised collection of " statistics " will, it is suggested, enable us to measure the economic value of the affections and desires of every sort in so far as they are reflected in our estimates of money. It must be at once conceded that we can and habitually do make comparisons of desires widely differing in kind and degree by reference to money, and the new method, so far as it is applicable, appears to meet Mr. Ruskin's demand that the accidental or disturbing forces must be of the same nature as the primitive forces.

§ 9. Assuming, therefore, that the phenomena of buying and selling, and the industrial activities to which they have reference, can be conveniently isolated, it is legit-

imate to make them the subject of a separate science.
But can they be conveniently isolated, and if so, is the
science which deals with them to be called Political
Economy? Such are the questions which arise next
in logical order. Since unity in the phenomena of the
universe and in human knowledge is an essential condition of all science, it is often rightly urged that only
one science exists. The recognition of many sciences
is a matter of convenience which posits a certain sacrifice of exactitude. The exact demarcation of scientific
boundaries is a constant matter of dispute. The contention of the supporters of a science of Industry is that
the phenomena with which it is concerned are sufficiently like one another and unlike other phenomena
to form the object of a separate science. That this
science will impinge upon other sciences, *e. g.* ethics and
politics and hygiene, is admitted. But this impact is
not so frequent and so constant as to destroy the virtual
independence of industrial phenomena.

Now there are many difficulties in the way of admitting this virtual independence. If we regard the problem on the side of " production," the organic character
of man obliges us to insist that every act of his life has
an effect, and often an important one, upon his productive powers for good or evil in various ways. Intemper-
ance, the exercise of football, the kind of books he reads,
the friendships he forms, and a thousand other more
detailed habits and acts of a non-economic nature,
directly affect him as a worker. The modern economist
replies, " Well, in so far as they affect the money-value
of his work and the wages he gets, we will consider
them." Similarly with the problem on the " consump-

tion " side : every individual peculiarity of nature, habits, etc., will affect those desires which find expression in the way he spends his money. " Well," says the modern economist, " let us consider them so far as they are reflected in his demand for commodities."

This sounds plausible, and is perhaps feasible, and yet it is noteworthy that these very economists who claim that Political Economy is confined to the investigation of the ways in which a man makes and spends his income, do not, in fact, confine their treatment of the life and character of man to his desires reflected in money. Having abandoned the old economic man, and striving to see man as he is, they are almost inevitably drawn away from their investigation of him as a " getting and spending " animal to the direct consideration of various other conditions of his life which underlie his getting and spending processes. In the early economists this inconsistency was confined to occasional pious or humane reflections or aspirations, but J. S. Mill having set the example of elaborate dissertations upon methods of social reform and the future of the labouring classes, has been generally followed by later writers. It is true that these speculations and humane disquisitions have something to do with the getting and spending of money ; but it is not true that the social problems there discussed — the influence of machinery, the eight-hours day, the possibilities of co-operation, the functions of the State — are discussed in direct or sole reference to " getting and spending." On the contrary, various non-economic goods, such as leisure, honesty, intellectual and æsthetic tastes, friendship and the social virtues, are treated not as economic factors actually ascertained in their monetary

influence, but as human functions which have some definite relations of their own to the functions of production
and consumption. Now, when an economist discusses
the reactionary influence of contentment, leisure, domestic happiness upon the wealth-producing faculties in an
à priori way, or when he points out how raising the
character of civic life will react upon the efficiency of
industry, his arguments are so many tacit admissions
that the segregation of purely industrial phenomena is
not, in fact, the convenient hypothesis for Political
Economy which he averred it was.

But perhaps the most convincing testimony to the
loose-jointedness of the current economic science was
afforded by the astounding diversity of meaning attaching to the term in general use to describe the subject-
matter of that science. Mr. Ruskin has indeed most
ample ground for his sarcastic commentary upon J. S.
Mill's declaration, that " Every one has a notion, sufficiently correct for common purposes, of what is meant
by wealth." [1]   In fact, we find almost every economist
with a special definition of his own ; some including
everything with an exchange-value whether it is material or not, others excluding non-material goods ; some
including, others excluding, human skill, honesty, and
serviceable human qualities ; some insisting upon permanency as a condition of wealth. Whatever definition is
taken, new difficulties arise by reason of the shifting
character of industry and social institutions. The liberation of slaves causes a reduction of national wealth,
the enclosure of common lands an increase ; when brew-
ing and baking are no longer done at home new indus-

[1] J. S. Mill, " Principles of Political Economy," Introd., p. 2.

tries and new orders of industrial wealth come into
being. Most of the work of women, domestic in character, is not "productive of wealth" because its results
are not exchangeable. The natural resources of a country, its climate and conformation, its rivers, etc., are
they to be classed as wealth? The highways, public
buildings, and other strictly non-saleable property, in
what sense is it wealth?

Such questions, and they may be multiplied almost
indefinitely, indicate that "wealth" and "the industrial
system" are not such clearly separable divisions of the
totality of things as could be desired for the establishment of a science. The actual and increasing trans-
gressions made by political economists outside the limits
laid down by their own definition are a most convincing,
because an unconscious, testimony to the uncertainty of
their position.

§ 10. It is not, however, essential to Mr. Ruskin's
position to deny that "the industrial system" can be
made the subject of a special study. There might be a
science of marketable goods estimated at market prices.
But he repudiates the claim of such a science to be
called "Political Economy," as he also denies its ability
to impose any rule of conduct upon life. If such a
science exist, let it be called what it actually is, Mercantile Economy.[1]

Against this Mercantile Science, the science of avarice,
as he conceives it, Mr. Ruskin places Political Economy,
which he says "consists simply in the production, preservation, and distribution, at fittest time and place, of
useful or pleasurable things." [2]

[1] Unto this Last, p. 41.   [2] Ibid., p. 41.

Mr. Ruskin habitually ignores the academic question how far Political Economy is a science, how far an art. An " economy" of any kind, he would urge, is distinctively " a doing," but as it is " a doing" which implies not only a knowing how to do but a knowing what the results of doing will be, it may be said to contain a science. In reality he is justified in ignoring the distinction by the all-embracing character of Political Economy as he conceives it. Though the science of making money may be distinguished from the art, the " laws " of the one being in the indicative, the laws of the other in the imperative mood, the same does not hold when Political Economy is at once the science and art of life. An individual or a nation which knows the laws of making and spending money may not wish to determine expenditure or taxation in sole accord with rules deducible from these laws ; but a valid science of the " production, preservation, and distribution, at fittest time and place, of useful and pleasurable things," implies the practice of the art.

§ 11. This vital distinction between Mercantile and Political Economy brings us to the very heart of Mr. Ruskin's social criticism. His Political Economy stands not one but two removes from the current teaching.

In the first place it breaks down the barrier separating industrial processes from other serviceable human activities, bringing under wealth " all useful or pleasurable things," whether exchangeable or not, and bringing under production of wealth all wholesome human energies. Though, in his earlier treatment, Mr. Ruskin occasionally wavers, showing a disposition to confine his Political Economy to the same " industrial " activities which form the subject-matter of Mercantile Economy, only substituting a standard of justice and humanity for the accepted " commercial " standard, this is no more than a dialectical position temporarily occupied for " fighting purposes." His full, final conception of Political Economy, as a science of human welfare, includes within its scope not merely the processes by which men gain a livelihood, but all human efforts and satisfactions.

Mercantile Economy claims to concern itself with the processes by which men earn a living. But what is a living? asks Mr. Ruskin, and answering with Words-worth, " We live by admiration, hope, and love," he demands that Political Economy shall take direct cogni-sance of this higher livelihood.

This treatment is based, not upon a " sentimental," but upon a strictly scientific criticism. Mercantile Economy assumes that man as an industrial animal, a getter and spender of money, is a separate being from man as a friend, a lover, a father, a citizen, or that he can conveniently and justifiably be regarded as separate for " economic " treatment. Now Mr. Ruskin insists that the organic unity of a man as a conscious, rational being, with a capacity for regarding his life as a whole and forming a plan for its conduct, imposes a correspond-ing unity upon the science which is to treat of human conduct, that the interaction of conscious forces within man is so constant and so intricate that it is not really convenient to make the separatist assumption required by Mercantile Economy. \ " Goods " which are not " wealth " in the " mercantile " sense, the fruits of good-will and self-sacrifice, friendship, family affection, neigh-bourly or civic feeling, intellectual efforts, not destined for the market, are, both in their " production " and their

" consumption," in vital relation to industrial goods. The activities employed upon such " goods " have the most intimate reaction upon the distinctively " industrial " activities, while the enjoyment of these higher moral and intellectual goods is a chief determinant of the nature of demand for mercantile wares. This deep essential truth Mr. Ruskin illustrates by taking the instance of domestic service, and showing that the best work cannot be got out of a servant by treating his labour as a mere marketable commodity, and ignoring the personality or " soul," which necessarily enters into services. So, enlarging on the theme, he shows how every sort of work given out in industrial processes is in its nature and result the expression, not of an " economic man," a human mechanism, but of a conscious, rational, and emotional being. The appeal is made not to a mere cluster of self-seeking industrial instincts, but to the whole nature of man, and it is the whole man who in some sense responds. Treat a man as something less than a man and you fail to get even the best industrial results out of him. Why? Not merely because you ought, as a fellow-creature, to treat him with due regard to moral obligations, but because you are proceeding on a wrong hypothesis. The assumption, then, of the economist in theory, and of the business man in practice, that a " worker " may conveniently be treated simply as a repository of a certain sort of labour-power, to be elicited by wages in order to be stored in material wares, is a false assumption which invalidates the subsequent reasonings of the theorist, as it impairs the practice of the entrepreneur. The attempt to make a separate science of industrial wealth, based upon the conviction that man's actions in the getting and spending of money form what Professor Marshall calls "a tolerably homogeneous group," breaks down, because the organic unity of man is too strong for this separatist treatment. Industry is a department of the conduct of life which is not sufficiently distinct from other departments to form the subject-matter of a separate science. All this line of criticism is brought to a head by Mr. Ruskin in his indictment of the narrowing down of the term Wealth to signify an accumulation of material marketable goods. The philological reference which identifies wealth with human welfare is not a mere play of fancy, but an assertion of the testimony of language to that substantial truth of the unity of human life and conduct which has been implicitly denied by the degradation which the term has undergone.

§ 12. The next essential reform in Political Economy is the deposition of the money-standard of value and the substitution of a vital standard. This gives us the deepest line of cleavage between Mr. Ruskin's Political Economy and that of the "orthodox" teachers. The value of any stock of mercantile wealth is to the latter what it will fetch in money or in other goods if it is sold. Value, according to Mr. Ruskin, consists in the power to sustain life. "To be valuable is to avail towards life." In a word, he proposes to substitute for the money-measurement of wealth adopted by the business man and the mercantile economist a standard of human utility. According to the mercantile economy, a cask of raw whisky or a roulette-table has the same value as a stack of corn or a shelf-full of "best books," if it commands the same price in the market; the fact that the former commodities get their value from depraved tastes and injure human life by their "consumption," while the latter serve to maintain physical and intellectual life, does not affect their value. Now, economists from early times had distinguished between exchange-value and value-in-use. But orthodox practice had taken exchange-value as the central point of theory, following the practice of the business man. The latter is not, as "economic man," concerned with the capacity of his wares to satisfy the purposes of human life; if there is an "effective demand" for the goods he makes or deals in, that is enough for him. As to the results of the consumption of his goods, that is the purchaser's look-out. *Caveat emptor!*

Certain economists had given some slight perfunctory attention to the vital services of goods that were sold, by tracing the influence of their consumption upon labour-power, deploring the consumption of luxuries by labourers and so forth; but such criticism formed no integral part of economic theory. Mr. Ruskin's adoption of vital use as the standard and measure of value must therefore be regarded as the most revolutionary of his positions. It may be summed up in his eloquent but strictly scientific formula: "THERE IS NO WEALTH BUT LIFE. Life, including all its powers of love, of joy, and of admiration. That country is the richest which nourishes the greatest number of noble and happy human beings; that man is richest who, having perfected the functions of his own life to the utmost, has also the widest influence, both personal and by means of his possessions, over the lives of others."[1]

[1] Unto this Last, p. 156.

§ 13. It is not enough to recognise that Mr. Ruskin has substituted for the objective commercial standard of money a subjective human standard. Though economists are primarily interested in exchange-value, there is a growing tendency among recent thinkers to insist upon subjective utility as the ground of exchange-value; but the acceptance of this view by Jevons and his followers does not make them any nearer to Mr. Ruskin's theory, for none of the economists goes behind the present actual desires of men as reflected in their industrial conduct. Political Economy, as they conceive it, deals with what *is*, not with what *ought to be*. As a science it is concerned with what men actually do and want, as an art with the economical ordering of their doings for the satisfaction of these actual wants.

Now Mr. Ruskin deliberately lays down an ethical standard of conduct for the art of Political Economy, the acceptance of which entirely alters the nature of the science. The true "value" of a thing is neither the price paid for it nor the amount of present satisfaction it yields to the consumer, but the intrinsic service it is capable of yielding by its right use. Of commercial goods, or any other class of goods, those which have a capacity of satisfying wholesome human wants are "wealth," those which pander to some base or injurious desire of man are not wealth, but "illth," availing, as they do, not for life but for death. Thus he posits as the starting-point of Political Economy a standard of life not based upon present subjective valuations of "consumers," but upon eternal and immutable principles of health and disease, justice and injustice. A man or a nation is wealthy in proportion as he or it is enabled to satisfy those needs of nature which are healthy, and thus to realise true capacities of manhood. The mercantile economist says he is a practical man concerned with what is, not with what ought to be. Mr. Ruskin as political economist insists that "what ought to be" is a practical standard of conduct for the consistent science of Political Economy : the "ought" which lies outside the narrow utilitarianism of the mercantile economist falls within the range of broader human economics, and becomes the most important " is."

§ 14. The third great reform in Mr. Ruskin's method has reference to the term " Political." Although the first great English treatise upon Political Economy bore the title " Wealth of Nations," the science in the hands of Adam Smith's successors had never taken a true " social " or " national " standard even for the computation of commercial wealth. The *laissez faire* assumption that each individual, in seeking to get most for himself, must take that course by which he would contribute most to the general well-being, implied a complete failure to comprehend the organic structure of society. A nation was conceived of as a mere aggregate of its constituent members ; the good of the whole as the added good of all the separate parts. The current " Political Economy " did indeed recognise the utility of private co-operation of groups of individuals within a nation for the production of wealth, but the incentive to such co-operation was not the production of wealth for the nation but of profits and wages for the separate co-operating members.

The conviction that the greed of individuals and groups of individuals within a nation would induce them to such industry as would yield a larger total aggregate of material forms of wealth than could be obtained by a direct national ordering of industry, might or might not be reasonable, but an economy in which the good of the "polis" is neither the conscious good nor the directing influence could scarcely deserve the name political. The fact was that the economy of Ricardo and Mill was never "political" in any proper sense; its economic laws were merely generalisations of the discreet action of individual business men in their buying and selling processes; it was simply the economy of the shrewd Lancashire mill-manager "writ large" and called political. Because it was a profitable thing for the mill-manager to buy his raw material, his machinery and labour, in the cheapest market, to order his mill by the most thorough subdivision of labour, to get the largest possible output from his iron or his human mechanisms, to produce not the best goods but those which would sell so as to yield the larger margin, to get for himself a market by ousting his competitors; because it was good business for *any* manufacturers to pursue this course of conduct, it was good for *all* manufacturers to do so, and for the nation of manufacturers and shopkeepers as an aggregate. Even the Free Trade policy, in which the old economists came nearest to a conscious realisation of National Economy, was seldom presented in a national form, and was more generally proved and illustrated by the advantages accruing to individuals or special interests within the nation by untrammelled intercourse with individuals and trades in other nations.

The conception of a really "Political Economy," to

which Jevons once rose in a single rhetorical flight when
he said that " the great problem of economy may, as it
seems to me, be stated thus : ' Given a certain population
with various needs and powers of production, in possession of certain lands and other sources of material :
required the mode of employing their labour so as to
maximise the utility of the produce,' " [1] found no place in
the authoritative text-books, not even in those of Jevons
himself.

Now Mr. Ruskin, though he did not philosophise upon
the " organic " nature of the State, did always insist
upon imputing to it that nature, premising that both the
science and the art of Political Economy should be constructed from the standpoint of the well-being of the
whole society. The state with which his " economy " is
concerned is not merely an industrial and a political,
but, in accordance with his view of life and art, distinctively a moral organism : justice is the life of his state
as it was the life of Plato's. This organic conception
everywhere illuminates his theory and his practical constructive policy ; it gives order to his conception of the
different industrial classes and to the relations of individual members of each class ; it releases him from the mechanical atomic notion of equality, and compels him to
develop an orderly system of interdependence sustained
by authority and obedience, and in the radical problem of
distribution it drives him to have recourse to the analogy
of the human body which is the type of organic life.
" The circulation of wealth in a nation resembles that
of blood in the natural body. The analogy will hold
down to minute particulars. For as diseased local deter-

---

[1] Theory of Political Economy, p. 289 (2d ed.).

mination of the blood involves depression of the general
health of the system, all morbid local action of riches
will be found ultimately to involve a weakening of the
resources of the body politic." [1] Other sociologists, with
more parade of scientific terminology, *e. g.* Herbert
Spencer in England and Schäffle in Austria, have developed this industrial physiology, but the full worth of the
analogy still waits recognition alike in its bearing upon
the theory of production and of distribution of wealth.

This organic conception of industry is essential in
order to justify the epithet " political," and the fact that
it was wanting in the inductive science of the mercantile
economists dominated by an individualist philosophy, is
a fatal defect.

§ 15. We can now sum up Mr. Ruskin's radical
reforms in the structure of Political Economy.

Whereas the current theory took for its subject-matter
material marketable goods and the processes of making
and distributing them, measured in terms of money, and
regarded from a distinctively individual standpoint, Mr.
Ruskin's theory took for its subject-matter all kinds of
" goods," including those highest goods which are immaterial and unmarketable, and the processes of making
and distributing them, measured in terms of " life " and
regarded from a social standpoint.

The work of Mr. Ruskin then consists in this, that he
has " humanised " Political Economy. Every fact and
every process is stripped of its materialistic or its monetary garb and shown in its naked truth as " vitality."
The " essence of wealth " consists neither in bank-
balances nor in the lands, houses, goods they represent,

[1] Unto this Last, p. 49.

but in " authority over men." [1] Here is " sentimentalism " with a vengeance! Hood in his " Song of a Shirt "
had declared, " It isn't linen you're wearin', it's human
creatures' lives." Mr. Ruskin, by his powerful grasp of
industrial physiology, proves that every " demand for
commodities " is a demand for life or death, according
as the work embodied in these commodities is good or
evil in its nature and in the conditions under which it is
performed. " Value," according to the professional
economists, is not a property which anything possesses,
a thing has no " value " inherent in it, the " value "
depends upon the quantity of other things which it ex-
changes for. Value, according to Mr. Ruskin, is the
life-sustaining properties of anything, which are neither
dependent upon other things nor upon the opinions which
people form about it. " The thing is worth what it *can*
do for you, not what you think it can." [2] Cost of Production, according to the text-books, was the quantity of
money paid to get work done, or, in the more recent
treatment, the amount of labour-power measured by
time or some objective standard; cost of production,
according to Mr. Ruskin, is expenditure of life. The
only standard of utility recognised by the orthodox
theory is a monetary measure of desire. Mr. Ruskin's
utility means promotion of life and happiness. By thus
vitalising and moralising every term and every process,
Mr. Ruskin forms the outline of a Political Economy
which is primarily concerned with the production of
healthy life, the manufacture of " souls of a good quality."

§ 16. It is important to recognise the distinction between the " vitalising " and the " moralising " processes

----

[1] Unto this Last, p. 63.   [2] Queen of the Air, § 125.

here imputed to Mr. Ruskin. The reduction of money-cost and money-measured utility to the pains of production and the pleasures of consumption, estimated in accordance with the actual desires and feelings of those who produce and consume, would be a vitalising process, marking a distinct advance in the humanisation of Political Economy. Such an analysis would doubtless condemn the false economy of our white-lead industry and other painful, pernicious, or toilsome work, by showing that the money-wages were no true measure of the cost in human suffering, as it would explode the bloated bubble of utility imputed to expensive luxuries. But to take the imperfect or distorted desires and tastes of existing workers and consumers as a final standard of valuation, is but a halfway house at which Mr. Ruskin never consents to tarry. Neither order nor progress is possible or conceivable without ideals; no science or art of wealth can be founded upon the short-sighted, mistaken, and shifting desires of the moment; the welfare of an individual or a nation implies a standard of true humanity to which the desires and caprices of the moment must be referred. For the false short-range expediency of passing pleasures and pains, must be substituted a just and orderly conception of social well-being. Thus the practice of Political Economy demands an ideal alike of the individual and the social life : a just ordering of life which will lead to happiness.

Though Mr. Ruskin is stern in his denunciation of the doctrine of utility and the school of utilitarians, with their " greatest happiness of the greatest number," this repugnance is directed against the hedonism by which most of the utilitarian prophets delivered over the con-

duct of life to fleeting pleasures and pains, without providing for the attainment of the conditions of abiding
happiness. Indeed, Mr. Ruskin himself in his Political
Economy, so far as his conception of the end is concerned, may not unaptly be classed as a utilitarian. For
though the operating motives upon the individual man
are to be the principles of Justice and Honesty, the result is measured in terms of happiness. "The final
outcome and consummation of all wealth is in the producing, as many as possible, full-breathed, bright-eyed,
and happy-hearted human beings."[1]

In passing from Mercantile Economy to Mr. Ruskin's
science and art of Social Economics, we do not abandon
the self-seeking motives or the attainments of satisfaction
as the goal ; we enlarge the scope and expand the nature
of these conceptions by rationalising and moralising the
"self" which is seeking satisfaction. The domination
of Justice and Honesty within the soul enlarges and
purifies the self by imposing sacrifices of the narrower
self in favour of a wider self which grows as we identify
our good with that of others; it expands and orders our
conception of happiness by imparting a broader and more
complex character to our plan of life ; sensations which
are "just, measured, and continuous" evolve a true
standard of utility for the conduct of life. When Mr.
Ruskin insists that "the essence of the misteaching of
your day concerning wealth of any kind consists in the
denial of intrinsic value,"[2] he is denouncing the lack
of principle which underlies the so-called philosophy of
utilitarianism in its refusal to furnish any satisfactory
check upon short-range expediency of conduct.

[1] Unto this Last, p. 65.   [2] Fors, Letter xii. (i. 250).

Now, to Mr. Ruskin these defects of Political Economy, its materialism, its faith in competition and enlightened selfishness, its monetary standard of value, were primarily moral defects, and his crusade against the current teaching was inspired by moral energy. It is this moral character which has led many to discount the value of his criticism as "sentimental." We have already seen that sentiments and the ideals which they imply are essential to any orderly interpretation of economic phenomena, and that in this sense Mr. Ruskin's Political Economy is "scientific."

§ 17. 1 have dwelt at some length upon Mr. Ruskin's criticism of the unscientific basis of current "Political Economy" because defenders of that study have often accused Mr. Ruskin of attacking not the "science" but an art which, they say, he has wrongly foisted upon them. This accusation derives a certain speciousness from the fact that his fiercest resentment is aimed against the practical support which he holds to be given by "economists" to the iniquity and inhumanity of competitive industry. But even here, it will be seen later on [1] his attack is in reality directed against certain dogmatic "principles" of the science, and not primarily against the art.

The partition between science and art in Political Economy has always been peculiarly thin, and writers from Adam Smith onwards have been as much concerned with the application of their theories to free trade, taxation, money, and the maintenance of individual bargaining, as with the construction of those theories.

Mr. Ruskin did not, as is sometimes alleged, mistake

[1] Chapter V.

the indicative for the imperative mood in the " economists ; " the confusion was chiefly their own. It is true
that in his proposals for a wider " Political Economy "
he himself was more directly concerned with the art than
with the science. But for all that it must not be supposed that he ignored the need of scientific basis.
Doubtless the claim which he himself preferred was to
have laid an ethical basis of the art of social life rather
than a " scientific " basis. He would probably have repudiated " a science of ethics." But in the stress laid
upon the basis of " economic " conduct, we may not
ignore the testimony which modern sociology accords to
the scientific nature of his work.

Mr. Ruskin's statement of the end of " economic "
activity as the production of " life," " souls of a good
quality," furnishes the necessary hypothetical end or goal
required to give meaning to Sociology as a science and
to Social Progress as an art. The modern teaching of
evolution, so far from dispensing with " final causes," is
unintelligible, and falls into anarchy without them.
However dimly conceived, the ordered movement of
" evolution " requires the hypothetical goal just as it requires the hypothesis of efficient causes. Not only the
practical reformer, but the student of social movements,
must posit some such end as that which Mr. Ruskin
sets before us in asserting the aim of Political Economy
to be " the multiplication of human life at its highest
standard." [1]

Sociology requires the scientific imagination to leap
over the interstices of known phenomena in order to
construct out of a medley of ill-assorted facts a scientific

[1] *Munera Pulveris*, § 7.

law of change in conformity with some idea which has been imposed upon phenomena before it is illustrated by them and explains them; as this scientific imagination transcends in its theory the phenomena of the past, so it produces the lines of progress discovered in the past, into the future, manufacturing ideals. This construction of ideals is an essential task of a truly scientific mind: all great discoveries come from such intellectual acts of faith.

Biologists and sociologists, correlating the processes of organic life in conformity with preconceived and well-verified laws of progress, are everywhere engaged in giving intellectual form to a science and art of life such as Mr. Ruskin conceived and foreshadowed in his Political Economy. His conception of wealth is what sociology requires for its ideal; his " value " is in substantial conformity to this same scientific purpose. Take the following testimony of a great living biologist:

" Let us . . . leave the inmates of the academic cloister: walk out into the world, look about us, try to express loaf and diamond from the objective side in terms of actual fact, and we find that physical and physiological properties, or ' values,' can indeed indefinitely be assigned: the one as so much fuel, its heat-giving power measurable in calorimeter, or in actual units of work, the other a definite sensory stimulus, varying according to Fechner's law. This is precisely what our author means in such a passage as the following, which, however absurd to the orthodox, is now intelligible enough to us :

" Intrinsic value is the absolute power of anything to support life. A sheaf of wheat of given quantity and weight has in it a measurable power of sustaining the substance of the body ; a cubic foot of pure air, a fixed power of sustaining its warmth, and a cluster of flowers of given beauty, a fixed power of enlivening or animating the senses and heart." [1]

Our claim is not that Mr. Ruskin has formed a system of sociology, or that he has advanced far towards such a system, but that he has pointed the way to such a science, and has laid down certain hypotheses of fact and terminology such as are consistent with advances made independently by other scientific men. By insisting upon the reduction of all economic terms, such as value, cost, utility, etc., to terms of " vitality," by insisting upon the organic integrity and unity of all human activities, and the organic nature of the co-operation of the social units, and finally by furnishing a social ideal of reasonable humanity, Mr. Ruskin has amply justified his claim as a pioneer in the theory of Social Economics.

[1] "John Ruskin," by Patrick Geddes (Round Table Series), p. 26.

CHAPTER IV.

MR. RUSKIN'S THEORY OF SOCIAL ECONOMICS.

§ 1. It is not unnatural that the term "criticism" should have acquired a censorious or condemnatory meaning which does not rightly belong to it; for a judge may often with propriety leave the virtues of a man or a thing to stand upon their own patent merits, and devote his time and attention chiefly to exposure of faults, which, either by escaping notice for what they are, or by some semblance of goodness or utility, may remain as hidden dangers. Such criticism will always be a special function of reformers; but it is only a short-sighted and partial view of their work of criticism which will regard it as negative and destructive merely: all criticism in the hands of such men will be reformatory in purpose, the distinctively critical work only serving

103

as the foundation of constructive work, which will proceed continuously from it.

It is in this sense that Mr. Ruskin ever ranks as critic; there is in him nothing of the intellectual " wrecker;" his analytic faculty directed against the faults of a bad system of art, education, or social order is always charged with the spirit of repair, which is eager to exert itself in imposing order upon chaos, supplanting noxious weeds by wholesome fruit-bearing plants, and preparing the barren ground for useful cultivation.

In approaching the social doctrine of Mr. Ruskin, it has been convenient to regard him as the assailant of current economic thought, partly because this rightly represents the historical evolution of his social work, and partly because this hostile attitude towards current teaching marks with dramatic emphasis his positive contribution towards the right handling of the social problem.

We find this destructive and constructive work almost inextricably· interwoven in the fabric of nearly all his books, and the form thus imposed upon his thinking has often proved a stumbling-block to the full comprehension and acceptance of his teaching.

But this is only part of the larger character of superficial disorder which prevails in most of his writings, and which nothing but a sympathetic appreciation of the free laws which govern " the literature of power " is able to unravel. In order to understand the method of a thinker, we must understand his purpose.

The sound and consistent structure of Mr. Ruskin's social theory has seldom gained full recognition, because it is nowhere presented in that continuous systematic

form of statement which is commonly adopted by
teachers who address the intellect. He never addresses
the intellect alone; in his writing there always lurks a
double appeal: he ever seeks to touch the heart as well
as to convince the understanding. The system which
underlies this process is thus one of literary rather than
of logical order, and the blending of passion with argument, which it involves, is apt to cause confusion and
distrust in those who like to have their reasoning dry.
Moreover, this literary mode of exposition, proper
though it was for Mr. Ruskin, often beguiled him into
the opposed errors of discursiveness and excessive con-
densation.

§ 2.   In no one of his books do we find a full, clear,
and consistent statement of his social principles. "Unto
this Last," "Munera Pulveris," and "Fors Clavigera,"
each and all profess such utterance; large and just
principles of exposition are laid down, but the performance, noble though it be, is nowhere a complete
fulfilment of the initial promise. Not merely must his
full teaching be gathered from many quarters in order
to yield a consistent body of doctrine, but even then we
shall find considerable lacunæ in the application of the
basic principles.

The most systematic of his books, "Munera Pulveris,"
serves to illustrate this statement. At the opening we
find a full definition of the scope of his work. "The
essential work of the political economist is to determine
what are in reality useful or life-giving things, and by
what degrees and kinds of labour they are attainable and
distributable." [1]

---

[1] Munera Pulveris, § xi.

Now here is laid down with admirable succinctness the fundamental antithesis between the cost or labour which goes into making "goods," and the utility or enjoyment to be got out of them. A right consideration of Industry from the human or social standpoint requires that the goods considered as "wealth" shall be resolved into these costs and utilities, and shall be estimated with equal reference to both. One of the gravest accusations which lies against the commercial economists is that they look too exclusively to the products and not sufficiently to the processes of production, rating the prosperity of a people by the sum of its material goods, without considering how far this gain is offset by increased duration, intensity, monotony, and unwholesomeness of work. In his broad declaration, "There is no wealth but life," as in his unceasing stress upon the need of good work for all men, Mr. Ruskin has laid down as the foundation-stone of social theory the organic relation between work and life, between production and consumption. It was therefore to be expected that in "Munera Pulveris" "wealth" would be resolved into both its human constituents, human cost receiving the same attention as human utility, and that the laws of the natural and moral interaction between work and life would be expounded. A logical analysis of Ruskinian wealth would take the concrete forms which constituted "commercial wealth," and, after ascertaining how much cost of painful or injurious effort went with the making of each of them, how much vital use would be got out of each of them by the consumer into whose hands it passed by distribution, would rate the true "wealth" embodied in these forms by the surplus of utility over cost. Such analysis is suggested, but is only partially applied in " Munera Pulveris." The defective treatment is due to an acceptance of a narrower meaning of wealth, which, by making it consist in " things in themselves valuable," eliminates direct regard for labor-cost, and throws an undue stress upon utility.

He opens with a clear and logical distinction between value and cost. " Value is the life-giving power of anything; cost the quantity of labor required to produce it;"[1] but instead of rating the " wealth " contained in goods equally by the lowness of their cost and the height of their value, he looks to the latter only for his standard measure. This gives a one-sided character to his analysis — the value or " utility " side is worked out with admirable skill, but the " cost " side is slighted, while the organic relation between the two is left out of sight.

§ 3. In order to reduce a stock of commercial " utilities," with which Mercantile Economy concerns itself, to the real " utility " or human satisfaction which alone " Political Economy " regards, three tests must be applied, three questions answered.

(1) What is the nature of the goods and services which rank as " utilities ? "

Mercantile Economy pays no regard to the inherent qualities of goods, whether they are well made or ill made, pure or adulterated ; or to the kind of desires they serve to satisfy, whether they are wholesome or morbid, moral or immoral. Utility is only seen reflected through demand. A demand for bad books or shoddy clothing which prompts £100,000 of purchases is just

[1] Munera Pulveris, § xii.

as good as a demand which offers the same sum for wholesome bread or noble works of art.

Now, to Mr. Ruskin the prime test of value is the " essential utility " of the goods, their capacity to satisfy a good human want. According to the excellence of use embodied in a thing will it rank as valuable. Things which make for life in their consumption are " wealth ; " things which, being essentially noxious, make for death, are " illth."

In the preface of " Munera Pulveris " Mr. Ruskin illustrates this distinction in the realm of art by comparing certain pictures of Tintoret, which were left to rottenness and ruin in Venice after the Austrian siege, with the " elaborately finished and coloured lithographs representing the modern dances of delight " which were selling freely in the streets of Paris.

" The labour employed on the stone of one of those lithographs is very much more than Tintoret was in the habit of giving to a picture of average size. Considering labour as the origin of value, therefore, the stone so highly wrought would be of greater value than the picture ; and since also it is capable of producing a large number of immediately saleable or exchangeable impressions, for which the demand is constant, the city of Paris naturally supposed itself, and in all hitherto believed or stated principles of Political Economy was, infinitely richer in the possession of a large number of these lithographic stones . . . than Venice in the possession of those rags of mildewed canvas flaunting in the south wind and its salt rain. . . . Yet all the while, Paris was not the richer for these possessions. Intrinsically the delightful lithographs were not wealth, but polar contraries of wealth. She was, by the exact quantity of labour she had given to produce these, sunk below, instead of above, absolute Poverty. They not only were false Riches, they were true Debt, which had to be paid at last — and the present aspect of the Rue Rivoli shows in what manner." [1]

§ 4. (2) " Intrinsic value " is the first qualification of wealth. But it must be supplemented by " acceptant capacity," *i. e.* the ability of the consumer to get out of the " utility " the good it contains. "A horse is no wealth to us if we cannot ride, nor a picture if we cannot see, *nor can any noble thing be wealth except to a noble person.* As the aptness of the user increases, the effectual value of the thing used increases ; and in its entirety can coexist only with perfect skill of use and fitness of nature." [2] It is this thought which links Mr. Ruskin's Art of Education to his Political Economy, and furnishes one more condemnation of the commercial measurement of wealth by quantity of material forms. It has only just begun to dawn upon the minds of our most enlightened political economists that the prosperity of a country can be enhanced as much by educating the consumer as by improving the arts of the producer. The character-test is enforced in a passage of " Unto this Last," where some persons are denounced as " inherently and eternally incapable of wealth."

§ 5. (3) A third test of " wealth," not explicitly applied [3] by Mr. Ruskin, follows as corollary from the

---

[1] Preface, p. xi. Written in 1871, after the siege of Paris.

[2] Munera Pulveris, § 14.

[3] Though implied in " Munera Pulveris," §§ 56, 57.

requirement of "capacity." The amount of utility got
out of anything will depend, not only upon its intrinsic
quality and the nature of the person who possesses it,
but also upon the quantity of it which he possesses.
A loaf has intrinsic value; it has effectual value to a
worthy man, but only in so far as he has not already
sufficient bread. In other words, the greatest effectual
utility is got from any article when it goes to satisfy the
intensest human need. We must look, therefore, not
only to the nature of the thing and the nature of the
consumer in order to know the "wealth" that attaches
to any goods, but also to their distribution. A given
quantity of commercial goods will attain their maximum
value according as they are distributed so as to satisfy
the greatest needs.

If, therefore, a commercial economist shows us
£1,000 worth of goods, before we can obtain from
him any knowledge of their true value, we must ask

(1) What good human purposes can they serve?

(2) What kind of persons will get them?

(3) How much will each of these persons get?

§ 6. This analysis of commercial into human utility
is sound and complete. But Mr. Ruskin's "science"
demands that a precisely analogous process be applied
to the "cost" side of the problem. The doctrine of
intrinsic value must be applied to "cost." As utility is
measured in terms of life, so cost must be measured in
terms of death. This is affirmed on page 58 in general
terms, but the full and lucid analysis of utility is
balanced by no corresponding analysis of cost in
"Munera Pulveris." For the economics of work we
must turn to an earlier book, "The Political Economy

of Art,"[1] and even there we do not find any orderly
treatment of the whole scope of human work, but only
a just consideration of the work side of the problem in
art-production.

In order to make the analysis of Labour (Cost)
correspond with the analysis of Utility or Value, we
must investigate

(1) The intrinsic nature of the work in relation to
the worker. Some work is essentially degrading by its
physical conditions, *e. g.* that of the iron-puddler or the
stoker on board ship. Other work is fraught with danger to health or moral character so grave that only ignorance or penury could induce workers to undertake it.
To this class belong some processes in the manufacture
of white lead, phosphorus matches or chemicals, some
work in public-houses or other places of entertainment.
The " cost" of such work is incalculably large : set off
against utility by a human standard, it can never " pay ; "
it must always involve a net loss of human life.

Labour that is toilsome, monotonous, carried on amid
ugly and noxious surroundings, uninteresting and unedu-
cative, involves " cost." Labour which is wholesome
physical or mental exercise, pursued in moderation, involving skill and the expression of individuality, educative of capacity and character, is not really labour,[2] for
it involves no loss of life. It is in reality a source of
wealth as great as the consumption of utilities, and Mr.
Ruskin's full theory requires that it be so reckoned.
The term " intrinsic cost" is required to balance " intrinsic value."

---

[1] Afterwards published as " A Joy for Ever."
[2] Labour = lapse = loss (of life), § 59.

(2) This doctrine of "intrinsic cost" requires to be supplemented by consideration of the capacities of the workers. Their industrial nature, strength, skill, etc., must be known if we would discover the true or "effectual" cost. A given quantity of a certain labour imposed upon trained and strong men during a normal working day may involve slight "cost;" imposed upon weaker women or children, its cost may be enormous in human injury and suffering. Race, sex, age, natural ability, education, and training are all leading factors in determining subjective "cost." Where labour which might fall lightly upon adult shoulders is imposed upon the unripened strength of "half-timers" the "cost" both to individual and society is incalculably great, though commercially it is "cheap labour," because the money paid for it is small. We must know who supplies the labour before we can tell the cost.

(3) Finally, in estimating the cost as we estimate the utility of a quantity of goods, we require to know how the labour is distributed, — whether it is spread in reasonably short periods of moderate intensity over a large number of workers, or is inflicted in heavy and protracted toil upon a small number driven to put out an excessive exertion, or involves seasons of overtime alternating with seasons of idleness. The lightest and most interesting work becomes a painful and injurious toil if it is continued too long, while the most strenuous physical or mental effort may be light and wholesome if undertaken in small pieces. Thus any given quantity of labour-time in mining, type-setting, machine-tending, etc., may vary infinitely in the amount of the vital "cost" it involves, according as it is distributed.

§ 7. To all these considerations of cost Mr. Ruskin was fully alive ; not one fails to find eloquent expression and illustration in his works. But neither in " Munera Pulveris " nor elsewhere has he gathered them together so as to confront them with his analysis of value or utility. This lack of systematic setting has injured his reputation as economic thinker. Had he placed side by side his analysis of human cost and human utility, showing, as indeed he has shown in many incidental passages, the just and natural relation between cost and utility ; how the quantity and quality of consumption react upon the volume and character of work ; how good conditions of skilled and interesting work form an education of the consumer and the citizen, reacting in their turn upon demand ; how the effort of one class to consume without producing obliges another class to produce without consuming ; how such violations of physical and moral law are fraught with double injury alike to those who overwork and those who overfeed, — had Mr. Ruskin in " Munera Pulveris " or elsewhere plainly and orderly set forth these principles of the subjective political economy, their strictly scientific character could not have evaded recognition.

By neglecting formally to complete his statement of principles, by scattering his theory amid passages of passionate appeal, whimsical flights of philology, vigorous tirades against materialism and utilitarianism, Mr. Ruskin has hidden the really consistent ground-plan of his economic teaching so that it is difficult to discover and apprehend as a perfect whole.

§ 8. Other elements of incompleteness in Mr. Ruskin's social theory require notice. One of his radical reforms

in the structure of Political Economy, we have already
seen, consisted in breaking down the barrier between
marketable and non-marketable goods. By identifying
wealth with life he has expanded the science and art of
wealth so as to include human activities which lie outside the industrial arts, not merely humanising the character, but expanding the area of political economy. This
being so, we should naturally expect that considerable
attention would be devoted to the principles governing
the just relation between industrial and non-industrial
wealth and the human faculties respectively employed in
producing and consuming each. The science of efforts
and satisfactions, which Mr. Ruskin's analysis is always
reaching after, requires elaborate search into the organic
relations subsisting between the different kinds of effort
and satisfaction, in order that a rational standard of good
life may be established which shall economise most perfectly the powers of individual life, and so harmonise
them in the play of social life as to secure a true
" political economy."

    This work is implied in and flows from Mr. Ruskin's
fundamental principles, but nowhere has he attempted
even to mark its outlines in social theory, though, in the
actual experiments of social reform which he planned in
later life, he contributes many wise suggestions regarding
the distribution of human activity in different forms of
work and enjoyment.

    § 9. One other strongly marked feature of his intel-
lectual character has impaired the productivity of his
social teaching. Either because his intellectual principles were firmly set before Darwin, Wallace, and
Spencer had firmly impressed upon their age the lead-

ing ideas of evolution, or from a certain blend of scorn and apprehension with which he greeted the more abstract doctrines of the natural sciences, Mr. Ruskin's social views are defective in the sense of continuous development.

His assertion of the eternity and immutability of value best exhibits this trait. "The value of a thing . . . is independent of opinion, and of quantity. Think what you will of it, gain how much you may of it, the value of the thing itself is neither greater nor less. For ever it avails, or avails not; no estimate can ruin, no disdain repress, the power which it holds from the Maker of things and of men." [1]

Now here Mr. Ruskin comes very near to reviving one of the mediæval superstitions about "substance" as an "entity." The value of a thing, what it avails for life, may, as we have seen, be independent of opinion, in the sense that a drunkard's high valuation of "gin" does not raise its essential value. But the value of a thing must vary with its quantity; the value of a glut of corn can at best be a potential not an actual value; where there is no hunger to satisfy, it cannot avail for life. A still more radical objection underlies his assertion of the immanence of value in "utilities" independently of the estimate of consumers. In discussing "acceptant capacity" in "Munera Pulveris," Mr. Ruskin allowed that there would be no value in a horse for one who could not ride. Now this admission indicates that in his theory he takes man as he is, counting wealth what is good for actual man, "illth" what is bad for him. With this criterion we must insist that the effi-

[1] Unto this Last, p. 118 ; *cf.* Munera Pulveris, §§ 32-34.

cient value of anything may vary infinitely according
to the stage of development an individual or a society
has reached. A picture of Tintoret, an opera of Wagner,
would have no value whatever if presented to a savage
people, for though the intrinsic nature of these goods
was not affected, their actual power to raise life would
be absent. Indeed the very essence of culture in an
individual, civilisation in a nation, consists in a rising to
new levels, at which goods, which were valueless before,
ripen into value, while the valuation of all other goods
is altered. This conception of an orderly and natural
development of a standard of consumption is a corner-
stone of " human economics." Progress largely consists
in giving value to new objects and in the adjustment of
old values which enter into a " standard of life." To
conceive value as some power immanent in a thing
and unchangeable in quantity, implies the adoption of
a stereotyped ideal of society, and, more than this, it
implies a conception of a homogeneous humanity which
is not even ideally true. Mr. Ruskin was possibly misled
by the " specific ideals " of his early art theory into supposing that there was one specific ideal of society independent of race, place, age, and all other conditions.
" Modification of organism by environment," attended
by " reaction of organism upon environment," are
phrases which would have awakened Mr. Ruskin's ire,
but for all that they express important truths required
to complete the principles of Social Economics which
he avowed. Had Mr. Ruskin been less scornful or suspicious of the rising science of biology, he might have
greatly strengthened the ethical supports on which he
relied by evidences from that source. For in tracing

the laws of the physical life of animal organisms, and
those of the life of societies, analogy has long since been
resolved into identity, and an ever-increasing number of
biologists are willing to carry biology into sociology, and
to recognise that " the economic problem of the maintenance of man is but one special case of the vast problem
of the modification of organism by environment, exactly
as the descent of man is a special case of the origin of
species." [1]

The law of just distribution of wealth, to Mr. Ruskin
primarily a moral problem, is seen to rest upon a necessary physical basis, so soon as we learn to trace through
all the changing processes of vegetable and animal life
the natural interdependence and interaction between
nutrition and function, the intake of food and the output of energy in work. Once let us grasp comprehen-
sively the truth that society is rightly classed as an
organism, and the great principle of apportionment
of work and its products contained in the formula,
" From each according to his powers, to each according
to his needs," no longer rests only on a sentimental or a
purely moral basis; it becomes the necessary application
of a natural law of progress in every department of
organic life.

§ 10. There are indeed those who suggest that the
cosmic laws applicable to all lower forms of life, and to
man as an animal, are overruled or even reversed by
new laws governing the rational conduct of man in
society. Thus Huxley, for example, has endeavoured
to contrast social with cosmic development, urging that

---

[1] Proceedings of the Royal Society, Edinburgh, 1884 (quoted,
Geddes, " John Ruskin," p. 33).

" social progress means a checking of the cosmic process at every step, and the substitution of it for another,
which may be called the ethical process, the end of
which is not the survival of those who may happen to
be the fittest, in respect of the whole of the conditions
that exist, but of those who are ethically the fittest." [1]
The loose logic of this distinction resides in the words
" in respect of the whole of the conditions which exist;"
for among these conditions ethical fitness must rank ;
and if this is found to be the chief determinant of survival, it can only hold this position by successfully competing with other non-ethical conditions, and if it prove
the stronger, the test it imposes is evidently a truer
representative of " the whole of the conditions " than
another test of individual fitness which *ex hypothesi* is
weaker. In point of fact, Huxley's distinction contains
the negation of all continuity of development; if his
contrast of ethical and cosmic were valid, it implies,
first, a sundering of human society from other animal
societies, and, secondly, the conception of ethical
motives entering suddenly into the history of man so
as to reverse the earlier modes of human action. The
conformity of the life of human societies to the laws
which govern other infra-human societies, the identity
of certain principles of healthy growth in social organisms with those of individual organisms, does not dera-
tionalise or in any way degrade the former. On the
contrary, this identity and continuity of organic processes, which, by continuous strengthening of social
forces raise the struggle for life to a higher plane, in
which the struggle of societies plays a more important

[1] Evolution and Ethics, p. 81.

part, imposing a more social test of "fitness" upon the struggles of individuals, are essential for the realisation of rational order in the universe. The crude dualism which Huxley posits receives little support from thoughtful biologists, while ethical philosophers more and more incline to give a negative reply to the oft-put question, "Are God and Nature then at strife?"

Through his refusal to accept the teaching of evolution in human life, Mr. Ruskin has been led to impart too statical a character to his "Political Economy," and too uniform a type to his ideal society. Sociology, in its conception of social progress, admits not one but many types of civilisation; political and industrial societies must take many different paths of progress moving towards, sometimes consciously realising, widely different ideals. There can be no single abiding, universal form of political or industrial society; wealth, value, and all terms expressive of utility to man must shift according to the changing needs and capacities of man.

Mr. Ruskin did not, of course, explicitly deny this necessity of continuous progress. But his criticism shows him possessed too strongly by the conviction that the injustice, waste, ugliness, and other evils of society were maladies which, properly treated, would restore society to a primitive natural state of health. Curative measures were needed to overcome the maladies, a good regimen to preserve the restored health. Social health presented itself to him rather as an accomplished order than as a means of progress. His own strong love of order, and his unusually dogmatic temperament, led him to conceive social reform as a work of restoration, a realisation of definite principles of social good in a pattern commonwealth, where peace and contentment would prevail, and when stable and rational authority would be subject to no disturbing influence.

But this disorder and uncertainty in the teaching of social principles, this undue stress upon the absoluteness and the permanence of his ideals, must not be allowed to blind us to the fundamental excellence of Mr. Ruskin's Political Economy.

He has laid a solid foundation of social economics as the science of the relation of efforts and satisfactions in a society. By insisting upon the reduction of money-measured " cost" and " utility" to subjective or human " cost" and " utility," he has taken a truly scientific and not, as commonly supposed, a sentimental position. It has been humorous to hear the dull drudges of commercial economics speaking contemptuously of an economist whose logic is far keener than their own, and whose work will hereafter be recognised as the first serious attempt in England to establish a scientific basis of economic study from the social standpoint.

Upon this human basis the fuller economic theory of the future will be built. In America and upon the continent of Europe not a few professional economists of note are engaged in working out the biological factors involved in the various forms of " cost" and " utility," so as to throw fuller light upon the economy of production and consumption. It is becoming more widely admitted that both the starting-point and the goal of economic activity is human life, and that all economic terms must be reduced to the standard not of money but of man. The art of Political Economy demands

such enlargement and humanisation of the science as
shall enable it to direct and govern social conduct. The
admission of this claim does not imply, as is sometimes
represented, the degradation of a science by making it
subservient to practical utility. The visible failure of
the orthodox Political Economy to throw light upon
social or even distinctively industrial problems proves
that a narrow group of phenomena has been falsely
specialised, and that a standard of valuation has been
taken which has sterilised the study. Mr. Ruskin's first
claim as social reformer is that he reformed Political
Economy.

CHAPTER V.

FLAWS IN THE SCIENCE AND PRACTICE OF MODERN
INDUSTRY.

§ 1. Detection of flaws in the structure of industrial science.
§ 2. Growing acceptance of Mr. Ruskin's teaching of the
economy of high wages. § 3. Over-specialisation as a malady
of modern industry. § 4. The need of good work for all. § 5.
Consumption the industrial goal — Detection of the fallacy of
unlimited saving. § 6. "Demand for commodities not a demand for labour" refuted. § 7. Currency based on intrinsic
values — No credit.

§ 1. In the last two chapters we have examined the
vital differences in scope and nature between the Political Economy of Mr. Ruskin and the current Mercantile
Economy. But Mr. Ruskin by no means confined himself to a general repudiation of the claims of the latter.
Much of his closest analysis and his choicest ridicule
are devoted to exposing specific flaws in the structure of
commercial science, which he further charges with offering support to the immorality of business conducted for
individual profit. Perhaps the most caustic summary
of his position is contained in the following words:
"While I admit there is such a thing as mercantile
economy, distinguished from social, I have always said
also that neither Mill, Fawcett, nor Bastiat knew the
contemptible science they professed to teach." [1]

[1] Note by Mr. Ruskin to "A Disciple of Plato," by Mr. William
Smart.

Such scornful language, applied to able and honest specialists, has done much to prevent Mr. Ruskin's arguments from receiving the attention they deserve. But the undue depreciation and the captious criticism in which he sometimes indulged must not deter us from recognising the acuteness of many of the points he presses. The inherent difficulties which arise in every department of social science from the complexity and shifting character of its phenomena, the few opportunities of scientific experiment, the difficulties of securing just and reliable terminology, attach, as we have seen, in no ordinary measure to Commercial Economy; while the conditions of its late and comparatively obscure growth have prevented it from receiving an adequate share of the attention of the keenest and most far-sighted intelligences of our century. The result has been a too facile establishment of dogmas enrolled in specious phraseology and sustained by the authority of a few able men who have been prematurely accredited as the builders of a complete science of industry, whereas they are only entitled to be regarded as pioneers groping in the obscure beginnings of a science.

When a man with Mr. Ruskin's mental equipment approached the text-books of this commercial economy he could hardly fail to detect considerable flaws. The unconscious pressure of class interests and prejudices, flowing often through honest and efficient channels, is always operative in the intellectual world, framing hypotheses, moulding theories, driving home conclusions to support the intellectual or material vested interests of the educated classes. This is not the judgment of a cynic. No one who faithfully follows out the progress

of any science, medicine, law, theology, philosophy,
geology, politics, can fail to see the innumerable subtle
ways in which the dry light of the intellect is humidised
by passion and class interest. Just in proportion as
the science is applicable for the guidance of an individual or a nation in matters where self-interest weighs
heavily, is this injurious influence operative. In the
selection and rejection of ideas and phrases, the formation of theories, the admission and the valuation of
different kinds of evidence, even in the basic processes
of observation, bias creeps in. The study of industrial
facts and laws among a people, passionately devoted to
the pursuit of industrial gains, is subject to these falsi-
fying forces in no ordinary measure.

Free competition of individuals upon the basis of
existing distribution of property was at once the passion
and the intellectual conviction of the hard-headed men
who, during the first half of this century, had in their
hands the making of Commercial Economy. It was not,
indeed, their conscious design to make a science which
should yield an intellectual, or a moral, support to the
existing industrial order; but any one who closely
follows the growth of the study from Adam Smith to
Jevons can see that it was in fact made to yield such
support. Though much valuable work was done in
the collection of industrial facts, and much acuteness
was evinced in the deductive reasoning from economic
principles, these principles themselves, the corner-stones
of the scientific edifice, were often exceedingly defective
both in substance and in wording, and each of these
defects were serviceable for the maintenance of the
industrial power of " the classes." Moreover, these

defects lay thickest in those parts of economic theory which had particular relation to the distribution of wealth among the different sections of the industrial community. A full justification of this imputation is not here possible; but its validity may be briefly evidenced by asking what has now become of the maxims, " Industry is limited by capital," " Labour receives advances from a wage-fund," " A demand for commodities is not a demand for labour," " Value depends upon cost of production," " Rent of land stands by itself as a surplus, not paid out of the product of labour, and forming no element in price." Is there any one of these central dogmas of the Political Economy of 1860, which commands the general allegiance of modern teachers of commercial science? Several of them, notably the wage-fund doctrine, and the cost theory of value, may be said to have almost disappeared, while the others, so far as they survive, present a strangely battered or transformed appearance.

Now, though academic reformers of industrial science give small attention and less credit to John Ruskin, it is none the less true that his criticism in "Unto this Last," "Munera Pulveris," and "Fors Clavigera" furnishes, in several important instances, the first clear and effective refutation of the mortal errors of the above-named doctrines.

§ 2. Let us take in order the leading heads of Mr. Ruskin's criticism. Commercial economists sought to sustain the credit of this system by representing the laws of this economy as " natural," and therefore " inevitable" in their operation. This character was particularly claimed for the Law of Supply and Demand as a necessary determinant of wages. From the earliest beginning of " economic systems " the working classes and their sympathisers had been bluffed by the show of some such natural law. The bare subsistence wage of the French artisan was represented as natural by the Physiocrats, " Il ne gagne que sa vie ; " Adam Smith saw forces which tended inevitably to keep the wages of common labour at a minimum ; his successors fortified their wage-fund theory by the cheerful doctrines of Malthus, teaching that " natural law " prevented wages from remaining above subsistence level, owing to the stimulus given by higher wages to an increase of the labouring population, which, by flooding the labour market, must speedily bring down any temporary rise. The wage-fund doctrine, whether supported by the Law of Population or not, represented wages as fixed in quantity at any given time by natural causes affecting the growth of capital, upon which no action of the workers themselves exercised any influence. Supported by a Law of Rent that professed to stand upon a basis of fixed physical conditions, and an equally rigid law of the tendency of profits to a minimum by the competition of capital, the whole structure, especially upon its distribution side, laid bold claim to a " natural and necessary " character. Mr. Ruskin's general attack upon this claim was a double one. He asserted, and proved by an appeal to facts, that these laws obtained their natural and necessary appearance by false abstraction. Taking wages in particular, he showed that they were not universally or even generally determined by the exclusive action of competition, but that custom, good feeling, and other considerations did actually enter in to determine rates of wages. Knowing that one chief object and result of this doctrine of necessary wages was to defend as socially advantageous the buying of labour on the cheapest terms, he followed up his denial of the facts by an exposure of the false economy of cheap labour. | Political economists supported the payment of the lowest market wages by affirming that by this procedure the greatest average of work would be obtained from the servant, and therefore the fullest benefit to the community, and through the community to the servant himself. Mr. Ruskin replies, "That, however, is not so. It would be so if the servant were an engine, of which the motive-power were steam, magnetism, gravitation, or any other agent of calculable force. But he being, on the contrary, an engine whose motive-power is a Soul, the force of this very peculiar agent, as an unknown quantity, enters into all the political economist's equations without his knowledge, and falsifies every one of their results. The largest quantity of work will not be done by this curious engine for pay, or under pressure. It will be done only when the motive force, that is to say, the will or spirit of the creature is brought up to its greatest strength by its own proper fuel; namely, by the affections."[1] This is not a sentimental, but a strictly business consideration. When Mr. Ruskin wrote these words, the notion of the Economy of High Wages was confined to a handful of Owenites, who were condemned by all sound, practical men as "cranks." There are now few teachers of Commercial Economy who either maintain that wages tend to rest at a subsistence level for any class of labour

[1] Unto this Last, p. 10.

by the operation of economic " laws," or who defend
the utility of buying all labour for the lowest price at
which it can be got. / The experience of many enlightened business men has made visible advance in
the direction of Mr. Ruskin's teaching: a widespread
conviction obtains, even in the business world, that a
decent standard of subsistence is a necessary condition
of efficient and reliable work, and that contentment and
mutual good-will between employer and employed are
the best security of business success. The countless
experiments in " bonuses " and " progressive wages," in
" profit-sharing " and " copartnership," attest the growing recognition of " soul " as an agent in production.
It is true that many of these experiments are motived
by interested considerations, seeking to utilise contentment and efficiency of labour in order to secure steadier
and higher business profits. But none the less they
appeal to motives entirely outside the ken of the earlier
political economist, and subvert utterly the old reliance upon a competitive market price as the standard
of " good business." But the most notable progress
in this direction has been made by public bodies in
the conduct of public business. State departments,
municipal councils, boards of guardians, and other
public authorities are not only learning the false
economy of low wages, but are supporting their wiser
policy by the very arguments of precedent and social
theory which Mr. Ruskin presents in " Unto this Last "
and " Fors." " We do not sell our prime-ministership
by Dutch auction ; nor on the decease of a bishop,
whatever may be the general advantages of simony,
do we (yet) offer his diocese to the clergyman who will

take the episcopacy at the lowest contract. . . . The
natural and right system respecting all labour is, that
it should be paid at a fixed rate, but the good workman
employed, and the bad workman unemployed. The
false, unnatural, and destructive system is when the
bad workman is allowed to offer his work at half
price, and either take the place of the good, or force
him by his competition to work for an inadequate
sum." [1]

The social folly and the false economy of a town
council paying its employees a rate of wages insufficient
to evoke good social service, and to secure them and
their families against the necessity of coming upon the
poor rate or charitable funds, in old age or times of
disablement, is so palpable as to require no serious
argument. But for the private employer the net economy of paying a "living wage" is sometimes less obvious.
Where sound, skilled work is required, in order to produce high qualities of goods, the enlightened self-interest
of the employer may make for this policy; but when a
low efficiency suffices to make low-class goods which can
command a profitable sale, self-interest of the profit-
monger may defend the sweating wage. It is this fact
that gives a fighting aspect to trade unionism. The
common rule with its standard wage and standard-work-
ing-day, which trade unionism seeks to force upon entire
trades, is in strict accord with the principles laid down
by "Unto this Last." As is shown by the classical
authority upon the labour movement,[2] the true policy of

---

[1] Unto this Last, pp. 18, 21.

[2] "Industrial Democracy," by Sidney and Beatrice Webb, vol.
ii., chap. xiii.

trade unions is to carry down into the lower grades of
labour the principles of remuneration and other conditions of employment which, both in public and private
work, have always been applied to the higher grades of
officers and managers. Competition is not to disappear,
but is merely to be shifted from price to quality of work ;
it is to be applied, not so as to select the least efficient
man at the lowest pay (for the more efficient man will
be most likely to refuse the lowest pay), but the most
efficient man at a rate of pay determined by some
reasonable estimate of decent maintenance. Thus economic practice is gradually creeping after a saner ideal,
in the payment of labour and the placing of contracts.
Mr. Ruskin's condemnation of the economic teaching
which gave theoretic sanction to the folly and the
immorality of a false system of competition is sustained
by an ever-widening circle of experience.

§ 3. His criticism of the defence of unlimited division
of labour by the teachers of industrial economy is not
less trenchant or less salutary. Low cost of production,
large quantity of goods, low prices for consumers, these
are correctly attributed to increasing division of labour
by commercial economists. Adam Smith builds his
theory of " The Wealth of Nations " upon the economy
of the division of labour and its accompanying increase
of productivity, and the tests of low cost and low prices
have seldom been seriously questioned. In modern English economics the defence of Free Trade doctrine by
exclusive reference to the interests of consumers, and
the pivotal position assigned to utility in the theory of
value, have prevented the claims of the producer from
receiving due attention. It is not necessary to accept

Mr. Ruskin's full theory of social economics to recognise the scientific inaccuracy of this position. Why should the utility of the consumer be more considered than the disutility (the cost) of the producer? If division of labour increases the real cost of the producer, this loss should not be ignored, but should be set against the alleged gain of the consumer. Now, Mr. Ruskin's indictment of excessive specialisation or division of labour is twofold: its injurious effect on the life and work of the producer is affirmed; the reality of the consumer's gain is denied.

Commercial economy says that the " cost of production " is lowered by division of labour, but this only means that less wages are paid to labour for the smaller amount of energy put into the making of a given article: it takes no account of the quality of that energy. Now, the quality and interest of work is all-important to the worker; anything which degrades that quality or destroys that interest imposes a " cost " upon the man which finds no register in the wages he is paid or the price of the article he makes. Mr. Ruskin insists that the effect of division of labour, especially under the reign of machinery, is to degrade the humanity of the worker by confining him to the performance of some single narrow routine task which calls for no exercise of his individual taste and skill, feeds no genuine interest, and educates only one activity, starving all the others in order to impart to this a purely mechanical accuracy and perfection. " It is not the labour that is divided, but the men — divided into mere segments of men, broken into small fragments and crumbs of life." " It is a sad account of a man to give of himself that he has spent his life in opening a valve, and never made anything but the eighteenth part of a pin." Mr. Ruskin by no means stands alone in this indictment of modern industry. Emerson, Carlyle, Tolstoy, William Morris, and many others of our wisest teachers agree in regarding over-specialisation as one of the most destructive vices of our age and a chief source of modern discontent. The revolt of art against modern social conditions, the prominent part taken by artists in every revolutionary movement, are animated chiefly by the recognition that modern industrial economy is the enemy of good work. The product is severed from the process; the product is all-valued, the process is ignored. The distinctive conditions of industrial work are, first, narrowness, the confinement to a single set of actions; second, monotony, the assimilation of the man-worker to a mechanism; third, irrationality of labour, by dissociating the work of each worker from the conscious attainment of any complete end.

The broader attitude adopted by Mr. Ruskin towards the use of machinery is reserved for fuller treatment. Here it must suffice to say that he is not an indiscriminate enemy of machinery. Nor does he oppose division of labour, involving, as it does, a certain wholesome sacrifice of all-round development of individual faculties for a social good, which again reacts beneficially upon the individual life by imposing service to a wider human end. It is the reckless, excessive, unconsidered sacrifice which degrades and brutalises workers by absorbing all their time and energies in narrow routine work that he condemns. This is the charge against industry. Against the science of industrial economy he charges the direct defence and encouragement of this reckless policy, and an ill-balanced and short-sighted estimate of wealth, which measures it exclusively in terms of quantities of marketable goods. Adam Smith indeed, in one of his most eloquent passages,[1] admits the dangers of the policy upon which his theory of wealth is built, but few of his followers have ever raised their voices to repeat his caution. The notion that work is of necessity a disagreeable means to a desirable end, the attainment of commodities, is still firmly rooted in current economic theory, and the protests of literary or artistic meddlers has made little palpable impression.

But social movements of to-day are more and more concerned with the " costs " imposed upon labour by division of labour, and with the risks incurred by sacrificing the well-being of producers to the supposed interests of consumers. The greater part of our industrial legislation, our factory and employers' liability acts, the energies of the trade unions, and, in particular, the movements by legislative or private action to secure a shortening of the working day, constitute a persistent and a growing public protest against the tyranny of the consumer practised in modern industry and defended by Political Economy. When economic theory has accepted a really scientific setting of value, and comes to recognise the exact equivalence of cost and utility in determining value with the necessary reduction of cost and utility to terms of life, it will be once more forced to admit the fundamental sanity and importance of Mr. Ruskin's criticism. Meanwhile it lags far behind the policy which the labour movement and all keen-

[1] Wealth of Nations, Book V., chap. i., part iii., art. 2.

sighted social reformers are pressing upon civilised communities.

§ 4. Mr. Ruskin's criticism carries him much further than mere protests against the injuries inflicted on the workers by excessive specialisation of work. The true wealth of nations requires that just as much attention be given to reducing the real cost of work, by enhancing its educative and health-giving character, as increasing the real utility of commodities. The wholesome and pleasurable life of man requires him to work and to work well. " To do as much as you can heartily and happily do each day in a well-determined direction, with a view to far-off results, with present enjoyment of one's work, is the only proper, the only essentially profitable way." [1] Political Economy had always assumed that progress implied a diminution of the quantity of labour expended in producing anything; to Mr. Ruskin it implies an improvement of the quality of labour expended. The two positions are not of course contradictory; Mr. Ruskin approves division of labour and machinery in so far as they reduce the quantity of painful, dangerous, or tedious toil, but an improvement of quality may be as serviceable as a diminution of quantity. To the commercial economist labour was a bad thing, and it (or at any rate its cost) was to be kept at a minimum; to Mr. Ruskin labour is a good thing, if done in moderation and under sound conditions. To raise the character of production is as important as to increase the quantity of consumption. Indeed, Mr. Ruskin goes further, in insisting that an increase of consumption purchased by a growing degradation of the

---

[1] Ruskiniana in Igdrasil ; *cf.* Fors, iii., Letters lxiv. and lxvii.

quality of production is a net loss. Either the increased
quantity of commodities is consumed by a class of
drones living an idle, luxurious life in bold defiance
of the natural and moral laws which bind work to
enjoyment; or, in so far as they are consumed by those
who produce them, the degraded conditions of mechanical labour impair the wholesome capacity of enjoyment.
It comes to this, that only good work can produce real
utilities : excessive division of labour, in degrading the
character of labour, degrades the quality of commodities,
and a progress estimated quantitatively in increase of
low-class material forms of wealth is not true progress.
Reformed political economy will measure social progress
just as much in terms of work as in terms of wealth :
how to get for every man a proper quantity of good
work will be just as important as how to get for him the
proper quantity of consumption. All this is contained
in Mr. Ruskin's attack upon the economic doctrine of
division of labour.

§ 5. These criticisms of the economic policy of buying in the cheapest market and of the division of labour
are primarily directed against industrial practice, and
only secondarily against the current teaching of economics which assumed and supported the validity of these
practices. But some of Mr. Ruskin's keenest thrusts are
directed at the technical doctrines of the current text-
books. In this fight he is invariably bold and generally
skilful, though not always successful. Perhaps one of
his best services in this department is his convincing
exposure of the fallacies of the teaching regarding capital for which J. S. Mill in particular was responsible.
The doctrine of the social utility of unlimited saving, the

assumptions that industry is limited by capital, and that demand for commodities is not demand for labour, are successfully exploded by Mr. Ruskin in various skilful analytic passages garnished with quaint illustrations. Mr. Ruskin rightly insisted that if any order was to be \put into the current teaching it must definitely accept ,consumption as the economic goal.[1] The admission of consumption as the end implies a limitation of the quantity of capital which at any given time can serviceably function, and since capital proceeds from saving, the quantity of saving which is socially useful is determined by the rate of consumption. The folly of unlimited parsimony is disclosed by humorous analogies from gardening, in which he points out the futile policy of postponing the production of the flower by an indefinite elongation of the stalk.

The definition and the structure of commercial economy point, in spite of occasional disclaimers, to the making of capital or productive goods as the end. Mr. Ruskin insists that capital is no end, that it is not consumption that has to justify itself by showing that it is "productive" (as the economic text-books with unconscious humour suggest), but capital, by showing that it produces something different from itself which can be and will be consumed. "It is a root which does not enter into vital function till it produces something else than a root, namely, fruit. That fruit will in time again produce roots; and so all living capital issues in reproduction of capital; but capital which produces nothing but capital is only root producing root; bulb issuing in bulb, never in tulip; seed issuing in seed, never in

[1] Unto this Last, p. 150.

bread. The Political Economy of Europe has hitherto devoted itself wholly to the multiplication, or (less even) the aggregation of bulbs. It never saw nor conceived such a thing as a tulip." [1]

This truth that capital is limited by consumption has made slow progress among English political economists because of the intricate ambiguity of meaning attached to the term Capital, but among continental thinkers and in America the fallacy of unlimited saving is gaining ground.[2] That industry is limited by capital is shown to be just as true, and no more true, than that industry is limited by natural resources and by labour,[3] for all three requisites are equally essential in their just proportions.

§ 6. But in his treatment of this topic, Mr. Ruskin's chief service consists in his refutation of Mill's proposition, " A demand for commodities is not a demand for labour." Those who are inclined to question his aptitude for economic controversy may read with profit the second letter of vol. i. of " Fors," containing his concise and thoroughly effective exposure of the three separate fallacies contained in the argument by which Mill pretends to prove that a consumer of lace who stops his purchases of that commodity, and invests his savings in some other business, causes increased employment of labour.[4] The reluctance of our academic economists to abandon this dogma, so firmly rooted in " authority " and so serviceable a defence of unrestricted saving, is

[1] Unto this Last, p. 145.
[2] *Cf.* recent works of Professors Ely and Hadley.
[3] Munera Pulveris, § 50.
[4] The same fallacy is more briefly exposed in " Unto this Last," pp. 151-2.

humorously illustrated by the treatment of recent text-books. Professors Marshall and Sidgwick "retire" this "fundamental proposition on capital" into the obscurity of foot-notes,[1] covering their withdrawal by a qualified but utterly confused defence.[2] Professor Nicholson is the first British economist who has had the courage in an authoritative text-book[3] to admit the "obvious falsehood" of Mill's position, though he makes no acknowledgment whatever of the far more effective refutation given twenty-five years before by Mr. Ruskin, nor does he perceive that his admission involves, as it rightly does, the complete abandonment of the doctrine of "Parsimony," or the utility of unlimited saving.

§ 7. The most highly technical department of industrial science is currency. Probably few of those scientists and business men who are engaged in fighting the battle of the standards, or in building their highly intricate and often wholly illusory monetary systems, would condescend to read the passages in which an "amateur" states what he conceives to be the basic principles of a sound and socially serviceable currency. But those who understand the special weakness of all specialists, their detailed elaboration of superstructures built upon a foundation of general assumptions which

---

[1] Marshall, "Principles of Economics," Book VI., chap. ii. (note); Sidgwick, "Principles of Political Economy," Book I., chap. v. (note).

[2] Marshall, in a recent new edition of his "Principles," makes up his mind at last to a definite withdrawal of the dogma.

[3] J. S. Nicholson, "Principles of Political Economy" (1893), pp. 101–3. A whole series of economic writers, from the Earl of Lauderdale and Malthus to the present day, protested in vain against the acceptance of the doctrine of Parsimony, which gave a specious justification to this theory of Capital.

have been commonly received upon authority, and have not been subjected to a strict, patient, and unbiassed examination, may be inclined to give serious attention to the clear and original analysis presented by so powerful a mind as that of Mr. Ruskin. His theory of currency, presented in " Munera Pulveris" and elsewhere, has not, indeed, the interest which attaches to his more violent " heresies," but it is a lucid presentation of certain fundamental principles which, rightly grasped, point towards financial reforms after which statesmen and trained financiers are tardily and darkly groping their way.

Mr. Ruskin's reasoning upon this subject is more than usually compact in its presentation. The best summary is contained in the chapter of " Munera Pulveris " called " Coin-keeping." Currency he defines in the following terms : " The currency of any country consists of every document acknowledging debt which is transferable in the country."[1] " Legally authorised or national currency, in its perfect condition, is a form of public acknowledgment of debt, so regulated and divided that any person presenting a commodity in the public market shall, if he please, receive in exchange for it a document giving his claim to the return of its equivalent (1) in any place, (2) at any time, and (3) in any kind."[2]

The true and full purposes of such public currency require (1) that a more stable standard of exchange-values than gold and silver should be found, for " the

---

[1] Students of Monetary Science will recognise a kinship to the theory of Money championed by M'Leod, but Ruskin nowhere indorses the inclusion of all private Credit in Money, which is the kernel of M'Leod's teaching.

[2] Munera Pulveris, § lxx.

right of debt ought not to rest upon a basis of imagination, nor should the frame of a national currency vibrate
with every miser's panic and every merchant's impru-
dence." We ought, therefore, to base our currency
upon several substances, not one, and upon " substances
of true intrinsic value." This insistence upon the
superior stability of a composite basis is in accord with
the teaching of Jevons and the most liberal economists.
The theory of taking substances of intrinsic value as the
basis of currency, implying, as it must and would, the
ability of farmers, manufacturers, and other owners of
" goods " to deposit these goods in " public store-
houses " [1] and obtain credit notes for them, places Mr.
Ruskin in line with the advocates of Free Money as a
protection against the monopoly of private bankers and
money-lenders, and the dangers and waste of our private
credit notes. An honest government not issuing any
currency of forced acceptance (a deceitful form of taxation), and permitting no dishonest speculation, would
never find itself embarrassed in the theory or working
of currency.

Mr. Ruskin lays his finger upon the chief source of
our instability of values and our financial crises when he
denounces speculation. His further treatment of the
subject in " Fors " proves his keen apprehension of the
truth that speculation permeates the entire system of
private credit in modern commerce, that such credit,
though highly serviceable to the individual trader, is of
doubtful benefit to society. Upon this matter, indeed,
he expresses himself in no measured words. " This
system of mercantile credit, invented simply to give

[1] Fors, iii., Letter lviii.

power and opportunity to rogues, and enable them to live upon the wreck of honest men — was ever anything like it in the world before? That the wretched, impatient, scrambling idiots, calling themselves commercial men, forsooth, should not be able to see this plainest of all facts, that any given sum of money will be as serviceable to commerce in the pocket of the seller of the goods, as of the buyer; and that nobody gains by credit in the long run! It is precisely as great a loss to commerce that every seller has to wait six months for his money, as a gain that every buyer should keep his money six months in his pocket. In reality there is neither gain nor loss — except by roguery, when the gain is all to the rogue, and the loss to the true man." [1] Mr. Ruskin is probably right in holding that the common mode of swelling currency by private "bills of exchange" is a socially foolish policy, and ought to be unnecessary even as an individual convenience, if the theory that "all commerce is exchange of commodities" worked out properly by making it as easy to sell as it is to buy.

It is only the greater difficulty which owners of commodities experience in selling than owners of money experience in buying that impels manufacturers and merchants, competing with one another, constantly to tempt buyers by offering easy terms of payment. Such elasticity of credit is but one more testimony to the most salient defect of our present industrial mechanism, the existence of productive power in excess of what is needed to satisfy the demands of current consumption. Under-consumption, involving, as it must, the inability

[1] Fors, Letter xxvi. (ii. 33).

of producers to find purchasers with ready money, is a constant stimulus of inflated credit. Sound business, as Mr. Ruskin clearly sees, does not rest upon credit. A striking testimony to this truth is afforded by the fact that the most important structural change in modern industry, the growth of joint-stock companies, is attended by a return to the custom of ready-money payments. Mr. Ruskin's persistent advocacy of ready money, both in wholesale and retail transactions, is not merely a sound moral principle but a true economic policy.

Finally, his insistence that all money means power over labour, authority over men, proves that he has brought his currency teaching into true organic relation with the rest of his political economy, which is more than can be said for most of our writers on the subject. The possession of money means, ultimately, the power to demand work, and Mr. Ruskin rightly insists that the true vital significance of a quantity of money depends upon the economic condition of the workers. Where a large, poor, and degraded class of workers exists, the possession of £5 gives me the power to force an injurious quantity of bad work out of weaklings who are unable to refuse my demands; in a fairly ordered society of skilled and comfortable workers, the possession of the same sum would only give me power to put some of those workers to wholesome and moderate labour. Thus, the mere knowledge of the quantity of money owned by a person or a nation tells us nothing of the underlying human facts. Money must be reduced to subjective or vital " cost " before its significance is understood.

CHAPTER VI.

§ 1. Denunciation of competition in general terms. § 2. Work
motived by pay injures the worker. § 3. Bad influence of competition upon quality of "goods." § 4. Qualifications of the
charge of immorality. § 5. Incisive exposure of the unfair
nature of bargaining. § 6. Proposal for a scientific basis of
exchange. § 7. Mr. Ruskin's doctrine of "No profit in exchange." § 8. Doctrine of the illegitimacy of interest. § 9.
Source of error in Mr. Ruskin's economic reasoning. § 10. Distinction of charitable loans for need and loans for investment.

§ 1. Mr. Ruskin's attitude towards competition as a
method of determining prices and payments of any kind
is one of unqualified hostility. The disutility and the
immorality of industrial competition are charges he is
never tired of pressing. "Government and Co-operation
are in all things the Laws of Life; Anarchy and Competition the Laws of Death." [1] He accuses the current
economic teaching of misrepresenting the processes of
bargaining and competition so as to conceal their immoral and anti-social character. Adam Smith's doctrine
of "the invisible hand," by whose guidance every industrial man, in following his own individual gain, was
necessarily impelled to conduct which contributed to the
welfare of society, indisputably underlay the current
teaching, furnishing a utilitarian sanction. It was,

[1] Unto this Last, p. 102.

143

indeed, no business of theirs, economists averred, to justify the morality of economic processes, nor to defend the motive of enlightened self-interest, by which " economic men " were actuated ; but this analysis of industry did serve, in fact, to palliate self-seeking conduct by showing that it fulfilled, and by suggesting that it was " intended " to fulfil, a social purpose, as well as by presenting such an account of the processes of bargains as to teach that each man got what he deserved, and that substantial justice was done by the existing methods of appointment of wealth.

§ 2. Now, addressing himself first to this defence of the " competitive system " of industry, Mr. Ruskin vehemently repudiates both its morality and its utility, the latter not only because he believes that what is immoral cannot be ultimately useful, but because he denies that the self-seeking motive of the " economic man " does actually impel him to a socially profitable line of conduct. Competitive industry, he contends, is doubly degrading to the character of those engaging in it, both in the conscious motive it indulges and in the character it imposes upon work. Since profit, not excellence of work, is the admitted motive, the individual producer is purely self-engrossed, his selfishness not being tempered by any sense of social service ; in all the processes of buying and selling this selfishness is accentuated by the constant sharp antagonism between himself and his competitors. Any dim perception that competition involves some indirect co-operation towards a common social end is kept in the background of consciousness by the unceasing sense of struggle. A system which thus concentrates all thought upon profit, instead of upon quality of work or excellence of achievement, inevitably damages the character of work, and does not secure the utility it professes to serve. Good work can only be the result of a conscious effort to work well. A sense of enjoyment accompanies all true effort of the artist; no worthy art-work is produced for pay. In every process of art or industry, just in proportion as the work and its result are not valued for themselves, and are by their very conditions incapable of such valuation, will the product be base. Large quantities of common routine machine-made goods may be turned out by wholly unenjoyed and toilsome labour undergone for pay, but none of the worthier forms of material or immaterial wealth can be thus produced. Work undertaken merely for pay is essentially degrading to the worker; and blinded as our age is by the spurious ethics of commercialism, it has sufficient sound feeling to attest this truth by the degrees of honour it imputes to different kinds of workers. *[Why* are soldiers, doctors, preachers, held in high social esteem?[1] Because, though all live by their calling, the conditions of their labour are such as to give them an independent interest in the success of their work, and not to keep their minds fixed upon the pay they are to get for it. Again, in manufacture, just in so far as an employer or a worker is able to take a genuine pride and interest in his work, apart from the profit or wage which it brings, will he do good work, and that work do good to him. Where a carpenter (not a subdivided cabinetmaker) or a tailor (not a presser or a button-holer) is engaged in turning out by skill a complete article, even modern industrial

[1] Unto this Last, pp. 25-28.

conditions preserve for him a certain dignity of labour, which is endorsed by the general estimate of his fellows. Why is it that merchants, and still more retail shopkeepers, have always been held in low esteem? Mr. Ruskin's answer is conclusive. "A great deal of the vulgarity and nearly all the vice of retail commerce, involving the degradation of persons engaged in it, depend simply on the fact that their minds are always occupied by the vital (or rather mortal) question of profits." [1] The carpenter is interested in his work, and knows that he is making a useful article; the retailer is interested in persuading people to buy goods for their highest price, and knows only that he is making profit. Just in proportion as men's minds are set on profit, it is not their "interest" to do the best work of which they are capable; it is rather their "interest" to do the worst work which will enable them to earn their pay. This is Mr. Ruskin's answer to the argument that love of profit will evoke good work by competition. Competitive profit-seeking may serve to prevent the making and the selling of bad articles where badness can be detected by consumers, but it is a direct stimulus to the practice of every art of adulteration and concealment which can escape detection, and can thus become the " custom of a trade ;" while it offers direct and prohibitive discouragement to any excellence of work which cannot recommend itself by specious show to the consuming public. The skill really stimulated by profit-seeking consists far more in keeping down expenses (not " human cost ") of production than in improving the quality of products.

[1] Unto this Last, p. 28.

§ 3. Similarly the direct influence of keen competition between manufacturers or merchants is not fraught
with the social advantage claimed for it by *laissez faire*
economists. The normal result of competition is not
to induce manufacturers to make and merchants to
sell to customers better commodities at the same price at
which worse commodities were sold before, but to make
and sell at lower prices worse commodities pretending
to be the same. This is the explanation of the " cheap
and nasty " goods which all deplore, but which the
poor must buy, and which sweating businesses will
therefore make and sell. Thus one chief natural effect
of competition is to glut markets with low-class commodities, and to debauch the taste and injure the persons
and the pockets of consumers.

Mr. Ruskin does not, indeed, deny that improvement
of quality and true cheapness may and do result from
the stimulus of competition,[1] but such gains are chiefly
confined to articles the true character of which cannot
be concealed, and which are bought by people of some
taste and education, who know what they are buying.
False cheapness will always deceive the poorer and more
ignorant buyers, and many articles are permanently and
generally deteriorated for all classes of purchasers by the
pressure of competition, which has gradually converted
some insidious dishonesty into the custom of a trade.

To these evils must be added the immeasurable waste
involved in the actual processes of competition, the end-
less multiplication of agents, touters, and advertisements
of every kind, almost the whole of which must be debited
as social loss.

[1] *Munera Pulveris*, § 62 (note).

§ 4. To dwell in detail upon the charges pressed against competitive industry is unnecessary. Most of them will be admitted by all thoughtful persons, though some considerable qualifications and offsets may be demanded. The selfishness of profit-seeking and competition educates, it may be claimed, intellectual and moral qualities of industry, thrift, foresight, self-command, enterprise, and courage, which, even though devoted primarily to selfish ends, have also social worth, when circumstances draw them from their narrower occupations. The struggle for life and livelihood, it is contended, has never been so narrowly self-seeking as is sometimes alleged : in some degree it has always been a struggle for the life of others, directly and consciously, for the support and welfare of family and dependents, in some measure, at any rate, for the good of a trade or a locality ; the very Manchesterism, which is sometimes taken as the type of commercial selfishness, expressed itself in a policy which evoked a powerful common interest in a trade, and often a laudable self-sacrifice for this wider organism.

Ignoring these actualities of modern commerce, Mr. Ruskin painted too dark a picture. The commercial man, even under the reign of steam-driven machinery, is not the mere " covetous machine " which the " pure theory " of the older economic text-books sometimes assumed him to be. At the same time the wide and glaring discrepancy between the higher teaching of ethics and Christianity, on the one hand, and the practice of industry on the other, is undeniable. The man who loved his neighbour as himself in business would quickly find his way into the bankruptcy court. It can scarcely be denied that the net moral result of competitive industry is to promote conscious discord between man and man, to dissociate and not to unite human interests, to inure men during six days of the week to an attitude of mind repugnant to that teaching of the seventh day, which in theory they profess ought to govern the whole conduct of the week.

Mr. Ruskin, therefore, even though he exaggerated the intensity of selfishness involved in commercial competition, and denounced in too unqualified terms its social inutility, must be held to have established his main charge, that a deep antagonism exists between our moral theory and our common practice in the affairs of life which most occupy our energies. This antagonism inevitably retards social progress, and all reasonable men must favour such reforms as shall make industry a conscious social bond between man and man instead of a conscious severance.

§ 5. When Mr. Ruskin proceeds to specify in more detail the character of those bargains by which commerce is conducted, he is not so exact in his reasoning or so successful in substantiating his charges. That the law of supply and demand works unjustly, that bargaining does not secure a fair or just price, that exchange is conducted on a basis of fraud and force, these are his accusations against industry, and commercial economy he charges with aiding and abetting these wrongs by misrepresentations of the processes.

In his treatment of this theme he renders one signal service. Although commercial economy never positively affirmed the justice of bargaining as a means of exchange and of distribution, its teaching undoubtedly conveyed the impression that substantial justice was achieved by these processes. The suggestion was that, when an act of sale took place, seller and buyer made an equal gain from the transaction. The unusual candour of Professor J. E. Cairnes, who said, "I am unaware of any rule of justice applicable to the problem of distributing the produce of industry," never made its way into the current teaching of economics which still rested on the assumption that competition harmonised the interests of the individual with the interests of society, all working together for the best. Mr. Ruskin's flat denial of any tendency towards fair or equal apportionment of gain in an act of purchase or exchange, is sustained by exact analysis of economic processes.

His simple statement of the working of supply and demand is not to be gainsaid. "In practice, according to the laws of demand and of supply, when two men are ready to do the work, and only one man wants to have it done, the two men underbid each other for it; and the one who gets it to do is underpaid. But when two men want the work done, and there is only one man ready to do it, the two men who want it done overbid each other, and the workman is overpaid."[1] In uncivilised communities force and fraud have always been chief means of acquiring property; in modern industrial societies it is supposed that a just and rational system of exchange has been substituted. But when we closely investigate the actual working of exchange, we find the elements of fraud and force surviving, only hidden. The bargain of a baker with a starving man rests upon a

[1] Unto this Last, p. 82.

display of economic force which is present more or less in every bargain.

It may be urged that Mr. Ruskin's instance improperly assumes inequality by making two sellers face one buyer or *vice versâ*. But the answer is, that over the larger portion of the field of exchange, the number of willing and effective buyers is either larger or smaller than the number of sellers, and the closer competition set in motion among those who find themselves in danger of being left out in the cold, does give to the other side the advantage of monopoly which Mr. Ruskin's simple case serves to illustrate. Nor is it merely a question of numbers: the relative strength of economic resources of the two parties bargaining is the real criterion. In many kinds of bargains there is no direct competition at all upon one side or the other; in hiring labour, for example, the direct needs of employer and labourer chiefly determine the price of the labour, and the more urgent need of the labourer tends to give the advantage to the employer. Even when a number of employers are genuinely competing on the one side, and a number of labourers on the other, there is still no provision for determining a " fair" wage, in the sense of a wage which is equally beneficial to labourer and employer: an equality in numbers and resources of the two sides still tends to give the larger gain of the bargain to one of the two parties.

§ 6. But while Mr. Ruskin is quite justified in his conviction that force lies at the root of bargaining, and that " robbing the poor because he is poor " is an underlying principle of exchange, his insistence that equity in exchange consists " in giving time for time, strength for strength and skill for skill,"[1] is of doubtful validity. Absolute equality of time, strength, or skill, even if the two latter things were measurable, would not furnish the true basis of equality of personal services, which morality seems to demand. Ideally, at any rate, the individual capacity of each person must be taken into account in considering how much time, strength, or skill is required to balance the same time or intensity of labour in some other person. It is, therefore, unsafe to endorse Mr. Ruskin's declaration that "it is easier to determine scientifically what a man ought to have for his work, than what his necessities will compel him to take for it."[2]

The only definite attempt to substantiate this claim of a scientific basis of wages, and therefore of exchange, is the reference to a physiological standard of "cost," the clearest expression of which is contained in a letter addressed to the *Pall Mall Gazette* in 1867 :[3] "Let any half-dozen London physicians of recognised standing state in precise terms the quantity and kind of food, and space of lodging, they consider approximately necessary for the healthy life of a labourer in any given manufacture, and the number of hours he may, without shortening his life, work at such business daily, if in such manner he be sustained. Let all masters be bound to give their men a choice between an order for that quantity of food and space of lodging, or the market wages for that specified number of hours of work." In considering Mr. Ruskin's doctrine of "intrinsic value," attention has already been called to the just, scientific

<hr>

[1] Unto this Last, pp. 82-3.　　[2] Ibid, p. 90.
[3] Reprinted in "Arrows of the Chace," ii. 97.

instinct which leads him to resolve both " cost" and " utility " into their physical equivalents.[1] Here, too, as in many other instances, we find expert economists following in his footsteps. The writers of the ablest modern treatise upon industrial reform advocate, as the basis of our wage system, the recognition of a National Minimum, " determined by practical inquiry as to the cost of the food, clothing, and shelter physiologically necessary, according to national habit and custom, to prevent bodily deterioration."[2] For centuries, in fact, the money wages of most English labourers were regulated by rough reference to their physical requirements as indicated by the price of bread. But though the idea of a physical replacement of energy given out in work forms a sound basis for a minimum wage, to make it the sole regulator of the price of labour would be to ignore entirely the claim of the labourer to share the gain arising from the productivity of labour over and above a mere replacement. It would, in fact, mean a return to the notion which denied all " profit" to labour, and kept wages at a natural minimum of subsistence. Moreover, so long as a wage system exists, it will be necessary to consider not only the " cost" side of the wage question, but also the " utility " as represented in the demand for different kinds of labour. To fix wages according to a standard of physical health, under existing circumstances, would stereotype the economic condition of the working-classes, and hand over to the capitalist-employer all increased value arising

---

[1] *Supra*, ch. iii., p. 69.
[2] "Industrial Democracy," by Sidney and Beatrice Webb, vol. ii., p. 774.

from industrial improvments or growing needs of the consuming public. Taking Mr. Ruskin's proposal in further detail, the impracticability of any sufficiently exact agreement as to the physical needs of various classes of workers might be urged. This objection would be fatal against an attempt at a delicate and precise determination of the needs of different classes of labourers, in relation to locality, sex, age, health, and other factors; but it need not prevent the establishment of a broadly-marked " national minimum " such as Mr. and Mrs. Webb suggest. In other words, though Mr. Ruskin's proposal has a distinct scientific worth, it cannot fulfil the large purpose he claims for it. But this failure to furnish an exact scientific standard of exchange does not in the least degree invalidate his exposure of the immorality and waste involved in determining all payments by reference to the economic force of the competing and bargaining parties.

§ 7. In pressing his charges against competitive industry, and the economic interpretation of it, Mr. Ruskin, however, puts forward two highly disputable doctrines. The first is embodied in his teaching that there is no profit in exchange. Since this is one of the gravest difficulties in Mr. Ruskin's " economics," it demands close consideration. In his first statement of the doctrine (" Unto this Last," p. 129), he carefully distinguishes " profit " from " advantage." " In exchange there is only advantage, *i. e.* a bringing of vantage or power to the exchanging persons. Thus, one man by sewing and reaping, turns one measure of corn into two measures. That is Profit. Another, by digging and forging, turns one spade into two spades. That is Profit. But the man who

has two measures of corn, wants sometimes to dig ; and
the man who has two spades wants sometimes to eat. . .
They exchange the gained grain for the gained tool : and
both are the better for the exchange ; but though there
is much advantage in the transaction, there is no profit.
Nothing is constructed or produced." [1] The orthodox
economist's first comment is that something is produced
by exchange, viz., utility, for things in the possession of
those who need them more are more useful than when
in the possession of those who need them less. Mr.
Ruskin, however, admits an advantage accruing to both
parties, but objects to call it profit. Economists can
hardly blame him for insisting upon narrowing the
meaning of a word, which, by its vagueness, has been
the source of so much trouble in economic literature.
It is, however, not easy to understand what Mr. Ruskin
gains by this materialistic conception of profit, confining
it to the construction of new material gain. He is, as
we know, a stickler for etymology ; but there is no
linguistic propriety which prevents the increased utility
assigned to goods by exchange from meriting the title
" profit." Probably the real source of the distinction is
his conception of value as a quality intrinsic and un-
alterable in amount attaching to forms of wealth. The
mere act of exchange cannot increase this quality impressed on goods " by the Maker of men and things."
There is therefore no " profit " or " advance " of value
by exchange. Nor does Mr. Ruskin's conception of the
standard of exchange induce him to take a different
view. Labour-time is the basis of exchange, and the
act of exchange can hardly be said to consume labour-

[1] *Unto this Last*, pp. 29, 30.

time. There is, therefore, according to his economic code, no reason for assigning increased use-value (his " value,") or exchange-value (economic value), as the result of exchange.

Mr. Ruskin's denial of " profit" to exchange, though a perverse and arbitrary judgment, would, however, be innocent if it had not visibly misled its author into later criticisms of exchange, which, if they have any meaning, signify that there can be no two-sided gain in exchange. This strange obliquity shows itself only a few pages later, in " Unto this Last" (pp. 132–3), where he condemns the whole science and practice of exchange, on the ground that the " advantage" of exchange depends on cheating. " If I can exchange a needle with a savage for a diamond, my power of doing so depends either on the savage's ignorance of social arrangements in Europe, or on his want of power to take advantage of them, by selling the diamond to any one else for more needles. If, farther, I make the bargain as completely advantageous to myself as possible, by giving to the savage a needle with no eye in it (reaching thus a sufficiently satisfactory type of the perfect operation of catallactic science), the advantage to me in the entire transaction depends wholly upon the ignorance, powerlessness, or heedlessness of the person dealt with. Do away with these, and catallactic advantage becomes impossible."[1]

Mr. Ruskin does not appear to recognise that, even in the cases of exchange, where one party is immeasurably stronger or craftier than the other, a residuum of real gain or advantage must accrue to the weaker party, at any rate just such minimum advantage as is sufficient

[1] p. 133.

to induce him to be a party to the bargain. The materialistic conception of "profit," which he has adopted, brings him back at times almost to the doctrine of the French physiocrats, who held that agriculture was the only occupation which produced value. This ancient position is even more logical than that which Mr. Ruskin adopts, for the physiocrats insisted that "production" should be confined to the getting of actual material forms out of the earth, while Mr. Ruskin allows that profit may be made by altering the shape of material forms, though not, apparently, by altering their place or ownership. For it must be clearly understood that Mr. Ruskin denies profit to all trade, not merely to the activities of the merchant or retailer in the act of selling, but to the importer and carrier in the act of conveyance. It may perhaps be said that the issue is, after all, a verbal one, but Mr. Ruskin does not deny the services of merchant or retailer, but prefers to keep the term "profit" for productive work in a narrower sense of the word "production." But, at any rate, the distinction is most unfortunate, for it not only misleads his readers, but it has duped its author, as may be shown by the following passage of "Fors," which will also serve the further purpose of introducing the second serious error which impairs his indictment of modern industry :

"There are in the main two great fallacies which the rascals of the world rejoice in making its fools proclaim : the first, that by continually exchanging and cheating each other in exchange, two exchanging persons, out of one pot, alternating with one kettle, can make their two fortunes. This is the principle of *Trade*. The second, that Judas's bag has become a juggler's, in which, if Mr.

P. deposits his pot, and waits awhile, there will come out two pots, both full of broth ; and if Mr. K. deposits his kettle, and awaits awhile, there will come out two kettles, both full of fish! That is the principle of *Interest.*" [1]

It is a curious irony which makes Mr. Ruskin take such a materialistic view of wealth, so utterly inconsistent with his human standard, as to make him suppose that an increase of fortune, even reckoned in commercial terms, requires a corresponding increase in quantity of material forms. Why should not an improved method of exchange, by merely putting the right things in the right hands, be held to make fortunes ? for commodities, thus well disposed, are evidently worth more both in money and in real utility or power to contribute to human vitality. The charge that bargaining distributes unfairly the advantage of exchange need not lead us to a virtual denial of the productivity of trade.

§ 8. Mr. Ruskin's conviction of the illegitimacy of interest belongs to his later years. When he wrote " Munera Pulveris," the usury which he condemned meant, in reference to capital, taking an *exorbitant* rate of interest.[2] No special sin was attached to interest upon loans, except so far as it meant taking advantage of the borrower's poverty. But as soon as he began " Fors Clavigera " further doubts arose. The first letter shows him probing the economic defence of interest ; the eighth letter contains a general assault upon " capitalists' percentages ; " and by 1872 he had reached a settled conviction that all interest was wrong. The pamphlets of Mr. W. C. Sillar were largely instrumental

---

[1] Fors, Letter xlv. (ii. 435).   [2] Munera Pulveris, § 98.

in this conversion,[1] and in Letter xviii. of "Fors," he
sets forth his position in a most instructive passage.
After showing briefly that compensation for risk and
wages of management are legitimate payments which
form no true part of interest, he finds that the defence
of interest, as given by Professor Fawcett, consists in
treating it as " the reward of abstinence." " It strikes
me, upon this, that if I had not my £15,000 of bank
stock, I should be a good deal more abstinent than I
am, and that nobody would then talk of rewarding me
for it. It might be possible to find even cases of very
prolonged and painful abstinence, for which no reward
has yet been adjudged by less abstinent England. Abstinence may indeed have its reward, nevertheless ; but not
by increase of what we abstain from, *unless there be a law
of growth for it unconnected with our abstinence.* ' You
cannot have your cake and eat it.' Of course not ; and
if you don't eat it, you have your cake ; but not a cake
and a half! Imagine the complex trial of schoolboy
minds, if the law of nature about cakes were, that if
you ate none of your cake to-day, you would have ever
so much bigger a cake to-morrow ! — which is Mr. Fawcett's notion of *the law of nature about money ;* and, alas,
many a man's beside, — it being no law of nature whatever, but absolutely contrary to all her laws, and not to
be enacted by the whole force of united mankind."[2]
Hence he concludes that interest is a forcible taxation
or exaction of usury.[3] Now, this paragraph is interesting, because it thoroughly exposes the strength and
weakness of Mr. Ruskin's position. The playful soph-

---

[1] Munera Pulveris, § 98 (note).
[2] Fors, Letter xviii. (i. 366).   [3] Fors, Letter xxi. (i. 419).

istry of the two opening sentences may be set aside at
once, for though it is of course true that the most painful abstinence, that of the poor, get no reward of interest, that in no way meets the contention that interest is
the reward of a certain sort of abstinence, viz., that of
those who, possessing the power to consume at once,
postpone its exercise.   Since it is obviously open to this
ambiguous interpretation, the phrase " reward of abstinence " may not be the best term to describe the *raison
d'être* of interest.   For this and other reasons many
economists have preferred to rest the justification of
interest not upon abstinence but upon the productivity
of capital.   Mr. Ruskin's real underlying argument is
that capital is not productive, in the sense that it cannot
grow.   " Abstinence does not cause an increase of what
we abstain from," is his first argument, enforced by the
former of the two passages which I have italicised.   But,
jumping the metaphysics of causation, it may be answered that " abstinence " is a necessary condition of
an increase of wealth that is due to the presence and
use of what we abstain from.   By abstaining from some
immediate enjoyment, I can bring into existence and
keep in use certain admittedly serviceable forms of capital : the service these forms of capital render involves,
and is represented by, an increased growth of wealth,
and this increase, whether it be spoken of as " caused
by " my abstinence or not, is at any rate conditioned
by that abstinence : if I do not abstain, that wealth does
not grow, and since I shall prefer present enjoyment to
that abstinence unless I receive a portion of the increased
wealth, interest may be regarded as a necessary reward
of abstinence paid out of an increased product due to the

practice of the abstinence. That abstinence alone, in
the sense of a refusal to consume existing goods, will
not cause increase of those goods, is true enough; but
neither will labour alone, or any productive power or
condition, be effectual, except in co-operation with other
forces. The notion which sometimes crops up in Mr.
Ruskin's argument, as elsewhere, that "abstinence" or
"waiting" cannot be a productive activity, rests upon
an unconscious materialism in the conception of productivity, as if no action were productive except by
direct physical operation in shaping or moving goods.
The "waiting" of the capitalist is productive in much
the same sense as the inspection of the overlooker in
a mill; it is a condition of the effective functioning
of capital as the latter is of the effective functioning of
labour. "But the overlooker works in return for what
he gets, and the capitalist does not," it may be re-
torted. However, the use of the word "work" begs
a question. Abstinence may, and does in some capitalists, imply a painful exertion of will which, if it is serviceable in industry, has the same right and natural
need of a "reward" as labour.

The obvious fact that much of this abstinence involves
no pain at all is no more reason for denying the validity
of all interest, than the equally obvious fact that some
labour is a positive satisfaction to the labourer is a reason
for denying him his wages. The real gravamen of the
charge against capital is not for receiving interest, but
for the modes by which the capital is often accumulated.
There is, indeed, a legitimate presumption that capital,
the saving of which involves no real sacrifice, has been
acquired not by honest labour but by some form of eco-

nomic oppression in the processes of bargaining through which an income is derived. It is to these processes that we should rightly attach the condemnation which Mr. Ruskin and others fasten specifically on interest. The Ruskin of " Fors " has in fact abandoned the far sounder position of " Munera Pulveris," which condemned only exorbitant interest due to oppression as one among various modes of oppressive dealing.

Nowhere does Mr. Ruskin seriously attempt to meet the claim for interest upon the ground of the " productivity " of capital. In his brilliant sword-play with the Bishop of Manchester he carves very prettily the theology and ethics of the bishop, but he does not fairly meet the contention that interest upon invested capital stands on a different footing from loans made to poorer neighbours in emergencies. The instances he quotes of the fraud and tyranny which mark the proceedings of certain trading companies, the degrading influences of speculation and so forth, are doubtless valid evidence of certain abuses of capital, but constitute no proof whatever of his contention that interest upon all capital is derived from extortion.

This controversy serves, indeed, to make it clear that Mr. Ruskin identifies interest with usury ; but though his theological arguments for doing so are strong, his economical ones are weak.

§ 9. How was Mr. Ruskin really led from condemnation of extortion to condemnation of all interest? The answer to this question is, I think, contained in the second phrase which I have italicised in the passage from " Fors " quoted above. He there speaks of " the law of nature about money." In a word, he has fallen a victim to a famous fallacy which has in the history of economic thought proved fatal to many of the subtlest intellects the world has ever known. The intellectual repudiation of interest has nearly always arisen from the difficulty of conceiving that money could " produce " anything, either more money or more wealth of any kind. Aristotle's famous diction that " money is barren " expresses concisely the point of view which this " master of those that know " held in common with Moses and Jesus, most of the fathers of the Church, Bacon, Luther, Bossuet, and many wise men of all ages.

Mr. Ruskin goes out of his way to endorse Aristotle's saying,[1] and several passages in " Fors " make it evident that the notion, that the service for which interest is paid is a loan of money, is at the root of his condemnation.[2] If Mr. Ruskin, debating the right of interest, had kept clearly before him his own theory of the nature of money, as expounded in " Time and Tide " and elsewhere, viz., that the essence of money, as currency, is that it is a sign of command over wealth in general and ultimately over human services, he would have recognised that a man who makes a loan of money is really handing over a general command of all forms of material or immaterial wealth, and that upon the productive use of this wealth, not upon the productivity of " coins," depends the claim of interest. The loan of money and the receipt of money interest are only the outward and

<hr />

[1] Fors, Letter xlviii. (ii 483, note.)

[2] See especially " Fors," iii., pp. 380 and 382, Letter lxviii. ; iv. 119, Letter lxxviii.; *cf.* also " Arrows of the Chace," ii. 103, where Mr. Ruskin calls attention to the fact that money doesn't "grow."

convenient form of the transaction; the substance is a loan of tools or goods and the receipt of tools or goods in return.

§ 10. If this view is correct, it convicts Mr. Ruskin of serious error in his economic reasoning. But though the rejection of interest has so long relied upon this intellectual defence, it may be doubted whether its real strength has ever been derived from this source. Indignation at palpable abuse of power by usurers, and a certain sense of brotherhood, imposing upon those who have to spare the duty of lending freely to those in need — these strong moral bases of conduct have probably been more influential in moulding the policy of states and in dominating custom than economic reasoning about the barrenness of money. In ancient societies the opportunities for productive employment of private capital were exceedingly restricted, and loans of money made to tide over some season of need, or to repair some unforeseen misfortune, played a far more conspicuous part. The social virtues of neighbourly assistance and charity are always more prized and more practised in primitive societies than in developed industrial communities, and the morality of a nation is particularly directed to such a policy by its religious and ethical instructors.

Had Mr. Ruskin confined his attack upon interest to the reassertion of the humane charitable duty of free lending to the poor, his position would have been far stronger than the one he actually adopted. The social utility of a policy of free loans will depend upon the attitude we adopt towards charity in general as a mode of redressing or abating social injuries. Holding with

Mr. Ruskin that the existing economic processes which apportion wealth are void of moral sanction, and that the pressure of need therefore does not in general imply moral infirmity, we may very well regard such charity as an informal mode of redressing certain noxious inequalities of our economic arrangements.

So far as loans to the needy are concerned, this attitude has undoubtedly a strong moral support. But in times when most capital is employed, not for such purposes, but for business investments of a directly productive character, it is not possible to rely upon these moral motives for a general denial of the validity of taking interest. Mr. Ruskin, in common with many assailants of the theory of interest, appears to forget the vital difference between the " money-lender " and the " investor." Where money is invested there is no warrant for supposing that the borrower cannot at least hold his own ; and since such investments are evidently a source of profit to their employment, no reason can be shown why that profit should be taken by the manufacturer or the trading company to whom the " loan " is made rather than by the investor.

Indeed, the practical good sense of ancient communities, where " interest " was formally forbidden, generally made exception of cases where the loan was made to a person of substance, or was otherwise designed for profitable employment in business.

The belief that all business conducted for the sake of private profit is wrong, and prejudicial to the interests of society, is sometimes adduced as implying a condemnation of interest. But the argument is entirely beside the point. If all industry could be organised by society, and conducted for the common good, no special profit need be asked as the reward of social saving; but so long as individual saving is required for the maintenance of individual business, such portion of that saving as involves personal sacrifice has the same natural and moral claim to compensation as any other order of industrial sacrifice. Other times, other morals! Organise industry upon a social basis, then individual interest will be unnecessary and illicit, but not till then.

But, however wrong Mr. Ruskin may have been in his theory of interest, his exposure of the folly of those who taxed him with inconsistency in consenting to take interest for investments, after discovering interest was wrong, is exemplary. " I hold bank stock simply because I suppose it to be safer than any other stock, and I take the interest of it because, though taking interest is, in the abstract, as wrong as war, the entire fabric of society is at present so connected with both usury and war that it is not possible violently to withdraw, nor wisely to set example of withdrawing, from either evil." [1]   There is no more convincing testimony of the inherent incapacity for reasoning in the average sensual man than the charge of " inconsistency " brought against a Socialist on the ground that he does not attempt to cure a social evil by an individual remedy.

The chief harm done by Mr. Ruskin's economic errors is that they have furnished really vulnerable points upon which hostile critics have concentrated all their fire.   The social teaching of a man who denies the productiveness of exchange, and who challenges the validity of interest, it is urged, may be safely dis-

---

[1] Fors, Letter xxi. (i. 419).

regarded by all sane-minded and practical persons. So perverse is most men's judgment of criticism involving an unsettlement of convenient opinions, that they gladly seize upon some salient single weakness as a pretext for ignoring the deepest and most vital truths. Mr. Ruskin has remorselessly and accurately exposed the injustice inherent in all bargaining, and the existence of oppression in all forms of buying and selling, including the selling of the use of capital. But because he has found some special and separate fault in this last class of bargains which is not always there, his more fundamental criticism, which is valid, has been utterly disregarded by the great majority of cultured persons who yet pretend to think that Mr. Ruskin is a wise and wholesome teacher. "They read the words, and say they are pretty, and go on in their own ways."[1]

Well might such obdurate irrationality drive a man of Mr. Ruskin's temperament to madness, as he declares it did.[2] Here was a man of wide experience and of the keenest penetration into life, coining his very soul into passionate eloquence and searching analysis, in order to convince the intellect and stir the heart of his countrymen to see the deadly injustice and inutility of the existing social order, and the necessity of labouring energetically towards reform; and his words are — not unlistened to, and not unread, that were hard enough — but eagerly heard and willingly read, and yet impotent for conviction and for the guidance of conduct. That people should gush over his beautiful writing about Art and Literature, should "sympathise" with much that

---

[1] Fors, Letter lviii. (iii. 176).
[2] Fors, Letters lxvi. and lxvii. (iii. 343, 362-63).

he has to say about the ugliness of industrial towns, the miseries of the poor, the dangers of luxury, the need of social solidarity, and should go their own way in comfortable self-complacency, giving their usual subscriptions to " charities," and deprecating any radical change in this best of all possible worlds for the well-to-do — this surely is a more scathing indictment of his age and country than any that Mr. Ruskin himself uttered in his most impassioned moments.

CHAPTER VII.

§ 1. WHAT is the right ordering of human activities in a true commonwealth ? is the great practical question as it presented itself to Mr. Ruskin. In " Time and Tide " and " Fors Clavigera " he gives his answer, describing those changes necessary to establish a sound society upon right industrial and political principles. Certain axioms of social justice relating to work and property underlie his proposals. Every man must do the work which he can do best, and in the best way, for the common good and not for individual profit, receiving in return property consisting of good things which he has honestly got, and can skilfully use. [1] These general laws are applied to the circumstances of his age and country, so as to yield a body of definite proposals for social reform.

[1] Fors, Letter lxx. (iii. 411).

Education, government, industrial order, are naturally and necessarily involved in the art of social economics, as Mr. Ruskin conceived it, and his leading proposals may all be set in their ethical, political, or economic aspects. Perhaps these several aspects may best be harmonised by thus restating and answering the social question as it familiarly appeared to Mr. Ruskin. " How can society consciously order the lives of its members so as to maintain the largest number of noble and happy human beings ? "

§ 2. First, adequate care must be taken to provide good human material. Mr. Ruskin often bitterly complains that his most vital elements of teaching are precisely those which are ignored by his friends. Partly from prudishness, partly from sheer blindness, the fundamental importance attached by Mr. Ruskin to " the population question " is completely shirked by most of his professed followers and lovers. Mr. Ruskin was far too wise not to perceive that every great social question has one of its roots in physiology. The first provision for a sound society is that its citizens shall be well born, the second that they shall be well educated. We have come to a lip agreement at any rate on this second requisite, but the first is still wilfully and wofully ignored. Yet few who face the issue can or will deny the truth of the solemn declaration that " the beginning of all sanitary and moral law is in the regulation of marriage, and that, ugly and fatal as is every form and agency of license, no licentiousness is so mortal as licentiousness in marriage." [1] That society should tacitly sanction the transmission and increase of every form

[1] Time and Tide, § 123.

of hereditary disease, vice or folly, ignoring its first
duty, that of maintaining the standard of health, intelligence, and morals in the community, is quite the
most foolish and most wasteful abdication of responsibility in which any government can possibly indulge.
Mr. Ruskin's proposals for state " permission to marry,"
with rigid regulations as to age and income, qualified by
fantastic revivals of ancient ceremony, may seem impossible or intolerable, but the prohibition of definitely anti-
social marriages, the refusal to allow epileptics, criminals,
or the victims of any serious hereditary evil, to increase
and multiply at an incalculable cost to society, is one of
the plainest demands of social welfare.

§ 3. After provision for good birth comes the need of
good education. Mr. Ruskin has so much to say about
methods of education that it would be unwise to attempt
to summarise his fuller teaching here. A very brief
statement of the purpose and direction of his public
education, which must be under state control, and free,
liberal, and technical, will here suffice. Physical nurture
is coupled with education in his scheme. " I hold it ✗
indisputable, that the first duty of a state is to see that
every child born therein shall be well housed, clothed,
fed, and educated, till it attain years of discretion." [1]
This does not mean that children shall be taken from
their parents' homes and brought up in state establishments, for the maintenance of home life and parental
duties is a central feature in his conception of social
order ; but that society shall enforce the interest it possesses in the quality of its future citizens, by insisting
that they shall grow up with sound physical as well as

[1] Time and Tide, § 70.

intellectual surroundings. He fully recognises that the enforcement of such social duty involves that "the government must have an authority over the people of which we do not so much as dream." The nature of this authority will be presently disclosed.

All children, both of the operative and ruling classes, must first be taught "The Laws of Health, and exercises enjoined by them, and to this end your schools must be in fresh country, and amidst fresh air, and have great extents of land attached to them in permanent estate. Riding, running, all the honest, personal exercises of offence and defence, and music, should be the primal heads of this bodily education." " Next to these bodily accomplishments, the two great mental graces should be taught, Reverence and Compassion,"[1] the bases of moral conduct in life, and with them " truth of spirit and word, of thought and sight." The principal subjects of common education will be history, natural science and mathematics, the accurate teaching of language, the mother tongue being involved in all book studies. He makes a broad differentiation of education to conform with large local differences of life, which will probably control or determine later occupations. " For children whose life is to be in cities, the subjects of study should be, as far as their disposition will allow of it, mathematics and the arts; for children who are to live in the country, natural history of birds, insects, and plants, together with agriculture taught practically; and for children who are to be seamen, physical geography, astronomy, and the natural history of sea-fish and sea-birds."[2] Upon this broader foundation must be set the

[1] Time and Tide, § 75.   [2] Ibid., § 100.

technical education, by which a child learns the calling
by which it is to live.

Such is a brief outline of a state policy, towards
which civilised states to-day are surely but slowly
moving. The vast expenditure of labour and money
involved in such an education still staggers financiers
and other "practical" men, who have yet to learn that
no expenditure of public money or time is so profitably
invested for all purposes, industrial and social, as that
which is directly expended in raising the standard of
human life and character. The pinchbeck policy which
guides even our more liberal educationalists to-day will
furnish derision and amazement to a more enlightened
posterity. For after this ideal, as after many other
ideals of John Ruskin, history is slowly and dimly
groping its way.

§ 4. But how is this educated human faculty to be
used for public service? How is industry to be ordered?

Mr. Ruskin sometimes appears as the advocate of a
New Feudalism, in which class distinctions are to be
strictly preserved, and every man is to have a fixed
status. But though the stress he lays upon contentment
in men and stability in institutions, his artistic appreciation of clear lines of social and industrial demarcation
lends support to this view, it was not really his desire to
establish a stereotype caste system, which should deny
to society the services that individual genius or aptitude
is capable of rendering. The tools, the land, the capital,
the powers to him who can use it, is the gospel which he
always preaches. Education, therefore, is not to be
confined to fitting a man to work well in the condition

of life in which he happens to be born. If he has any
special aptitude, it must be discovered and utilised. "If
indeed no effort is made to discover, in the course of
their early training, for what services the youth of a
nation are individually qualified; nor any care taken to
place those who have unquestionably proved their fitness
for certain functions, in the offices they could best fulfil
— then to call the confused wreck of social order and
life, brought about by malicious confusion and competition, an arrangement of Providence, is quite one of the
most insolent and wicked ways in which it is possible to
take the name of God in vain." [1]

§ 5. But, while admitting the desirability of genuine
"equality of opportunity" for the assertion of individual
talent, and making due allowance for effects of environment,[2] Mr. Ruskin bases this order of industrial and
social life upon what he calls "unconquerable differences
in the clay of the human creature." [3]   He is distinctly a
believer both in class and individual differences, and to
the former he attributes a natural as well as a social
support. The children of unskilled labourers or mere
mechanics he conceives to be rightly destined by nature
and social convenience to unskilled and mechanical
labour, with lives ordered accordingly; skilled workmen
of different sorts will, by inheritance and by association,
be fitted to continue these crafts; the children of professional and governing parents will be best adapted to
continue these functions. His conviction of the utility
of keeping class distinctions both in work and life is so
strongly marked, and plays so prominent a part in his
scheme of society, that it appears certain that he thought

the transference from one grade to another would be confined to a few exceptional cases.

§ 6. The teaching of Plato,[1] and a fanatical abhorrence of the " radical " doctrine of natural equality, combined to enforce this belief in a natural basis of class differences, which furnished Mr. Ruskin with a principle of social stratification. It first relieved him from the necessity of maintaining the false and foolish thesis that all work is in itself equally worthy and ennobling. This doctrine, used indifferently by flatterers of the working-classes to dignify manual labour, and by conservative philanthropists to assuage discontent, finds no mercy in Mr. Ruskin's hands. He utterly denies that the work of a navvy or a miner well done is as ennobling as the work of a skilled carver in wood or iron. On the contrary, he insists that at the base of the industrial fabric there is a considerable amount of work to be done which is essentially low, and even degrading ; and there are persons born who are fitted by nature to do this work. " The fact is, a great number of quite necessary employments are, in the accuratest sense, 'servile' — that is, they sink a man to the condition of a serf, or unthinking worker, the proper state of an animal, but more or less unworthy of man." [2] In this class he includes not only such work as mining, stoking, forging — which is essentially brutalising in the heavy muscular toil it involves — but all " simply manual occupations." [3] After a flying and half-satirical suggestion, the futility of which he feels, that earnest Christians might voluntarily undertake this

[1] *cf.* Munera Pulveris, pp. 134-6.
[2] Time and Tide, § 119 ; *cf.* also § 104.   [3] § 127.

work as a sacrifice to the spirit of humility, he falls
back upon the existence of a large number of children
of whom nothing could be made, and who would therefore rightly " furnish candidates for degradation to
common mechanical business." [1] Such work seems to
him to require the continuance of a class of men who
shall in all essential facts, though not in name, be slaves ;
and that attitude of Mr. Ruskin, as of his master Carlyle,
which seems to defend or condone " slavery," has clear
reference to this social necessity. In " Munera Pulveris," however, there is an instructive passage which
considerably mitigates, though it does not remove, the
harshness of this position. " The highest conditions of
human society reached hitherto have cast such work
to slaves ; but supposing slavery of a politically defined
kind to be done away with, mechanical and foul employment must, in all highly organised states, take the aspect
either of punishment or probation. All criminals should
at once be set to the most dangerous and painful forms
of it . . . so as to relieve the innocent population as far
as possible ; of merely rough (not mechanical) manual
labour, especially agricultural, *a large portion should be
done by the upper classes ; bodily health and sufficient contrast and repose for the mental functions being unattaina-
ble without it ;* what necessarily inferior labour remains
to be done, as especially in manufactures, should, and
always will, when the relations of society are reverent
and harmonious, fall to the lot of those who, for the
time, are fit for nothing better." [2]

But though Mr. Ruskin, with Plato and Aristotle, tries
to brave it out that there are base mechanic natures in-

---

[1] *Time and Tide,* § 107.   [2] *Munera Pulveris,* § 109.

tended for such work, his humanity yet revolts against
the notion, and he looks forward to a policy which shall
reduce such work to a minimum, either by reform of
industrial processes or by keeping down as low as possible the demand for such base services. In connection
with this last point, we have an interesting distinction
between good and evil forms of luxury, judged not from
the effect upon consumers but upon producers. "You
may have Paul Veronese to paint your ceiling, if you
like, or Benvenuto Cellini to make cups for you. But
you must not employ a hundred divers to find beads
to stitch over your sleeve."[1] All comment upon the
alleged necessity of handing over "base mechanic"
occupations to a special class is best reserved until the
fuller classification is expounded. It must here suffice
to observe Mr. Ruskin's own evident dissatisfaction
with a plan which implies by his hypothesis the further
degrading of criminals and low types of humanity.

§ 7. Rising from this base we have grade upon
grade of skilled manual occupations engaged in producing good forms of material wealth. A civilised
society of consumers would demand sound qualities
of largely hand-made goods, and so "the arts of working in wood, clay, stone, and metal would all be *fine*
arts," or would at any rate have elements of skill and
individual character attaching to them. It would be
part of the scheme of physical education that "every
youth in the state . . . should learn to do something finely
and thoroughly with his hands,"[2] and even those who
were not chiefly occupied in these industries might usefully and pleasantly cultivate some branch of them in

[1] Time and Tide, § 131.   [2] Ibid., § 133.

leisure time, while within the trades themselves there
would be room "for nearly every grade of practical
intelligence and productive imagination." The organisation of these and other industries is not clearly or consistently indicated by Mr. Ruskin. His general form is
that of the guild, and in "Fors Clavigera" he proposes
that workmen shall range themselves under some twenty-
one classes, which he names, organising themselves
peaceably for the conduct of their several crafts,[1] and
acquiring the requisite land and capital. This proposal
to transform Trade Unions into Labourers' Unions or
Guilds, each apparently taking over the functions of
capitalist-employer, and regulating the quality of goods
and conditions of work, is a harking back to mediævalism, of which there are many signs in Mr. Ruskin's
social schemes. How this new order should be insti-
tuted, what should be the local or industrial lines of
demarcation, how the guilds should be governed and
their rules enforced, these important questions find no
full and satisfactory answers. It is implied both in
"Fors" and in "Time and Tide" that voluntary co-
operation of individuals should be the basis of action.
Those members of any trade who favoured order and
honesty should constitute themselves into a guild, elect-
ing their officers,[2] regulating methods of production,
qualities of goods, and prices. The central feature of
the system is the joint responsibility provided by the
guild for the quality of wares made by its members,
which would be secured by a method of warranty.
This warrant would, of course, only apply to certain

---

[1] Fors, Letter lxxxix.

[2] Fors, Letter lxxxix. (iv. 374); but see "Time and Tide," § 139.

common standard forms of commodity. "You could
only warrant a certain kind of glazing or painting in
china, a certain quality of leather or cloth, bricks of
a certain clay, loaves of a defined mixture of flour.
Advisable improvements or varieties in manufacture
would have to be examined and accepted by the trade
guild : when so accepted, they would be announced in
public reports; and all puffery and self-proclamation on
the part of tradesmen absolutely forbidden, as much as
the making of any other kind of noise or disturbance." [1]
For all warranted articles, prices, wages, and conse-
quently profits, should be annually fixed : while for
unwarranted articles made by guild members, each firm
should regulate its own prices and make its own arrangements with its workmen, subject to a penalty in case of
adulteration or fraudulent description. "Finally, the
state of the affairs of every firm should be annually
reported to the guild, and its books laid open to inspection, for guidance in the regulation of prices in
the subsequent year ; and any firm whose liabilities
exceeded its assets by a hundred pounds should be
forthwith declared bankrupt." [2]

Membership of these guilds was to be entirely
optional, no monopoly or official position was to be
assigned to them, outsiders could compete among themselves and with the guild for the custom of consumers,
as they now compete. If persons preferred to buy from
outsiders, they could do so at their pleasure and peril.
Two reasons are assigned for this permission of outside
competition : first, "that it is always necessary, in enact-
ing strict law, to leave some safety-valve for outlet of

[1] Time and Tide, §§ 78, 79. [2] Ibid., § 80.

irrepressible vice "— a wise and far-reaching thought,
which advocates of all forms of state coercion would
do well to ponder; secondly, in order to preserve "the
stimulus of such erratic external ingenuity as cannot be
tested by law." [1]

The guilds of producers are to have control also of
the retail trade, employing retail dealers as their salaried
officers,[2] though there also outside competition is pre-
sumably permissible. All "necessary public works and
undertakings, as roads, mines, harbour protections, and
the like," are to be owned and administered by the
public for the public profit, private speculation in these
matters being prohibited.[3]

§ 8. The organisation of agriculture is a source of
special solicitude to Mr. Ruskin, holding, as he did, that
peasant life is the backbone of a nation.

In the essential and historical priority accorded to
land reform he shows himself eminently a practical
reformer. His insistence upon fixity of rent and security of tenants' improvements as the most urgent needs,[4]
indicates a firm grasp of the existing agricultural situation.
His wide and close study of continental agriculture gives
especial authority to his treatment, and his books, "Fors"
in particular, are full of shrewd criticism and suggestion.

His wider scheme of the position of agriculture in the
ideal state is, however, fraught with peculiar difficulty.
A tempered feudalism, with nominal ownership and
some real control and responsibility vested in "great
old families," while complete security of tenure and
freedom of cultivation is secured to a peasant class,

---

[1] Time and Tide, §§ 79, 80.   [2] Ibid., § 134.   [3] Ibid., § 74.
[4] Fors, Letter xlv. (ii. 429).

forms the ideal in its large outline. "The right action
of a state respecting its land is, indeed, to secure it in
various portions to those of its citizens who deserve to
be trusted with it, according to their respective desires
and proved capacities; and after having so secured it
to each, to exercise such vigilance over his treatment
of it as the state must give also to his treatment of his
wife and servants; for the most part leaving him free,
but interfering in cases of gross mismanagement or
abuse of power. And in the case of great old families,
which always ought to be, and in some measure, however decadent, still truly are, the noblest monumental
architecture of the kingdom, living temples of sacred
tradition and hero's religion, so much land ought to be
granted to them in perpetuity as may enable them to
live thereon with all circumstance of state and outward
nobleness; *but their incomes must in no wise be derived
from the rents of it*, nor must they be occupied (even
in the most distant and subordinately administered
methods) in the exaction of rents. That is not noble-
men's work. Their income must be fixed and paid by
the state, as the king's is." [1] What the actual status
and the occupation of this feudal aristocracy, in the
midst of a population of virtually independent peasant
occupiers, paying rent to the state, would be, we are not
told; nor is it easy to conceive how, otherwise than by
existing beautifully, they would justify the state incomes
they receive. The separate account Mr. Ruskin gives of
the functions of his aristocracy does not, as we shall see,
throw much light upon this obscurity.

    The order of agriculture here indicated is seen to

[1] *Time and Tide,* § 151.

differ vitally from the proposed reforms of manufacture
and commerce. The later are, for the most part, achieved
by the growth of a voluntary state within a state: but
for the growth of the new agricultural feudalism, no
such natural origin is possible. It is conceivable, though
highly improbable, that the growth of Co-operative Movements, Unions of Employers and Employed, either
through development of profit-sharing schemes or
along the new line of Alliances of Labour Unions
and Masters' Federations, might lead to the establishment, in all or most industries, of voluntary associations
which should fulfil the functions of Mr. Ruskin's guilds.
But it is hardly conceivable that the present land system
should be revolutionised by the voluntary cession of the
right to draw rents and to control cultivation, enjoyed
now by private landowners. Such changes as are required by Mr. Ruskin's land system would require state
coercion, a practical nationalisation of the land,[1] which
might then be handed over to tenants paying state rents
and subject to state control, along with a sort of idyllic
suzerainty to some local magnate.

§ 9. That Mr. Ruskin does in fact oscillate between
voluntary co-operation and state action is illustrated
otherwise. The guild system above described represents the later thought of " Time and Tide " and
" Fors."

In the preface of " Unto this Last " we have the
government undertaking the functions which in his
later scheme Mr. Ruskin assigns to voluntary guilds.
In this earlier treatise " there should be established —
entirely under government regulation — manufactories

[1] See, however, " Fors," Letter lxxxix. (iv. 374.)

and workshops for the production and sale of every
necessary of life, and for the exercise of every useful
art," with the same safeguards of private competition
accorded in his later treatment, "interfering no whit
with private enterprise, nor setting any restraint or tax
on private trade, but leaving both to do their best and
beat the government if they could; there should, at
these government manufactories and shops, be authoritatively good and exemplary work done, and pure and
true substance sold; so that a man could be sure, if
he chose to pay the government price, that he got for
his money bread that was bread, ale that was ale, and
work that was work."[1]

That Mr. Ruskin never definitely abandoned this
idea of limited State Socialism for a thoroughly
thought-out scheme of voluntary co-operation may be
seen best by examining the functions of government
which he destined for the upper classes.

§ 10. The learned professions, the fine arts, and the
work of government are reserved for Mr. Ruskin's
aristocracy, because he holds they are by nature and
training best qualified to do this work. Apparently he
is willing to take the "upper classes" as they are, with
every allowance for the degrading influences of plutoc-
racy and the degeneration caused by luxury, and to
moralise and elevate them into a condition which will
justify their social and industrial supremacy. His
reasoning is based upon curiously simple and defective
generalisations of history and heredity. "The upper
classes, broadly speaking, are originally composed of
the best-bred (in the merely animal sense of the term),

[1] Unto this Last, xvii., xviii.

the most energetic, and most thoughtful of the population, who, either by strength of arm seize the land
from the rest and make slaves of them, or bring desert
land into cultivation, over which they have therefore,
within certain limits, true personal right; or by industry
accumulate other property, or by choice devote themselves to intellectual pursuits, and, though poor, obtain
an acknowledged superiority of position, shown by benefits conferred in discovery, or in teaching, or in gifts
of art. This is all in the simple course of the law of
nature; and the proper offices of the upper classes,
thus distinguished from the rest, became therefore in
the main threefold :

" A. Those who are strongest of arm have for their
proper function the restraint and punishment of vice,
and the general maintenance of law and order; releasing
only from its original subjection to their power that
which truly deserves to be emancipated.

" B. Those who are superior by forethought and
industry have for their function to be the providences
of the foolish, the weak, and the idle; and to establish such systems of trade and distribution of goods
as shall preserve the lower orders from perishing
by famine or any other consequence of their care-
lessness and folly, and to bring them all, according
to each man's capacity, at last into some harmonious
industry.

" C. The third class, of scholars and artists, of course,
have for their function the teaching and delighting of
the inferior multitude.

" The office of the upper classes, then, as a body,
is to keep order among their inferiors, and raise them

always to the nearest level with themselves of which those inferiors are capable." [1]

It is not to some ideally selected aristocracy of the future, but to the existing aristocracy, "however degraded," that he looks for the fulfilment of these high duties. This aristocracy, in accordance with the above-named functions, is divisible into three great classes. First, the landed proprietors and soldiers, essentially one political body (for the possession of land can only be maintained by military power); secondly, the moneyed men and leaders of commerce; thirdly, the professional men and masters in science, art, and literature. [2]

For doing this work these classes are to be maintained by salaries from the state, and not by casual fees; they are to be specially educated for their work in state schools, and are to be in every way regarded as public officers. Mr. Ruskin has no words of sufficient condemnation for the degrading influence of profit-mongering in the higher arts and professions; and fixed pay for fixed appointments is the principle he advocates. Here, however, as elsewhere in his reformed society, lurks some inconsistency. To Mr. Ruskin, in "Fors Clavigera," not only does it appear degrading to introduce competition for money into the professions, but even to make them necessary in the sense that they form the basis of a livelihood. There the state art-doctrine is announced that "food, fuel, and clothes can only be got out of the ground, or sea, by muscular labour; and no man has any business to have any unless he has done, if able, the muscular work necessary

<hr>

[1] Time and Tide, §§ 138, 139.   [2] Ibid., § 142.

to produce his portion, or to render (as the labour of
a surgeon or a physician renders) equivalent benefit
to life."[1] This requirement of direct vital service,
while it does not narrow Mr. Ruskin down to the
"bread labour" enjoined by Tolstoy, does involve the
insistence that "the mercenary professions of preaching, lawgiving, and fighting must be utterly abolished."
Such work is to be an honourable service rendered
gratuitously by skilled persons who have earned their
living by some physical work. "Scholars, painters,
and musicians," he concedes, "may be advisedly kept
on due pittance, to instruct or amuse the labourer after,
or at, his work."

§ 11. Although it would seem consistent with Mr.
Ruskin's fuller sense of social economy to derive his
governing power from all classes, cultivating natural
aptitudes wherever they might be displayed, his strong
appreciation of fixed orders shows itself in allotting
state authority to the land-owning aristocracy. The
sciences of war and of law are in particular assigned
to them. The scheme of state authorities which he
lays down is the following:

(1) The king, exercising, as part both of his pre-
rogative and his duty, the office of a supreme judge
at stated times in the central court of appeal of his
kingdom.

(2) Supreme judges, appointed by national election,
exercising sole authority in courts of final appeal.

(3) Ordinary judges, holding office hereditarily under
conditions, and with power to add to their number (and
liable to have it increased if necessary by the king's ap-

---

[1] Fors, iii. 370, Letter lxvii.

pointment) ; the office of such judges being to administer
the national laws under the decision of juries.

(4) State officers, charged with the direction of
public agency in matters of public utility.

(5) Bishops, charged with offices of supervision and
aid, to family by family, and person by person.

(6) The officers of war of various ranks.

(7) The officers of public instruction, of various
ranks. [1]

Reserving all comments upon the general characteristics of this aristocratic government until the following chapter, I must allude to one essential feature
provided in section (5). The typical character of modern anarchism, as Mr. Ruskin saw it in English society,
consists in people " minding their own business," and
not being " their brothers' keepers." In old feudalism
every one was some one's " man ;" owned some political superior to whom he was responsible for certain
services, and who in return was rightly bound to defend him and his family, their life, property, and status.
Never perhaps in the world's history has the particular
form of helpless, hopeless " liberty " which shows itself
in the poorer life of our great modern cities, elsewhere
appeared ; where families, grown up in want and ignorance, struggle for a bare subsistence, live in disorder
and degradation, and die without society giving to
them any systematic recognition whatever. The casual
and arbitrary interference of the police, the equally
casual enforcement of a few social regulations respecting the rudiments of sanitation, hygiene, and education,
the legal registration of a few cardinal facts of life and

[1] Time and Tide, § 153.

death — at certain odd intervals this machinery of social order impinges upon the " liberty " of the citizen. But there is no pretence of any genuine social education and social supervision. The state, the city, the parish have no real official knowledge or control of the lives of the great mass of the population. So long as this is so, there can be no government that is worthy the name. The responsibility of all to each and of each to all is the essential of true citizenship. To embody this responsibility in right human institutions is the real problem of government from the political point of view. Here, as elsewhere, Mr. Ruskin's fancy for names has stood much in his way. His insistence that it is the duty of a " Bishop " or " Episcopus," in accordance with the derivation of his title, to " keep an eye " on each body and soul in his diocese,[1] moved the ridicule of many who had not the humour or the sense to follow Mr. Ruskin's dialectics of reform. He was obliged to explain that what he really meant was that a public officer should be appointed for every hundred families or so, in order to render account of their lives to the state, so that public cognisance might be taken of the good and evil in their lives, that help, reward, and punishment might be rendered with intelligence and efficacy, by a society organised to give all possible support to the individual life, not merely in the way of restraint and prohibition, but of rewards and encouragements. These bishops or overseers were to fulfil the functions of pastors and biographers, keeping full records of all families within their charge, and above them should be set higher officers of state in

[1] Sesame and Lilies, § 22.

charge of larger districts.[1] Thus, and thus alone, could the full vital resources of a society be rightly known and utilised for public services.

This scheme is distinguished in two ways from the police superintendence which prevails in some countries. In the first place, it would be engaged not merely in marking a few leading facts of external life and conduct — chiefly the irregularities of life — but in keeping a just register of all essential facts. Secondly, it would presume a genuine spirit of humanity and sympathy animating the civic system, and softening the asperities of official investigation as commonly conducted by the perfunctory labours of uninterested officers.

§ 12. The scheme indicated in " Time and Tide," and elsewhere, makes no pretence to completeness of detail, and is not always clear or consistent in its main outlines. But, read in the light of his social ideals, the proposals have yet a powerful coherence and a genuinely practical value, which may be tested by observing the many independent social forces of our age which are moving towards a similar constructive policy. There are, indeed, as is admitted, not a few discrepancies in Mr. Ruskin's presentment. Such discrepancies seem to belong partly to differences of reform-focus. Sometimes he is asking and answering the question, What is the line of present practicable progress ? Sometimes again he gives his imagination and his logical faculty freer scope, and depicts the structure of a society under ideal conditions. But another difference arises in connection with " Fors Clavigera " and " Time and Tide." Both were later products, representing a somewhat disillu-

[1] Time and Tide, §§ 72-74.

sioned view of life: he no longer looked to a perfected state to order work and life in complete harmony; small, local, detailed experiment occupied him more, and his appeal was more addressed to individual well-wishers, and less to statesmen or wholesale economic reformers.

Yet ever and anon in the midst of his more detailed practical schemes, he returns to the larger ideal. The idea of an enduring and united commonwealth, a state in that meaning of the word which he dwells upon in "Sesame and Lilies," "without tremor, without quiver of balance, established and enthroned upon a foundation of eternal law, which nothing can alter or overthrow," [1] always had a powerful hold upon his imagination, and all schemes of partial co-operation to which he lent his voice may be regarded as purely provisional " concessa propter duritiem cordis."

The schemes of social reform, which I have outlined chiefly in his own words, never took such shape as can rightly justify their submission to detailed criticism. They may rather be regarded as speculative experiments, in part the application of large political and economic ideals which underlay his criticism, by whittling them down to meet the broadly conceived conditions of actual life, in part the enlargement into wider social forms of certain practical experiments which he was engaged in trying upon a small scale on his own account.

In spite of those brilliant flashes of convincing realism which he was able to impart into all his proposals, it is easy to see that their author has far too keen a knowledge of the present possibilities of human nature to indulge any swift hopes of realisation. The note of

[1] Sesame and Lilies, § 52.

disappointment, often of despair, is sounded many times, and more frequently than ever in "Fors." Though progress moves in many of the directions which Mr. Ruskin's imagination foreshadowed, his ideal society, as he sorrowfully allows, must rank with Plato's, though with Plato he likewise insists that for the good man such ideals are " practical." " In heaven there is laid up a pattern of such a city : and he who desires may behold it, and beholding, govern himself accordingly. But whether there really is, or will be, such an one, is of no importance to him, for he will act according to the laws of that city and no other." [1]

[1] Republic, ix. 592.

CHAPTER VIII.

§ 1. WHAT is Mr. Ruskin's proper place among Social
Reformers ? In attempting to answer this question, it
will be most convenient to begin by asking another. In
what sense is Mr. Ruskin a Socialist? Having already
collected much evidence upon this head, it is only necessary to focus it by a judgment which shall bear in mind
the different grades of loose meaning attached to the
term Socialism. Considered as a philosophic term,
Socialism is best taken to imply an organic view of
social life, which accords to society a unity not constituted of the mere addition of its individual members,
but contained in a common end or purpose, which determines and imposes the activities of these individual

192

members. In this sense Mr. Ruskin is a pronounced Socialist, enforcing his theory by analogies constantly drawn from the conscious organic life of animals, and ignoring those points of defect or difference which some philosophic Socialists admit, in comparing the organised structure of political and industrial society with human life in the individual man.

But even in theoretic discussions Socialism commonly means more than a bare adhesion to some organic view of social life. It implies at least a tendency to favour increased social activity in politics and industry, either through the instrumentality of the state or by voluntary co-operation for common ends. Now Mr. Ruskin distinctly favours the largest substitution of public for private enterprise, and a public superintendence and control of the details of individual life by the state. " Live openly " is not merely an ethical precept binding upon the individual good citizen, but a public interest to be enforced by public provision. Such freedom as is granted to individuals to hold and till land, to make and sell goods of any kind, proceeds from the positive, as distinct from the tacit, consent of society. Large sections of industrial work are to be directly ordered and managed by state officials. The guild system, though in some places treated as a voluntary co-operative movement, is in effect to be a public institution ; [1] and though provisional liberty is granted to buy and sell goods produced under free competitive conditions, this is evidently regarded as an imperfection which would disappear with the fuller growth of the sense of commonalty.

In this general economic sense, as approving the

[1] Time and Tide, § 3.

increased ownership and control of industry by the state, Mr. Ruskin, then, will also rank as Socialist. But how far is his teaching to be identified with that of the movement commonly described as Socialist, and in particular with the large continental organisation which has assumed that name ?

There are many close points of resemblance in social criticism. The general humanitarian revolt against the misery and the social injustice implied by poverty, the corrupting influences of luxury, and the base origin of riches has never been so eloquently voiced by any other " agitator." His insistence that " large fortunes cannot honestly be made by the work of any *one* man's hands or head," [1] always implying the " discovery of some method of taxing the labor of others," [2] his contemptuous repudiation of charity as a substitute for justice, his demand that property shall be set upon a sound basis both of origin and use, [3] are agitating doctrines which Mr. Ruskin never shrinks from driving to their logical conclusions. The plainest and most fearless statement of the case is in a letter to the *Pall Mall Gazette* in 1873, [4] which contains the words : " These are the facts. The laborious poor produce the means of life by their labour. Rich persons possess themselves by various expedients of a right to dispense these ' means of life,' and keeping as much means as they want of it for themselves, dispense the rest, usually only in return for more labour from the poor, expended in producing various delights for the rich dispenser."

§ 2. But Mr. Ruskin comes even nearer to continental

---

[1] Time and Tide, § 81.   [2] Munera Pulveris, § 139.
[3] Fors, iii. 411, Letter lxx.   [4] Arrows of the Chace, ii. 100.

Socialism on its economic side. Three of the most distinctive demands of Social Democrats are : First, the abolition of " the competitive system " of industry under private control for profit, and the substitution of publicly organised industry for use ; second, the abolition of rent and interest ; third, the establishment of a labour-basis of exchange. Now Mr. Ruskin's acceptance of these fundamental planks of the Socialist platform is well-nigh complete. That powerful chapter in " Unto this Last," entitled " The Roots of Honour," is nothing but a splendid moral pleading for the abolition of " profit " as an industrial motive, and the adoption of social service in its place ; and this principle was at once the earliest, the most constant, and the most consistent of his social teachings. His rejection, alike on moral and utilitarian grounds, of rent and interest, has already been subject of comment. His demands in this regard may be concisely summed up in the language of " Fors :" [1] " That the usurer's trade will be abolished utterly ; that the employer will be paid justly for his superintendence, but not for his capital ; and the landlord paid for his superintendence of the cultivation of land, when he is able to direct it wisely."

Not only is Mr. Ruskin a Socialist in his criticism of competition and profitmongers : he also adopts the corner-stone of the constructive economic theory of Marx and his followers, quantity of labour as the basis of exchange for commodities. " Equity can only consist in giving time for time, strength for strength, and skill for skill." [2] It is true that, when he is upon his guard, he insists upon qualitative differences of labour

---

[1] Letter lx. (iii. 226).   [2] Unto this Last, p. 83.

as grounds for differential remuneration,[1] but in his more abstract treatment of exchange value and prices he often adopts[2] labour-time as his standard, using language very similar to that which we find in the Socialist bible, " Das Capital," and utterly ignoring the influence of " utility," which receives so much attention from most modern economists.

The " right to labour," and the correspondent duty of the state to furnish work and wages in public workshops to all unemployed persons, are fully admitted in the preface to " Unto this Last," where he insists " that any man, or woman, or boy, or girl out of employment, should be at once admitted at the nearest government school, and set to such work as it appeared, on trial, they were fit for, at a fixed rate of wages determinable every year ; "[3] compulsion of the most stringent order being applied in the case of shirkers or confirmed idlers.

All these are crucial points, which place Mr. Ruskin's teaching in close sympathy with the tenets of revolutionary Socialism.

§ 3. There are, however, certain important limitations to his economic Socialism. His treatment of the whole land question sometimes brings him near to those individualists who look to peasant proprietorship as the economic basis of a healthy society. Possession of land by an occupying owner with inheritance and even the maintenance of primogeniture are the principles he lays down in " Fors."[4] It is true that the quantity of land to be held is to be limited by capacity to use it, and the king and the state overseers are to exercise a general

---

[1] *E. g.* Unto this Last, p. 94.
[2] *E. g.* Munera Pulveris, §§ 63, 64.   [3] P. xviii.   [4] Letter lxxxix.

power of superintendence and control, while a rent or tax is to be paid to the state. But the reiterated stress upon a possession which is virtually free ownership with hereditary tenure, is recognised by Mr. Ruskin himself [1] to be antagonistic to the " Land Nationalisation " which all revolutionary Socialists include in their programme, nor does he deal in any manner conformable to Socialist principles with the ownership and control of city lands and other land not used for purely agricultural purposes. Both land and houses are to all intents the private property of the occupants, for " no landlord has any business with building cottages for his people. Every peasant should be able to build his own cottage — to build it to his own mind ; and to have a mind to build it to." [2]

While Mr. Ruskin nowhere descends to the " peasant worship " in which Tolstoy indulges, the importance he attaches to the agricultural industries, established upon this basis of nominal state-tenancy but practical private ownership, removes him widely from the Socialism which regards town life and subdivided labour under machinery as the salient features of the new civilisation, and their economical ordering for the public good as the chief concern of revolutionary reformers.

Nor if we turn from agriculture to other industries do we find Mr. Ruskin consistently sound upon the principle of " public ownership and control." Carlyle and a certain temperamental individualism of his own, traceable in all strong men, had impressed upon him the need of a full application of the precept, " the tools to him who can use them." The whole tenor of his volun-

---

[1] Letter xcv.   [2] Eagle's Nest, § 200.

tary guild system with liberty to employers to remain outside and to compete with the public workshops, and the suggestion that the latter might be confined to the production of certain classes of standard necessary wares, is quite inconsistent with the teaching of Social Democracy in its modern form. Perhaps the single passage which best shows how far he stands from the full acceptance of economic Socialism is that in which he advocates an "interim" policy by which a master, after paying a standard wage and providing for sick and superannuated workers, shall "be allowed to retain to his own use the surplus profits of the business."[1] Yet even on this point there is a growing tendency in the more moderate wing of continental Socialists to accept some such provisional arrangement. The part of Mr. Ruskin's economic policy, which really severs him most distinctly from the main body of avowed Socialists, is the reversion to the mediævalism of a guild system, voluntary in its membership and self-governing in its constitution. But even with this notion sections of continental Socialists have sometimes coquetted, both in the early schemes for state-assisted industrial societies, which Schulze-Delitzsch advocated, and in the propagandism of the Catholic Socialist party, in whose platform the establishment of monopolist guilds under state patronage and clerical control generally forms the most imposing plank.[2]

§ 4. In the general spirit of his teaching and in the stress which he lays upon religious authority as a vital function in good government, Mr. Ruskin approaches far nearer to the position of the more radical school of

[1] *Time and Tide*, § 5.　　[2] See Nitti's "Catholic Socialism."

Christian Socialists than to the continental party of Social Democracy with their anti-religious tendency and their leanings towards the use of physical force.[1] It is true that Mr. Ruskin has a far stronger and more consistent intellectual basis than Catholic or Anglican Socialists have succeeded in impressing on their movement. Christian Socialists generally evade such economic analysis as yields a rigid condemnation of rent, monopoly profits, and other unearned elements of income, preferring to dwell upon the obligations which attach to riches, than upon the necessity of such drastic reforms of industrial institutions as shall make riches impossible. Though there are bold individual exceptions, this is a characteristic attitude of the party, which leans to charity rather than to justice as the typically Christian basis of reform. Though Mr. Ruskin never acquiesces in this policy, and in many powerful utterances denounces the notion of supposing that reformed expenditure of income can enable us to dispense with scrutiny of the origins of incomes, he falls not infrequently into a genuinely " sentimental " vein, which, detached from his revolutionary analysis of economic forces, is eagerly exploited by those who shrink from the application of his more heroic remedies. Let me quote one such instance from " Fors : " " Therefore, you who are eating luxurious dinners, call in the tramp from the highway and share them with him, — so gradually you will understand how your brother came to *be* a tramp ; and practically make your own dinners plain till the poor

---

[1] Important modifications are, however, now visible in the Social Democratic party in favour of abandoning a definitely anti-religious policy, and of a clearer recognition of peaceable evolution as an instrument of reform.

man's dinner is rich, — or you are no Christians; and you who are dressing in fine dress, put on blouses and aprons, till you have got your poor dressed with grace and decency, — or you are no Christians; and you who can sing and play on instruments, hang your harps on the pollards above the rivers you have poisoned, or else go down among the mad and vile and deaf things whom you have made, and put melody into the souls of them, — else you are no Christians." [1]

Literally understood, such advice is heroic, though, as I shall presently show, quite ineffectual as a means of social reform; copiously watered down it furnishes an attractive policy for many persons smitten with social compunction and prepared to make some not too great personal sacrifice for the cause of the poor, but not prepared to recognise or to cut away the economic roots of poverty.

It is only natural that the virtue of self-sacrifice, which, from the more rigid types of asceticism to the milder types of charity, has in all ages been accepted as the kernel of Christian holiness, should be used once more to salve the diseases of society, and Mr. Ruskin, whose Puritan forbears and early training had impressed upon his temperament a powerful strain of this asceticism, gave vivid expression to it when the spirit of prophetic denunciation seized him.

An even stronger bond of sympathy with Catholic Socialism is Mr. Ruskin's advocacy of a theocracy. Spiritual authority, derived from the Fatherhood of God, and administered on earth by divinely appointed bishops and by a hierarchy of " orders," penetrating all the

---

[1] Fors, Letter lxxxii. (iv. 225).

details of social life — such a vision found eager acceptance among many " churchmen," who look to a revival of the popular power of the priesthood, and are even willing to modify their stress upon " another life " in favour of a better life on earth, partly because the defences of " supernaturalism " have been weakened by the inroad of rationalism, partly because the growing sense of continuity between this world and another has genuinely raised the value of this life even for convinced believers in another. How far such Christian Socialists would be prepared to conform to the lines of demarcation which Mr. Ruskin laid down between spiritual and temporal authorities, may well be doubted. Perhaps only a small minority of them would accept his virtual abandonment of dogmatic religious teaching or his suggestion of a union of Churches. But the position of spiritual authority which Mr. Ruskin would accord the reconstituted Church is genuinely acceptable to many " advanced " men in the Roman and English Churches.

§ 5. This character, which most recommends Mr. Ruskin to the Churches, his stress upon " authority," serves to sunder him very definitely both from organised Social Democracy and from most milder economic movements in the same general direction. For his conception of the rightful operation of " authority," alike in spiritual and temporal affairs, induces a complete and vehement rejection of the forms of government generally identified with democracy. It is not merely a disbelief in the efficacy of representative institutions, but a deeper distrust of the ability of the people to safeguard or advance their true interests. Even those forms of organised self-help which have won the approval of many of our most conservative minds, the co-operative movement[1] and trade unionism, evoke in him a doubtful and imperfect sympathy.

Order, reverence, authority, obedience, these words are always on his lips, these ideas always present in his mind. Radical and revolutionary doctrines and movements, as he interprets them, imply the rejection and overthrow of these principles, and are denounced accordingly. Liberty and equality he scornfully repudiates as the negation of order and government. "No liberty, but instant obedience to known law and appointed persons; no equality, but recognition of every betterness and reprobation of every worseness."[2]

His detestation of liberty and equality brought him into strange company and into strange historic judgments. With Carlyle and the autocratic Tory party of the day he stood for "order and a strong hand" in the Jamaica business, taking a leading part on the Eyre Defence Committee. His hatred of republican government was manifested in express admiration for "the firm and wise government of the third Napoleon,"[3] words written when the infamous *coup d'état* of this mountebank monarch was still fresh in the memory of men. It is true that later events tempered this admiration, but Mr. Ruskin never ceased to dwell exultingly upon the spell-bound impotence of the French republicans before this shadow of a king.[4]

The whole trend of modern Liberalism, as he saw it, was towards anarchy, — a levelling of social and

[1] Time and Tide, §§ 4, 5.   [2] Fors, Letter v. (i. 101).
[3] On the Old Road, vol. i., § 259.   [4] Fors, Letter x. (i. 194-5).

political distinctions, the distribution of political power
upon a basis of arithmetical equality, and a decay of
habits of reverence and discipline.

Disclaiming respect for either of the great modern
political parties, Mr. Ruskin sometimes speaks of himself as "an old Tory," sometimes as an "Illiberal."[1]
The United States of America always served him as
a terrible example of the effect of liberal ideas and
institutions upon life and character. What was to be
expected from "a country so miserable as to possess
no castles,"[2] no aristocracy, where every one had the
same voting power, and elected his president and his
very judges. The specialty of America was evidently
"to teach people how not to worship."[3]

It is not difficult to understand how Mr. Ruskin
should be repelled by what he regarded as the final
and necessary effects of Liberalism — the levelling of all
distinctions between class and class, man and man ; the
disintegration of all moral and practical authority. His
theory of art, including the art of social life, is based,
as readers of "Modern Painters" will remember, upon
the validity of "specific characters," the reality of
"class" distinctions. Æsthetic satisfaction as well as
moral order requires this harmonious gradation ; organic
unity, whether in the composition of a picture or of a
society, depends on the co-operation of unequals, not
upon the mere accumulation or co-ordination of equals.
"The strongest man" is not, as one of Ibsen's heroes
says, "he who best can stand alone," for such a being,
independent of his fellows, is less than man. "For the

---

[1] Fors, Letter i. (i. 4).   [2] Fors, Letter x. (i. 193).
[3] Fors, Letter xii. (i. 249) ; *cf.* Time and Tide, §§ 141, 142.

true strength of every human soul is to be dependent on as many noble as it can discern, and to be depended upon by as many inferior as it can reach," is Mr. Ruskin's doctrine.

> All social order is built upon authority of superiors, which imposes upon inferiors an absolute, unquestioning obedience. This was the first and foremost of those "strange ideas about kings" which Mr. Ruskin had eagerly imbibed in childhood from Homer and from Scott.[1] The "people" were but common stuff to Homer: helpless scores of them fell in battle before the sword of Hector or Achilles; if a stray voice of theirs dared to offer counsel to the masters, it was

> answered with a jeer and a blow. Plato and Carlyle taught him the eternal need of an aristocracy of intellect.

> Naturally gifted with reverence and admiration for great men, Mr. Ruskin eagerly absorbed the hero-worship of Carlyle, and came to look upon history as "the biography of great men," though he retained some fuller sense of national as distinct from individual forces than did Carlyle. In no matter perhaps does the analytic power of Mr. Ruskin come into more frequent conflict with the temperamental emotional faculty than in the interpretation of history. Carlyle was so ridden by his hero-worship as to pardon almost anything, almost hypocrisy itself, to the forceful man of destiny, admitting Mohammed, Napoleon, and Frederick to the front rank of heroism. Mr. Ruskin's hero-worship is more consciously ideal: when he confronts the great men of history at close quarters he has an uncommonly shrewd eye for their defects. From Carlyle he had learned not only

[1] Fors, Letter x. (i. 190).

kingship, but theocracy, the doctrine of divine rights of monarchs. But when he generalised from history in a calmer mood he does not find either kings or priests after his heart. " You find kings and priests alike, always inventing expedients to get money; you find kings and priests alike, always inventing expedients to get power." [1] Yet, in spite of this, Mr. Ruskin is always harking back to an ideal government in which clergy and civil officers shall unite to rule, each supporting and correcting the other, " the clergy hallowing all worldly policy by their influence, and the magistracy repressing all religious enthusiasm by their practical wisdom." [2] Sometimes in earlier writings he seems to leave it doubtful whether the monarchical supreme power is to be one man or several, a king or a ruling oligarchy,[3] but in later years he steadily supports the " one man power."

§ 6. Such a conception of history and of government brought him into necessary collision with modern liberal democracy, with its formula of " natural equality," and drove him, as it drove Carlyle, into frequent assertions of an opposite doctrine of " natural slavery." He was not, however, carried into the preposterous pose of a defender of negro " slavery " in the common meaning of that term.[4] Indeed, if we take the various proposals of reform, we perceive that not a few are directly designed to give economic equality, as, for instance, the limitation in holding of land, the maximum limit upon incomes suggested in " Time and Tide," [5] and the care-

---

[1] The Eagle's Nest, § 216.   [2] The Old Road, ii., § 219.
[3] " On the Construction of Sheepfolds " (Old Road, ii., § 217.)
[4] Time and Tide, § 149.   [5] Letter ii.

fully devised schemes for levelling up education for all citizens. There is indeed reason to hold that Mr. Ruskin is much nearer to the more enlightened Liberals of his day and ours than he is willing to admit. The overbearing influence of Carlyle upon his politics is chiefly confined to the acceptance of a common terminology, and somewhat vague but violent attacks upon the revolutionary formula of the eighteenth century. With Carlyle he jeers at Parliament as an idle " talking-shop," and occasionally warns working men not to trust to it for reforms ;[1] but after all his only definite suggestion for getting good government is by suffrage of the body of citizens. He does not even object to universal suffrage, provided it does not imply equality of voting power: age, property, experience, and intellect should all be taken into account, and political power bestowed according to fitness.[2] Against no representative of radicalism does he fulminate so fiercely as against J. S. Mill. Yet Mill's scheme of an education test for the franchise stands upon the same principle as Mr. Ruskin's. Mill makes provision for the control of legislation by an intellectual aristocracy, and is as earnestly concerned as he to get the men of intellect at the top of affairs. Not merely in political but in economic reform the Mill of later years approximates more and more to Mr. Ruskin's views, substituting equality of opportunity for absolute equality. Even when Mr. Ruskin was writing his fiercest tirades against Liberalism, it is probable that the majority of Englishmen who owned that name cherished no such ideals of Liberty or Equality as those with which they were accredited. The empty

---

[1] *E. g.* **Time and Tide** (Preface).   [2] **Munera Pulveris**, § 129.

liberty of *laissez faire* was never more than the theoretic ideal of a small clique of economists and politicians, and the socialistic criticism of economic liberty had carried not only Mill, but a large section of the " radicals," away from the position of the French Revolution to a more positive conception of a social order. Mr. Ruskin himself seems hardly to recognise how far his historic and economic criticism had removed him from Carlyle. The latter's scorn for political economy had hidden from his eyes certain deep truths which Mr. Ruskin had unearthed. Carlyle had indeed certain intuitive glimpses of the economic power which the governing classes abused for their private enjoyment: his healthy respect for work led him to condemn idleness, history taught him the demoralizing effects of luxury, and so he came to suspect the power of the landowner and the rich commercial class. But he never dived into the intricacies of the connection between politics and industry as Mr. Ruskin did.

Mr. Ruskin was able to recognise that those very defects of irreverence and distrust of authority, which were the seats of moral and social disorder, were in large measure the results of economic causes, arising from the abuse of government by the governing classes. No writer of the age, except Mazzini, had so powerfully and clearly traced the common root of the social problem. Mazzini, strangely slighted by Mr. Ruskin, had laid his finger upon the very same defects in the old revolutionary formulæ which Mr. Ruskin had noted ; but, instead of formally renouncing liberty and equality, he strove more wisely to impart a fuller and more positive context to the former, and to lay a moral basis of

brotherhood for the latter. Both saw that economic
injustice was the soil from which sprung the vices of
political systems; both diagnosed that injustice in the
same way, though Mr. Ruskin far more completely and
acutely. But while Mazzini concluded that the needed
reform was that the people should control their economic as well as their political government, and must fit
themselves for doing so, Mr. Ruskin always denied the
possibility of popular government either in politics or
industry. And yet he saw even more clearly than
Mazzini the general law of this economic injustice
operative through history.

"The people have begun to suspect that one particular form of their past misgovernment has been that
their masters have set them to do all the work and have
themselves taken all the wages. In a word, that what
was called governing them meant only wearing fine
clothes and living on good fare at their expense. And,
I am sorry to say, the people are quite right in this
opinion, too. If you inquire into the vital fact of the
matter, this you will find to be the constant structure
of European society for the thousand years of the feudal
system; it was divided into peasants who lived by digging, priests who lived by begging, and knights who
lived by pillaging; and as the luminous public mind
becomes fully cognisant of these facts, it will assuredly
not suffer things to be altogether arranged that way any
more."[1]

When he thus closely realises the terrible defects
of aristocracy in actual history, and particularly in con-
templating the failure of the English upper classes to

[1] Crown of Wild Olive, § 136.

fulfil their duties of right government, Mr. Ruskin seems at times to understand and even to justify democratic movements. To this temper must be referred his occasional suggestions of reformed electoral machinery, his prophetic announcement to the working-classes of " the natural issue of the transference of power out of the hands of the upper classes, so called, into yours." [1] In looking at current events, he seems to recognise the inevitability of the democratic movement; and yet his wider survey of history and his theory of human nature oblige him to condemn the experiment of popular government, to turn his back upon the trend of recent history, which he so vividly describes in passages such as that which we have quoted, and to stake everything upon the miraculous reversal of modern movements by a voluntary self-reformation of the governing classes.

§ 7. In spite of wavering moments, this deep-rooted disbelief in democracy and a persistent disparagement of popular action stand as distinctive marks of Mr. Ruskin's teaching. The people cannot help themselves; the growing discontent with their condition, aroused by education, can never become the power for progress which their friends and flatterers pretend. The domination of the masses, either by this or by other means, is not really feasible, for " slavery," that is to say, unqualified and unquestioning submission to a superior will, is " an inherent, natural, and eternal inheritance of a large portion of the human race, — to whom the more you give them of their own free will, the more slaves they will make themselves." [2] The true instrument of

[1] Fors, Letter lxxxix. (iv. 361) ; cf. Letter lxxxix. (iv. 372).
[2] Munera Pulveris, § 133.

✗ social progress, as he conceives it, is the good-will and intelligence of the upper classes, the landowners and " captains of industry," whose functions have been already named, " to keep order among their inferiors, and raise them always to the nearest level with themselves of which those inferiors are capable." [1] This " raising" of " inferiors" may be safely carried on without risk of attaining any dangerous condition of equality, on account of " the wholesome indisposition of the average mind for intellectual labour." [2]

§ 8. Although he has sketched elaborate plans of political and industrial organisation, Mr. Ruskin is no true believer in public machinery, even when the working is in the hands of the illuminated " upper classes." Like most thinkers who have approached the social question from a distinctively " moral" standpoint, he finds the spring of progress in the individual will. " All effectual advancement towards this true felicity of the human race must be by individual, not public effort. Certain general measures may aid, certain revised laws guide, such advancement; but the measure and the law which have first to be determined are those of each man's home." [3]

✗ (In a word, the Socialism, to which Mr. Ruskin looks, is to be imposed by an hereditary aristocracy, whose effective co-operation for the common good is to be derived from the voluntary action of individual landowners and employers. There must be no movement of the masses to claim economic justice; no use of Par-

---

[1] Time and Tide, § 139.   [2] Fors, Letter xcv. (iv. 465).
[3] Unto this Last, p. 169.

liament to " nationalise " land or capital, or to attack
any private interest.

Reform must proceed from a moral appeal to the ✗
heart and the intelligence of individual members of the
ruling classes, who, according to Mr. Ruskin's diagnosis,
are now living idly or wastefully upon the labour of the
people. They must be invited to reflect upon the obligations which attach to their position of authority ; a
new heart must be put into them, that they may recognise the duty they owe to their inferiors, and, instead
of using their economic and social power to suck the
greatest advantage for themselves, may turn again to a
right recognition of the principle, " *noblesse oblige*," and,
as true " princes," furnish " initiative ; " as true dukes,
" leading ; " as " bishops," oversee the lives of the people ; as " lords " of agriculture, order the food supply ;
as " captains of industry," marshal the manufacturing
forces of the people for the satisfaction of the common
needs of all.

This conviction that genuine progress can only be ∠
attained by " the moralisation of the employing and
ruling classes " is not by any means a novel doctrine.
On the contrary, it is ever the typical attitude of a large ∟
section of the educated classes, who distrust the capacity
of the people for self-government, and fear violent attacks upon existing social institutions. The leaders of
the Comptist movement, closely following the same trend
of thought, imposed upon their ideal society an aristocracy with similar temporal and spiritual powers to those
which Mr. Ruskin assigns to his upper classes, and Mr.
Frederic Harrison looks to the same free moral action
of employers for the chief solution of the " labour prob-

lem." I name this body not for its numbers and direct
influence, which are small, but because they aptly illustrate a natural attitude of persons of superior mind who
bring moral reflection to bear upon social reform. This
same position is adopted by the Charity Organisation
Society, so far as it has any social philosophy. If individual employers and workers could be induced to moralise their lives, there would be no need of state action
or of any heroic remedy for social maladies. Whenever
religious or reflective persons of the well-to-do classes
approach the social question in some of its protean
aspects, they are generally driven to adopt this moral
individualism of Mr. Ruskin, though they are far from
accepting his searching analyses of commerce and of the
economic bases of class life. Such people think that
employers ought to be more "considerate" to their
employees; that landlords should seek to establish
something of the old "feudal" status in dealing with
their tenants, only exacting "fair" rents; "consumers"
should recognise a responsibility in the purchase of
sweated goods; and rich people in general should admit
the moral principle that "riches are a trust," and that
they are bound to administer this trust with some regard
to improving the condition of the poor by thoughtful and
personally conducted schemes of charity.

The chief recommendation, indeed the secret driving
motive of this attitude and policy, is that by throwing all
the moral onus upon *use* of riches it evades all questions
of their *origin*. Now, Mr. Ruskin has by no means
shunned this scrutiny of origin. His economic analysis has shown that the economic powers of landowner
and capitalist stand on an unsound moral basis, being

derived largely from oppressive bargains. Even while
he is engaged in working out his "new feudalism," with
its enlightened aristocracy, as often as the question con-
fronts him, he insists that beneficial expenditure does
not exculpate the rich man who has made his gains
wrongfully.[1] Indeed, as we have seen, his reformed
society deprives the landowner of his rack-rent power
and makes him a state land-agent, while the employer
in his ultimate development will govern industry for use
and not for profit.

Yet Mr. Ruskin, in common with these milder reformers, looks for his reform force to the voluntary good-will
of those very rulers whose financial and social power is,
according to his analysis, derived from extortion, and
whose characters have been corrupted by abuse of their
wrongful takings.

§ 9. There are, in fact, two fatal obstacles to the
efficacy of Mr. Ruskin's policy of trusting reform to
the initiative of the upper classes.

In the first place, history proves it to be impossible
so to convince the intellect and touch the hearts of any
large proportion of the owners of political or economic
power, that they will make a voluntary surrender of
that power, or will divert its use from a selfish chan-
nel to the public good. Mr. Ruskin proposes to divert
strongly established " vested interests " from private to
public uses, by persuasion of their owners. He sometimes represents it as a simple task : " If we once can
get a sufficient quantity of honesty in our captains the
organisation of labour is easy." [2] But in reality two
formidable barriers block the way. In the first place,

[1] Fors, Letter lx. (iii. 214).   [2] Unto this Last, Pref. xv.

he must convince these "captains" that their present conduct is "dishonest." At present, the vast majority of them are satisfied that, in taking all the rent, profits, and other emoluments they can get, and in spending them for their private purposes, they are strictly "within their rights." Now, supposing Mr. Ruskin's diagnosis of the present industrial system of competition and production for profit to be absolutely correct, is it possible to induce the "captains" to perceive and to admit its correctness? Any one who has ever tried to persuade another of the wrongfulness of any conduct consecrated by long use and concealed within a vast network of complex action, will be convinced of the impracticability of this method of reform. The great majority of "captains of industry" are, and will remain, intellectually incapable of following the economic analysis by which Mr. Ruskin or another may seek to convince their intellect: those who are capable of following it will refuse to do so, adopting some one of the many refuges or evasions which a man instinctively employs, when he is asked to arrive at an inconvenient judgment by long process of reasoning. In the next place, even were it possible to put the injustice of their present conduct plainly before our "captains," the generation of "honest" motives out of a mere intellectual conviction is by general admission extremely difficult: it is all the difference between seeing the right and doing it, when the doing implies a complete abandonment of a customary and agreeable line of conduct.

It is surely no cynicism to insist that the process of putting "honesty," not into exceptional members but into a sufficient proportion of the captains of industry to revolutionise the conduct of business, is utterly chimerical. Some appeal to humanitarian sentiment is possible; a widespread conviction that good wages and conditions of labour should prevail wherever " the trade will bear it," is quite practicable; benevolent employers here and there may be willing to compromise the present profit-seeking business by admitting employees to some share of " profits." But such *_* reversal of the whole spirit of industry as is required by Mr. Ruskin cannot be effected by arguments or moral appeals addressed to the body of employers.

§ 10. Moreover, supposing that individual employers were open to " conviction of sin " and to the adoption of the new principle of " industry for use," this method of reform would still be futile. The antithesis which is drawn in the Preface of " Unto this Last " between " individual " and " public effort " is ruinously false. It is perfectly true that every social reform requires that the individual members of that society shall accept and respond to a moral appeal : it is perfectly false that they can by moral action in their individual capacity apply a social remedy. The separate action of individuals can never attain a social end, simply because they are *ex hypothesi* not acting as members of society. Social evils require social remedies. A social remedy indeed need not in all, or even in most cases, imply public action in the sense of a recourse to political machinery. But organic co-operation is essential : the general will must *z* be the instrument of actual reform, though the first appeal may be to the intelligence and will of individuals.

§ 11. That this is no empty quibbling will easily

appear if one considers the operation of such industrial reform as Mr. Ruskin seeks to obtain by the individual initiative of " captains of industry." Here is a trade in which large manufacturers are closely competing with one another : they are paying the lowest wages to their labourers for the longest working-day, and are selling, at the lowest prices, the worst wares which the public will consent to buy. This is a typical industrial problem ; now find a remedy by individual moral action. Let Mr. Ruskin approach a competitor in this trade, and try to induce him to gradually transform his business, paying decent wages, refusing to take dividends, and putting sound wares upon the market. Suppose the manufacturer to be intellectually convinced and thoroughly desirous to mend his ways, he will, nevertheless, be forced to reply: " I cannot raise my wages without raising my prices; I cannot raise my prices without losing my trade, closing my mills, and turning my employees out of work ; I cannot knock off the dividends because my business depends on borrowed capital, and such capital cannot be obtained without payment of dividend ; I cannot improve my quality of wares because it would cost more to improve them, and the consumer would not consent to pay the higher price for the better article." No arguments to show the efficiency of " high wages " or the advantages of educating the consumer's taste are valid in such a case, for we are bound to assume that the intelligent self-interest of employers in this trade is convinced that it would not " pay " to give higher wages or to produce better wares. There is no means by which the individual desire for reform on the part of our manufacturer can express itself in his conduct. It may indeed be said that he can do "something" to raise the condition of labour, and the quality of wares; but he cannot do much, for he is bound to conform pretty closely to the general custom of the trade, on penalty of losing his share of it. Where competition does not press so closely, or where some monopoly or special advantage of market is possessed, the power of the individual manufacturer is, of course, correspondingly enlarged. It is possible for the American trust, or the water and gas companies in English towns, to moralise their business policy to a considerable extent. But this process of conversion implies a wholesale conversion of shareholders, which it is not possible to compass. To endeavour to reform the structure of business by moralising individual employers implies a failure to grasp the physiology of industry. The "moral" conduct of a converted individual, so far from gradually leavening the lump, would not even enable him to hold his own in the business world: if he were a capitalist-employer in ordinary business, his trade would pass away from him and he would be left stranded and impotent; if he were a shareholder, he could only rid himself of personal responsibility of profit-mongering by handing his shares to some less scrupulous person. It is worse than useless for well-meaning people, unskilled in the business world, to deceive themselves. Here and there an individual, of exceptional business endowments and trade advantages, may materially abate the pressure of competition upon his employees, and may exercise a wholesome pride in selling sound articles at reasonable prices. But even such a one cannot throw off the profit-making system

completely, still less can he furnish an example which
other employers, less favourably placed, can imitate. In
ordinary competitive trade, the man who refuses to play
the game according to the rules, must simply retire and
let another take his place. The honest example of a
morally enlightened individual has not that power of
permeating industry which is required by the gospel
of "moralising the employer." Honesty, beyond the
meagre limits of legality and the demands of purchasers, not merely is not the best policy, but is not
a possible policy where the making of dividends is a
condition of continuance in business.

§ 12. Just as impracticable in the long run is the
corresponding policy of individual reform applied at the
other end of the industrial system, the moral education
of the consumer. Something, doubtless, may be done
by "white lists" and by Consumers' Leagues, having
for their object the protection of purchasers from the
encouragement of "sweating," by affording them some
guarantee that the articles they buy have been produced
under "fair conditions." But this "something" is infini-
tesimally little. Those who, under this humanitarian
impulse, buy goods when they would not otherwise have
bought them, and who, in the nature of the case, pay
prices higher than they would have paid, can have no
really satisfactory guarantee that the innumerable processes which contribute directly and indirectly to the
production and distribution of most manufactured goods
are conducted on fair conditions. It is practically impossible to earmark goods so as to trace their industrial
history from the condition of raw material to shop goods,
or, conversely, to trace the different hands among which

the price paid for the shop goods is distributed in the intricate course of modern commerce. The guarantee is practically confined to the final process, and, even then, any considerable extension of the method of the Consumers' League would most likely be defeated by the ability of the specialist producer or vendor to deceive the amateur purchaser or his amateur adviser. In general, the consumer is not competent to ascertain the conditions of production and distribution of the many articles he buys, nor can he succeed in acquiring such competence; for, when it becomes necessary to outwit him, he will always be outwitted by the superior opportunities of a highly interested manufacturer or retailer. An unorganised or feebly organised method of attempting to solve a social problem is both scientifically false and practically futile.

§ 13. Mr. Ruskin's assumption that, because the will of individuals initiates all moral conduct, the solution of the social problem must proceed chiefly from individual, not from public action, is untenable. The education of ✗ the individual intelligence and moral sense is indeed one and the first essential ; but, unless it succeeds in stimulating him to public action in co-operation with his fellows, its influence is sterilised. Public action may, of course, take other forms than legislation and public administration ; it may operate through private organisations of business men or of citizens, the huge reticulation of voluntary societies which, in matters industrial, recreative, educational, and spiritual, have formed so distinguished a feature of our age and country ; or, taking powerful and definite shape as public opinion, it may grow into customs as strong and as coercive as any law.

But there is increasing reason to believe that the individual units of moral force, which are to turn industry
from private profit-seeking into public use, will be compelled to organise themselves into a "general will," and
to find expression through the most definite and concrete instruments of social government, the political and
administrative machinery of the state. The reason for
this expectation is not that the use of this more or less
clumsy machinery is in itself preferable to that of the
more flexible and less mechanical forms, in which the
moral will of a people may make for conduct; but that
our analysis of the industrial problem shows that the
more rigorous coercive treatment is essential to break
down the evil power which competitive industry for
profit places in the hands of the least scrupulous competitors. The conversion of the best, or even of the
average industrial competitor, is not enough; we must
needs restrain the worst, and such restraint requires and
justifies coercion and the application of the most effective
general machinery of coercion. Such public action, however, is not less moral in its origin and its supports than
the so-called individual conduct. The education of the
will of individual citizens is essential to its employment;
for public opinion alone can pass a law or secure its
effective administration when it is passed. The too
common notion, that legislation replaces and dispenses
with the need of other more elastic voluntary forms of
co-operation, is unsound; the advocates of state action
are not the enemies of private reform agencies, but the
friends. More and more, as citizens learn to conduct
public affairs for the public good, it will be recognised
that the best use of private organisations and even of

individual activity for the general good is to educate individuals for the performance of civic duties, to watch and to assist the administration of public functions, and to perform those public services which, by reason of their delicacy and the local individuality of their character, cannot conveniently be trusted to the more routine and mechanical agencies of government.

§ 14. Mr. Ruskin's refusal to accept democracy, and his reliance on the voluntary conversion of the ruling classes, is a radical defect of his social thinking, and ultimately rests, as all such errors must, upon a moral obliquity. His diagnosis of the moral claims of democracy is false. He looks upon it as a rebellion, instead of as a necessary development of the general will, a moral process of popular activity. The order which he so passionately desires cannot be reached by the moral means he advocates. It can only arise as the expression of the enlightened, rational, free will of the people. Socialism, either that of Mr. Ruskin or another, however far it goes, must either mean industrial democracy or nothing. A so-called Socialism from above, embodying the patronage of emperor or of a small enlightened bureaucracy, is not Socialism in any moral sense at all; the forms of government must be animated by the social spirit, must be the expression of the common organic genius of the people, if it is to have true vitality and meaning. Carlyle and Mr. Ruskin, with many others, declare democracy impossible, because such a spirit cannot emanate from the rude people. If this is true, then moral government is impossible. Mr. Ruskin is misled in his notions of democracy by assigning undue stress and validity to certain emphatic phrases which crude revolutionary experiments evoke. Democracy, as he would see it, is the assertion of absolute equality, and the negation of all reverence. This in effect constitutes his moral indictment. It is true that there have been and still are advocates of democracy against whom these charges hold good. But neither of them applies to the more rational modern conception of a democracy with representative institutions. Irreverence is not essential to the democrat, as Mr. Ruskin insists. It is, indeed, true that the canine fidelity, the absolute servility, and unintelligent obedience which Mr. Ruskin not uncommonly requires, is utterly alien from the spirit of democracy. But it is also alien from morality, which, in order to deserve its name, must be a " perfect freedom," a voluntary, rational service. It is the curious survival of an ascetic feeling of self-renunciation in conjunction with an admiration of those " strange ideas " of autocracy, which here obfuscates the clear moral vision of Mr. Ruskin. The reverence of one who understands, though he may not possess, the superior qualities of one set in authority over him, is something better than mere canine worship. This reverence, this enlightened appreciation of the character of others, is not inconsistent with democracy; it is, we must insist, the necessary moral support of it, and the education of rational democracy is vital and effective just in so far as it is calculated to evoke and sustain this sentiment.

§ 15. Neither does democracy stand or fall by any declaration of absolute equality. Mr. Ruskin's criticism of the notion that " all men are by nature free and equal " is valid, for as soon as this quality is expressed

in closer concrete form, it is discovered not to conform
to facts. Not only are men not in present fact equal,
but there is no reason to suppose that they ever will be
equal in nature and capacities. But the phrase has, for
all that, served a sound historic purpose as a dramatic
protest against inequalities bred not of nature but of
human oppression. There is also a sense in which it
expresses an important truth. In the eyes of society
and of the state, all citizens are presumed to be of equal
value, so far as the consideration of the public and the
bestowal of public benefits are concerned; it is convenient
to attach an equal sanctity to their lives and property,
not that ultimately and accurately any two members
are of equal value to society and equally deserving of
social consideration, but because the inherent difficulties attending human valuation and the necessary imperfections of public machinery are such that, for most
purposes at any rate, it will be socially expedient to
uphold and practise this maxim of equality, excepting
where explicit experience has testified the contrary, as
in the case of criminals or other proved anti-social persons. But outside this limited application of the doctrine, modern democracy does not make any demand
based upon a false assertion of natural or moral facts.
Equality of opportunity for social service and for self-
development is the only equality which is demanded.
How far this implies an absolutely equal access to
natural resources, to education, and to other social
opportunities, may be matter for discussion. Democracy does undoubtedly reject Mr. Ruskin's system of
hereditary castes; but its rejection would not be based
upon an abstract assertion of equality, but upon histori-

cal facts and scientific interpretations of heredity, which
would be taken to refute the practicability and social
utility of such a system.

§ 16. Whether, how far, or how fast a democracy can
be established, based upon rational reverence for real
and proved capacity, and therefore endowed with necessary checks upon the abuse of governmental powers in
politics or industry, and directed to secure for all its
members equal opportunities of consciously contributing
to the ends of the commonwealth, will be questions upon
which no close agreement may at present be expected.
Believers in the possibility of democracy do indeed reject Mr. Ruskin's contemptuous estimate of the capacities of " the common people," insisting that the common
rational faculties possessed by all, and the common experience of life, enable " the masses " to attain a practical wisdom which is of essential service in the work of
government. Not merely by furnishing a check upon
those abuses of power which always attend class government, but by a direct important contribution to the
knowledge of social needs and of the wisest means of
satisfaction, must the voice of the people claim to contribute to government. The organic conception of society, which Mr. Ruskin accepts, demands a self-government in which the whole of the self, the organic
experience and judgment of the whole rational system,
shall find direct conscious expression, a demand which is
entirely inconsistent with the dumb submission which
his ideal government would seem to impose upon the
masses.

The whole notion that social government is to be
specialised like medicine or shoemaking, in the hands of

particular class, involves a complete misconception
f the problem, confounding the expert drafting of
aws and administration, which are special arts, with
he wider rational ordering of social life to which the
ntire organic society must contribute. The comparison
f the wisdom and ability of various classes, and of indi-
iduals within these classes, as a basis for the quantita-
ive apportionment of governmental powers, is only one
f the many fallacies which lurk in a sectional or sep-
ratist solution of an organic problem. The wisdom of
nation for purposes of self-government cannot be un-
erstood as the mere addition of the wisdom of its sepa-
ate units. The real plea for democracy is the absolute
eed for the expression of the rational life of the whole
ational organism in the arts of government. Neither
he equal right of all individual members, nor the un-
qual capacities of separate classes measured by educa-
ion or by property, forms the true basis of rational
elf-government. Through the necessarily rude and im- ∠
erfect mechanism of franchise and elections must
reathe the conscious organic experience of national
ife, expressed in large general judgments and demands
rhich are really the will and voice of the people as a
nity, and which only appear to be the added judgments
nd demands of a number of separate individuals, be-
ause of the necessary defects of the mechanical instru-
ents of record. Democracy insists that the people as ⌐
whole is rational, and that government must express
his rationality. This does not exclude but implies a _
ecognition of the need of making full use of the capaci-
ies of skilled men for special governmental functions,
nd of assigning to these the requisite authority as lead-

ers both in the education and in the execution of the national will. Mr. Ruskin's criticism of democracy glances scatheless from the strong formula of Mazzini, " The progress of all through all, under the leadership of the best and wisest."

CHAPTER IX.

§ 1. So strong is the popular bent to caricature that
it is safe to conclude that the most general of all notions
about Mr. Ruskin is that he is a fanatical opponent of
machinery, a literary Luddite and railway wrecker, the
insanity of such an attitude being in part condoned by
the reflection that he is an artist, and therefore incapable of taking a sound practical view of the benefits which
factories and coal-pits have conferred upon our national
life.

Now, since certain " objections to machinery " are no
by-product of Mr. Ruskin's thought, but belong to the
very kernel of his criticism of life, they deserve closer
attention than the "average sensual man " is inclined to
accord them.

In order to clear the way, we must first ask, How far
does Mr. Ruskin object to machinery ? Quaint stories
of his " posting " up north in 1876 " quite in the old-

fashioned way," with a specially built carriage, postillion, and relays of horses, in order to escape the railway;[1] attempts to restore hand-weaving in Cumberland; his reversion to hand-made paper and handicraft of every kind in the production of his books; his constant and vehement denunciation of factory towns and factory life, have created an impression of a quixotic, indiscriminate opposition to modern industrial methods. With just reason, Mr. Ruskin complains[2] of the ignorance of critics who, trusting to vulgar gossip, accuse him of "condemning machinery," whereas he is himself the inventor and proposer of daring schemes for tide-mills, drainage, and other engineering exploits. Two important distinctions mark his real attitude. His opposition is directed primarily not against machinery, but against "steam-power" superseding not only human power, but the "natural" agencies of wind, water, and animal life.[3] The causes of his hatred of steam-power are manifold: the horror and the brutalising toil of mining, the foul impurity of a smoke-laden atmosphere, the ugly structure and degrading monotony of factories and factory towns, the devastation of beautiful localities by mines and mills, by railways and hordes of barbarian "trippers," the absorption of so much national energy and skill in economy of steam-production, — all contribute to his abhorrence.

His attitude may seem unreasonable: it may be urged that "steam," too, is a power of nature; that mining need not be, and indeed is not, a peculiarly unhealthy or degrading work; that much of the injuri-

---

[1] Collingwood, "Life," ii. 162.   [2] Fors, Letter lxxxv. (iv. 290).
[3] Fors, Letter lxvii. (iii. 873).

ous effect of smoke is preventable ; that factories need not be either ugly or unhealthy, and are becoming less so ; that steam-power, as the servant of humanity, confers enormous benefits in facilitating the production of material wealth and in widening the horizon of life for all people, by providing easy and swift communication of persons, goods, and ideas. Many of these pleas, in part, at any rate, Mr. Ruskin's mind was open to receive. Even railways he did not utterly eschew. For although in the opening letter of " Fors " he expresses a fierce desire " to destroy most of the railroads in England, and all the railroads in Wales," [1] in milder moments he draws a distinction between main lines — which for their large and obvious utility he would permit — and certain branch lines, whose smaller utility is far outweighed by their injury to nature and to rural life. In particular, and with sound reason, he opposed the introduction of railways into the finest valleys of Switzerland and into the heart of our own Lake Country, because he held that their presence destroyed the beauty which was the distinctive worth of these places. Those who think this exhibits an exclusive spirit, and consider that a Rigi railway, by making the glories of Switzerland accessible to larger numbers of people, confers a benefit so large as to outweigh the damage to scenery, fail to appreciate the sensitive genius to which wilfully-flawed beauty is a desecration and a source of keener pain than the presence of any ordinary ugliness or lack of harmony. All utilitarian calculations of the quantity of lower satisfaction afforded to a larger number necessarily failed to touch and to convince one who always held that the best

[1] Fors, Letter i. (i. 5).

is infinitely better than the next best. Mr. Ruskin's objections to the degradation of what is greatest and most beautiful in nature are neither perverse nor weakly " sentimental" to those who value quality of life.

§ 2. There are, however, cases where there is some reason to accuse him of being unduly swayed by " sentimental" considerations. Hand-weaving is one example. Where fine and skilful work is required, the hand-loom is most desirable and in large measure necessary, but neither the materials nor the inherent processes of weaving justify the prohibition of steam-driven machinery for the common sorts of cloths. Every one acquainted with the true history of hand-weaving in the olden times, or who watches the industry as it survives to-day in less advanced places, knows that in general it preserves hardly any of the character of fine manual labour: it is a dull, monotonous, routine work, wearing to muscles and to nerves, with scarcely any interest or scope for skill and originality ; moreover, the economic circumstances of its survival as a home-industry favour excessive work and under-pay. If any one is disposed to doubt this, let him visit some of the châlets in Swiss valleys, where enterprising Berne manufacturers are re-introducing common sorts of silk-weaving. It is doubt-less claimed that hand-woven goods are best in quality for wear, but to desire always the best goods at any cost of labour is undesirable : for ordinary purposes ordinary wares suffice, and steam-driven machinery both can and should produce them. A certain fallacy of mediæval picturesqueness has sometimes carried Mr. Ruskin, with Carlyle and other good company, into extravagant work of " restoration." To this same " sentimentalism," or

falsely grounded sentiment, we must attribute the indiscriminate denial of machinery to agriculture.[1] If Mr.
Ruskin had enjoyed personal experience of agricultural
work, he would have known that much labour, quite as
heavy, dull, and brutalising in its effect upon the nature
of the labourer as the work in mines and iron-works
which he so earnestly deplored, has been taken from
agricultural workers and put upon the tireless back of
the steam-driven machine-plough, reaper, thresher,
digger, etc., and that the net result of this new agriculture is to lighten labour, and to leave to labourers
a larger margin of free energy for their leisure time.

But though Mr. Ruskin is undoubtedly carried too far
in his protests against the encroachments of machinery
in industry, we are not at liberty to neglect what is true
in his indictment. Perhaps the following passage from
" Fors " gives the best conspectus of his whole position :
" The use of machinery in agriculture throws a certain
number of persons out of wholesome employment, who
must thenceforth either do nothing, or mischief. The
use of machinery in art destroys the national intellect;
and, finally, renders all luxury impossible. All machinery needful in ordinary life to supplement human or
animal labour may be moved by wind or water ; while
steam, or any modes of *heat power*, may only be employed
justifiably under extreme or special conditions of need,
as for speed on main lines of communication and for
raising water from great depths, or other such work
beyond human strength."[2]

§ 3. What is really interesting and important is Mr.

---

[1] Crown of Wild Olive, § 157 ; Time and Tide, § 152.
[2] Fors, Letter lxvii. (iii. 374) ; *cf.* Letter xliv. (ii. 413).

Ruskin's general protest against the mechanisation of work and life. The tendency of machinery, as he sees it, is to subdivide labour so that no one any longer shall make anything, shall see the end or utility of his labour, or shall even complete a single process. Subdivision of labour really subdivides the man, makes him less than a man, — a mere servant or a machine in one narrow routine process. Not merely does it degrade him by narrowing the scope of the work, but the skill, freedom, and control of the workman is gone, and he becomes a mere machine-tender. This is a mortal injury: it denotes the difference between a man who uses a tool and a tool that uses a man. Now, according to Mr. Ruskin, a prime need of humanity is the performance of skilled manual work. Purely mechanical work "invariably degrades,"[1] and the thought that it is necessary is an ever-haunting trouble to Mr. Ruskin, who does not adequately realise that it is the chief function of machinery to solve his difficulty, and that mechanical work is from its very nature the only work a machine can do.

The universal need of good and interesting work is a first principle of the art of life according to Mr. Ruskin, and machinery, in so far as it enslaves the worker, impugns this principle. Like many others, he seems often to assume that machinery will gradually convert a larger and larger proportion of workers into machine-tenders. There is no evidence that this is so. The most highly developed manufacturing machinery — *e. g.* a modern flour-mill — requires the smallest quantity of tending, and such labour as it does require partakes of the nature of skilled engineering rather than of mechanical routine.

[1] Fors, Letter xliv. (ii. 413).

The tendency to subdivision of labour which preceded modern machinery, though it has undoubtedly been intensified by machine processes, was a more warrantable source of distrust than machinery itself. It is by no means the case that manufacturing machinery is engaging the labour of an increasing proportion of our English workers; and though steam-transport by sea and land is a growing source of employment, most of the workers here are not under the direct governance of the machinery with which they co-operate.

§ 4. But for Mr. Ruskin's broader charge against modern industry, of "mechanising" life by an excessive specialisation, which sacrifices the individuality of the man, by absorbing his productive energies in a single narrow routine process, there is ample warrant. Industrial economy, looking only to the increased production of goods and the consequent gain of the consumer, has ignored the vital needs of the producer. In this way "free" competition has enslaved the individual worker to society, by confining him to the constant repetition of some small single task, to which he must give all his time and energy in order to gain a livelihood, starving and wasting by atrophy all the other human faculties with which he was endowed by nature. Similarly, on a larger scale, "free trade," so far as it is determined by purely commercial considerations, narrows and enslaves the national productive life, insisting that whole districts of England shall be monotonised by cotton, iron, pottery, at the behest of a world-market. The protest which Mr. Ruskin, in common with Carlyle, Emerson, Arnold, Morris, and most of our wisest teachers, raises against this insane policy, is not, as sometimes represented, a

mad crusade against inevitable laws. These protestants
do not refuse the gains of effective co-operation, which
come by using the special qualities of men and nations;
they merely insist that the practice of dividing labour
shall be moderated by a due consideration of the interests of the producer, and that the consumer shall not
ride roughshod over him. It is desirable that work
shall be highly specialised, but not that the energy of the
worker shall be monopolised by this specialised work.
Hence the need of protecting labour against excessive
hours of labour and the " driving " tendency of modern
machine-production. The legitimate use of division of
labour requires that a large margin of leisure and of
energy be given to every worker for the free and
healthy exercise and use of his other faculties. The
farther division of labour is carried, the shorter should
be the routine working day, the longer the time for
other kinds of work and play. This is the " true inward-
ness " of the agitation for shorter hours; it is not a plea
for idleness, but for the healthy use of unspecialised
faculties. Such demand is based upon no merely " sentimental " considerations or regard for a more pleasurable
life, valid as these considerations are. It is a necessity
of sound individual and national life. Over-specialisation is the destruction of physical and intellectual life.
True manhood requires some just apportionment of
time and energy to the different departments of a
human life : a man who digs all day, or thinks all day,
or plays all day, is less than a man, for all these things
are needed to complete humanity.

§ 5. When, therefore, Mr. Ruskin indicts the idle
wealthy class, he is actuated not merely by a sense of

justice, but by a consideration of the wholesomeness of work. The worst effect of division of labour falls upon those who are relieved from the necessity of labouring at all. " Whoever will not work neither shall he eat" is a physical as well as a moral law. Like other laws, it may be evaded: sport, the return of our aristocracy to the " hunting" stage of their barbarous ancestors, is a chief form of this evasion. But the attempt to eat and digest a dinner without previously deserving it by some voluntary output of physical " work " must, and in the long run does, defeat itself. Mr. Ruskin, fortified by moral considerations and directed by economic analysis, insists that some hand-labour is required of all.[1] Not only should the idle classes earn the bread they eat by the skill of their hand and the sweat of their brow, but the intellectual classes require a physical counterbalance to their specialised brain-work. The extravagances of modern sport are chief testimony to a wasteful economy, exhibiting an erratic, often a wantonly destructive use of forces which, properly directed, might yield sound social service, without any diminution of the interest and enjoyment they afford to those who give them out. Mr. Ruskin's attempt to introduce road-making as a pastime for Oxford undergraduates, though it failed to compete with the attractions of the river and the football field, was nevertheless a serviceable protest against abuse of recreation. Tolstoy has insisted that the working day of every healthy man should contain some routine muscular work, some skilled exercise of eye and wrist, and some definitely intellectual work, and Mr. Ruskin would agree with him. Tolstoy, indeed, goes

[1] Crown of Wild Olive, § 151.

somewhat farther in his praise of agriculture than even
Mr. Ruskin would be prepared to go, demanding apparently that " bread-labour " in the literal sense shall form
part of the regular work of every one, and thus imposing
upon all alike the conditions of a rural life. But while
Mr. Ruskin allows more division of labour than Tolstoy,
and does not insist that every one shall dig and plough,
he does require physical work from all, and holds life in
great industrial towns of the present type to be inconsistent alike with individual and national health.

§ 6. On one point his teaching seems less " scientific "
than Tolstoy's, and not quite consistent with his practical experiments. We have already seen [1] that he not
only regarded the " degrading" occupation of mining,
forging, etc., as essentially " servile," but included in
this category all " simply manual occupations." This
conviction that nature had provided an inferior grade of
labourers, belonging essentially to the Helot class, who
would be best adapted for such low work, and would
suffer less from doing it than others, seemed to furnish
him a moderately satisfactory solution for the question,
" Who will do the hard and disagreeable work ? " This
specialisation of human nature enabled him to reserve
" the rough and hard work" for " the rough and hard
people." [2] " It is in the wholesome indisposition of the
average mind for intellectual labour that due provision
is made for the quantity of dull work which must be
done in stubbing the Thornaby wastes of the world." [3]

Apparently the manual work which he would impose
upon all other classes is to be skilled work, not that

[1] Chapter VII.   [2] Fors, Letter lxxxii. (iv. 208).
[3] Fors, Letter xcv. (iv. 464).

mechanical work which "invariably degrades."[1] Here
Mr. Ruskin is surely wrong and Tolstoy in essence right.
Simple mechanical work, either of a muscular order, like
digging, or lighter, like most mill labour, when done in
moderation, not only is not degrading in itself, but is
positively useful as a part of the day's work. Both for
physical exercise and for moral discipline some mechanical, routine, manual work is desirable. To put it all
upon a specialised grade of servile beings, which is Mr.
Ruskin's proposal, would be a double wrong: first to
these slaves by depriving them of their share of interesting and educative work, some of which is their due;
secondly, to the other classes, by over-stimulation of
nervous and mental powers through lack of a wholesome
admixture of routine-work. In an *obiter dictum* Mr.
Ruskin declares there is no harm in a man "thinking all
day if he can." There is a curiously defective grasp of
humanity in such a statement. The direct reply is that
a person who thinks all day will not think sanely, for he
is not leading a sane life. Critics, like Tolstoy and
Edward Carpenter, rightly insist that specialised intellectual castes of persons, who have absolutely thrown off
all physical labour, are driven to justify their unnatural
life by producing an abortive brood of study-bred theories and researches, artificial products of literature,
science, philosophy, theology, and art, which are not
truly sound or serviceable, because their makers are not
in true contact with the common life. Whitman touches
the quick of the matter, "Now I re-examine philosophies
and religions. They may prove well in lecture-rooms
and yet may not prove at all under the spacious

[1] Fors, Letter xliv. (ii. 413).

clouds, and along the landscape and flowing currents."
Theories of life spun by the over-wrought brains of
those who are not living a whole life cannot themselves be whole. It is only right to acknowledge that
this too has been Mr. Ruskin's contention through all
his teaching: no one has done more to expose theorising
not based upon first hand knowledge of nature and
human life, or to refute the exaggerated claims of
academic sophisms. It is only in the failure to recognise the right place of mechanical labour in every life
that Mr. Ruskin consistently errs. The specialisation of
routine work which he sanctions is both a physical and
a moral mistake. Due attention to the physiology of
work indicates the need of routine manual exercise for
all; the necessary mechanical work, divided amongst
all, would be a gain to all instead of a wearisome and
degrading toil to a single class. The industrial ordering
which would be necessary to give to all their proper
share of unskilled and skilled manual work doubtless
involves grave difficulties; but that the ideal of healthy
individual life in a well-ordered society demands such
apportionment, there can be no reasonable doubt.

§ 7. But it is not merely in the direct interests of the
producer that Mr. Ruskin and other artists have revolted
against the dominance of machinery and the excessive
division of labour. The commercial economists, sanctioned by "common sense," have assumed, without
warrant, that the consumers gain by every increase
of routine-made goods which implies the narrowing of
the labour of the producers. This economic view takes
a too quantitative and a too objective estimate of wealth.
It is by no means sure that an increase of material

goods of routine character is of service to consumers already provided with the necessaries of physical life. One who is no fanatical machino-clast may well doubt whether the flooding of markets with vast quantities of low-class machine-made goods has been an unqualified gain to consumers. Let us bear in mind the necessary limits of machine-production. A machine can economically function only when a large number of persons will consent to consume a large quantity of goods of precisely the same size, shape, and general character, and without any of those "art" qualities which belong to the skill and finish of good individual workmanship. Now the general policy of replacing hand-made by < machine-made goods may be, and in many cases is, entirely justified, but it is a bad education for the taste of the community. In a really progressive society, not only the interest of the producer in doing good work, but of the consumer in getting the result of good work, will impose restrictions upon machine-economy. In speaking of "taste," I do not mean only the nicer æsthetic discrimination which distinguishes between an oil painting and an oleograph, and which detects the inherent imperfections in photography. Throughout the whole field of commodities there exists a necessary war between the individual consumer and machine-production. Take tailoring for an example. Coats can be cut out quickly and cheaply by machinery, upon one condition, viz., that those who are to wear them will consent to forego a precise fit and take an average fit. No two individuals are exactly the same in figure, and therefore a machine-cut coat, constructed to suit many persons, can never be an exact fit for any one of them;

it may be sufficiently near for "practical purposes," but a person who is "particular" will always demand a hand-cut coat. So in every other case, machine-economy requires individuals to merge their individuality and to consent to conform to a common type. Now lack of individual taste or lack of money may induce large numbers of persons to make this sacrifice; but educated persons do it unwillingly, and if they have money they refuse to do it. In a community of widespread wealth, with growing education, this will always form a natural check upon machine-economy. How far and in what precise direction this check will operate is disputable. All persons will and must consent to conform in some respects and to consume common routine goods. Few will insist that their buttons shall be hand-made, that the flour they eat shall be ground by hand. But wherever the consumer desires to express his individuality in his consumption, and can afford to do so, he exercises a demand for commodities which cannot be supplied by machinery, but constitute a "special order" to be executed by the skill of a human worker. The best work, therefore, must always remain outside machine-economy. It is here, then, that the character of the consumer comes in as an important factor.

The rapid mechanical improvements of our age have corrupted and repressed the taste of the consuming public, stimulating a demand for increased quantities of goods rather than for improved qualities. It is not of course right to ignore or to depreciate the immense services machinery has rendered in enabling the poorer classes to acquire increased stores of the common comforts of life, from which they were for-

merly precluded. Much, if not most of this common ✗
work of satisfying the grosser material needs, is rightly
performed by machinery applied to manufacture, trans-
port, and (*pace* Mr. Ruskin) even to agriculture. But '
it is of the utmost importance that, after these common
needs are thus satisfied, further progress in consumption
shall take a qualitative more than a quantitative character. For here the vital identity of interests between producer and consumer is seen. So long as consumers sink
their individuality, and seek merely to enlarge the number of their material needs, and to express their "prosperity" in more food and clothing, larger houses, and
gross expenditure on coarse external show, they are
forcing upon vast numbers of workers a monotonous
life of machine or routine work. When, on the other
hand, increased prosperity means the demand for a better
and a higher life, more taste and variety in material
goods, luxuries which are the product of art or skilled
workmanship, increased expenditure upon intellectual
goods, a wholesome reaction takes place upon the condition of employment all over the industrial field. This ✗
is the choice of life for an individual or a nation, between
a quantitative and a qualitative self-expression. Mr.
Ruskin has performed no greater service than in pro-
testing against the lamentable assumption that the industrial prosperity of a nation consists in the quantity
of marketable goods she can produce by the most economical use of machinery and division of labour. We
may not agree with him in the narrow limits he would
assign to machines; we may recognise a legitimate and
most serviceable co-operation between machinery and
human skill in the production of fine qualities of

wealth, machinery more and more taking over the rough, coarser, routine groundwork, and leaving to human art the more delicate manipulation and finish which gives character and tone; we would not seek to stereotype for any nation or any age the kinds of consumption in which its individual taste will seek expression. But though machinery is not the enemy, and may even be made the servant of art, we feel that Mr. Ruskin is right in his preachment against the grave danger of mechanising life at the present time.

I have confined my illustrations to industries engaged in producing material wealth. When we examine Mr. Ruskin's views on education, we shall see how powerfully he emphasises the same dangers in the production of intellectual wealth, the mental factory system by which quantities of stereotype intellectual wares are forced on the body of consumers through schools and printing-presses, the mechanism of churches, political organisations, and social conventions of every kind.

Thus we perceive that Mr. Ruskin's hostility against machinery is far from being, as some would represent it, a mere fantastic revolt against machinery, ugliness, and smoke. It is part of a wider feeling that production so carried on is "unnatural," in the sense that it takes away the initiative and the productive force from man, and the familiar friendly forces of animals, wind, and water, and hands them over to a lower power, which enslaves human labour, and drives it by imposing conditions of unnatural routine and unwholesome tension. There is a characteristic passage in which Mr. Ruskin objects to forcing flowers and fruit: "The vile and gluttonous habit of forcing never allows people properly to taste anything." [1] Here we have the same root of hostility, the interference with the beauty and order of natural processes, with the result that the two human gains of gardening are lost, the wholesome work in free air on natural soil, the timely fruits of labour in their due season. The whole of his criticism of modern industry in its double and related injury to " producer " and " consumer " lies in this illustration.

§ 8. The largest and most dramatic form of the danger of machinery is the modern industrial town. Modern Manchester and Leeds are typical machine-made products; they exist primarily not as " cities," for the wholesome social life of citizens, but as work-shops, for the most economical production and distri-bution of machine-made goods. Mr. Ruskin is filled with voluble indignation whenever he approaches the subject; to him these are monstrous wens on the fair face of England, huge areas of grimy, ugly streets, buildings unredeemed and unredeemable by architec-ture, the exhausted atmosphere noxious with foul vapours, and black with smoke from giant chimneys ; the popu-lation are engaged in a degrading struggle to get rich at the expense of one another, or to scrape together a miserable livelihood. No sound human life, no true work can thrive in such conditions. That the inhabitants of such a place can be content, or even proud of their town, is in itself the most striking proof of its degrading influence on character. His condemnation is upon every count, hygienic, industrial, intellectual, and moral. He holds that " no great arts were practicable by any people unless they were living contented lives, in pure air, out

---

[1] Fors, Letter xlvi. (ii. 458).

of the way of unsightly objects, and emancipated from
unnecessary mechanical occupation."[1] Still more evil
is the fate of those ancient towns which have fallen
from their old estate into modern industry, — such a
town as Abingdon, where the county-gaol, police-office,
and a large gasometer are the most conspicuous features. But perhaps the most scathing realism is found
in his account of the suburban villadom which is the
typical expression of middle-class character and aspirations in a modern town. In " Fors " he gives us the
following account of the district between Sydenham and
Penge, within his memory one of the fairest regions of
the South of England : " That same district is now covered by, literally, many thousands of houses, built within
the last ten years of rotten brick, with various iron
devices to hold it together. They, every one, have a
drawing-room and dining-room, transparent from back
to front. They have a second story of bedrooms, and
an underground one of kitchen. They are fastened in
a Siamese-twin manner together by their sides, and each
couple has a Greek or Gothic portico shared between
them, with magnificent steps and highly ornamented
capitals. Attached to every double block are exactly
similar double parallelograms of garden, laid out in new
gravel and scanty turf, on the model of the pleasure
grounds in the Crystal Palace, and enclosed by high,
thin, and pale brick walls. The gardens in front are
fenced from the road with an immense weight of cast
iron, and entered between two square gate-posts, with
projecting stucco cornices, bearing the information that
the eligible residence within is Mortimer House or Mon-

[1] Fors, Letter ix. (i. 177).

tague Villa. On the other side of the road, which is laid freshly down with large flints, and is deep at the sides in ruts of yellow mud, one sees Burleigh House, or Devonshire Villa, still to let, and getting leprous in patches all over the fronts. . . . Of the men, their wives and children, who live in any of these houses, probably not the fifth part are possessed of one common manly or womanly skill, knowledge, or means of happiness. The men can indeed write, and cast accounts, and go to town every day to get their living by doing so; the women and children can perhaps read story-books, dance in a vulgar manner, and play upon a piano with dull dexterities for exhibition; but not a member of the whole family can, in general, cook, sweep, knock in a nail, drive a stake, or spin a thread. They are still less capable of fine work. They know nothing of painting, sculpture, or architecture; of science, inaccurately, as much as may more or less account to them for Mr. Pepper's ghost, and make them disbelieve in the existence of any other ghost but that, particularly the Holy One: of books they read *Macmillan's Magazine* on week days and *Good Words* on Sundays, and are entirely ignorant of all the standard literature belonging to their own country, or to any other. . . . They cannot enjoy their gardens, for they have neither sense nor strength enough to work in them. The women and girls have no pleasure but in calling on each other in false hair, cheap dresses of gaudy stuffs, machine-made and high-heeled boots, of which the pattern was set to them by Parisian prostitutes of the lowest order: the men have no faculty beyond that of cheating in business; no pleasures but in smoking or eating; and no ideas nor any capacity of forming ideas, of anything that has yet been done of great, or seen of good, in this world."[1] Such is the character of the industrial town as reflected in the life of the Philistine class, according to Mr. Ruskin.

§ 9. Causally related to this dominance of the industrial town is the decay of the country. The most distinctive fact in the external life of modern England is the decline of agriculture and the progressive diminution of the agricultural workers. Industrial economy regards this change with indifference, or rather with complacency, as testimony to the increased productivity of town life. To Mr. Ruskin it is an unmitigated evil, equally injurious to town or country, for the noxious influence of town life is not even confined to the towns. Every big town is a huge sucker, draining in the best blood from the country and using it up in two generations, reaching out its antennæ in the shape of railways and water-pipes to ruin the scenery, polluting the rivers and converting lakes into reservoirs : within forty miles of London it is scarcely possible to buy pure milk, poultry, vegetables, or any agricultural product, owing to this greedy suction of the metropolis. All this occurs with what object? to maintain an ugly, unhealthy, immoral, and almost useless city life, where a small class live in luxurious idleness or mischievous activity, a large class in sordid and toilsome penury, and where the " City " so-called is not the home of citizens but the gambling-hell of cunning merchants and speculators. Such is the picture Ruskin presents in many passages of his later books.[2] The startling vividity of his language possibly

---

[1] Fors, Letter xxix. (ii. 99-101).
[2] E. g. Fors, Letter xliv. (ii. 410, etc.).

repels as many readers as it convinces: and some exaggeration may well be admitted. Neither the health nor
the character of town dwellers has suffered to the extent
which Mr. Ruskin's contrast would indicate, nor is the
work so purely selfish, useless, or mechanical as he often
represents. And yet we feel the indictment to be substantially correct. Commercial economy has succeeded
in blinding the public to the dangerous significance of
the absorption of national life and energy in machine-
made towns. The endeavour to civilise the towns, so as
to make them sound social centres, may do much to mit-
igate the worst phases of the maladies upon which Mr.
Ruskin dwells; but it is difficult to believe that a nation,—
three-quarters of which are dwellers in towns and chiefly
in large towns, can preserve intact the vigour of physique
and character which is essential to the progress of a
nation.

Even those who are coming to look upon England as
one small field in our imperial estate should find some
difficulty in reconciling to their intelligence such local
specialisation as shall make England a purely manufacturing and commercial area, no longer breeding in rural
life the bone, muscle, and brain which have made the
empire, but depending for its force and progress in the
future upon colonial lives. To many, we are aware,
this movement seems inevitable; the forces making for
large town life in England seem to them natural and
necessary. The industrial destiny of England has indeed been so incessantly dinned into our ears during
this century, that it seems to some the only destiny.
More money can be made by going to work in large
towns; that appears a final irrefutable argument. And

indeed we are not sanguine about its speedy refutation.
But, with Mr. Ruskin, we may remind ourselves, that it
is only within recent times that we have submitted all
values of individual and national life to the arbitrament
of the counter. A wider view of our history does not
mark us as an exclusively, or even a distinctively, industrial nation, or one which only counted commercial
gains. It is quite true that so long as, and in so far as,
we allow purely monetary consideration of profits and
wages exclusively to settle for us where we shall live,
what air we shall breathe, what company of nature or of
man we shall keep, what work we shall do, what kind
of home, what kind of children we shall have, the recent
townward movement is necessary. But if, with Mr. Ruskin, we consent to take a wider social outlook, nay, even
if we are guided by a more truly enlightened self-interest, we shall refuse to confine our calculation to monetary values, and to leave out of view all the higher and
nobler " goods " which, by their nature, are above money
and above price, — air, sunshine, scenery, elbow-room,
attachment to land and home, neighbourhood, the character and interest of work, leisure and spare energy for
self-cultivation and enjoyment. These goods are inherent in sound rural life, and cannot be permanently
ignored by a people capable of education and of progress.
Many of them are imperfectly procurable in the rural
life of modern England, as Mr. Ruskin clearly recognises. Drastic reforms of land-tenure and of social government are essential to win for rural work and life that
wholesome stimulus to individual energy, and that social
order which are essential to agricultural prosperity and
to the production of sound manhood and womanhood.

The urgent need of these reforms absorbed more and
more of Mr. Ruskin's thought in later years, for he
rightly saw that the dangers of mechanical, unnatural
town life can only be met by educating a truer and more
discriminative valuation. In order that the agricultural
life may be valued more highly it must become more
valuable: it must not be the worn-out relic of a dead
feudalism with all incentive taken from work, all intelligence and hope from life, as is the case in agricultural
England to-day: it must be a restored yeomanry with
adequate control of soil, competent to work it, and
able to secure, by wholesome co-operation, all requisite
advantages of intellectual and spiritual life.

CHAPTER X.

§ 1. ALWAYS a teacher, and always reflecting upon methods and processes, it was inevitable that Mr. Ruskin should have fresh, free, and vigorous ideas about education. A peculiar interest attaches to the profound conviction which marks all that he says upon the training of the young. For though all of us profess to believe in "education," few of us even now truly realise it as an organic process of developing the capacities of a human soul; for the most part we only believe in processes of learning, the result of which is an attainment of knowledge; or at the most we believe in a certain sharpening of aptitudes for the practical work of life. Even where sound principles of teaching are acquired, the stress upon intellectualism is commonly so strong as to narrow and deform the true meaning of education, which is "the leading human souls to what is best, and making what is best out of them." All specialism, even the specialism of a science of Pedagogics, is prone to stereotype ideas and processes, which ill accords with the watchful freedom and delicate plasticity of method that is required for the moulding of souls.

It is essential to Mr. Ruskin, as social reformer, that he should have clear ideas on education of the young. For what marks him off most distinctively from others is the repudiation of all mechanical or merely external methods of reform, and his insistence upon individual and social character as the means and the end.

The understanding of the nature and sources of social wrong and social waste, the feelings of pity and indignation which stimulate redress, the patient labour undertaken for a distant common good, the "habits of gentleness and justice" which shall keep a new and better order safe and strong, — these things are only possible by education of true civic character. In order to "elevate the race at once," we must work upon the malleable nature of children. All Mr. Ruskin's books, but especially "A Joy for Ever," "Sesame and Lilies," and "Fors," are rich in contribution towards this art of education, abounding in critical and constructive suggestions. In no sense a pedagogic expert, nor making much use of technical language, his wise and humane thoughts furnish an admirable, independent support and corroboration of the more scientific methods connected with such names as Herbart, Pestalozzi, Froebel, which are slowly but surely winning their way into our schools, while serving to check by their simplicity and sweetness any tendency to hardness and elaboration which a science is apt to put on with its esoteric terminology. Moreover the keeping a social ideal always before our eyes is a wholesome counterpoise to the individualism which, for many purposes, is a sound and necessary principle for the practical educationalist, who finds his greatest difficulties in the idiosyncrasies of particular children.

§ 2. Seeing that, however much we pretend to divide it, life is one, it was inevitable that Mr. Ruskin should find in existing education copies of all the representative vices of industrial society.

As a nation, our disinterested love of ideas, our reverence for " sweetness and light," have not been strong enough to keep our educational system free from the domination of the industrialism which so thoroughly absorbs the national energy.

In " Sesame and Lilies" he inveighs against the enslavement of education, even among the middle and upper classes, to the " gospel of getting on." The " success in life," which education is to win for boys, is conceived in terms of lucrative employment, or as the satisfaction of social ambition : " what is sought is an education which shall keep a good coat on my son's back, which shall enable him to ring with confidence the visitor's bell at double-belled doors, which shall result ultimately in the establishment of a double-belled door to his own house." [1] Even Mr. Ruskin was probably unaware of the countless subtle ways by which money-making and social snobbishness everywhere creep into the schools of " the classes," poisoning the intellectual and moral atmosphere both of our great historic

[1] Sesame and Lilies, § 2.

schools and of the select private establishments designed far less to make good men and women than to feed the pride and exclusiveness of that very caste to which Mr. Ruskin yet chiefly looked for the redemption of England. As for the public education of the people, though pioneers have ever striven to hold up the banner of the ideal, and are still labouring to humanise the system, it will be true to say that the real national support of popular education is the conviction that without reading, writing, and the first four rules of arithmetic, a man is at a disadvantage in getting and spending money. It is felt that a nation of shopkeepers should at least secure for its members the capacity to " keep accounts ! "

If a detailed and veracious history of the beginnings of the modern Technical Education movement could be written, it would give an instructive and a humorous corroboration of Mr. Ruskin's charge upon this head. With the national avarice inflamed by fears of competing Germany, Technical Education, a vague, formless conception, floated upon a sea of our most potent national beverage,[1] was foisted upon our raw County Councils, who, not even pretending to know what was to be done, set about to do it, sucked, pulled, or goaded on to start rash experiments, to subsidise useless or pernicious schools, and to deal out money to any institution which could bring sufficient pressure on them. What technical education was, how it should be conducted, no one knew ; but every one seemed agreed that it could be successfully imposed upon the foundation of our elementary system, — the most fatuous notion that

[1] The " Whiskey Money," earmarked by Mr. Goschen for Technical Education.

ever entered the head of official man. Slowly and stupidly, at huge expense, we are learning something practical about the unity and organic character of education, how that education, conducted with a single eye to the shop, will not even successfully cater to our avarice, but requires some mean basis of general culture to stand upon.

In one of the best-known passages of " Sesame " Mr. Ruskin denounces the shortsighted penury of the state in its patronage of art, science, and literature, for leaving its duty to the spasmodic benevolence of private individuals, and merely encouraging certain narrow forms of science and art with a strict view to business, that we may learn to sell canvas as well as coal, and crockery as well as iron.

§ 3. The end of education being conceived in mortal error, it follows that the standard or test of educational success is vitiated. The real meaning of the charge of " materialism " often brought against our nation and age, is that we judge success by quantitative measures. As we measure the wealth of nations or persons by the amount of money or of other property they possess, so we measure education by quantity of attainment in knowledge.

" Payment by results " is a most enlightening phrase in our educational system. In order to work such a system, you must regard education as a process of acquisitiveness, engaged in accumulating lumps of knowledge of various sorts and sizes, which are deposited in the brain, and which can be produced, measured, and expressed in " marks " at regular periods of stock-taking. Needless to say, under the sway of such an idea, a school becomes a factory of knowledge, engaged in putting into the heads of little boys and girls the largest quantity of measurable facts within a given time, a process definitely and purposely encouraged by the free permission given to their parents to use these children for wage-earning, so soon as their heads have been once packed with the required quantity. This is a crude form of evil, widely condemned by all thoughtful persons, but very slow to disappear from a school system where "economy" is always understood to refer to current expenditure of money: surviving even in "high-class" schools under the direct encouragement of parents who, for the most part, have and can have no other guarantee that they are "getting what they pay for," than the examinations which their children pass.

With their lips all schoolmasters and most parents condemn "cram," and "cram" of the cruder sort is perhaps diminishing; but our educational system still insists upon the cultivation of so many "subjects," imposed for the most part upon unwilling recipients, that even the better-ordered schools retain much of the factory character. A factory implies mechanism. Insisting, as he did, that no good thing can come out of a machine, least of all would Mr. Ruskin admit mechanical methods into education. We are not always aware how grave this particular danger is to a nation of our temperament. Our virtues as well as our vices favour it. Not only are we, as a nation, little amenable to the direct attraction of ideas of truth and beauty, but our very love of order, the source of our national strength, drives us to mechanism in education. Take an extreme and a peculiarly painful example.

56

JOHN RUSKIN.

Criminals are persons of disordered, abnormal minds, requiring for their judicious care and healing not less but more delicate individual consideration than persons of normal character. But how do we deal with these cases in our prisons which profess to be reformatory, *i. e.* educational establishments? We rigidly mechanise the entire life by fixed routine of times, places, occupations; having the care of men who have sinned against society we reconcile them to society by desocialising them; knowing by our most familiar proverb that " man is a social animal," we proceed to dehumanise him by removing all social support and sympathy. The most delicate organic operation, that of repairing bad or diseased character, we seek to compass by machine methods, so that the very virtue of our prison system, the absolute good order which prevails, constitutes its most damning indictment. This illustrates in one great public department the grave danger which besets all our education, the application of mechanical instead of organic treatment. If a school were a factory, and if the object really were to turn out large quantities of intellectual goods of certain common brands, the mechanical method would be the correct one. But we cannot hope to make " souls of a good quality " by such a method.

§ 4. With the mechanical utilitarian conception of education the moral and economic vice of competition is naturally allied. So long as you look to quantity of wares alone, with little regard to quality, and with liberty to adulterate as much as you can, keen competition is an excellent spur to production. Prize scholars warranted to put down on paper the correct formal answers to routine series of questions relating to prescribed areas of knowledge, can be produced better under a competitive system than in any other way; for acquisitiveness is thus best fed alike in pupil and schoolmaster. Mr. Ruskin's denunciation of com- ∠ petitive examination thus belongs to his general condemnation of mechanism in education.

Here Mr. Ruskin does yeoman service in a cause which all true educationalists have at heart. The barbarous method of goading boys and girls to knowledge by appealing to the lust of self-assertion, and by setting each one's head and heart against his fellow's in the pursuit of intellectual wealth, is even more base and more unnatural than the corresponding policy in material industry. The limitation of supply of the best materials of industrial wealth affords there a " natural " basis of antagonism, only to be overcome by the growth of social sentiment; whereas no such limits apply to intellectual wealth; one man in gaining knowledge need not make another lose, or by increasing his store reduce the store of another. It is only when the true ends of education, knowledge and self-development, are deliberately set aside, and some false end, pride of place, or some extraneous prize, is thrust forward, that the appeal of a competitive examination is made effective. But while thoughtful reformers are sensible of the folly and the immorality of corrupting the love of ideas in the young, in making learning a means to a narrow selfish end, there is some fear that this cause is injured by the undue preaching of counsels of perfection. There is this root-difficulty in all education, that the application of the ideally best motives presumes a more complete attainment of rationality in the learner than can *ex hypothesi* actually exist. Just as in the early physical training of a child, certain habits of necessary conduct must be authoritatively imposed, because the intelligence is too crude and unformed to understand their rationality ; so in intellectual education we cannot always trust to the inherent attractiveness of ideas to stir the sluggish energies of a young mind to move along an unexplored path. For this cause some alloy of coercion and of appeals to lower motives may temper the purely rational motive. The same general distinction which applies in industrial competition holds also here. Where competition acts as a spur to excellence of work, concentrating the thoughts upon the work in hand, and does not cause malicious brooding and contrivance to secure the failure of another, it occupies a legitimate place. The distinction is a sound and useful one, though the margin between use and abuse may be easily transgressed. Only as education actually attains its end of informing and enlightening the soul can this alloy of irrationality and selfishness be cast off, and the goodness of ideas be allowed freely to work upon us by their pure worthiness alone.

Mr. Ruskin is not, as sometimes is supposed, the undiscriminating enemy of competition. No one draws the just distinction more convincingly than he. " I want you to compete, not for the praise of what you know, but for the praise of what you become ; and to compete only in that great school where death is the examiner and God the judge." [1]

How far Mr. Ruskin was prepared to sanction

[1] The Eagle's Nest, § 212.

the further compromise enjoined by the imperfectly rational nature of all learners I cannot say. But in every field of endeavour such compromise is valid, and any refusal to practise it involves some waste of energy.

After all due allowances are made, the abuses of competition in our schools have been very grave, and Mr. Ruskin's outcry has been of the greatest service in stimulating revolt against this tyranny of commercialism over education.

§ 5. Another radical criticism of current education requires consideration. The mechanical and quantitative spirit not merely prevails in our school curricula and methods, in more subtle ways it enters and contaminates the best culture of our nation. In our choicest academic circles, everywhere where " culture " is most prized, the tendency to identify education with acquirements and accomplishments, and with the collection and satisfaction of many interests and curiosities about nature, men, and books, is clearly perceptible. Mr. Ruskin does not, indeed, follow Tolstoy in his reactionary condemnation of intellectualism, but he does distinctly and powerfully denounce the excessive valuation set upon intellectual attainments held as possessions and ornamental appendages of life.

" A man is not educated, in any sense whatsoever, because he can read Latin or write English, or can behave himself in a drawing-room ; but he is only educated if he is happy, busy, beneficent, and effective in the world. Millions of peasants are, therefore, at this moment better educated than most of those who call themselves gentlemen ; and the means taken to educate the lower classes in any other sense may very often be productive of a precisely opposite result." [1]

This passage may serve for a convenient bridge from Mr. Ruskin's critical to his constructive principles in education.

As in the fine arts, as in all industry, so in education, his teaching contains two spinal thoughts, — the rightful dominance of moral ideas in directing the formation of character, and the need of an accurate first-hand and vital study of the facts of nature and of human life.

These are not idle platitudes; on the contrary, they are implicitly denied and practically set aside in most schemes of education.

The common meaning given to the unqualified word "education" by all classes attests the undue weight of the intellectual side.   Physical, æsthetic, and moral claims are indeed making some way, but the tendency to treat them as separate and subordinate departments is still general, and shows the deep-rooted mechanism of our methods.   It is the lack of harmony or unity of thought which explains the excess which rude, ill-ordered physical exercises have attained in our aristocratic schools, and the slight perfunctory attention given to physical training in the schools for the poorer classes. The woful neglect to provide any food and direct training to the æsthetic tastes and the moral faculties, as an integral part of the education of children, furnishes, however, the most signal illustration of our national defect in the work of education.   This is due partly to a failure of philosophic grasp, partly to the fore-named spirit of commercialism, which naturally post-

[1] Stones of Venice, iii., Appendix vii.

pones and ignores such training as cannot be tested and justified by directly measurable results. The practical mind, which rules education through the public and the private purse, still adopts an attitude towards æsthetic and moral education which is fraught with deep injury. Æsthetic education is still relegated to a sphere of " accomplishments," desirable, perhaps, where time and money can be afforded to procure them, but luxuries in " education," while the crudest forms of moral training are given under the head of religious instruction.

The vital influences of education, according to Mr. Ruskin, are two, — Nature and Humanity ; the badness of our common education consists in ignoring or perverting these holy sources of power.

To make a child of Nature and a Human Being is the end of education.

§ 6. It is not " sentimentalism," but a deep sense of physical and moral truth, which impels Mr. Ruskin to insist upon a free outdoor life, amid pure and beautiful natural surroundings, as the first essential of education. All readers will remember the verses of Wordsworth, which he quotes in " Lilies," beginning :

> " Three years she grew in sun and shower,
> Then Nature said, ' A lovelier flower
> On earth was never sown.
> This child I to myself will take :
> She shall be mine, and I will make
> A lady of my own.' "

This free, friendly, constant intercourse with field and forest, stream and mountain, the flow of the seasons and the changes on the face of nature that they bring, are vital and essential needs of the education of healthy and happy childhood, and it is their denial which is the first great waste and injury to life done by our industrial life in cities. Mr. Ruskin sets aside the fatuous reply which tells us that country-bred people do not notice or love nature as well as town-bred people. In the first place it is false; in the second place it misunderstands the vital use of nature, which does not consist in sentimental seeking of beautiful effects of scenery, but in the free and hardly conscious sympathy with the life of nature which rises from familiar dwelling with her processes.

This education of nature is neither to be won by occasional emotional excursions nor by analytic study prompted by purely intellectual interest. Mr. Ruskin is often unduly contemptuous and suspicious of the genuine advance in education made by giving more attention to the natural sciences. To bring dead bits of nature into the schoolroom of a crowded city for dissection, in order to teach botany or biology, is a proceeding which rouses his animosity, and incites him to utter language about " science " which he has sometimes had occasion to regret. But while the advance of natural science in school teaching is a distinct gain, alike in scope of training and in actuality, upon the old monopoly of language and mathematics, it must be admitted that it does by no means serve the highest educational purpose of which nature is capable, and that Mr. Ruskin is fully justified in insisting that contact with " wild and fair nature " is essential to lay the just foundation of sane and wholesome emotions. Beauty of nature is needed first. " All education to beauty is, first, in the beauty of gentle faces round a child; secondly, in the fields." Even here there is a tendency of modern pedagogy to err. In his admirably sympathetic account of Mr. Ruskin's educational methods, Mr. Jolly seems to me to strike a somewhat false note in the stress he lays upon the use of outdoors as "an uncovered class-room." There is a distinct danger in the conscious strain to get direct educational value out of everything. Nature will not do for her children what Wordsworth claims, if she is regarded as "an outer uncovered class-room"[1] to be promenaded by a pedagogic showman with a pointer. The greatest uses of nature are unconscious, free, secret gifts which come, like every happiness, when they are not sought. All this is quite consistent with the intelligent and accurate study of natural objects and processes, and even with the discernment of the operation of scientific laws. It is only a question of stress, the amount of time given to receptivity, and a recognition of the uses of idleness, which Wordsworth himself so beautifully illustrated and justified, that "majestic indolence so dear to native man," the "broad margin to life" which another lover of nature craved.

Mr. Ruskin is surely right in demanding that our scientific interests shall not crowd out the unthinking sympathy, and that there is a danger here which requires recognition. It is above all the atmosphere of nature that we need to breathe with free unconscious drafts. In the field excursions and country rambles which more enlightened teachers are grafting on to school life, care should be taken that these unconscious influences of nature, the "vital feelings of delight"

[1] "Ruskin on Education," by W. Jolly, p. 42.

which come to the young from the everlasting youth
and beauty of natural processes, be the first consideration, and that the guidance of the intellectual curiosity
towards "laws" and causality of every sort shall be
secondary and incidental.   Field clubs and geological
excursions are excellent things, but so to feed the collecting appetite of a child that it approaches nature
chiefly as a quarry or a herbarium is to produce a peculiarly offensive sort of prig.   When the acquisitive spirit
has got so strong a hold over national life as it has in
England, there is a genuine risk of this perversion of
educational energy.

§ 7. For the cultivation of taste, the æsthetic sense,
Mr. Ruskin, therefore, rightly insists upon a fuller recognition of the passive and insensible influences shed
upon the soul by beautiful and stimulative material
surroundings.   This does not mean the absence of
human effort and design.   Not merely by going out
freely to nature will a child drink in ideas of beauty
which shall mould his form and character : the true
teacher's art will largely be engaged in making an art
atmosphere of the schoolroom, which shall give dignity
and interest to the more definite instruction of teachers
and books by its grace and suggestiveness.   Cheap furniture and bare walls are no proper features of a schoolroom.   The school demands "refined architectural
decoration," every form of "noble" luxury should be
there, everything which can by its presence inform the
eye and ear and stimulate the imagination and the intellect.   Modern psychology bears out Mr. Ruskin in the
emphasis it lays upon the sub-conscious factor, the
great accretion of impressions slowly gathered from

large general surroundings, which yet plays a vitally important part in determining thought and emotion : to leave the plastic mind of young children open to a base, ugly, or depressing environment is to inflict upon them an incalculable wrong which can never be properly repaid in later life.

Whatever is beautiful and interesting in nature and art should be in the schoolroom, so far as it can aid in this passive formative work, or lend support to more active education.

§ 8. For convenience in characterising Mr. Ruskin's educational views I spoke of Nature and Humanity as two founts of influence. But it is of course essential to his thought that the separation should never be retained. Nature as a source of influence must feed Humanity : education must give man's place in nature and enable him to hold that place.

When, therefore, the end of education is stated in a simple way, it must always be related to some ideal of humanity, whether abstractly as with Mr. Herbert Spencer, who says, " To prepare us for complete living is the function which education has to discharge," or more concretely in Mr. Ruskin's well-known formula, " You do not educate a man by telling him what he knew not, but by making him what he was not." But, while no one is likely to deny that the goal in education is formation of character, there is a danger to which the teacher by the very necessities of his work is peculiarly prone, the too individualistic conception of humanity. To many of our ablest and most intelligent teachers education is the training of perfect human beings, the ideal being represented as the harmonious development of the different parts of their nature as free isolated individuals. In order to comprehend rightly the sense in which "humanity" is the educational end, the place and work of the human being in society must be clearly understood. In the modern science and art of teaching, psychology, which almost necessarily confines itself to the study of the individual soul, is not adequately reinforced by sociology. The practice of teaching demands so constant an attention to the idiosyncrasies of the pupils as to lead teachers too much to confine themselves to considering what each child needs for his individual development, and to neglect the claims which society has and intends to exercise in after life. Yet, as no one lives for himself alone, the end of education cannot be regarded as the perfection of individuals as such. Not only industry but social life in general requires a certain sacrifice of free individual development, represented by a specialisation of certain powers and a comparative neglect of others. This, of course, is only a sacrifice, so long as we regard individuals as separate self-sufficient units, which they are not: the so-called sacrifice becomes a gain as soon as we recognise the social character of man, which requires that he be formed not merely with regard to his individual perfection, but with regard to the perfection of the social organism of which he is a part. This proper balance and adjustment of the claims of individual and of society in the human purposes of education, none of our great teachers has grasped so vitally as Mr. Ruskin, for none of them has quite so clear and powerful a vision of the true society.

§ 9. That education has been too purely intellectual in its aims, too mechanical in its methods, has been the

grave charge of our wisest censors. Matthew Arnold
laid his finger upon the kernel of error when he insisted
that our defect was lack of " humanity " in school teaching. Schools, however, are by no means entirely to
blame. Humanity, which has its roots in " sensations
that are just, measured, and continuous," cannot rely
upon school life alone. The home is the first and the
most potent sphere of human influence. England rather
prides herself upon home life, but yet when we faithfully
compare the actual possibilities of home for the mass of
our city-bred children with the human requirements, we
shall understand why savagery is so slowly rooted out
from our national habits. " This is the true nature of
home, — it is the place of peace ; the shelter not only
from all injury, but from all terror, doubt, and division.
In so far as it is not this, it is not home ; so far as the
anxieties of the outer life penetrate into it, and the in-
consistently-minded, unknown, unloved, or hostile society
of the outer world is allowed by either husband or wife
to cross the threshold, it ceases to be home; it is then
only a part of the outer world which you have roofed
over, and lighted fire in." [1] There are then grave dangers
to be guarded against in the home of " the upper or undistressed middle classes," whom Mr. Ruskin was here
particularly addressing. For the mass of our children
not merely the moral but the material basis of a true
home is still wofully defective. None know better than
our teachers in primary schools how intimately every
problem of education is linked with reforms of the economic structure of society. But while the daily events
of home life, the intimate dealings with friends and rela-

[1] Sesame and Lilies, § 68.

tions, the gradually expanding horizon of neighbourhood must ever be the most powerful and continuous educa‑ tion in humanity, the school, as Mr. Ruskin conceived it, can do much that it does not do, or do properly. So long as narrow considerations of economy and sectarian jealousy are allowed to cramp and pinch the financial resources and the moral freedom of our schools, so long will the taunt that they are factories for the production of cheap clerks, have point. When we have national sense and dignity enough to recognise what truly " pays," we shall insist upon the literal realisation of one of our most devoted modern pioneers of education, who demands " not a poor education for the children of the poor, but the best possible education for the children of the nation."

§ 10. Such an education requires not the bare bones of the three R's, with penurious allowances of facts in geography, history, hygiene, as its most liberal diet; but a far larger, nobler, more profitable " economy." At present every cheap piano or swimming-bath is grudg‑ ingly granted or more commonly refused, as a wanton luxury likely to pamper children and to waste time; every meagre school accessory in the shape of instru‑ ments and " objects " is regarded with suspicion by school authorities; every trivial step of liberality is won by a wasteful struggle. Even now almost every ele‑ ment which is distinctively human, and therefore useless in the Gradgrind sense, is rigidly banished from the schools of the people; and even in the public schools of the " classes," in spite of recent progress, it is subordi‑ nated to drill in language and mathematics. In how many of our schools is history made a really vital sub-

ject? What use is actually made of this infinite storehouse of human wisdom and morality? For the vast
majority of our children, history still means a painfully
acquired accumulation of dates and facts regarding
battles and dynasties, unanimated by the spirit which
cannot be produced for inspection and examination.
The greatest literature (for our purposes at any rate)
which the world has ever known lies either utterly
neglected as an instrument of human culture in our
schools and our universities, or else is insulted by being
made a subject for vain repetition or philological ped-
antry. It is not too much to say that local examinations have displayed an almost diabolical perversity of
ingenuity in slaying the love and perverting the understanding of Shakespeare in the minds of myriads of
English boys and girls of the middle classes.

It is Mr. Ruskin's perception and abhorrence of the
inhumanity of our school teaching which leads him to
that denunciation of the three R's for which he has been
so much criticised. He not only refused to teach the
three R's in his schools of St. George, but gave as his
reason for objecting to reading and writing that " there
are very few people in this world who get any good by
either." But such sensational protests must not be
taken literally, as representing his true convictions.
In his careful, detailed schemes he provides " a children's library, in which the scholars who *care* to read
may learn that art as deftly as they like by themselves,
helping each other without troubling the master." [1] So,
too, he would have taught other rudiments. His feigned
rejection of the three R's may be understood as a dra-

[1] Fors, Letter xcv. (iv. 470).

matic protest against the barbarous notion which has ele-
vated them into a national education, and which still
insists that the State has done its duty to its children in
providing this utterly inadequate equipment for the voy-
age of life.   There lurks a terrible prophetic significance
in the following wise words from his "Crown of Wild
Olive:"[1] "Education does not mean teaching people to
know what they do not know; it means teaching them
to behave as they do not behave. It is not teaching the
youth of England the shapes of letters and the tricks of
numbers, and then leaving them to turn their arithmetic
to roguery and their literature to lust."   There is only
too great reason to believe that the plague of gambling,
which is sapping the moral life of the working classes
to-day, and the twin evil of the monstrous consumption
of the lowest orders of sensational journalism, are the
natural and necessary results of a national education
which ends in teaching to read and to calculate the
odds, without even tempering these processes with
humanising elements.

§ 11. Let me set against our present schools the
school as Mr. Ruskin sees it. It must be the first and
most important of all public buildings, and must impress
the senses with a beauty and dignity of architecture. It
must be at once a library of best books, an art-gallery of
sound models, a museum of minerals and other natural
objects. Its walls must be hung with historical paintings, and not as now with maps and physiological diagrams, which should be kept for special purposes, and
not form part of the general character of the school.
Workshops are to be attached, always a carpenter's,

[1] § 144.

where possible a potter's shop. Everywhere a garden, playground, and cultivable land should surround the school, so that scholars could be employed in fine weather largely out-of-doors. Not only the three R's shall be reduced to an insignificant position, but grammar shall be altogether banished. Not that words are to be less studied than now, quite the contrary. Elocution and literature shall teach the just and powerful use of language. Almost utterly neglected now, these studies shall occupy foremost places, cultivating the twin powers of the tongue and the pen in the use of words. Instead of a barren, artificial, mechanical analysis of words, elocution and literature will teach their human uses. Such study will not be less exact because more humane. Readers of " Sesame " will remember the almost superhuman standard of exactitude he requires in reading and speech, the painful digging, crushing, and smelting he enjoins in order to get the full true meaning of good sentences, the necessity of cultivating " the habit of looking intensely at words, and assuring yourself of their meaning, syllable by syllable, — nay, letter by letter," the insistence that, in speaking, " a false accent or a mistaken syllable is enough, in the parliament of any civilised nation, to assign to a man a certain degree of inferior dignity for ever." [1] In such a school the essentials of physical and moral health will be taught to all as a matter of course. A " sound system of elementary music " is regarded as a necessity. Literature shall be used, not only for teaching language, but for the " story," as history, travels, romance, or fairy-tale. " In poetry, Chaucer, Spencer, and Scott, for

[1] Sesame and Lilies, § 15.

the upper classes, lighter ballad or fable for the lower.
. . . No merely didactic or descriptive books should be
permitted in the reading-room, but so far as they are
used at all, studied in the same way as grammars; and
Shakespeare, accessible always at play-time in the library
. . . should never be used as a school-book, nor even
formally or continuously read aloud. He is to be
known by thinking, not mouthing." [1] Drawing should
be taught to all, being essential for the accurate performance of most skilled manual work. Geometry,
astronomy, botany, zoology, will have their proper
place, and Mr. Ruskin has many bright thoughts about
teaching them. " And finally, to all children of whatever gift, grade, or age, the laws of Honour, the habit of
Truth, the Virtue of Humility, and the Happiness of
Love." [2]

Such would be common properties of all schools; the
elements which would enter into the education of every
child whose natural capacity fitted him to receive them.
Upon such foundations would be constructed the proper
specialisation which should recognise class, life-work,
and locality. This we have already touched upon in
relation to the ideal organisation of industry. The
detailed stress which he lays upon Moral Education
consists in an intense realisation of the practical uses
of education in enabling men and women to perform
effectively their duties towards themselves and their
neighbours. It is here that he breaks away from that
language too commonly adopted by educationalists, who
speak as if the drawing out of the faculties was an end
itself, as if the goal of education was the mere produc-

[1] Fors, Letter xcv. (iv. 470).   [2] Fors, Letter xciv. (iv. 447).

tion of a prize human being who should exist beautifully. To Mr. Ruskin the object of education is not to perfect the functions of the human being in order that they may be in sound condition, but with the strictly ulterior object that they may do their work well, and bring use and happiness to their owner and to others. It is this note which is significant in his elements of moral teaching. "Moral Education begins in making the creature to be educated, clean and obedient. This must be done thoroughly and at all cost, and with any kind of compulsion rendered necessary by the nature of the animal, be it dog, child, or man. Moral Education consists in making the creature practically serviceable to other creatures, according to the nature and extent of its own capacities; taking care that it be healthily developed in such service. Moral Education is summed when the creature has been made to do its work with delight and thoroughly." [1]

§ 12. Modern educationalists will recognise nothing new in these lines of reform except in the rich realism of detail which Mr. Ruskin's creative imagination wove around all his projects. Its significance is that it furnishes an independent corroboration of the rightness and utility of the teaching of great specialist reformers. But where Mr. Ruskin transcends the work of the specialist in educational reform, is in making such work an integral part of his wider social reform. In order properly to mark this connection I must crave particular attention for the two deepest and most distinctive notes of his educational theory. First is the need of manual training for all children, not merely as a part of whole-

---

[1] Fors Clavigera, quoted by Jolly, p. 117.

some physical exercise, but as a preparation for the useful manual labour which we have seen he requires from all in a rightly ordered society. But without waiting for a reconstructed society in which every one does his share of the necessary manual labour, there are powerful reasons for recognising manual instruction as an integral part of the education of all children. Educational reformers from Xenophon to Froebel have emphasised the natural union of " head and hand " as the first principle of education. Not merely is dexterity of hand and eye a useful accomplishment, while the foolish and immoral contempt which " gentility " affects for manual work is scotched in childhood; the direct intellectual gain is still more important. Children who draw their intellectual pabulum from books alone, and whose experience embodies no regular and systematic experience of the nature of matter in relation to human service, the qualities of useful substances, and the tools and modes of work by which these substances can be wrought into serviceable forms, grow up to manhood and womanhood and pass on through life with an utterly defective grip on the earth on which they live and the material environment of life. This is the supreme meaning of Mr. Ruskin's insistence upon direct free contact with Nature and the practice of manual work. Human life without these has no bottom; the gentlemen and ladies without this education may get a reflected knowledge through books and conversation; they may, as managers of businesses, politicians, philosophers, littérateurs, deal with the hard facts of work and life, but their treatment will be feeble and unsubstantial, because they have not the knowledge of the meaning of the words they use and of

the ideas these words represent, which contact with the
material facts alone can give. Take for example the
thinking and speaking of politicians and political economists regarding important issues of working life. How
can a member of Parliament know how a measure affecting land will actually affect the agricultural labourer,
if he does not know from personal experience what digging or mowing is, or how a prison should be ordered if
he does not know the sort of effect produced upon the
temper and the nerves by turning a crank or pulling a
cart? How can an economist theorise regarding "unskilled" labour when he does not know what driving
wagons or carrying sacks of grain means physically? I
do not suggest that no man must theorise on matters the
precise nature of which he has not experienced, but that,
if he is safely to theorise, he must have had direct experience of facts and feelings belonging to the same
order as those involved. What applies to politicians
and economists, who are directly engaged in determining, practically or theoretically, large and intricate issues
regarding human work upon matter, applies in various
degrees to all other persons who think, read, and speak
about workaday affairs. We have the loose habit of
supposing that every one knows what such words as
wood, iron, horses, ploughing, sawing, stoking, cotton-
factory, warehouse mean, and that the meaning of most
persons who use the words is the same. In fact, however, the difference of meaning is almost infinitely great
between such words as used by persons who have been
in familiar contact with the things and actions, and as
used by those who have only seen them casually, or perhaps even only read about them. The waste of intellec-

tual effort, often the positive injury, due to defective
realisation of the meaning of common words is seldom
rightly appreciated. Different gradations of reality, due
to different focuses, are the direct cause of the widest
and most unbridgeable differences of judgment. Mr.
Ruskin therefore wisely insists that the education of all
shall include direct contact with, and familiar experience of, representative facts and feelings belonging to
the various departments of material nature and human
work upon matter.

Not merely for use but for enjoyment is this necessary. What can the noblest poetry of nature, and the
finest pictures of natural scenery mean to the average
Cockney, who has of necessity but a shadowy and
fourth-hand impression of the images which are given?
Direct experience of nature, and of man's action upon
nature is a necessary food of the vivid imagination;
without it the greater part of language, thought, and
life is utterly deficient of reality. We speak of the
eloquent descriptive powers of a Ruskin, the superb
analogies of a Browning or an Emerson, as if they
were acrobatic feats of the creative imagination flying
in the void; no such thing! they are built upon and
are definitively and naturally linked with direct, close,
personal observation of, and experiment on, concrete
facts. The vital realisation of language necessary for
the safe and wise conduct of all intellectual processes
can only be got by laying this solid, physical foundation of experience. The release of the intellectual life
from direct and constant contact with the common
processes of the material world, both in early education, and in the false over-specialisation of later

years, is a source of incalculable damage to the nature
and worth of intellectual work itself.

§ 13. But if every man and woman must stand with
feet firmly planted upon the solid earth, their thoughts
must not be kept to earthy things. If it is hard
to solidify the pulpy intellectualism of the modern
school by imparting concrete experience of material
facts, it is still harder to obtain the subordination of
both learning and intellectual training to emotional
purposes, which is Mr. Ruskin's second great deside-
ratum. Education rooted in nature and manual work
must grow towards " habits of gentleness and justice."
The oft-quoted line of Wordsworth ever clearly points
for him the goal of education, " We live by admiration,
hope, and love." This is not a sentimental *façon de
parler*, but a literal sentiment of what he means, and
means with an intensity and worth only to be gauged as
we understand his capacity for admiring, hoping, and
loving. Education aims at giving value to life, and the
real value for individual or for nation is the value of its
finest quality. From this standpoint, physical education
is our duty to our bodies, in order that we may
have accuracy and delicacy of sensations wherewith to
build objects worthy of admiration and love. So intellectual education is no more to be regarded as existing
for its own sake than art for art's sake; we need to
know truths about nature and man, the best that has
been thought and said, in order to strengthen and
inform this life of the soul.

It is unreasonable to predict that all open-hearted and
free-minded educationalists will adopt the language of
Mr. Ruskin regarding the end of education, or will assign

the dominance which he sometimes assigns to moral
as distinguished from intellectual or æsthetic ends. The
appearance of this dominance of morals is sometimes
forced upon him by the necessities of habitual language
which, for certain conveniences, distinguishes the good
from the true and the beautiful. Wherever this distinction is assumed as valid, the logical priority is given
to " the good," as the goal alike of education and of
life. But this should not mislead us into supposing
that Mr. Ruskin really harboured any deep-rooted
Hebraism or specialised puritanism in conceiving the
nature of " the good " as realised in conduct. His
goodness of " behaviour " comprises not merely all that
is conveyed in morality, and is conceived as " duty," but
all that is excellent in the search for truth and beauty.
" All literature, art, and science are vain, and worse, if
they do not enable you to be glad, and glad justly." [1]
Such gladness is not even regarded as a natural adjunct,
something that is added unto us if we follow the path of
duty. It is an essential aspect of the end, " all education being directed to make yourselves and your children
capable of Honesty and capable of Delight." [2]

Alike in this conception of the starting-point of
education from Nature and manual work, and of the
goal, Mr. Ruskin's views are in close general accord
with the best thoughts of the scientific school of educational reformers. But though in respect for Nature
and for Humanity there is a growing willingness to
follow these right lines, when the old traditionary barriers can be broken down, it ought to be recognised that
the majority even of the most liberal educationalists fall

[1] Eagle's Nest, § 177.   [2] Time and Tide, § 61.

far short in one important regard. "Habits of gentleness and justice" is a phrase of which full meaning is only realised by a clear acceptance of the larger body of Mr. Ruskin's social teaching. This is the real reason why his views upon education must be studied as an essential part of his broad work as social reformer. Our duty towards our neighbour, contained in gentleness and justice, is a barren platitude so long as we ignore the searching analysis of ungentleness and injustice in the existing order of society; so long as we seek to detach educational reform from the wider and equally radical reforms of industrial and social structure, by which alone "habits of gentleness and justice" can be realised in the common life.

It is idle to think that infusing Sloÿd into the curriculum of schools, more out-door life, the teaching of hygiene, attention to music and elocution, and definite instruction in morals — excellent as all these things are in humanising education — will be able to bear true fruit of just and gentle manners, if we neglect the weightier matters of the law of justice and gentleness in the organisation of society for the commonwealth.

§ 14. So much for theory; but Mr. Ruskin was not only a theorist in education. His occupation of the Slade Professorship of Fine Arts at Oxford was one large liberal experiment in education, by which he sought at once to impress the true significance of Fine Art, and the obligations of a professor in a seat of learning.

As Mr. Cook has well remarked,[1] Mr. Ruskin illustrated with peculiar felicity the three functions of a

[1] "Studies in Ruskin," by E. T. Cook. p. 38.

University Professor, — Research, General Instruction, and Professional Teaching. Each department he strove to liberate from the perfunctory or mechanical character which has sterilised so much of the ripest scholarship and the profoundest intellect in our universities. With honest and accurate work he ever sought to associate freedom and delight, and while not infrequently scandalising the sober dignity of academic personages by the wayward humour of his habits and utterances, he did more, during the years of his residence,[1] to humanise and invigorate the atmosphere of university life than any other teacher of his age. Of his special labours of research in art history and criticism, and of the strictly professional teaching, I need say nothing here, except to remind readers that the characteristics of his theory were always present in his practice. He continually strove to keep the imagination of his hearers alive to facts by calling in the direct aid of the eye : illustration both by models, standard works of art, diagrams, and specimens of every kind was organically interwoven with exposition. So again the mind was ever kept alert and mobile by fanciful and unexpected devices, introduced by way of dramatic emphasis, or to carry the listener along the line of analogy to see some hidden law of art. Mr. Ruskin was contrasting the way in which modern French art looks at the sky with that in which Turner saw and drew " the pure traceries of the vault of morning." " See," he said, " what the French artistic imagination makes of it," and a drawing done by Mr. Macdonald from a French handbook was disclosed,

[1] First elected, 1870 ; re-elected, 1873 and 1876 ; resigned, 1879 ; re-appointed, 1883 ; resigned early in 1885.

showing the clouds grouped into the face of a mocking
and angry fiend. When the audience had had their
look and their laugh, Mr. Macdonald modestly pro-
ceeded to turn his sketch with its back to the wall
again. "No, no," interposed Mr. Ruskin, "keep it
there, and it shall permanently remain in your school,
as a type of the loathsome and lying spirit of defama-
tion which studies man only in the skeleton and nature
only in ashes." [1]

But always free and stimulating, Mr. Ruskin was
strict and even exacting in his demands upon pupils
who put themselves under his charge for professional
study. Art was a tender plant in the somewhat austere atmosphere of Oxford study, and the rigorous rules
imposed upon the Ruskin Drawing School chilled the
incipient zeal of the artistic undergraduate, and even
when the early rigour was relaxed, his school never
attained popularity in the University, though Oxford
ladies soon came to attend in fair numbers. Mr. Ruskin,
however, incurred much expenditure of labour and of
money in the carefully arranged collection of drawings
grouped for various educational purposes, which still
enrich the Drawing School at Oxford.

The double purpose of this collection, as indeed the
double purpose of all his teaching, was, first, to furnish
standards of criticism, models of the various schools and
styles of art, for reference in forming taste and judgment; secondly, to supply the serviceable tools for a
working School of Art in which pupils were learning
to produce. Nowhere is the thoroughness and detailed
originality of Mr. Ruskin's educational method so

---

[1] Studies in Ruskin, pp. 59, 60.

finely illustrated as in the equipment of this Drawing School.

His more exoteric teaching, the series of lectures given to the Oxford world, and later to the wider reading world, fulfilled a much larger and more directly important function. There was a deep inner propriety of time and place in the earnest prophetic voice which, from a professorial chair at Oxford, proclaimed a new and revolutionary doctrine of art, in protest at once against the engrossing commercialism of the outer world and the cold-hearted intellectualism which was stealing over the intellect of England in her chosen and ancient homes of learning. The very attitude of liberty he gave himself in the treatment of art savoured of revolution, and was so regarded by the mediocre respectability of the University. That a man told off to deal with a special field of culture should trespass freely over the fields of neighbouring professors, who were supposed to know and teach the desired truths in various sciences, histories, and literatures, was a terrible outrage of established order. This rough shaking of academic proprieties was not one of the least services Mr. Ruskin has rendered in his life. The shock was particularly needed, for one of the chief intellectual dangers of the age is a too precise specialism, which, by sharply marking out into carefully defined provinces the domain of learning, runs a constant risk of losing the wide standard of humanity, and cultivating triviality under the false name of thoroughness. Mr. Ruskin's discursiveness may, perhaps, have been over-emphasised, but it served as a wholesome and much needed protest. Moreover, he rightly felt that one of the most urgent needs in art education was a recognition of the place which Fine Art holds in the general education of life. The relation of Art to Literature, to Science, to Morals was, therefore, to him not merely a legitimate but the most vitally important theme ; and the great service of his Oxford teaching, alike for Art and for Humanity, consists in the persistent enforcement of this teaching.

His conviction of the deep importance of free personal intercourse between teacher and taught, so often dwelt upon in " Fors," was illustrated by his own example. Not a few of our most influential writers and artists came under the spell of his personality during these years, for Mr. Ruskin retained, like many great teachers, even amid the physical infirmity of increasing age, the charm and brilliancy of youth, the quality of direct and spontaneous sympathy with the needs and spirits of the young. Not merely in his own field of activity, wide as that was, did his influence appear ; no one was more eager for the honour and welfare of the University. At the same time, that certain spirit of reaction, which made him the relentless enemy of liberalism in every shape, haunted him also in Oxford, the most mediæval and conservative of places. It came under the guise of opposition to science. Mr. Ruskin, though of many sciences he had more than a smattering, was never fair to scientific men or to their methods. The rapid progress of the physical sciences frightened him, and he foresaw under the unchecked sway of the scientist a mechanical life of the mind corresponding to the mechanical rule of industry. His final severance from Oxford was a characteristic expression of this fear. A vain struggle against the establishment of a physiological laboratory, which represented to him the endowment of vivisection and the desecration at once of the sanctity of animal life and of true human purposes in science, obliged him to relinquish his attempt to humanise Oxford by means of art.

CHAPTER XI.

WOMAN'S PLACE AND EDUCATION.

§ 1. The essentially right life for woman. § 2. Woman's work within and without the home. § 3. Mr. Ruskin's temperamental bias in the intellectual subordination of women. § 4. Historical justification of the struggle for " rights " as a provisional not a final policy.

§ 1. To none of the doctrines and practices of modern " liberalism " was Mr. Ruskin more vehemently hostile than to those which find general expression in " the emancipation of woman." His resentment to all such movements was indeed so deep as rarely to find expression in his writings. What he has to say in direct criticism is condensed into a scathing brevity which never condescends to reason. In " Fors " he refers to " the enlightened notion among English young women, derived from Mr. J. Stuart Mill, — that the ' career ' of the Madonna is too limited a one, and that modern political economy can provide them . . . with ' much more lucrative occupations than that of nursing the baby.' " [1] " Arrows of the Chace " also contains a brief letter to a Swiss journal which contains the same uncompromising testimony : " Je ne puis trouver des termes assez forts pour exprimer la haine et le mépris que je ressens pour l'idée moderne qu'une femme doit cesser d'être mère, fille ou femme

[1] Fors, Letter 407 (i. xxiv).

pour qu'elle puisse devenir commis ou ingénieur." [1] Of women's suffrage he is far too contemptuous to discuss it. The position of woman was one of his most absolutely fixed principles through life, connected as it was with the central idea of home. A woman was to be primarily a useful, secondarily a beautiful, home-maker and home-keeper.

Occasionally Mr. Ruskin expresses himself in unqualified language, which seems to sanction the idea of drudgery or the narrow position of an average *haus-frau* in the middle classes of society to-day. For instance, he declares that " the essentially right life for all womankind is that of the Swiss paysanne." [2] But then he partly idealised that life, as he saw it through the glasses of the Swiss novelist Gotthelf, or as brightened by romantic memory, and partly he designed to offer a dramatic protest against the notion of frivolity and uselessness which he saw to inhere in the English idea of " ladyhood." He did not really mean that all women were to be farmers' wives like the heroine of " Ulric the Farm Servant," but that they were all to undertake useful service in the performance or the superintendence of manual labour connected with the life of the home. It is because agriculture is to him the basic industry that the life of the farmhouse is the type of " the essentially right life for all womankind." The testimony of all history to the abuse of male physical power, in imposing an almost intolerable burden of servile drudgery upon the " paysanne," is simply ignored by Mr. Ruskin, who, in his idyllic picture of true agricultural life, assumes relations of affection and comradeship which would give

---

[1] Vol. ii. 224.   [2] Fors, Letter xciv. (iv. 455).

happiness to any home. While the farmer looks after the cattle and the crops, and superintends the outdoor labour in the fields, his wife manages the dairy and the fowl-yard, and concerns herself with the housework and the food supply. Here is a division or co-operation of labour imposed by nature and convenience : no trouble-some question arises of what is a man's, what a woman's work, or of competition between the two. The direct ordering of the home and of the industries which gather closely around the home is woman's work in every well-appointed peasant life.

§ 2. To all other kinds of life the same general rule applies. " Lilies " is written for the women of the well-to-do classes ; but, while it does not suppose a farm life, it applies the same principles of life. Manual work will not there absorb so much attention ; the graces and re-finements of life hold larger place, and demand a higher intellectual and emotional education. But the same central idea is present, woman as the Angel of the House, responsible for the making of the home, con-cerned with the arts of consumption rather than with the arts of production. As in the primitive society man goes out to the chase and to the fight, while woman tends the hut and the peaceful industries of growing and grinding corn, making clothes, etc. ; so in the more complex civilisation of to-day, the more arduous and ad-venturous work of body or of mind, outside the house, is by nature and by moral considerations of utility reserved for men. Mr. Ruskin utterly disapproves of women go-ing out into the arena of industrial or professional com-petition, struggling with men or among themselves for wages, profits, and fees. He does not discuss the ques-

tion whether women can or cannot do good work and
" hold their own " in fair competition of the trades or
professions, but he deprecates the preference of such
success to the higher success attainable in the arts of
home, and the reaction such entering of the competitive
life will exert upon the character of women. That
motherhood and the related duties of the home, which
nature has reserved for women, can either be repudiated
or treated as a secondary consideration is, in Mr. Ruskin's eyes, the most pernicious doctrine which can be
preached to women. It not only ignores the true laws
of economy of effort, by belittling the importance and
difficulties of the home arts, but, more fatal still, it mis-
interprets the differences of sex character which dominate the issue. " The man's power is active, progressive,
defensive. He is eminently the doer, the creator, the
discoverer, the defender. His intellect is for speculation and invention; his energy for adventure, for war,
and for conquest, wherever war is just, wherever conquest necessary. But the woman's power is for rule,
not for battle, and her intellect is not for invention or
creation, but for sweet ordering, arrangement, and decision." [1] Within the sacred circle of the home, guarded
against the coarseness, the selfishness, and cruelty of the
outside life, woman is to queen it, as " the centre of
order, the balm of distress, and the mirror of beauty."
There is a certain poetic vagueness, a certain lack of
substance and actuality in the eloquent description of
woman's place in " Lilies," and the simple answer given
to a correspondent through " Fors " is more directly
instructive. " Woman's work is: I. To please people.

[1] Sesame and Lilies, § 67.

II. To feed them in dainty ways. III. To clothe them.
IV. To keep them orderly. V. To teach them." [1] Here,
in further explanation, it is suggested that "young
ladies" shall practise plain cooking, dressmaking (a sew-
ing-machine is here sanctioned!), ironing, etc., a little
housemaid's work, spare minutes of gardening (have
nothing to do with hothouses!), and reading books that
are owned, not borrowed. This furnishes a solid material basis of work, upon which the more refined arts and
graces required to enable her " to sympathise in her
husband's pleasures, and in those of his best friends,"
may be engrafted. The public function accorded to her
is not the franchise or the sitting on elected bodies, but
the overflow of charity beyond the limits of the home,
the personal offices of affection and care bestowed upon
neighbours.

§ 3. The whole trend of woman's education is
designed to conform to this conception of her place
and power. But the eloquent passages of " Lilies "
which sketch this education betray a certain temperamental basis, which justifies critics in affirming that Mr.
Ruskin preaches the subordination of women. In the
division of functions to accord with natural powers
and social convenience, there is nothing to warrant the
ascription of superior value to one sex or the other;
indeed, no basis of comparison is possible. We can
only say that the two kinds of work are equally essential to the organic life of a family and a society; the
work of ordering the home and the arts of home consumption are just as skilled, just as serviceable, as the
work in which man is to engage. It is only when we

---

[1] Fors, Letter xlvi. (ii. 444).

come to consider the intellectual life, and the education
for it, that Mr. Ruskin offends the sense of equality by
a subordination of the woman to the man.   The useful
and necessary distinction between thought and feeling is
driven to a dangerous falsehood of extremes when we are
told that woman is not " to think for herself," but that
man is to be the thinker: the influence of moral goodness and wisdom accorded to her as her supreme gift
cannot compensate for this denial of the rights of intellect.   To say that excessive devotion to the intellectual
struggle for truth, as to the industrial struggle for
wealth, may be more injurious to a nature not made
for combat than it is to man's nature, follows consistently from the different characters accorded by Mr.
Ruskin to the sexes.   But to deny freedom of thought
to women, to insist upon making their cultivation of the
understanding only a means to the exercise of sympathy,
is a sin against their individuality.   A man may pursue
knowledge for itself as a part of the perfection of his
nature, as well as for the social services it enables him
to perform.   Not so a woman. " All such knowledge
should be given her as may enable her to understand,
and even to aid the work of men; and yet it should
be given, not as knowledge, not as if it were or could be
an object for her to know, but only to feel and to
judge." [1]   Now it is possible for Mr. Ruskin to maintain that knowledge shall not be described as an end in
itself, any more than art; but to make the knowledge of
a woman subordinate, not to her own wider conduct
of life, but to the work of a man, is to impose intellectual serfdom.   Without impugning Mr. Ruskin's con-

[1] Lilies, § 72.

ception of the place of woman in the home, I find it impossible to accept his statement that "it is of no moment to her own worth or dignity that she should be acquainted with this science or that." What is demanded is surely not that subordination of intellectual life which consciously estimates learning either by the food it offers to the emotions in general, or by its special service in enabling a wife to sympathise with her husband's thoughts, but that organic co-operation of intellectual and emotional life which makes a rich and roundly formed individuality in a woman as in a man. If, as Mr. Ruskin assumes, woman's special influence lies through the emotions, the education of these faculties must have more importance accorded to them; but that does not warrant us in impairing the good cultivation of those intellectual powers which are required to co-operate with the emotions in every act of judgment, by consciously regarding knowledge as a means. The intellectual life, so far as it is cultivated, must be cultivated as directly contributory to the worth of womanhood. Otherwise woman cannot exercise wisely and effectively that controlling influence in the family which Mr. Ruskin would accord to her. Apart from this intellectual subjection of women, his general scheme of education, rooted in physical freedom and joy, and feeding the imagination and the sympathies with all that is best and most beautiful in nature, in art, and literature, is rich in suggestiveness and in liberality of treatment. It may even be admitted that his precept, that while women may learn everything which men learn they must learn them differently, flows consistently from his premises. There is a subtlety of wisdom, drawn from

personal experiences, in his express prohibition of
theology, as fraught with peculiar danger to women,
in view of a natural tendency to " complacently and
pridefully bind up whatever vice or folly there is in them,
whatever arrogance, petulance, or blind incomprehen-
siveness, into one bitter bundle of consecrated myrrh." [1]

§ 4. Mr. Ruskin's views regarding women must not
be set aside lightly as " old-fashioned." The oldness of
the fashion was indeed to him a powerful testimony to
their natural rightness. But neither here nor on any
other matter was he a thoughtless conservative. The
position he assigns to women fits in his organic conception of society as truly as the social and industrial grades
which he desiderates. It belongs to the perpetual and
soulful protest against the liberating and the levelling
tendencies of thought and practice, based upon a shallow
philosophy of natural rights, which found in the equal
self-assertion of all individuals the basis of a well-har-
monised mechanical society. " Let women fight it out
with men in a fair field and no favour " is a logical im-
plication of the *laissez faire* philosophy. Those who
regard society as an elaborate mechanical structure,
built upon individual rights, naturally take this view,
and consider society will be best served by competition
of the sexes. Those who, like Mr. Ruskin, regard
society as an organic, not a mechanical, unity, insist
that a free fight between the separate molecules will not
produce that unity, but that, on the contrary, the organic
nature imposes, with all the weight of central authority,
a serviceable division of labour and life upon the parts.

How comes it, then, that so many professed Socialists

[1] Sesame and Lilies, § 73.

are staunch advocates of the " rights of women," as one
of the main factors in the movement of social progress ?
It is not difficult to answer this question. It arises
from an important fact of modern life which Mr. Ruskin and the Comtists, who take the same general lines
upon " the woman question," conveniently ignore. The
" emancipation of women " is a just provisional arrangement. If economic justice had been won, or were in
speedy course of being won, and an ideal society were
visibly rising, in which there would be a settled place
for every man and woman, with secure livelihood, as a
member of a working family, the struggle for the rights
of women might be as foolish and injurious a thing as
Mr. Ruskin and Auguste Comte maintained it was. But,
with the slow change of human heart and human actions,
we are confronted not merely with the necessity of working towards ideals of society, but with the need of pallia-
tives for terrible existing evils. Now the oppression of
the individuality of women by man-laid laws and customs,
created and supported by brutal force, is everywhere a
corrupting influence in wholesome family life. Women
have not that place and power which Mr. Ruskin finds
for them in the idealised Swiss peasant life, or in the
cultured and comfortable class life of " Sesame and
Lilies," and because they have it not, they cannot exercise those educative and ennobling influences upon the
young to which Mr. Ruskin, like all true reformers,
looks as the *primum mobile* of efficient social progress.
Moreover, the very economic conditions, against which
Mr. Ruskin wages war, present a flat contradiction to
the assumption that every woman is made for motherhood and the guardianship of a home. It is the large

proportion of women who, in a monogamic society, are superfluous for motherhood, and whom the present industrial conditions drive to the necessity of seeking a livelihood in competitive industry, whose cause stands in the forefront of the battle for liberty and rights of equal competition. Under present circumstances, this battle for liberty is true progress, and not the retrogressive policy which it would be in the face of a speedy realisation of an ideal new order. The stress upon liberty and rights is not essentially an evil thing. Old tyrannies must be crushed, old wrongs undone; this destructive policy is historically sound, and is both necessary to and continuous with the growth of a new organic process of construction. The revolutionary movement of the eighteenth century was not wrong in taking liberty and equality for its watchwords: the breaking down of the old trade restrictions, the law of settlement and the various chains which fettered the free action of capitalist and labourer in commerce, the destruction of ancient and obsolete privileges and authority in politics, — these things were necessary to the shaping of those new ideas and that new order which Mr. Ruskin strove to forward. But in this movement of liberty men had taken too narrow a basis of action; this is why the liberation of women has lingered so far behind, that it seems to Mr. Ruskin, and to not a few others, the injurious survival of an obsolete view of life. This is not the case. The negative freedom, even the freedom to vote and to compete which women seek, they rightly seek in the just order of historical development; it is their belated share of eighteenth century progress. Such freedom is only injurious where it is

interpreted as a sufficient end: where no such finality
is read into it, and it is regarded as a means of education and activity, needed to enable women to bear their
proper part in the evolution of a sound industrial society,
it is seen to lie along the right road of progress. Mr.
Ruskin set his eyes so earnestly upon a distant ideal
that he refused to make the true allowance for historical
processes. If the just spiritual relation of the sexes
which he craves existed now, and the family, at any
rate, was founded in affection and cheerful co-operation,
the movements which Mr. Ruskin deplores would rightly
be deplorable; but in the actual relations of women to
society, even the unsexing which he deprecates, with all
the self-assertion and the hardening which it brings, is
necessitated alike by the wrongs of the present and the
hopes and needs of the future. If some of the bellig-
erent advocates of women's rights regard emancipation
as an end, and competition of the sexes for all trades
and professions as a permanent and desirable factor in
social order, it is only because the dust and perturbation
of the present struggle has blinded them, as it blinded
many of the keenest thinkers and the bravest fighters
for male liberty in the last generation.

CHAPTER XII.

§ 1. As in education so in other matters Mr. Ruskin
was eager to practise what he preached. But in practice he drew a just distinction between what is ultimately desirable, and what is now practically serviceable.
Though he understood quite well that justice is unattain-
able in modern commercial transactions, he did not, as
a few have done, determine to have nothing to do with
buying and selling, and " to come out of the whole
affair." Here he was a teacher, drawing professional
salaries, a maker and seller of books, a specialist
buyer of pictures and other art treasures, as well as
a purchaser and consumer of general commodities.
What did common sense, enlightened by honesty, require of him? Certainly not to give up buying pictures and selling books, for these were among his most
serviceable functions to society. In his later years, at
any rate, having given away, or put to other social
use, his paternal inheritance, he could not fulfil his art

296

mission otherwise than by selling books. Mr. Ruskin
was no believer in an ascetic doctrine of self-renunciation, but in a life of honest and delightful self-expression
attainable for all. Had he refused to sell his books and
teaching, he would in no sense have illustrated his sane
theory of life. He was no disbeliever in commerce and
exchange. What he sought to do was to deal fairly
with others, as bookseller, as owner of houses and other
property, and as buyer of goods and services. His
method of buying he explains in the beginning of " Unto
this Last," as illustrated in the case of domestic service.
He did not make labourers compete against one another
so as to get his labour at the lowest market price, but
fixed what he regarded as a reasonable wage, such wage
as would enable the worker to do his work in comfort
and with good-will towards his master, and chose the
best labour available at this price. This was the theory
of sound wages, which he preached and practised, not
only in the treatment of domestic servants and other
workers whom he employed directly, but in the indirect
processes of buying commodities, by which also he
exercised power over men. If a picture was offered
him at a price he considered fair, and he had the means
to buy it, he paid the price ; if he made an offer, it was
not the lowest offer which he thought might be accepted,
but one which he thought to represent the present value:
bargaining he utterly eschewed. It may be forcibly
urged that, when one abandons the arbitrament of the
market, no true standard of " fairness " in price or wages
remains. This criticism is strictly valid, and yet it does
not prevent us from tempering the harshness of market
competition in particular cases, and in applying a rough

personal standard of justice. The appointment of most highly skilled officials, as we have seen, implies the legitimacy of such a standard, and the claim of Mr. Ruskin that it should be substituted everywhere for unchecked competition is one which he sought to enforce in all his private dealings.

§ 2. He fully recognised that this was a very rough approximation to justice, but it was all that the time and conditions render possible to the individual who cannot, however much he strive, " come out of the whole affair." In conformity with this true principle of compromise, Mr. Ruskin, even after he recognised the economic and moral wrong of rent and interest, took his rents and defended the action. His present obligation was to be a good landlord, and for this purpose, in 1864, he enlisted the help of Miss Octavia Hill, who helped him to attempt improvements in working-class dwellings on his property in Marylebone and other parts of London. Later on he sold to Miss Hill his London property. The proceeds of the sale, several thousand pounds, seem to have gone the way of nearly all the means he had inherited. It was no theory of his, as we have seen, that he should give away all the money which he had not earned. Yet, in fact, that seems to have been done, and even more. If we take account of the various large sums expended upon philanthropic and educational schemes, we shall find that the great bulk of his inherited property and his earnings went in these ways. A full and interesting account of the larger items of this expenditure is given in Letter lxxvi. of " Fors," from which it appears that of the fortune of £157,000, with certain houses and lands besides, which formed his inheritance, almost the whole of the money had been expended by 1877, while plans were already formed disposing in advance of considerable further sums derivable from the remaining property and current earnings. It is, indeed, impossible to allocate, out of the free but by no means lavish expenditure of a directly personal kind, which Mr. Ruskin admits, the proportion which is really and finally spent upon himself; for travel and art purchases, which expressed his most expensive tastes, were yet capital in the fuller and more liberal sense. The common phrase, " There were no limits to his generosity," was literally true of Mr. Ruskin ; no man of means ever treated his money more in the spirit of a public trust, and none ever administered that trust more wisely. To some who have followed closely his modes of outlay this latter statement may seem dubious, but Mr. Ruskin rightly understood that many of his schemes were risky experiments, and he also understood that even an experiment which fails may be a wise expenditure of money and effort.

§ 3. Before describing the largest of these experiments, it will be well to illustrate Mr. Ruskin's commercial dealings by brief reference to his conduct as bookseller. For the greater part of his literary life he held full control over the making and selling of his books, and imposed conditions both on their production and their sale which were in strict conformity with his conceptions of honesty and industry. To put a thoroughly sound article into the hands of those who wanted it for use at a reasonable price, without imposing injurious physical or moral conditions upon the labourers employed, and without employing advertise-

ments, or middlemen, or any of the arts of competition
and self-recommendation commonly in vogue, such was
the problem.   To meet these requirements, it was essential to trust no process to ordinary commerce.   The
earlier books were indeed published in the usual method,
chiefly by Messrs. Smith & Elder, but in 1872 Mr.
Ruskin began the experiment with Mr. George Allen
which was destined to have such important and lasting
results.   He had long kicked against the abatement and
discount system practised by publishers and booksellers,
and engaged Mr. Allen to sell " Fors Clavigera," which
was first printed by Messrs. Smith & Elder.   Mr. Allen
was then adopted as joint publisher with Messrs. Smith
& Elder for the Revised Series of Mr. Ruskin's works,
and after 1873 the entire publishing was placed in his
hands.   Mr. Allen, an engraver by trade, was himself a
pupil of Mr. Ruskin, and close personal relations have
always subsisted between them, Mr. Ruskin, especially
in the earlier years of the experiment, taking an active
part in the direction of the business.   The first thing to
secure was sound material and wholesome skilled processes.   Hand-made paper was often used, and in all
cases special attention was given both to paper and to
type.   To the preparation and printing of the plates the
most extraordinary care was habitually devoted to secure
thorough and honest work.   The printing itself was
done by Messrs. Hazell, Watson, & Viney at Aylesbury,
where every regard was paid to the health and comfort
of the workers, as well as to the excellence of the work
done.   But the most interesting experiment, both in its
industrial and its financial aspects, was the publishing
business, conducted for so many years by Messrs. Allen

at the little country village of Orpington, in Kent. There, in the back garden of Mr. Allen's private house, stood the warehouse, which contained the stock of Mr. Ruskin's books. For many years all these books were supplied to readers direct from Orpington without the interposition of any retail bookseller's profits. In other words, a private reader could get his single volume from Messrs. Allen upon the same terms as were given to a large retailer who took dozens. Mr. Ruskin was strongly opposed to all unacknowledged profits, and to the differences of real and nominal prices brought about by competition. A known, fixed, fair price for a sound and tasteful book was the principle from which he never willingly departed. At Orpington, not only the publishing in retail was accomplished, but much skilled work of engraving. Since no credit beyond the barest necessary limit was allowed and his prices were high, the success of this novel business was extraordinary. For a long time the powerful objection which Mr. Ruskin entertained for cheap literature, and the costly methods of production required by his æsthetic and economic principles, were a real grievance against him in the eyes of the larger public. In the case of " Fors," a work destined for all sorts and conditions of men lying far outside the range of his art public, the influence of Mr. Ruskin must have been greatly impaired by his refusal to use advertisement and retail booksellers. How many working men would be likely to forward at irregular intervals their 7d. or 10d. — the price was raised after 1874 — to an unknown person in a Kentish village in order to buy a pamphlet with an obscure Latin title, though it was designed particularly for their benefit?

Nothing, it may be said, except the rich inherent merits of the books would have enabled them to make their way, neglecting not merely all the more pushful modes of competition, but even the legitimate publicity of the retail counter. Not until, relenting in his later years, and recognising that considerable cheapness of production was now consistent with sound work, he came to sanction the cheaper editions of his books which, beginning with " Sesame and Lilies," have at length embraced most of his important works, did the influence of Mr. Ruskin's revolutionary teaching begin to tell upon the larger thinking public. So long as the ordinary volumes cost 13s. unbound, and the illustrated ones 22s. 6d., it was impossible that their ownership should transcend the " upper and the undistressed middle classes." The more recent arrangements of publication, while abiding by Mr. Ruskin's principles in the main, have departed in some important particulars. The removal to London of Messrs. Allen's publishing house, the allowance of a fixed discount to the trade, the use of ordinary methods of advertisement, have doubtless enhanced enormously the sale of Mr. Ruskin's books. How far Mr. Ruskin is thoroughly reconciled to these departures from his more primitive methods we cannot say, but the new arrangement entered in 1886 with his publisher, whereby the latter sells his works for proportionate profits, doubtless implied a larger liberty to adopt ordinary business methods.

§ 4. The largest of Mr. Ruskin's practical schemes of reform consists in the work of the St. George's Company, or Guild, as it was commonly called after 1877. This work is intimately connected with " Fors

Clavigera," which had as one of its chief direct aims its establishment. In the first letter of "Fors" he lays stress upon the need of clearing himself from all sense of responsibility by forwarding a practical proposal to deal with the material distress around him, and in the fifth letter he gives a brief but well-defined account of the scheme he had in mind. For many years he had been preaching two great economic and moral truths, " that food can only be got out of the ground, and happiness only out of honesty," and he was anxious to demonstrate the feasibility of an experiment upon these lines. The fundamental position of agriculture as the basis of national life impressed him with ever greater force precisely because the spirit of the age was against it, and was driving the agricultural population from a healthy and useful life upon their native soil into the noxious atmosphere of the large industrial towns, to engage in a wild, wasteful, and selfish struggle for existence. The work of St. George's Company was first designed as a practical protest against this demoralising tendency. To raise a fund in order to buy some land which should be cultivated by manual labour, with as little (water-driven) machinery as possible, worked thoroughly so as to bear the fullest increase, the labourers to be paid fixed and sufficient wages, to live in cottages of their own, with sound education for their children upon Ruskinian lines, and every opportunity of wholesome recreation for themselves, was the scheme as it took early shape. The fund itself was to serve the purpose of a noble charity, an act of higher justice by which persons of means might contribute a tithe of their annual income to the salva-

tion of society. As " Fors " advanced, so the practical
scheme took wider character; idle hands were to be
set upon reclaiming barren soil, townfolk were to be
invited to return " back to the soil," young couples of
the higher classes, who were willing to accept a rough
life, were to be welcomed. There was to be a skilled
overseer appointed by the Trust, the tenants were to
build houses for themselves under certain restrictions,
and were to own the full produce of the land, except
the tithe which they should pay to the Guild fund. By
1874 a considerable industrial side was added to the
proposed experiment, an artisan class was to be appended, carpenters and smiths, etc., so that the society
should be as far as possible completely self-sufficing for
all ordinary purposes. As the plan matured in his
mind and in the pages of " Fors," it became more
ambitious until it grew into a pattern of the elaborate
ideal society described in " Time and Tide," with a
master and marshals under him, and under them the
resident landlords, who should control districts, and be
responsible for the tenantry, tradesmen, and labourers. [1]
Thus was the work of the Company of St. George from
a small beginning upon a few acres of land expanded
into a copy of the New Feudalism.

The Company itself existed primarily to " float " and
" finance " this scheme; it was not expected that the
Companions should be tenants or workers under the
scheme; advice, good-will, and a tithe were to be their
contribution.

But as the idea took fuller shape in Mr. Ruskin's
mind, the Company itself, as a spiritual brotherhood

[1] Fors, Letter lviii.

of persons determined to live an honest life and serve their fellows, grew into a powerful interest, and its rules and constitution were carefully thought out. The solemn declaration which a Companion of the Guild was called upon to sign is an important document, in that it contains in bold relief the leading essentials of the art of a true and honest life, as Mr. Ruskin conceived them, thus defining the spiritual forces upon which he relied for social deliverance.

The " statement of creed and resolution " runs as follows : [1]

" I. I trust in the living God, Father Almighty, Maker of heaven and earth, and of all things and creatures, visible and invisible.

" I trust in the kindness of His law, and the goodness of His work.

" And I will strive to love Him, and keep His law, and see His work while I live.

" II. I trust in the nobleness of human nature, in the majesty of its faculties, the fullness of its mercy, and the joy of its love.

" And I will strive to love my neighbour as myself, and, even when I cannot, will act as if I did.

" III. I will labour, with such strength and opportunity as God gives me, for my own daily bread ; and all that my hand finds to do, I will do with all my might.

" IV. I will not deceive, or cause to be deceived, any human being for my gain or pleasure ; nor hurt, or cause to be hurt, any human being for my gain or pleasure ; nor rob, or cause to be robbed, any human being for my gain or pleasure.

[1] Letter lviii.

" V. I will not kill or hurt any living creature need-
lessly, nor destroy any beautiful thing ; but will strive
to save and comfort all gentle life, and guard and
perfect all natural beauty, upon the earth.

" VI. I will strive to raise my own body and soul
daily into all the higher powers of duty and happiness ;
not in rivalship or contention with others, but for the
help, delight, and honour of others, and for the joy and
peace of my own life.

" VII. I will obey all the laws of my country faithfully, and the orders of its monarch, and of any persons
appointed to be in authority under its monarch, so far as
such laws or commands are consistent with what I suppose to be the law of God ; and when they are not, or
seem in anywise to need change, I will oppose them
loyally and deliberately, not with malicious, concealed
or disorderly violence.

" VIII. And with the same faithfulness, and under
the limits of the same obedience, which I render to the
laws of my country, and the commands of its rulers, I
will obey the laws of the Society, called of St. George,
into which I am this day received ; and the orders of its
masters, and of all persons appointed to be in authority
under its masters, so long as I remain a Companion,
called of St. George." [1]

§ 5. " Fors Clavigera " enables us to follow the course

---

[1] It is interesting to compare this Confession of Faith with that
of Mazzini set forth in his " Faith and the Future " (Essays of
Mazzini, edited by Bolton King [Dent & Co.], pp. 74–77), where the
same trust in God and Humanity is realised in a fuller and more
scientific conception of human progress with less reference to
purely personal conduct, and with more dependence upon
organised political and other social activity.

of the early history of St. George's Company, especially upon its financial side, with considerable minuteness. This history is at once interesting testimony to the pertinacity of Mr. Ruskin and to the extreme reluctance of the not inconsiderable number of professing followers and admirers to translate their following and their admiration into terms of cash in aid of this great social experiment. Mr. Ruskin, himself, lost no time in seeking to establish financial confidence by providing for the payment of his tithe, though he bargained at the outset that some £5,000, out of the £14,000 represented by the tithe, should be devoted to a related scheme for establishing a Mastership for Drawing at Oxford. The sum thus earmarked for St. George's Company in July, 1871, was no less than £10,000,[1] though for certain good reasons the amount actually paid from this source seems to have amounted to £7,000.[2] Sir Thomas Dyke Acland and the Right Hon. W. Cowper Temple were appointed the first trustees of the fund, though not identified with the approval or execution of the schemes involved. But the "generous public" hung back, and in May of the next year Mr. Ruskin complains somewhat mournfully of the lack of volunteers in his St. George's war. "Not a human creature, except a personal friend or two, for mere love of me, has answered,"[3] though next month he records the receipt of £30, "the first money sent me by a stranger."[4]

After three years "begging for money" he had

---

[1] Fors, Letter viii. (i. 156).
[2] Fors, Letter xii. (i. 228.) £2,000 extra were apparently expended on series of drawings for the Oxford School (Fors, iii. 2).
[3] Fors, Letter xvii. (i. 332.)   [4] Fors, Letter xix. (i. 382).

obtained " upwards of two hundred pounds," and makes
the characteristic observation, " Had I been a swindler
the British public would delightfully have given me two
hundred thousand pounds instead of two hundred, of
which I might have returned them, by this time, say,
the quarter in dividends; spent a hundred and fifty
thousand pleasantly, myself, at the rate of fifty thousand
a year; and announced, in this month's report, with
regret, the failure of my project, owing to the unprec-
edented state of commercial affairs induced by strikes,
unions, and other illegitimate combinations among the
workmen." [1]

The account he presents of the total receipts of subscriptions during four years up to the close of 1874
includes a total sum of £370, 7s., contributed by twenty-
four persons mostly in the form of gifts, only seven persons having enrolled themselves as annual subscribers. [2]
The total funds then stood at £7,000 in stocks and £923
in the bank account, practically the whole of which was
contributed by Mr. Ruskin himself. Under these circumstances he did not hasten his experiment; he had
no intention whatever of sinking his capital in a large
purchase of land for founding a communist colony, as
not a few of his readers seemed to imagine. He wished
for the present to utilise only the interest upon the
funds for current expenses, until he should have obtained
more money and more helpers. Not until late in 1875
did the Company take action, and then upon a very
humble scale. A private friend, Mrs. Talbot, had presented three acres of rock and moor at Barmouth, with
eight rickety cottages which swallowed up their rents in

[1] Fors, Letter xxxvi. (ii. 261).   [2] Fors, Letter xlviii. (ii. 497).

repairs, hardly a hopeful cradle of agricultural reform. Nothing seems to have come of this, but in 1877 a somewhat more ambitious scheme was set on foot. At the suggestion of Mr. Swan, a former pupil at the Working Man's College, and at this time curate of the museum at Sheffield, Mr. Ruskin met a little circle of professed communists at Sheffield, and, though they remained outside the Guild, he was persuaded to assist them to try the experiment of a community. For this purpose the Guild purchased a farm of some fourteen acres of land named Abbeydale, at Dore, just outside Sheffield, for a price of £2,287, with an arrangement that the communists should pay back the money, without interest, in instalments, within seven years, at the expiration of which period they should be owners of the land.

From the very beginning the experiment seems to have been a failure, as, indeed, might have been predicted. No notion is more fatuous than the quite common one that since labour and land are the prime requisites for the maintenance of life, any labour put on any land can earn for the labourers a sufficient livelihood. These communists had neither the requisite knowledge, the requisite capital, or even any serious intention of working the land by their own labour. No solid attempt was made to establish a community, and after some endeavour to organise the working of the land under more efficient outside management, the bulk of the " communists " resigned and the Guild found itself saddled with the land.

Several other bits of land came gradually into the possession of the Guild. In 1877 Mr. George Baker, then Mayor of Birmingham, gave twenty acres of woodland in the prettiest part of Worcestershire. A little later, the Guild also obtained possession of a little estate, Cloughton, near Scarborough, consisting of a couple of acres and a cottage. But while all these remained the property of the Guild, they were quite unsuitable even for a nucleus of important agricultural reforms, and in fact very little was done in this direction.

Frequent attacks of ill-health which came upon him during the period covered by "Fors," and which, as the eighties advanced, deprived him of the ability to undertake the steady pursuit of any new enterprise, kept these agricultural experiments in embryo. Had Mr. Ruskin's influential friends afforded him the faith and the practical support which he once expected, some serviceable results might have been obtained; but virtually the whole burden of the work had fallen upon him, and with his collapse of health it came to a standstill. The failure seems to have been recognised by Mr. Ruskin himself as early as 1884, for, in the "Master's Report" issued for that year, he alludes to the causes of delay, and suggests that he " may probably have to bequeath to the succeeding master the prosecution of the objects of the Guild in that direction."

Though the Guild retains in its possession several pieces of land, the ownership of which is still vested in two trustees, nothing is being done to carry out the designs of Mr. Ruskin. In fact, it would be quite impossible without far larger resources, both of land and money, to conduct an experiment which should properly embody the essentials of Mr. Ruskin's plan with any prospect of success.

§ 6. The most serviceable outcome of the work of the Guild is the Ruskin Museum at Sheffield. No one who bears in mind the part assigned to ocular demonstration in his scheme of education will undervalue the importance of this unique experiment. It had long been a design of Mr. Ruskin to furnish an exemplar of the true museum as a treasury of art and a means of delight and instruction in the finer sorts of human work. Having acquired a piece of land at Walkley, two miles from Sheffield, with a cottage upon it, Mr. Ruskin in 1875 chose this for the first home of his museum. In Letter lix. of "Fors" he explains why Sheffield, the most uncompromising and most irredeemable of steam towns, is yet the most suitable location for the first of St. George's schools.

"Of such science, art, and literature as are properly connected with husbandry, St. George primarily acknowledges the art which provides him with a ploughshare, — and if need still be for those more savage instruments, — with spear, sword, and armour.

"Therefore, it is fitting that of his schools 'for the workmen and labourers of England,' the first should be placed in Sheffield. . . .

"Besides this merely systematic and poetical fitness, there is the farther practical reason for our first action being among this order of craftsmen in England; that in cutler's ironwork, we have, at this actual epoch of our history, the best in its kind done by English hands, unsurpassable, I presume, when the workman chooses to do all he knows, by that of any living nation."

To this he adds elsewhere the further reason that "Sheffield is in Yorkshire, and Yorkshire is yet in the main temper of its inhabitants Old English, and capable, therefore, yet of the ideas of honesty and piety by which

Old England lived : finally, because Sheffield is within easy reach of beautiful natural scenery."

For some years this cottage perched on a hill, with an extensive view over the valley of the Don, was the humble shell of his " King's Treasury." From the beginning it was Mr. Ruskin's rigorous design to put the very best pictures, drawings, models, the most perfect examples of natural objects and of the skilled labour of men's hands in his museum, and to arrange them to accord with the principles of classification which he had thought out for purposes of appreciation and instruction. Mere variety, rareness, or curiosity were no objects to him. It was not mere bovine wonder which he sought to evoke, but intelligent understanding of the excellent works of nature and of man.

After the lapse of some years the cottage at Walkley was found inadequate for the growing store, and an ampler home was sought. In 1890 proposals were made by the Corporation of Sheffield with the object of housing Mr. Ruskin's treasures in a more convenient and accessible place. A number of private gentlemen undertook to provide £5,000 for a permanent museum. The St. George's Guild, however, refused to accept any condition of permanency, wishing to be free to utilise the whole or any part of the collection, if desirable, in other places. At length Mr. Ruskin agreed with the Corporation that the collection should be placed in the newly acquired public park at Heeley for the term of twenty years. The Corporation of Sheffield undertook to house and maintain the museum, appointing a committee for the purpose, upon which Mr. Ruskin and the two trustees of the Guild accepted seats. The only funds, however,

available for purchases of new objects, in fulfilment of
the purpose of the museum, are such moneys as remain
in possession of the St. George's Guild and the bene-
factions of private individuals. The utmost care has
been exercised by the curator, Mr. William White, who
superintended the transfer from Walkley, and has devoted himself to the museum for the last eight years,
to follow scrupulously the design of Mr. Ruskin; and
every addition to the collection has kept in mind the
definite intentions of the founder, whose spirit pervades
the institution.

The museum is still kept in accordance with the first
intention, primarily as a place of education, and its
method is still dominated by the principle that "a
museum directed to the purposes of ethic as well as
scientific education must contain no vicious, barbarous,
or blundering art, and no abortive or diseased types,
or states of natural things." For many years after its
foundation, Mr. Ruskin continued to employ his own
unrivalled skill and the money of the Guild to enlarge
the early nucleus of the collection. Particularly did he
labour, by his own hands and by the employment of
other skilled artists, to complete, as far as possible, the
record of the sculptural details of the churches and
palaces which still stand as examples of the best periods
of Italian and French architecture. Since Mr. Ruskin
has been compelled to relinquish all personal part in
this work, it has been carried on by members of the
Guilds and friends. Though funds have to be strictly
economised, some valuable additions have been recently
made to the library, and the collection of engravings,
including a copy of Turner's Liber Studiorum and

various series of engravings of his water-colour drawings, many of the finest lithographic plates of Prout,
and fine examples of the early masters of Italy and
Germany. Mr. White, in particular, has followed Mr.
Ruskin's footsteps in Italy, collecting photographs of
buildings and sculptures, and filling up the lacunæ
of his records. The valuable collections of minerals,
and of architectural casts upon which Mr. Ruskin bestowed so much expense and trouble, are carefully
arranged, and wherever profitable, printed or written
descriptions are appended. The library contains many
rare and beautiful works, enriched by plates illustrative
of the animal and vegetable kingdoms, besides works
relating to the fine arts.

Every effort has been expended to make the museum
a home of material associations with Mr. Ruskin by
securing some adequate representation of every picture,
building, sculpture, or natural product which serves to
illustrate or to interpret his books. Though this purpose imposes a more restricted scope than that which is
taken by the general museums of the country, every one
acquainted with the width and variety of the subject-
matter of Mr. Ruskin's treatment will recognise that the
collection can suffer from no narrow specialism. Strict
care is taken to avoid confusing the mind and senses
of the visitor by multiplicity of disordered detail; a
thoughtful system of rotation is practised in the exhibition of the more educative drawings and pictures, only
a limited number being placed on view at the same
time.

The walls of the rooms are garnished with suggestive
and stimulative texts from Mr. Ruskin's writings. The

first room, for example, containing stones and other specimens of natural history, thus enforces the first principles of all intelligent study. "You will never love Art well till you love what she mirrors better." "Pleasant wonder is no loss of time." "All judgment of Art is founded in the knowledge of Nature." "There are so many things we never see." Not only by these bold proclamations, but by a thousand subtle incidents in the choice and the ordering of the treasures from nature and art, the reader of Mr. Ruskin's books is touched by the sense of his familiar personal presence: everywhere his mind and hand seems at work, his fine particular enthusiasms shine forth, his very prejudices are carefully conserved. Among the minerals, his special studies in the Silica class, in particular the agates and crystals, take prominence, recalling his early geological papers and his fascinating "Ethics of the Dust." The strict limitations of the Library and Print Department carry a distinction of their own. Here we find choicest illuminated Codices, Missals, and other religious works recalling the spiritual life of "the middle ages," with volumes of noted "Voyages and Travels," whose interest stretches back to Mr. Ruskin's early boyhood. In Literature the severest choice is exercised: Homer, Chaucer, and the French favourite Marmontel are represented by fine copies, together with a few of the later English prose writers. There is, however, no intention to provide a library, even of "best books;" it is the art side of literature in print, illustration, binding, etc., that is presented, though it is in strict accordance with Mr. Ruskin's universal principle that greatness of subject-

matter should be essential, and that no mere skill or
beauty of treatment should secure admission for slight
or unworthy subjects. The rule is even enforced to the
total exclusion of prose fiction, so that Sir Walter Scott
is only represented by his " Life of Napoleon."

It is, however, in pictures and in architectural casts
that the special interests and teaching of Mr. Ruskin are
most powerfully expressed, both in subject and in treatment. Numerous studies of the finest works of the early
Italian masters, whose greatness it is one of the peculiar glories of Mr. Ruskin to have rediscovered for the
modern world, are here presented in such a fashion as
to draw intelligent attention to the detailed qualities
of colour, composition, or sentiment. Verrocchio and
Carpaccio, two of the greatest rediscoveries, are represented, the former by a rare original, the latter by a
series of studies of paintings representing the Legend of
St. Ursula, and by numerous other studies.

Sculpture and architecture are exhibited in their close
natural relations, both through paintings and casts, with
especial reference to the great masterworks which form
the subject of Mr. Ruskin's most eloquent and convincing criticism, St. Mark's and the Ducal Palace at
Venice, the Duomo at Florence, Rouen Cathedral, etc.
Here is none of the crude unordered intellectualism,
the air of freaks and whimsicalities, the intrusion of
ugly and degraded elements of life which find place
in the untempered " realism " of the ordinary museum.
In the great personal atmosphere of the Ruskin Museum
the visitor can scarcely fail to gain certain clear and
noble ideas about the beauty and order of nature,
and the true treatment which wise human art accords

to them. The spell of this illumination is rudely broken, as he steps from the small park containing the museum into the mean, ugly, cramped streets of Heeley, the dismal new suburb of the great ogre town whose grimy arms and pestiferous breath have gathered in their stifling embrace so much of the fair country which lies around it. The social lesson afforded by this contrast is quite undesigned, for when this new home was chosen for the Ruskin collection, eight years ago, the windows of the museum commanded an unbroken view over the beautiful Derbyshire hills, now blocked by intervening streets and factory chimneys.

The faithful, though but partial, record of the labours of a long, strenuous, and multifarious life devoted to the education of a nation in true paths of art and just order of society, this museum forms a unique and abiding memorial to the genius and humanity of our greatest modern teacher. There have been but few lives capable of such a memorial; where the sanctum of closest personal associations naturally opens out into the many-vistaed vision of a new society of happy and noble human beings, lovers of all that is good and beautiful in nature and in art, and bound by a common conscious purpose of working out the illimitable progress of humanity towards a goal of perfect brotherhood.

§ 7. The most fruitful effort of Mr. Ruskin in the direction of practical industrial reform is in the revival of hand-weaving, wood-carving, and other home or small industries. It will be borne in mind that two motives impelled him to this course, — first, the desire that workers should do skilled and interesting work with their hands under wholesome and humane conditions;

secondly, that people should be able once more to know and to use good, sound, serviceable stuff, instead of cheap shoddy stuff. The experiment most closely associated with Mr. Ruskin is the St. George's Mill at Laxey, in the Isle of Man. Here, as in many other remote parts of the country, was a decaying hand-industry in spinning and weaving cloth. It was held by most people inevitable that these old-time industries should yield place to the new steam machinery and the factory life. Mr. Ruskin, among his many heresies, held that this was neither necessary nor desirable. Learning of the gallant, but apparently hopeless struggle of the spinners in Man, he took up the cause, found a serviceable right-hand man in Mr. Rydings, put new spirit into the old body by means of some capital and organisation, and established a new market among his friends and followers. He had a water-mill built at Laxey, to which farmers around brought their wool and were paid in yarn or in finished cloth, as in times of yore. All the processes of carding, spinning, and weaving were here carried on, some of the yarn being used for home knitting and weaving, some being woven at the mill. Here was made under old industrial conditions a sound cloth, all wool, warranted neither to shrink nor to change colour, and to "last for ever." For some time Mr. Ruskin himself took an active part in the management of the St. George's Mill, until in 1883 he found it necessary to hand it over to the care of Mr. George Thomson of Huddersfield.

Mr. Thomson, a Yorkshire manufacturer, and one of the trustees of St. George's Guild, has himself adopted much of the social teaching of Mr. Ruskin, and has applied it to his own woollen and worsted business at Huddersfield. Converting his manufactory into a co-operative association, he made financial arrangements for direct participation in ownership of capital by the workers engaged in the mill, devising means by which an increasing proportion of the shares should pass into their hands, so that the actual producers became participators in the profits. The perfected intention of the scheme has been that half the net profits should go to the workers, the other half passing, conformably to the Rochdale co-operative idea, to the customers. Since the latter have been mostly the retail co-operative societies, the entire experiment has a particular interest attached to it as a novel attempt to heal the industrial breach between capital and labour on the one hand, producer and consumer on the other.

Another experiment close after Mr. Ruskin's heart, and in which he took peculiar interest, was the revival of the old spinning industry in the cottages of Westmoreland, brought about by his friend Mr. Albert Fleming, producing " the soundest and fairest linen fabrics that care can weave or field-dew blanch." This was the case of reviving a dead, not a dying, industry. The old spinning-wheels, once part of the furniture of every cottage, had disappeared for generations, and models were with difficulty raked out from lumber-closets. However, at length a cottage was turned into a spinning-school, equipped with the necessary wheels, and lady friends assisted Mr. Fleming in giving the needed instruction to the cottagers. " Next came the weaving. In a cellar in Kendal we discovered a loom; it was in twenty pieces, and when we got it home, not all the collective wisdom of the village knew how to set it up. Luckily we had a photograph of Giotto's Campanile, and by help of that the various parts were rightly put together. We then secured an old weaver, and one bright Easter morning saw our first piece of linen woven, — the first purely hand-spun and hand-woven linen produced in all broad England in our generation."

Such is the account of the beginning of the Langdale linen industry given by Mr. Fleming.[1] This occurred in the winter of 1883, and is the first of a large number of similar revivals in different parts of the country. It was not designed as the complete basis of an industrial life, but only as a by-industry for the fireside in the evening after the day's work was done. In 1897 some twenty-five women were engaged in spinning and others in embroidering the linen, the best workers earning 5s. to 6s. a week. A great variety is produced for all sorts of domestic purposes, bleached or unbleached or dyed, according to fancy.

§ 8. The Home Arts and Industries Association, which holds an exhibition every year, and issues a report, is evidence of the great influence which Mr. Ruskin's teaching and example has exercised upon this movement in different parts of Great Britain and Ireland. The following statement of the aims of this Association is ample testimony to this influence. It seeks:

"1. To train the eyes and fingers of its pupils, thereby not only adding to their resources and powers of employment, but increasing their value as workmen, and making them more fit to earn a livelihood in whatever occupation they may adopt.

---

[1] "Studies in Ruskin," by Mr. E. T. Cook, p. 164, etc.

" 2. To fill up the idle hours of boys and girls, especially at the age when they have left school and not taken up a regular trade, by providing occupation of a kind which will keep them happily employed at home.

" 3. To promote pleasant and sympathetic intercourse between the educated and the poor, and to enable the possessors of art-knowledge and culture to impart their gifts to those who are without either.

" 4. To revive the old handicrafts which once flourished in England, but which have now almost died out, and to encourage the labouring classes to take a pride in making their homes beautiful by their own work."

Classes organised in various places, largely by voluntary effort of unpaid teachers, are at work. In a few instances an already existing industry is organised and a market found for it, as in the hand-woven cloth of South Wales. In a few other cases a new art-industry has arisen, as in the " Della Robbia Pottery " of Birkenhead, giving full remunerative employment to skilled artists in design and execution. But in most instances the lines which mark off the work of the Association from other organisations of a more strictly business order are closely observed, the work being of a voluntary and informal nature, more recreative and educational than professional, and not forming the basis of a complete commercial livelihood. The chief occupations are hand-spinning, weaving, and embroidery of different fabrics, and work in wood, metal, and clay, though a great variation of minor handicrafts are also practised, such as embossed and cut leather work, bookbinding, and basket-making. A few of the classes are associated with South Kensington Science and Art Department, certain others are partly supported by County Councils, but most are free from official support and its accompanying control, and represent voluntary organisation and working.

The rapid growth of this interesting movement is evidenced by the fact that, beginning with 40 classes in 1884, it has now considerably more than 500 classes at work. While many men and women of influence in art and in society have taken an active part in endowing and establishing centres of this work, notably Mr. and Mrs. G. F. Watts, and Lady Brownlow, the inspiration has in large measure come visibly from Mr. Ruskin. In the neighbourhood of his northern home a number of hand industries, the embodiments of his teaching, indicate his direct influence. Among the most interesting of these is one which bears his name, the " Ruskin Linen Industry " of Keswick, in which teaching is given at cottage homes in spinning, weaving, embroidery, and lace, and the more ambitious experiment in teaching a variety of handicrafts undertaken by Mrs. and Miss Harris at Kirkby Lonsdale in Westmoreland.

Nor does this work stand by itself as a gallant attempt to stem the inevitable encroachments of machine industry, as some would represent. It is rather to be regarded as an informal educational current in a wider and more potent movement of modern taste, marking not a protest, but a progress, a demand for the free individual expression of art-power in all forms of plastic material both for use and decoration, and a corresponding demand on the part of the consumer that his individual tastes and needs shall be satisfied.

It is, in a word, a practical informal attempt of a

civilised society to mark out for itself the reasonable limits of machine-production, and to insist that "cheapness" shall not dominate the whole industrial world to the detriment of the pleasure and benefit arising from good work to the worker and the consumer. Such a movement neither hopes nor seeks to restore mediævalism in industry, nor does it profess hostility to machinery, but it insists that machines shall be confined to the heavy, dull, monotonous, and therefore inhuman processes of work, while for the skill of human hand and eye shall be preserved all work which is pleasant and educative in its doing, and the skill and character of which contribute pleasure and profit to its use.

CHAPTER XIII.

SUMMARY OF MR. RUSKIN'S WORK AND INFLUENCE.

IN trying to mark as clearly as we may the place which Mr. Ruskin occupies among the social reformers of his age, it is of paramount importance to keep in mind his artistic temperament and training. For though the energy and inspiration of his social teaching was distinctively moral in character, the basis of his discontent with existing industrial and social conditions, and the forms of his constructive policy, are referable to the demands of an artistic nature. The definite social evils which first appealed to him were the bad workmanship imposed upon most workmen by the industrial conditions of their age, the degradation of the outward form of cities, and in particular of public and domestic architecture, the dominance which conventional and mechanical modes of work had obtained both in the fine arts and in the industries, and in general the power exercised by irresponsible wealth to corrupt the finest human qualities, and to uglify the outward aspects of life. It was the search into the causes of bad art, and of false ideas about art, that inevitably led him to detect the poisoning of the springs of individual and social conduct, and to trace in the greatness and the fall of nations the operation of forces which, chiefly economic in their outward working, are distinctively spiritual in their natural sources. This constant widening of ideas and sentiments, from art in its narrow connotation to an art which should include all sound work, and thence to the conception of an art first of individual then of social life, was, to a mind like Mr. Ruskin's, endowed at once with powerful and fearless analytic and constructive faculties, an inevitable process. Whereas the tendency of industrial economists, labouring for the cause of social reform, has almost invariably lain towards a separation of work and enjoyment, the processes of production and consumption, with an almost exclusive stress upon the latter, as if social as well as individual welfare consisted in the multiplication of commodities; the social revolt from the ranks of literature and art has made distinctively for the gospel of work, — work for all, good in quality, and valued for its own sake as well as for its result. This is the common note in the social teaching of men so widely different in many of their principles of life and modes of conduct as Emerson, Carlyle, Zola, Ibsen, William Morris, and Tolstoy. With such men this gospel of good work is no mere moral platitude, but a definite protest against the severance of work and life, process and result, producer and consumer, which the excessive specialisation of industry has forced upon modern life.

§ 2. The distinctive part which may be assigned to Mr. Ruskin in this many-voiced protest will be best

marked by a brief comparison of his general attitude
with the equally uncompromising attitude of two of his
contemporaries, — William Morris and Tolstoy. Many
principles all three have in common, — the rejection of
commercial competition and profit-seeking as destructive
of good work, and of the sense of brotherhood; the insistence upon the need and duty of manual labour for
all, and a repudiation of the sophistry by which the intellectual and cultured classes seek to evade this natural
law; a denunciation of the machine-made town, and a
leaning towards the simplest forms of rural life. Both in
their work of criticism and of reconstruction there are
many important points of agreement. Yet the widest
temperamental differences of attitude towards work and
life separate the three thinkers. Taking "News from
Nowhere" as at once the fullest and most concrete
expression of Morris's social reform teaching, we find
it resolved into a single precept, "Do as you like." A
society in which every one at once does what he likes,
and likes what he does, is the ideal that is presented.
All sense of pain and irksomeness is brushed away
from labour; duty either towards oneself, one's neighbours, or society nowhere presents itself as a necessary
motive. The artist even now likes what he does; therefore, place all work on the footing of an art, the necessary work will all be done for its own sake, and for the
sake of the pleasure got from doing it. Now Mr. Ruskin
is at once more definitely moral and more practical. He
perceives that much work is not inherently and immediately desirable; that most of the finest art-work is
based upon toil and monotony of preparation; that
neither a sense of duty nor social compulsion can be

utterly dispensed with as motives to labour, and that
the sense of moral obligation, and the painful endurance it often imposes, are not antagonistic to individual
and social good, though the promptings of passing self-
interest are opposed to them ; but that, on the contrary,
this duty and this toil are important factors in the
building up of character in men and nations. Mr.
Ruskin goes far with Morris, insisting that as much
work as possible should be made good and interesting,
and that all should share such work ; but he neither sees
the feasibility nor admits the desirability of abolishing
from work those qualities of self-sacrifice which imply
the subordination of the present interests of a narrow
self to the longer interests of the larger social self. Yet
he by no means carries his doctrine of self-sacrifice in
art and life to the extent which Tolstoy has carried it
in his later teaching. It is not indeed easy to represent
Tolstoy's doctrine without appearing guilty of parody.
It must suffice to say that the great Russian writer
seems to deny pleasure and the love of beauty any legitimate position as motives to the artist ; by imposing com-
municability of feelings and ideas as the standard of art,
and the desire to inform others, and so to further social
sympathy as the only genuine art-motive, he has made
that self-sacrifice or toil for others which Mr. Ruskin
recognised as one of the incentives of true individual
work, the one absorbing motive. At one with Tolstoy
in recognising that art ought not to be a thing apart, a
specialism to be practised by a few, but an essential
factor in the life of all, according to their several capacities and the requirements of the work in which they
are engaged, that the distinction between fine arts and

arts or industries not so fine is only a matter of degree, Mr. Ruskin yet would utterly refuse to endorse Tolstoy's rejections of professional technique and his insistence that spontaneity of expression is the only art-power. Moreover, Mr. Ruskin is ever a strenuous pleader for enjoyment as a right to be accorded every one in a well-ordered society: the joyful exercise of every physical and intellectual faculty belongs to his idea of a free and healthy individual life: the asceticism of Tolstoy has no place in his social order.

In his view of the use and need of social discipline, even in the form of public coercion, he is divided from both Morris and Tolstoy. In the ideal society of the former coercion has no place, because it is no longer necessary in order to induce men to do the best they can for society; while the scheme of Tolstoy is grounded upon the assumption of the immorality of all application of physical force. Thus, compared with these extreme teachers, Mr. Ruskin ranks as a common-sense philosopher, not representing all work as capable of yielding present pleasure with Morris, nor idealising the moral powers of man with Tolstoy.

It may perhaps be claimed for Mr. Ruskin that his philosophy, alike of art and of social reform, combines and even merges the supposed antagonism of Hellenism and Hebraism more completely than that of any other modern thinker. To many, indeed, it has always seemed that Hebraism is the sentimental taproot of his thinking. Whether there is any right ground for this supposition, beyond the fact that, recognising the current neglect of the moral factors which enter into art, he laid dramatic emphasis on this defect in his art-teaching, may well be doubted. As to the other form which the quarrel of "artists for art's sake" have often fastened upon Mr. Ruskin, it arises from a narrowness of understanding on their part. An artist who, quitting the scope of some special art, proceeds to universalise art in the art of living, must necessarily seem to sin against art in the narrower sense; the planning out of social life as an organic whole changes the focus as well as enlarges the subject, and the philosophic and spiritual focus adopted for the larger work abrogates the "absolute freedom" of any single art, however fine.

§ 4. He has unwittingly deceived many and offended not a few by giving forth his art of life under the title of Political Economy, sometimes expanding that term to its utmost capacity so as to embrace the whole science and practice of social life, sometimes, for combat, contracting it within the recognised orthodox limits.

As social reformer he has conferred signal services both in criticism and in construction of the theory and the art of social economics. The three deepest and most destructive maladies of modern industrial society he has exposed with more intellectual acuteness and with more convincing eloquence than any other writer. These are, first, the prevalent mechanisation of work and life; secondly, injustice as an economic basis of all bargaining; thirdly, the definite forms of waste and injury to work and human character arising from trade competition.

On the constructive side he has laid a true scientific foundation of a science and art of social economics by insisting upon (1) the reduction of commercial to human "costs" and "utilities" as the true foundation of a theory of wealth; (2) the inclusion of non-commercial as well as commercial values, *i.e.* the maintenance of the organic unity of the related faculties of effort and enjoyment; (3) the establishment of a social standard of goodness or happiness as an ideal.

To this it must be added that he made the most searching inquiry into the human processes involved in production and consumption.

"Honest production, just distribution, wise consumption," — these words summarise the reforms the necessity of which he laboured to enforce.

§ 5. Those who complain of Mr. Ruskin, as they complained of such men as Carlyle and Emerson, that he presented no such closely ordered philosophy of life as would satisfy the intellect, mistake, not so much the character of Mr. Ruskin's teaching, as the necessary limitations of human thought and language. Of all these men it may be said that they had an intuitive perception of the inability of human reason to afford such intellectual satisfaction. The necessary imperfections of language, the very processes of division and definition which reasoning involves, by their very nature baffle the mind in the search for that harmony and unity of design which alone can afford such intellectual satisfaction as is desired. The utmost straining after the appearance of intellectual completeness can only produce a delicately adjusted structure of artificial terminology, the innumerable rifts of which cannot but appear on closer analysis. Mr. Ruskin rightly judged that sound sensations and emotions, and the sane valuation of things derived from them, supply a truer unifying force in the art of life than metaphysics can

give. The unity and harmony of life are more powerfully and more consciously realised in the cultivation of
full human sympathies by such men as Mr. Ruskin,
Emerson, or Browning, than by the most highly desic-
cated scheme of philosophy ever made in Germany. No
modern thinker evinces a stronger grasp of the " wholesomeness " of life ; no resolution of false dualism by
philosophy is more effective than that clear and manifold perception of the truth that " the laws above are
sisters of the laws below " which came to Mr. Ruskin,
as he followed out, through history and the intimate
study of the fine arts, the subtle threads of union between the material and the spiritual life. The sources
of wholesome physical life, pure air and water, free communion with the powers of the uncontaminated earth,
are but the material counterparts of the sources of
spiritual life, admiration, hope, and love. As the body
draws its sustenance from the one source, so the mind
is fed and energised from the other. The artist requires to be rooted in Nature, and to interpret her by
the light of the love of ideas. So with the art of life, in
which every one should be an artist ; sound conditions
of material work and life are the bases of worthy humanity. Modern industrial life demands reform, because
it suffers from two mortal diseases which war against
this right ideal of human society ; first, it deprives men
of this sound physical basis of life ; secondly, it poisons
the springs of spiritual life and of intellectual honesty
by permitting the dominion of selfish lust directed to
the attainment of low material ends.

§ 6. The defective sympathy which Mr. Ruskin shows
for not a few of the modern social ideas and move-

ments which seem to make for progress, is a common
fault of those great originative geniuses who, to quote
the language of Oliver Wendell Holmes, "carry in
their brains the ovarian eggs of the next generation's
or century's civilisation."

A suggestive comment upon this quality of miso-
neism is made by the Italian sociologist Lombroso, who
says, "The men who create new worlds are as much
enemies of novelty as ordinary persons and children.
They display extraordinary energy in rejecting the discoveries of others; whether it is that the saturation, so
to say, of their brains prevents any new absorption, or
that they have acquired a special sensibility, alert only
to their own ideas, and refractory to the ideas of
others."[1]

Whatever may be the scientific explanation, there
can be no question but that a mind of the intensity and
concentration of Mr. Ruskin's is, in fact, "possessed"
by certain leading ideas originating from within to the
exclusion of ideas from without. If this is a defect, of
which we make no question, it is a penalty which so
high a quality must be content to pay.

§ 7. In this concluding chapter something remains
to be said regarding the distinctively literary methods of
Mr. Ruskin in their influence upon the force of his teaching and the acceptance of his ideas.

It is a matter of serious doubt whether his brilliant
literary qualities have aided or retarded the acceptance
of his thought. Wit and imagination, eloquence and
passion, those qualities which are essential to the "literature of power," exercise a curious double and con-

[1] The Man of Genius, p. 17.

tradictory influence upon the mind of most English readers. While our enjoyment and appreciation of such writing is both keen and genuine, this very relish awakes our suspicion; our cautious temperament shrinks from any full abandonment to the feelings, and our very admiration of emotional power is provided with an automatic check.

Mistaking our ability to distinguish those "sensations" which are "just, measured, and continuous," rooted in the facts of nature and of human life, from those which are the spurious products of mere literary artifice, we commonly seek to guard ourselves by discounting at extravagant rates all those elements which appeal to our emotions and not to our understanding. Though the great literature of all nations and all times stands as testimony to the use of impassioned language in the service of truth, the "common sense" of our nation has always refused acceptance of this fact. The "practical" man still looks with suspicious scorn upon "works of imagination," and the great masterpieces of prose fiction, which are the typical product of our modern literary genius, are not fully recognised as useful vehicles of truth.

This is not to be explained merely by attributing it to a national distaste for ideas and a correspondent mistrust of ideals. It is primarily due to a false psychology, based on defective temperament, which seeks wrongly to isolate the ratiocinative faculty, and considers that the imaginative faculty has no proper place either in the discovery or the teaching of truth. It is this notion which underlies the popular distrust of an attractive style; even J. S. Mill was felt by some to be too literary for a "serious thinker." A solid and convincing treatment of political economy or any "social science" ought to stick to the stony facts, and build out of them a durable, intellectual edifice. The discovery of social truth should be conducted by a solemn marshalling of the several orders of concrete phenomena, and their formal interpretation by the application of laws based upon inductive reasoning and expressed in carefully defined terminology; the teaching of such truth should be conducted by a steady pressure of closely consecutive reasoning, a syllogistic uncoiling of propositions which shall insert or insinuate them into a vacantly receptive understanding in one continuous line.

Now Mr. Ruskin neither gets his truths nor conveys them in this manner. We have already entered a twofold defence of his scientific method of inquiry. We have pointed out, in the first place, how the "facts" which can be ascertained by the elimination of human feeling, through the dry light of the intellect, are not the sort of facts he seeks; human facts, true social facts, require for their finding the penetrative and constructive powers of the human imagination. Economic facts, which are to be measured, not objectively in terms of money, but subjectively in terms of human life, cannot be learned except by the organic application of all the interpretative powers of man, sympathetic as well as ratiocinative. Again, we have shown that when the subject-matter has once been placed in position for strict intellectual analysis, Mr. Ruskin, though not infallible, is far more competent than most of his detractors, and is quite capable of excluding passion and imagination where pure reasoning has rightful sway.

Now the same vital difference in method affects
Mr. Ruskin's mode of teaching. Much of this teaching
consists in attempts to make facts felt, to vitalise knowledge. Social facts conveyed in statistics, or in abstract
terminology, are mere formal acquisitions of the intellect; they may be serviceable for proving or disproving
propositions in the practice of intellectual gymnastics;
but when it is sought to relate them to other classes of
fact, so as to yield a basis of conduct, they are useless
in this condition. Now, since Mr. Ruskin's conception
of social economics breaks down — as we have seen it
must — the barrier between science and practice, he is
rightly insistent that all his facts shall be vitally appreciated by those whom he teaches. One illustration may
serve to show how right he is in holding that no merely
quantitative statement of truth is valid. Mr. Charles
Booth's computation that thirty-four per cent. of Lon-
doners are living upon a weekly income per family of
less than twenty-one shillings seems a definite statement
enough, but it has really no meaning; it is not grasped
even by the intellect until we have reduced it to terms
of humanity. Now this is not achieved merely by com-
putations of rent and prices of food, or by assessment of
the physical requirements of an average family. All
such knowledge we must have, but the moral force of
the imagination is needed to interpret the facts, and to
present them to the mind as an organic whole in their
bearing upon the ideal life of the Londoner before we
have truly comprehended them. Mr. Ruskin's first great
task as teacher was to present facts in this humanised
form, so as to enter the hearts of his readers, as well as
their understandings. It is for this that he strained to

the utmost his great literary powers. To those accustomed to more formal modes of instruction, and who
harbour suspicions of rhetoric, his free discursive and
richly allusive mode of speech has been a source of
perplexity, and even of annoyance. " Fors" is full of
passages which seem to pompous sober-sides misplaced
levity or malicious exaggeration.

In such a spirit, for instance, the ordinances and
the dignitaries of the Church are often roughly handled.
Such a passage as the following is typical of the satirical
language which pervades " Fors," and which is an offence
to many :

" Meantime, the bishop, and the rector, and the
rector's lady, and the dear old Quaker spinster who
lives in Sweetbriar Cottage, are so shocked that you
drink so much, and that you are such horrid wretches
that nothing can be done for you! and you mustn't
have your wages raised, because you *will* spend them
in nothing but drink. And to-morrow they are all
going to dine at Drayton Park, with the brewer who
is your member of Parliament, and is building a public
house at the railway station, and another in the High
Street, and another at the corner of Philpott's Lane, and
another by the stables at the back of Tunstall Terrace,
outside the town, where he has just bricked over the
Dovesbourne, and filled Buttercup Meadow with broken
bottles ; and, by every measure, and on every principle of calculation, the growth of your prosperity is
established ! " [1]

What an inimitably truthful picture of a whole
large segment of social life, and yet the corruption of

[1] Fors, Letter xxiii. (iv. 13).

the faculty of observation is such that there is an almost instinctive tendency to reject it as caricature ! Or read the brilliantly sportive treatment of " English Roast Beef " in an earlier letter,[1] or any of the numerous illustrations of his charge against the clergy that " they teach a false gospel for hire."

Many of these passages are supposed by readers accustomed to the amenities of literature to be wild outbursts of irresponsible wrath, only excusable by imputing to the writer a total lack of self-control. Mr. Ruskin, however, in most cases neither desires nor deserves such excuses. He claims to be judged by the standard of great literature, which knows none of these amenities, and which does not confuse temperance with suavity. Isaiah, Jesus, Paul, Dante, Milton, and other prophets of righteousness did not mince their words; it is their spirit and their freedom of speech which Mr. Ruskin claims. Strong things need strong names ; a strong man in literature and in life calls these things by their names. When Mr. Ruskin denounced in sharp, short, passionate phrases the corrupt torpor of the Church, the degrading selfishness of commercial profit-mongers, the miserable and sordid vulgarity of suburban villadom, the godless irresponsibility of the " classes," the anarchy which masquerades as Liberalism among the masses, the evil tyranny of mechanism in commerce and in art, — when he sought by scorching instances to brand these evils into the hearts and understandings of his hearers, ought we to hold out our hands in finicking deprecation, with protests against " such terrible aspersions," " such irre-

[1] Fors, Letter xxv. (ii. 9, 10).

JOHN RUSKIN.

sponsible abuse," "such outrageous caricature?" Ought
we not rather first to ask whether the language does not
substantially convey the truth, whether the denunciation is not justified? Mr. Ruskin always insisted on
"the truth and soberness" of "Fors." That much of
his language was highly "heated" he sought not to
deny, but rather to justify, as helping him to tell the
truth, "that manner of mental ignition or irritation
being for the time a great additional force, enabling
me to discern more clearly, and say more vividly, what
for long years it had been in my heart to say." [1]

The greater part of what passes for exaggeration in
Mr. Ruskin's statements of fact is simply due to his
keen perception of the truth and his powerful mode
of expressing it, even if something must also be allowed
for the legitimate emphasis of the literary setting, that
idealisation of a specific truth which he has always
insisted on as a right function of all art.

These accusations of unfair and reckless exaggeration commonly proceed from those who have not
studied Mr. Ruskin's writings sufficiently closely to
know that epithets which sound at first reckless and
casual are chosen with conscious care. The writer
of "Sesame" did, indeed, lay down a counsel of perfection for the conscientious study of language, but no
modern writer came nearer to a following of the counsel.
"My own literary work," he writes in "Præterita,"
"was always done as quietly and methodically as a
piece of tapestry." [2]

This was true even of the meanderings of the
"Fors:" though choice of subject was often left to

---

[1] Fors, Letter lxxxviii.　　　[2] Prœterita, ii. 241.

the inspiration of some casual event or letter received, treatment was always dictated by conscientious scrupulosity. Those who complain that Mr. Ruskin did not "stick to one subject at a time," are probably mistaken through not knowing what "one subject" is.

Mr. Ruskin sometimes buried his main track too long under the patches of biography and heraldry; he often overrated both the culture and the perspicacity of his readers, but for all that his educative method was radically sound. He knew that the first duty of the teacher is to catch his hearer. The professor in his lecture-room, addressing students who have voluntarily devoted themselves to the continuous following of a narrowly marked line of study, is in a very different position from the self-elected teacher who wishes to seize the reluctant crowd and compel them to come in. His just instinct led him to understand that quite the first duty of such a teacher is to keep the minds of his listeners open and alert, and not to deaden the sensitive apertures of their minds by a constant monotony of dull instruction. No one more completely grasped and more subtly practised the vital as distinguished from the logico-mechanical method of teaching. In order to keep the attention fresh and receptive, he constantly varied the approach, changed the topic with fluent versatility, leaping from analogy to analogy with surpassing nimbleness of illustration, now leaving his main highway to explore some pleasant by-path, anon returning with a swift curve of the road back to his theme. So, sometimes by dogmatising, sometimes by suggestion, by pathetic or humorous appeal, by quick and close research into the meaning of words, by minute logic-chopping, taking every instrument of rhetoric and reasoning as it came to hand, never forging it by artifice, but always finding it, he played upon the mind of his public with multiform effect. Was the result ordered knowledge? Yes. Where he sought to convince the understanding, he convinced; where he sought to impart facts or trains of reflection, these stand out clearly enough from the rhetorical environment which is their setting; the sense of proportion is seldom ultimately lost, the merely incidental is seldom allowed to overshadow or weigh down the essential.

§ 8. Mr. Ruskin was never cajoled by words to loose his grip of the things which words purport to represent. In all his writing he was definite and practical. But to him the "things of the mind" were the most real things. The reality of ideas and sentiments, the practicality of sane ideals, this was his preachment to a nation falsely proud of being practical, because it has been successful in a narrow "doing" directed almost exclusively to narrow material ends.

To clarify the vision, to elevate the aim, to humanise, and so to dignify, the ends of conduct, are the persistent endeavours of John Ruskin's teaching. His hope and his appeal as reformer of society is to those misdirected or ill-directed forces of character which have made us so successful as individuals and as nations in the grosser forms of activity, and which, well economised for nobler purposes, might secure for us a "greatness" measurable neither in miles of territory, millions of population, nor in volume of commerce, but in "the multiplication of human life at its highest standard."

1.

WAR.

Mr. Ruskin's curious praise of war demands separate attention. A certain tendency to worship force *quâ* force, which, in spite of disclaimers, sometimes manifests itself in him, as in Carlyle, is partly responsible for his view. The romantic aspect of war which he got in childhood from Homer and from Scott never passed from him; the vivid dramatic presentation, both of the horror and the glory, evinces a certain unreality. The love of mastership, and of the self-assertion of strong men, casts a glamour over war, the most pronounced form of self-assertion. This sentiment is less a manly than a womanly quality; it is found rather in physically weak, sensitive men than in robust ones, arising from the idealisation of a quality by those who possess it not. Mr. Ruskin does not see war as it is or was; he does not see it as those few literary men who have experienced it face to face see and describe it, men like Mazzini and Tolstoy. Perhaps the pages we would most willingly delete from his works are those containing the address to young Woolwich students, reprinted in " The

Crown of Wild Olive," which defend " the game of war "
as that occupation in which " the full personal power of
the human creature " finds effective expression, and
which, " when well played, determines who is the best
man."[1] It is true that both here and elsewhere wars of
sheer aggression for selfish ends of territorial or commercial aggrandisement are denounced. But few defend wars ostensibly undertaken for gain. The sanction
and incitement given by Mr. Ruskin to the English nation " to undertake aggressive war, according to their
force, wherever they are, assured that their authority
would be helpful and protective," however laudable as
a theory of national conduct, is one of the most dangerous pieces of advice that could be tendered to a people
always able to persuade themselves that their interference is " helpful and protective," when it extends the
influence of England over a new area of the world. It
is true that the wars approved by Mr. Ruskin belong to
national knight-errantry and not to selfish rapacity; but
in permitting the indulgence of the war-spirit outside
the limits of pure self-defence, he gives free operation
to dangerous forces without providing any adequate
checks.

This defence of war comes under two heads:

" All the pure and noble arts of peace are founded on
war; no great art ever rose on earth but among a nation of soldiers."[2] Egypt, Greece, and Rome are the
examples he claims to have most in mind.[3] But are the
finer arts of these nations to be regarded as in any sense
the direct fruits of war? Egypt, at any rate, was never
a warlike nation. Most nations which have founded a

---

[1] Crown of Wild Olive, § 101.   [2] Ibid., § 116.   [3] Ibid., § 89.

civilisation, rendering the cultivation of fine arts possible, have certainly been at some time compelled to fight for their existence. A great national spirit, brought into self-consciousness by a struggle for existence, as was the Greek spirit by the Persian wars, has sometimes found expression afterwards in art and literature. But this merely indicates that national genius is not so closely specialised a power as it may seem to those who classify nations by some specific contribution they seem to make to the world's history in some particular period of their growth, as art and philosophy to Greece, law-making to Rome, astronomy, mathematics, etc., to the East, and so forth.

Some nations were great in war at the same time as they were great in " the noble arts of peace ; " this, to some extent, was true of Greece and Rome, but it was not true of Egypt, China, Phœnicia, and Holland. " Commerce," says Mr. Ruskin, " is barely consistent with fine art, but cannot produce it." This is untrue of Holland and Italy. No such causal relations as are here suggested are indeed capable of proof ; neither concomitance nor sequence proves causation. What Mr. Ruskin had to show, in order to sustain his thesis, was that some natural and necessary connection exists between the destructive art of war and the constructive arts of peace. This he has not shown, and could not show.

But his most curious defence of war is the ennobling influence upon the national character which he imputes to it. " It has been impossible for any nation, except a warrior one, to fix its mind wholly on its men, instead of on its possessions." In other words, the transition from a military to an industrial organisation of society, which Herbert Spencer regards as a distinctive mark of civilisation, is really a mark of degradation. The sentence just quoted is open to multifarious criticism. Are the virtues of the warrior — discipline, courage, self-restraint — an adequate compensation for the brutalising influence of his occupation? The thoughts of the soldier *quâ* soldier are not set upon making men, as Mr. Ruskin would insist, but upon slaying men; the cultivation of martial virtues are valued as means to this end. If the "profit" of a commercial mind, the end of commercial activity, is debasing, is "slaughter," the end of military activity, less debasing, for this is the fair comparison? Again, it may be asked, are these "virtues" of the soldier sound moral qualities at all? Is not the discipline formal, the self-restraint unreal, the courage largely animal bravery? Is not the evil education of war manifested by the inability of soldiers to conform to the laws of peaceful societies? These are some of the questions which occur, nor are they really answered by the distinction between a mercenary and a citizen army which Mr. Ruskin draws, approving the latter and reprobating the former. Reversion to a totally unspecialised military system is now impossible, as Mr. Ruskin must have known. There is, however, a peculiar weakness in the assertion, that war makes against greed in an age like this, when most wars are "for markets." Mr. Ruskin might have known that more than half the fighting of the world has been directly animated by a desire to take the land, the food, or the trade of others. That he should have taken his stand with Tennyson in the shallow criticism of "Maud," which makes the soldier a

superior creature to the merchant, is indeed deplorable.
No one who turns from " Crown of Wild Olive " to Emerson's essay upon " War " can fail to detect the shallow
sociology of Mr. Ruskin. The obtuseness of such a
judgment is the more remarkable in him, because even
in the lecture upon war to the Woolwich students, he
showed " the ghastly ludicrousness " of the thing[1] by
quoting the very language in which Carlyle exposes the
imposture of these national quarrels, in which the poor
blockheads who do the fighting are made the tools of
the governing classes. " Straightway the word ' Fire! '
is given, and they blow the souls out of one another, and
in place of sixty brisk useful craftsmen, the world had
sixty dead carcasses, which it must bury and anon shed
tears for. Had these men any quarrel? Busy as the
devil is, not the smallest! They lived far enough apart;
were the entirest strangers; nay, in so wide a universe,
there was even, unconsciously, by commerce, some mutual helpfulness between them. How then? Simpleton!
their governors had fallen out; and instead of shoot-
ing one another, had the cunning to make these poor
blockheads shoot."

Nay! Mr. Ruskin understood far better than Carlyle
what was the nature of this " cunning; " how the love
of money was the root of this particular evil. He saw
what the mind of the nation, in spite of our modern
business education, is so slow to comprehend, the distinctively financial origin of modern wars, and the financial aftermath of its glories. The plain truth is so
plainly set in the Preface of " Munera Pulveris," that
it is probably set aside as humorous parody by most

[1] Crown of Wild Olive, § 99.

readers, such being the usual treatment of the truth when it is inconvenient. "Capitalists, when they do not know what to do with their money, persuade the peasants that the said peasants want guns to shoot each other with. The peasants accordingly borrow guns, out of the manufacture of which the capitalists get a percentage, and men of science much amusement and credit. Then the peasants shoot a certain number of each other until they get tired, and burn each other's homes down in various places. Then they put the guns back into towns, arsenals, etc., in ornamental patterns (and the victorious party put also some ragged flags in churches). And then the capitalists tax both annually, ever afterwards, to pay interest on the loan of the guns and gunpowder." [1]

In one curiously bold passage he presses this economic lesson closer home, and drives it into the discovery, almost the justification, of that very revolutionary classwar which he so deeply and so constantly deplores.

"Wars between nations (fools and knaves though they be) is not necessarily in all respects evil. . . . But Occult Theft — Theft which hides itself even from itself, and is legal, respectable, and cowardly — corrupts the body and soul of man, to the last fibre of them. And the guilty Thieves of Europe, the real sources of all deadly war in it, are the Capitalists, — that is to say, people who live by percentages on the labour of others; instead of by fair wages for their own. The *Real* war in Europe, of which this fighting in Paris is the Inauguration,[2] is between these and the workmen,

---

[1] Munera Pulveris, Pref. xxvi ; *cf.* Fors, Letter viii. (i. 150).
[2] Written July, 1871.

WAR.   347

such as these have made him. They have kept him
poor, ignorant, and sinful, that they might, without his
knowledge, gather for themselves the produce of his
toil. At last, a dim insight into the fact of this dawns
on him; and such as they have made him he meets
them, and *will* meet." [1]

In his preface to a pamphlet on "Usury,"[2] he re-
affirms and illustrates at some length the judgment
briefly expressed in "Unto this Last." "It is entirely
capitalists' (*i.e.* usurers) wealth which supports unjust
wars." Had Mr. Ruskin searched more closely into the
nature of just wars, he would have found reason to
modify the language of his address to the Woolwich
students, and to regard even "just wars" as necessary
evils with essentially brutalising consequences upon those
who engage in them.

Mr. Ruskin's account of the intimate relation between
war and usury receives striking confirmation from a
great modern authority upon finance, who writes as
follows: "Debt, too, is a great determining factor everywhere in the imposing of taxation. Of late years the
passion for warlike display has entered into competition
with it, but this passion could not, in most cases, be
gratified, were it not for the facilities given for creating
fresh debts. . . . Supreme over all . . . is the debt
born of wars, and of the love of warlike display. The
more this folly is indulged in, the deeper is the hold
the great masters of usury have upon the springs of
a nation's life. Not only do the obligations they create,
for future generations to bear, draw more and more of

---

[1] Fors, Letter vii. (i. 140).
[2] Reprinted in "On the Old Road," ii. 243.

the substance of the people into the pockets of money-
lenders, but they frequently necessitate, by their intolerable pressure, a leaning on the help of great finance
houses to a degree which places the political institutions
of a country more and more under their thumb." [1]

[1] Mr. A. J. Wilson, *Contemporary Review*, March, 1898.

APPENDIX.

II.

SOME information regarding the Ruskin Societies at Birmingham, Liverpool, and Glasgow may serve to illustrate the strong hold which Mr. Ruskin's books and personality are gaining over people of thought and culture throughout the country.

The largest of these Societies is that established in Birmingham in 1896, the President of which is the Dean of Ely, and the Honorable Secretary and active organiser Mr. J. Howard Whitehouse. It numbers about four hundred members. The objects of the Society are stated in the Syllabus as follows:

" 1. To form a centre of union for students and others interested in Mr. Ruskin's writings.

" 2. To promote the study and circulation of his works by means of lectures, discussions, and the issuing of such publications as may be deemed advisable.

" 3. To influence public opinion in relation to art and ethics on lines which he has indicated.

" 4. Generally, to encourage such life and learning as may fitly and usefully abide in this country."

The work of the Society comprises a series of lectures given during the winter session upon subjects conformable to the objects of the Society, and includes addresses by such men as Mr. W. G. Collingwood, Dean Farrar, Mr. Walter Crane, Mr. Kineton Parkes, Mr. A. E. Fletcher. Special meetings are also arranged for more intimate discussions of aspects of Mr. Ruskin's work. A library exists for the use of members, containing books written by Mr. Ruskin and others relating to his works.

Lastly, this vigorous Society possesses a quarterly journal, entitled " St. George," the early issues of which merit the highest praise alike for their matter and their form. " St. George " contains articles or reports of lectures delivered before the Society, reviews of works of literature and art, and some admirable notes.

The Birmingham Society (which takes the additional title suggested by Mr. Ruskin of " The Society of the Rose ") adopts and prints in its reports an extract from the Creed of St. George's Guild.

The Liverpool Ruskin Society, containing a smaller number of members, also displays great activity. Its lecture work appears to have a more special reference to the social and economic part of Mr. Ruskin's teaching, and, in addition to general meetings of the Society, group meetings of members are held for the study of special books, such as " Unto this Last," and Carlyle's " Past and Present." A library of Mr. Ruskin's books exists.

An interesting development is the educational and social work undertaken by the Society. Classes for youths and men, and for girls, are held during the winter months. " Practical instruction is given in artistic needlework, in which few and simple materials are used, so that the girls may learn that true decoration of person and home does not depend on lavishness of money or material, but is the reward of the virtues of patience and industry, waited upon by the gifts of skill and imagination."

A noteworthy attempt at a literal fulfilment of Mr. Ruskin's economic teaching is the St. Anthony's Bank.

"This bank has been formed in imitation of the ancient custom of the Christian Church, of lending money to help those who had fallen into distress, and to whom temporary help might be the means of preventing increased difficulty and sorrow. Loans will be granted (without interest or expense) in cases approved by the Committee of Management, and preference will be given to cases of misfortune. Lender and borrower will act in money matters in simple and brotherly relations, the loan being for the good of the borrower, who will be expected to repay conscientiously, with the knowledge that the money is being set free for a similar help to others."

The Glasgow Society has the distinction of being by far the oldest of the Societies, having originated in 1879. Among its Honorary Presidents is the Master of Balliol, and it contains several well-known names among its officers and council. Its specific aims are three: (1) To encourage and promote the study and circulation of Mr. Ruskin's writings; (2) To form a centre of union for " Ruskin students ;" and (3) " To promote such life and learning as may fitly and usefully abide in this country."

In addition to the ordinary lecture syllabus, and a valuable library, a Lectures Extension Committee exists, which arranges lectures upon Mr. Ruskin's writings, and upon social and art questions closely related to them. A considerable number of lectures by well-known Ruskin students has been delivered in neighbouring towns under the auspices of this Committee. Readings in Ruskin are also a recent new feature of the Society's work.

Several smaller Ruskin Societies exist in other British towns, and many in the United States of America.

While these Ruskin Societies owe their origin and special inspiration to the writings of the master, the vital quality of their influence is shown in the impulse given to follow the disinterested pursuit of culture in many fields, and to undertake work which is the natural fruit of the seed sown by John Ruskin, and not a mere attempt to copy his designs.

The relation which members of these Ruskin Societies, and innumerable scattered disciples throughout the country, adopt towards their avowed master, has been expressed with excellent felicity by the Secretary of one of these Societies in a private letter, which I have permission to quote : " We like to regard ourselves as truth-seekers, and in all our study and work together we have never felt any reason to doubt the wisdom of putting our full trust and confidence in Mr. Ruskin, as not merely a great and noble teacher, but as the teacher who has seen clearly into the causes of social chaos, and pointed out for us the true principles of healthful and noble national life. Gentler in the use of his power than Carlyle, as clear in vision, with an appeal that reaches the heart with greater force, we have good hope that his life-work will be an ever-increasing influence for good in promoting all social movements."

INDEX.